HIS SHOCK VALENTINE'S PROPOSAL

BY
AMY RUTTAN

MILLS &
BOON

Published in Great Britain 2016
By Mills & Boon, an imprint of HarperCollins*Publishers*
1 London Bridge Street, London, SE1 9GF

© 2016 Amy Ruttan

ISBN: 978-0-263-25428-0

Ou[...] [...]cyclable
pro[...]
Th[...] [...]al
en[...]

Pri[...]
by[...]

Dear Reader,

Thank you for picking up a copy of *His Shock Valentine's Proposal*.

Montana is a state I never really had on my bucket list. And then one summer, on a drive out to Alberta to visit family, I had the privilege to travel through it. From Broadus to Billings, and up through Great Falls, I fell absolutely head over heels in love. Mountains, sweeping plains and badlands… They say Montana is 'Big Sky Country' and they're right.

After that visit I knew I had to set a story in Montana. Especially in the mountains, nestled against the border of Alberta—a province that was also never on my radar until I had to travel there for my sister-in-law's wedding. I fell in love with Alberta too on that trip.

What struck me about travelling through Montana was its vastness. All that land and barely a person in sight. It's a place to get lost and to find yourself. It's a perfect place for my heroine Esme to hide.

Montana is also a place I wouldn't mind raising my kids. Fresh air, mountains, plains—it's a beautiful land. It's also where my hero grew up. Carson doesn't want to leave Crater Lake, or the family practice he's inherited. And he certainly doesn't want a relationship after his heart is broken. But when he's faced with competition in the form of a new doctor in town, maybe love will soften his heart after all?

I love hearing from readers, so please drop by my website, amyruttan.com, or give me a shout on Twitter @ruttanamy.

With warmest wishes,

Amy Ruttan

This book is dedicated to Montana. Your beauty, even four years after I visited you, still haunts me and makes me long to spend endless summers wandering through your mountains, your plains and your badlands.

This book is also for James, who spent his third birthday in Montana on our cross-country trek and loved every second of it. Love you, buddy.

Born and raised on the outskirts of Toronto, Ontario, **Amy Ruttan** fled the big city to settle down with the country boy of her dreams. Life got in the way, and after the birth of her second child she decided to pursue her dream of becoming a romance author. When she's not furiously typing away at her computer, she's mom to three wonderful children.

CHAPTER ONE

"WHAT DOES SHE think she's doing?" Carson grumbled to himself.

"Looks like she's planting flowers in a pot," Nurse Adams remarked.

Carson turned and glanced at his father's nurse, who had worked in the practice longer than Carson had. Actually, she was technically his nurse now. He hadn't realized she'd snuck up behind him. Like a ninja.

"I didn't ask for your opinion."

She looked down her nose at him in that way she always did when he was little and causing mischief in his father's office. A look that still sent shivers of dread down his spine and he realized he'd taken it a step too far.

"If you didn't want my opinion, Dr. Ralston, you shouldn't be talking out loud in *my* waiting room."

"Sorry, Louise." He rubbed the back of his neck. "Just hate seeing all these changes going on in Crater Lake."

Her expression softened. "There's a building boom. It was inevitable that another doctor would come into town and set up shop."

Carson frowned and jammed his hands in his trouser pockets as he watched the new, attractive doctor in town planting flowers outside the office across the street. Crater Lake was changing and he wasn't sure he liked it too much.

His father had been the lone physician in Crater Lake for over forty years, long before Carson was born. It was a practice he'd taken over from his grandfather; now Carson had taken over the practice since his parents retired and moved south to warmer climates.

There had always been a Ralston as the town's sole practitioner since Crater Lake was founded in 1908. Something his father liked to remind him of constantly.

The only other time there had been a notion of two town doctors was when Danielle had lived with him for a time after medical school, but that had been different. They were supposed to work together, get married and raise a family. It hadn't lasted. She hadn't liked the slow existence or the winters of living in northwest Montana.

Luke is a doctor.

Carson snorted as he thought of his older brother, who was indeed a licensed practitioner, but Luke didn't like the confines of an office and preferred to be out in the woods tracking bears or whatever he did up on the mountains. Luke didn't have the same passion of upholding the family tradition of having a Ralston as the family practitioner in Crater Lake. That job fell on Carson.

The new doctor in town, Dr. Petersen, stood up, arching her back, stretching. Her blond hair shining in the early summer sunlight. He didn't know much about the newest resident of Crater Lake. Not many people did. She'd moved in and kept to herself. Her practice hadn't even opened yet and though Carson shouldn't care he couldn't help but wonder about her, who she was.

The door jingled and he glanced at the door as his brother came striding in, in his heavy denim and leather, a hank of rope slung around his shoulder.

Louise huffed under her breath as his brother dragged in dirt with his arrival.

"Slow day?" Luke asked as he set the rope down on a chair.

"Yeah. I have the Johnstone twins coming in about an hour for vaccinations."

Luke winced. "I'll be gone before then."

Louise stood up, hands on her ample hips. "Would you pick up that filthy rope? My waiting room was clean until you showed up! Honestly, if your parents were still here…"

Luke chuckled. "You make it sound like they're dead, Louise. They're in Naples, Florida. They live on the edge of a golf course."

Carson chuckled. "Come on, let's retreat to my office. Sorry, Louise."

Carson glanced back one more time, but Dr. Petersen had gone back inside. His brother followed his gaze out the window and then looked at him, confused.

When they were in his office, Luke sat down on one of the chairs. "What was so interesting outside?"

"There's a new doctor in town," Carson said off-handedly.

Luke grinned, leaning back in his chair. "Oh, I see."

"What do you see?"

"I've seen her. I'm not blind."

Carson snorted. "That's not it at all."

Luke cocked an eyebrow. "Then what is it?"

"It's a new doctor in town. It's threatening our family practice."

Luke shrugged. "It's your practice, not mine."

So like his brother. Not caring much about the family practice. Not caring about generations of Ralstons who'd sweated to build this practice and this town up. Well, at least he cared.

Do you?

Carson pinched the bridge of his nose. "I thought you were against the town expansion and the building of that ski-resort community."

"I am. Well… I was, but really there was no stopping it."

"You could've attended a few town meetings," Carson said.

When had Luke stopped caring so much?

It wasn't his concern and by the way Luke was glaring at him Carson was crossing a line. His brother quickly changed the subject. "I guess my point was that it didn't look like you were checking out the competition the way you want me to think you were."

"I'll work that out later." Carson moved around and sat down on the other side of his desk. "What brings you down off the mountain and what in heaven's name are you going to tie up with that rope?"

Luke grinned in the devilish way that used to cause their mother to worry. It usually meant that Luke was about to get into some serious trouble.

"Nothing much. I actually just came for some medical supplies. I'm taking some surveyors deep into the woods."

"And the rope is to tie them to the nearest tree and use them as bear bait?"

"The thought had crossed my mind, but like you,

little brother, I took the Hippocratic Oath. I swore to do no harm."

"Hmm."

"You need to liven up a bit, little brother. You're too tense."

Carson snorted. "Look who's talking. You know the local kids refer to you as the Grinch in the winter. One of the Johnstone twins thought you were going to come down and steal Christmas last year."

"Because I told her that. She spooked my horse."

"You're terrible with kids and have a horrible bed-side manner," Carson said.

"I'm great with kids. Dad just knew you were more of the office type of person and I like to run wild."

Must be nice.

The thought surprised him, because he should be used to Luke's lifestyle after all this time. Luke always got to run free, do what he wanted. Carson was the re-liable one.

Dependable.

Never took risks.

Carson shook his head. "As long as you're not naked while running wild then I don't care."

Luke grinned. "I didn't know how much you cared."

Carson couldn't help but chuckle. "You need to get your butt out of my clean office before you give Louise a heart attack and get yourself back up that mountain. I have patients coming in soon. Patients who think you're going to steal their Christmas."

"Right. So, do I get the medical supplies? I may not have regular office time but I technically have part ownership."

"You know where they are. I don't have to tell you."

"Thanks." Luke got up.

"Take your rope, too."

Luke winked and disappeared into the stockroom while Carson leaned back in his father's chair and scrubbed a hand over his face.

Luke had one thing right. He was tense. He worked too much.

You're wasting your surgical talent here. Why didn't you take that internship at Mayo? Why are you giving up a prestigious surgical residency to become a general practitioner?

Danielle's words haunted him.

Lately, they had been bothering him more. Ever since the old office building across the road had been bought and he'd got wind that a new doctor from Los Angeles was moving into town. There weren't many full-timers in Crater Lake. The ageing population was a threat to the small town and now with this resort community going in, it would bring more people, but not people who would be here all the time and Carson couldn't help but wonder if the time of the small-town doctor was gone.

Perhaps he had wasted his life? Maybe he should've cared less about the practice like Luke. Maybe he would've become a great surgeon.

More and more lately it seemed he was thinking these thoughts. He didn't take risks, but he was happy with the choices he made.

This was the path he chose and he was happy.

He was happy.

Who are you trying to convince?

He groaned inwardly. He didn't have to let the ghosts of his past haunt him.

Get a grip on yourself.

Carson shook those thoughts away.

No, he was doing what he'd always wanted to do. Sure, he'd been offered several amazing residencies, but surgery was not what he wanted to do.

He liked the small-town life; he liked the connection he had with the people in Crater Lake. He would be stifled in a big city; he'd be trapped in a busy hospital in the OR for countless hours. This he preferred.

Still...

It irked him that another doctor had moved into town, but he couldn't stop it and frankly he hoped she was up to the challenge. She was from California. He doubted it very much that she would be able to survive her first winter here and that thought secretly pleased him.

Louise knocked and then opened his door. She looked worried. "Dr. Ralston, Mrs. Johnstone is in the waiting room. She needs to speak with you."

"Is everything okay? I thought the twins' appointment was later?"

Louise's lips pursed together. "She's here to cancel her appointment and take their chart."

"Hold on!" Esme called out. She had no idea who was banging on the front door of her office. She wasn't open yet. The big day was at the end of the week. If it was a delivery they could've read the sign and come along to the back alleyway.

Only the banging was insistent. It sounded almost angry, which made her pause. Perhaps she should take a peek out the window. The last thing she wanted was it to be the tabloids outside pounding on her door. Not that they'd bothered with her for the past three months.

She'd dealt with enough press in LA before she'd

hightailed it to the solitude of the mountains. Of course, when she'd chosen Crater Lake as her new home, she'd known that there was going to be a resort community, but she hadn't realized another high-end spa and hotel was going up.

Esme could handle a small ski-resort community, but a huge high-end spa and hotel? That was not what she wanted. Small. Sleepy and in need of a friendly and eager town physician. Of course, once she'd spent all her money on buying her practice she really hadn't been able to change her mind. The building she had bought had been on the market for five years.

She knew there was an *old* family practice in town. Dr. Ralston had been practicing medicine in Crater Lake his whole career and his father before that and his father before that. It was time to breathe some new life into Crater Lake.

The pounding reminded her why her inventory of medical supplies was being interrupted and she glanced out of the window of her primary exam room.

"Whoa."

The handsome man standing in front of her office was definitely not paparazzi or press. He didn't have a camera or a recorder, or even a smartphone on him. He was well dressed in casual business attire. His brown hair combed neatly, clean shaven, but definitely an outdoorsy type of guy, because she could see his forearms where he'd rolled up the sleeves of his crisp white shirt were tanned and muscular.

He was a well-dressed country boy and Esme had a thing for country boys. Always had, but that was a hard thing to find in Los Angeles.

Unless you counted the country singers she'd treated,

and she didn't. Of course, when she'd thought she'd found the perfect guy it had turned out she hadn't and she was terrified by who she'd become and about what he wanted from her.

Don't think about Shane.

Well, whoever this guy was, he was off-limits. She wasn't here to get involved with anyone. Besides, he was probably married or taken. One thing Esme had discovered about her new place of residence was that Crater Lake was mostly filled with older people and young families. It wasn't a happening place for singles and that was fine by her.

She was here to hide, not find happiness. She didn't deserve that. Not after what she'd done to Shane.

Not after what happened in the OR with her last surgery. It was too painful. Love and friendship, they were not what she was here for. She was here to be a doctor. She was here to blend in, to hide so no one could find her.

He banged on the door again.

She ran her hand through her hair, hoping she didn't smell of sweat too much. Even though she had no interest in impressing him, she didn't want to scare off any potential patients because she gave off the impression of being smelly.

"Just a minute!" Esme called out as she undid the chain and bolt on her office door. She opened it. "Hey, look, I'm not open today."

"I'm aware," he said tersely. "Can I come in?"

"I don't even know you."

"Is that how you plan to treat residents of Crater Lake?" he asked.

What's this guy's deal?

"Okay, how about we start with introductions? I'm Dr. Petersen." She held out her hand, but he just glanced at it, ignoring her proffering.

"I know who you are, Dr. Petersen." His blue eyes were dark, his brow furrowed.

Oh, crap.

"You do? You know who I am? I'm sorry I can't say the same."

He was clearly annoyed and she didn't have time for this. "Look, I'm kind of busy today. Why don't you call my office and my nurse will call you about an appointment time? I'm pretty open for appointments as I'm not open for business just yet."

"You have a nurse?" he asked.

"Well, not yet, but I've interviewed some interesting candidates."

"I bet."

Esme frowned. "Have I offended you some way? If I have, I'm really sorry, but again I haven't opened yet."

"I'm aware you're not open yet. Of course, that really doesn't stop you from poaching patients."

Esme was stunned. "Who are you?"

"I'm Dr. Ralston. I was the Johnstone family's practitioner up until about two hours ago."

Okay, now she was really surprised. "You're Dr. Ralston?"

"Yes."

"Dr. C. Ralston?"

"Yes."

"I don't get it." Esme stepped aside to invite him in, but didn't even get the words out as he wandered inside and then sat on the edge of the waiting-room desk, his arms crossed.

"What don't you get? I can show you my ID."

"Dr. Charles Ralston has been practicing medicine in Crater Lake for forty years." She shut the door, but didn't lock it just in case this guy was crazy or something. "You guys either have the fountain of youth up here in Crater Lake or someone's records are incorrect."

A small smile played on his face, some of that fury fading. "Dr. Charles Ralston is my father. I'm Dr. Carson Ralston. I took over my father's practice when he retired five years ago."

"Oh, and I'm the fool who just poached some of your patients. Gotcha."

"Essentially."

Esme crossed her arms, too. "So how can I help you?"

"Stop poaching my patients." There was now a slight twinkle in his blue, blue eyes and he didn't seem as angry anymore.

"I'm really sorry, but your patient wanted to change. I couldn't turn them away," she stated.

"Look, you have to know when you come to a small town you don't go around stealing the patients of a practitioner who has been here for quite some time."

Esme raised an eyebrow. "Is that some kind of doctor rule? If so, I'm not aware of it."

"It's common courtesy." He didn't seem as though he was going to budge until she handed over the files to him. Although, she hadn't been given the files yet.

"I'm sorry to disappoint you, Dr. Ralston, but when I bumped into Mrs. Johnstone at the general store her twins took a shine to me and she wanted me to be her physician."

"What do you mean the twins took a shine to you?"

She grinned. "I mean I didn't scare them like the old, grumpy Dr. Ralston."

His mouth fell open in surprise for a moment and then he snapped it shut. "Okay, then. I won't bother you about it anymore."

"That's quite the defeatist attitude."

He shrugged and headed to the door. "If I'm old and grumpy then there is nothing more I can do."

A sense of dread niggled at her. "What do you know about them you're not sharing?"

Now it was his turn to grin with pleasure. "Nothing. Just good luck with the twins, but I will tell you that if you take any more of my patients it'll be war."

Esme couldn't help but laugh. "Are you declaring war on me, Dr. Ralston?"

"I believe I am, Dr. Petersen." He winked, chuckling to himself as he shut the door behind him and Esme couldn't help but wonder what she'd gotten herself into. She would have to keep her distance from Carson, though in a small town that was going to be hard to do, but she was going to try.

CHAPTER TWO

CARSON WAS GLAD that summer was coming, the days were longer, but then he really couldn't enjoy the extra daylight when he stayed late and he usually stayed late because he didn't have anything to go home to.

He had a big empty house that he used for sleeping. That was it. He'd built it for Danielle and him. Of course Danielle hadn't stayed long enough to live in it.

The sun was just beginning to set behind the mountains, giving a pink tinge to the glacier on Mount Jackson. He never got tired of it. He loved Montana and if he did have regrets about his past, staying in Montana wasn't one of them.

Still, the mountains, the scenery weren't any kind of companion, but at least the mountains would never betray him and wouldn't break his heart the way Danielle had done.

As he locked up the clinic he couldn't help but glance across the street at Dr. Petersen's clinic. The lights were still blazing. She'd opened at the end of last week, but Carson hadn't lost any more patients. Most of her patients seemed to be coming down from the resort community and with that new high-end hotel and spa going in there would be even more people coming.

There were a few timeshares that were in operation, but he knew the main lodge was still under construction, as his brother was still taking surveyors and construction workers out on the trails.

Once the main spa hotel lodge opened and the community got its own full-time doctor, a job he'd turned down, then Dr. Petersen might feel a bit of pain financially.

A twinge of guilt ate at him and he felt bad for declaring war on her.

"You declared war on her? How does that even happen?" Luke had had a good laugh over that.

Of course, the last time Carson had declared war on someone was when Luke and he had been kids. Carson had declared war on Luke when he was ten and Luke had been fifteen. Carson had gone about booby-trapping parts of the house. The ceasefire had come when Luke had set a snare and Carson had ended up dangling upside down in a tree with a sign that said bear food.

Their father had put a stop to all present and future wars.

Carson sighed. He hadn't been thinking that day in her surgery. She got on his nerves a bit and he had been put out that the Johnstone twins had thought he was grumpy and old. He honestly was glad to be rid of the little hellions.

It was the principle of the matter.

In all the years his father had practiced he'd never been called grumpy or old. He'd never lost a patient to another doctor.

There never was another doctor in Crater Lake.

A lot of new families had come into town over the past couple of years. Dr. Petersen was advertising. He'd heard her ad on the local radio station. Perhaps he needed to advertise. Maybe he was a bit too comfortable in his position and he was in a rut.

Carson rubbed the back of his neck.

He should go make amends with her.

He crossed the street and peered inside the clinic window to see if he could catch sight of her, get her attention, then maybe he could talk to her.

Before he knew what was happening there was a shout, his wrist was grabbed and he was on the ground staring at the pavement.

"What in the heck?" Carson shouted as a pain shot up his arm. He craned his neck to see Esme Petersen, sitting on his back, holding his left wrist, which was wrenched in an awkward position behind him. "Um, you can let go of me. I kind of need my arm."

"Oh, my gosh. Dr. Ralston, I'm so sorry." She let go of his wrist and got off his back. "I thought you were a burglar."

Carson groaned and heaved himself up off the pavement. "There aren't many burglars around Crater Lake. It's a pretty safe town."

"I'm really sorry for attacking you like that, but you scared me. Why the heck were you skulking around the outside of my office?"

"How the heck did you do that?" Carson asked, smoothing out his shirt.

"Do what?" Esme asked.

"Take me down?"

Esme grinned. "Krav Maga."

Carson frowned. "Never heard of it. What is it?"

Esme shook her head. "You still haven't answered my question. Why were you peering through the windows and generally acting suspicious? This doesn't have to do with the *war*, does it?"

"Kind of." Carson touched his forehead and winced. "I think I'm bleeding."

"Oh, my God. You are." Esme took his hand and led him to the open door. "Come inside and I'll clean that up. It's the least I can do."

"No, thank you," Carson murmured, trying to take his hand back. "I think you've done enough damage."

"No way. You owe me this." She dragged him into her very bright and yellow clinic waiting room. It was cheery and it made him wince. "You can head into the exam room and I'll take a look at the damage."

Carson snorted. "Are you going to charge me a fee?"

Esme rolled her eyes. "So petulant. I just may, since you were creeping around in the shadows trying to scare me."

Carson sat on the exam table as she came bustling into the room and then washed her hands in the sink, her small delicate hands. They looked soft, warm, and he wondered how they would feel in his. He couldn't think that way.

"I wasn't trying to scare you," he said.

"You said it was about the war you declared on me. Doesn't that usually involve trickery and scaring tactics?" Esme stood on her tiptoes and tried to get a box from a high shelf. She started cursing and mumbling under her breath as she couldn't quite reach it.

Carson stood and reached up, getting the box of gauze for her, his fingers brushing hers as she still tried to reach for it.

So soft.

His heart raced, he was standing so close to her,

and he looked down at her and she stared up at him in shock that he'd done that for her. He hadn't realized how blue her eyes were or how red her lips were and the color was accentuated by the white-blond of her hair. She kind of reminded him of a short, feisty Marilyn Monroe.

Focus.

Carson moved his hand away and tossed her the box of gauze. "If you can't reach it, you shouldn't put it up so high."

"I didn't. My nurse did. He is a bit taller than me."

"He?" Carson asked, teasing her.

"Sexist, too, are we?"

"Please."

"Sit down. You're such a whiner, Dr. Ralston."

Carson sat back on the table; his head was throbbing now. "Dang, you did a number on me. What did you call that again?"

"Krav Maga." Esme pulled on gloves. "Sorry."

"No, it's fine. You're right. I shouldn't have been... what did you call it?"

"Skulking." She smiled, her eyes twinkling as she parted his hair to look at his injury.

Carson winced again, ignoring the sting. It wasn't the sting that bothered him, it was her touch. Just the sudden contact sent a zing through him. It surprised him. It was unwelcome. He wanted to move away from her, so he wasn't so close, but that was hard to do when she was cleaning up his wound. "Right. Skulking. I shouldn't have been doing that outside your office."

She nodded and began to clean the wound. "So why were you?"

"I came to apologize."

Her eyes widened. "Oh, really?"

"Yeah. I shouldn't have come barging over here and accusing you of stealing my patients."

"So are you calling a truce?"

"I am. Ow."

Esme *tsked* under her breath. "It's just a scrape. Don't be such a baby."

"Do you talk to all your patients this way?"

"Only ones who whine so much." She smiled and continued to dab at his scrape. "There. I'll just put some ointment on it. Do you want a bandage?"

"No, thanks."

Esme shrugged and then rubbed some antiseptic ointment on the scrape.

"Ow."

"Doctors are the worst patients," she muttered.

"For a reason." Carson chuckled.

"I've never really understood that reason." She pulled off her gloves and tossed them in the medical-waste receptacle. "There. All done."

"Thanks."

"Are you sure you don't want a bandage? Maybe a pressure dressing." She was chuckling to herself and he rolled his eyes.

"Pretty sure." Carson sighed. He had to get out of the clinic before something else happened. Such as him doing something irrational. Only he couldn't move. "I better be going. Again, I'm really sorry for being such an idiot before."

She grinned. "Apology accepted."

Esme didn't really know what else to say. She felt very uncomfortable around Carson, but not in a bad way. In a very good way and that was dangerous. When their hands had barely touched a few moments ago, it had sent a zing through her. One that wasn't all that unpleasant. Actually, it had been some time since she'd felt that spark with someone. Of course, relationships never worked out for her. Men couldn't handle her drive and focus to commit to surgery and she had liked her independence and career too much. No one messed with her career.

Well, not anymore. She couldn't forget why she was a surgeon.

Hold on, Avery. Please.

Let me go, little sister. It hurts so much...let me go.

She'd dedicated her life to surgery. To save lives.

And until Shane, surgery had been her life. Her father had been so proud and she'd been training under Dr. Eli Draven, the best cardio-thoracic surgeon on the West Coast.

She'd thrown herself into her work. So much so, that she hadn't had time to date, until Eli had introduced her to his son.

She'd met Shane and surgery had become second, because he had always been taking her somewhere. Esme had been swept off her feet and, being the protégée of Dr. Eli Draven, she'd become too cocky. Too sure of herself. She'd thought she'd had it all.

Then in a routine procedure, she'd frozen. A resident had jumped in, knocking sense back into her and they'd worked hard to save the patient's life. But in the end they'd lost the fight.

Esme hadn't been able to go on, because in that moment—in that failure—she'd realized that she didn't know who she was anymore. She didn't know who she'd become, but it wasn't her.

Pulled back from her memories, Esme stared down at her hands, watching how they shook.

You're not a surgeon anymore, she reminded herself.

She'd come here to rebuild her life and right now she should be focusing on building her practice up, because every last dime of her savings had been sunk into this building. She'd bought the clinic, the license and the apartment upstairs.

This was her life now. She didn't have a retired parent to hand off a practice to her. Her stepmother had been a teacher and her father a cop.

They'd scrimped and saved to send her to the best medical school. Scholarships only went so far and she owed it to them to pay them back, since she could no longer be the surgeon they expected her to be.

She'd lost herself.

And she'd lost Shane. If only she'd come to the realization that he wasn't the man for her *before* she was in her wedding dress and halfway down the aisle on Valentine's Day. It was something she had to live with for the rest of her life.

Her father had made that clear to her. He'd been so disappointed. She'd let him down.

I don't know who you are anymore, Esme.

She didn't deserve any kind of happiness, or friendship. All she deserved was living with herself. Living with the stranger she'd become.

"Well, I have a bit of work to do tomorrow. I better

hit the hay," she said awkwardly, rubbing the back of her neck and trying not to look at him.

"Yeah, of course. I…" Carson said, trying to excuse himself when there was banging on her front door. Incessant and urgent.

"Who in the world?"

"Just stay here." Carson pushed her down into her chair, letting her know that he wanted her to stay put, before he headed out to the front door.

"As if," she mumbled, following him.

"I told you to stay in the exam room," he whispered as he stood in front of the door.

She crossed her arms. "You don't know Krav Maga. I do."

He rolled his eyes. "Fine."

Esme stood on her tiptoes and peered around him. When he opened the door a man let out a sigh of relief.

"Thank God I found you, Doc Ralston."

"Harry, what's wrong?" Carson asked, stepping aside to let the man in.

The man, Harry, was sweating and dirty, dressed in heavy denim, with thick work boots and leaving a trail of wood chips on her floor. He nodded to her. "Dr. Petersen."

"How can we help you… Harry, is it?"

"Yes, ma'am." He was twisting a ball cap in his hands and it looked as if he was in shock. "There's been an accident at Bartholomew's Mill."

"An accident?" Carson asked. "What kind?"

"Jenkins had a nasty incident with a saw, but there's bad smoke from a remote forest fire and we can't get a chopper in to airlift him to a hospital and paramedics are still two hours away."

Esme reeled at that information. She knew they were far off the beaten path, but medical help was two hours away? Why wasn't there a hospital closer?

"Let's go. I'll go grab my emergency medical kit." Carson slapped Harry on the shoulder. "I hope you don't mind driving, Harry. You know those logging roads better than me in the dark."

"No problem, Dr. Ralston."

"Can I help?" Esme asked.

Carson nodded. "Grab as many suture kits as you can."

Esme panicked. "Hospitals take care of suturing. We're not surgeons."

Carson shook his head. "Not around here. I hope you have some surgical skills. We're going to need them."

Harry and Carson disappeared into the night. Esme's stomach twisted in a knot. Suturing? Surgery? This wasn't what she'd signed up for.

When she'd moved here she'd put that all behind her. She wasn't a surgeon.

No.

Then she thought of Avery. Her brother bleeding out under her hands. She was being foolish. They needed her help. Someone was in pain. This wasn't an OR. She would make sure she wouldn't freeze up. She wouldn't. She couldn't. This was about sustaining a man's life until paramedics arrived. Esme rushed into her supply room, grabbed a rucksack and began to pack it full of equipment. Her hands shaking as she grabbed the suture kit.

I can do this.

Besides, she might not even have to stitch him.

Carson could handle it and nothing was going to happen.

This man wouldn't die.

This wasn't a surgery case. At least she hoped it wasn't.

CHAPTER THREE

ESME BIT HER lip in worry as they slowly traversed some windy hills up into the mountains. At least that was what she assumed by the bumps and the climbs that tried the engine of Harry's truck. She couldn't see anything.

She'd thought she knew what pitch-black was.

The sky was full of clouds and smoke from a forest fire, which Carson had assured her wasn't any threat to them. California had wild fires, but not really in Los Angeles, at least not when she was there. Then again, she wasn't a native Californian.

Fire, wilderness, bears, this existence was all new to her, but then this was what she wanted after all. This was a big wide place she could easily blend in. She was small here. A place she could hide, because who in their right mind would come looking for her here?

A large bump made her grip the dashboard tighter. She was wedged between Harry and Carson as they took the logging road deep into the camp.

Another bump made her hiss and curse under her breath.

Carson glanced at her. "You're mighty tense."

"Just hoping we don't die."

Harry chuckled. "We're not on the edge of a cliff. Our only threat is maybe a rock slide or a logging truck careening down the road, but since there are no trucks running we're pretty safe."

"I'll keep telling myself that we're safe, Harry."

He shook his head, probably at the folly of a city girl. Only it was a dark night like this when Avery had died. She'd only been ten years old, but the memory of her brother's gaping chest wound was still fresh. The feel of his exposed heart under her small hands, the warmth of his blood felt fresh. It was why she'd wanted to be a cardio-thoracic surgeon.

Why she'd worked so hard to be the best, because Avery had been a constant in her parents' strained marriage. Even though he'd been twelve years older than her.

He'd been her best friend and when he'd died, her world had been shattered. So she'd dedicated her life to surgery.

The nightmares of his death faded away but nights like this made it all rush back.

Carson slipped an arm around her shoulders and then leaned over. "Relax. You're okay."

She glanced at his arm around hers and she wanted to shrug it off, but it felt good there. Reassuring. It made her feel safe and she wished she could snuggle in. Esme let out the breath she hadn't realized she'd been holding in trepidation and leaned back against the seat, shrugging off Carson's arm. She could handle this. Alone.

"So what happened again, Harry?" Carson asked.

"Jenkins was overtired and nervous. Our new client, Mr. Draven, was headed out our way tomorrow. One wrong move and..." Harry trailed off.

Esme froze at the mention of the name Draven. *Dammit.*

Though it couldn't be Dr. Draven, her former mentor. Eli was a cardio-thoracic surgeon. Still the name sent dread down her spine.

Draven was a common name. So there was no way it would be Eli or Shane. Dr. Draven had money, but he invested it in medicine and science. All of Shane's money was tied up in his company. She doubted he would invest in lumber or a hotel in Montana.

Harry slowed the truck down and she could see light through the trees as the forest thinned out. There were floodlights everywhere and people milling around one of the buildings, which looked like an administrative building. Harry pulled up right in front of it.

Carson opened the door and jumped out, reaching into the back to grab their supplies. Esme followed suit, trying to ignore all the eyes on them as they made their way into the building. The moment the door opened they could hear a man screaming in pain.

Esme forgot all the trepidation about anyone recognizing her. That all melted away. Adrenaline fueled her now as she headed toward the man in pain. There was blood, but it wasn't the damage done by the saw that caught her attention. It was his neck, and as she bent over the man she could see the patient's neck veins were bulging as he struggled, or rather as his heart struggled to beat. Only it was drowning.

She'd seen it countless times when she was a resident surgeon, before she'd chosen her specialty. Before she'd become a surgeon to the stars. First she had to confirm the rest of Beck's Triad, before she even thought about trying to right it.

She didn't want to freeze up. Not here. Not in her new start.

"Dave, you're going to be fine," Carson said, trying to soothe the patient. Only Dave Jenkins couldn't hear him. "It doesn't look like he's lost a lot of blood."

"He's lost blood," she said, trying not to let her voice shake.

Just not externally.

Carson took off his jacket, rolling up his sleeves to inspect the gash on Dave's right arm. "It's deep, but hasn't severed any arteries."

The wound had been put in a tourniquet, standard first aid from those trained at the mill. It wasn't bleeding profusely. It would need cleaning and a few stitches to set it right.

"That's not the problem." Esme pulled out her stethoscope.

Carson cocked an eyebrow. "Really?"

"Really." She peered down at Dave. His faceplate, his eyes rolling back into his head. He was in obstructive shock. "Who saw what happened? There's more than a gash to the arm going on here."

"A piece of timber snapped back and hit Dave here." Esme glanced up as the man pointed to his sternum.

"The gash came after?" she asked.

"No, before, but Dave didn't get out of the way and he didn't shut off the machine after the first malfunction. He was overtired—"

"Got it." Esme cut him off. She bent over and listened. The muffled heart sounds were evident. A wall of blood drowning out the rhythmic diastole and systole of the heart. Drowning it. Cursing under her breath, she quickly took his blood pressure, but she knew when the man pointed to his sternum what was wrong.

Cardiac tamponade.

Dave wouldn't survive the helicopter coming. He probably wouldn't have survived the trip to the hospital.

"What's his blood pressure?" Carson asked.

"Ninety over seventy. He's showing signs of Beck's Triad."

"Cardiac tamponade?"

Esme nodded and rifled through her rucksack, finding the syringe she needed and alcohol to sterilize. "I have to aspirate the fluid from around his heart."

"Without an ultrasound?" Carson asked. "How can...? Only trained trauma surgeons can do that."

Esme didn't say anything. She wasn't a trauma surgeon, though she worked in an ER during her residency. She'd done this procedure countless times. She was, after all, the cardio God. She knew the heart. It was her passion, her reason for living. She loved everything about the heart. She loved its complexities, its mysteries.

She knew the heart. She loved the heart.

Or at least she had.

"It's okay. I've done this before. Once."

She was lying. She'd done this countless times. She'd learned the procedure from Dr. Draven. It was a signature move of his that he taught only a select few, but they didn't need to know that. How many general practitioners performed this procedure multiple times? Not many.

"Once?"

"I really don't have time to explain. It's preferable to have an ultrasound, but we don't have one. I need to do this or he'll die. Open his shirt."

Carson cut the shirt open, exposing Dave's chest where a bruise was forming on the sternum.

You can do this.

"I need two men to hold him in case he jerks, and he can't. Not when I'm guiding a needle into the sac around his heart."

There were a couple of gasps, but men stepped forward, holding the unconscious Dave down.

Esme took a deep breath, swabbed the skin and then guided the needle into his chest. She visualized the pericardial sac in her head, remembering from the countless times she'd done this every nuance of the heart and knowing when to stop so she didn't penetrate the heart muscle. She pulled back on the syringe and it filled with blood, the blood that was crushing the man's heart. The blood that the heart should've been pumping through with ease, but instead was working against him, to kill him.

Carson watched Esme in amazement. He'd never encountered Beck's Triad before. Well, not since his fleeting days as an intern. It was just something he didn't look for as a family practitioner. Cardiac tamponade was usually something a trauma surgeon saw because a cardiac tamponade was usually caused by an injury to the heart, by blunt force, gunshot or stab wound.

Those critical cases in Crater Lake, not that there were many, were flown out to the hospital. How did Esme know how to do that? It became clear to Carson that she hadn't been a family practitioner for very long. She was a surgeon before, but why was she hiding it?

Why would she hide such a talent?

It baffled him.

Because as he watched her work, that was what he saw. Utter talent as she drained the pericardial sac with ease. She then smiled as she listened with her stethoscope.

"Well?" Carson asked, feeling absolutely useless.

"He'll make it to the hospital, but he'll need a CT and possibly surgery depending on the extent of his injuries."

There was a whir of helicopter blades outside and Harry came running in. "The medics are here to fly him to the hospital."

Esme nodded. "I'll go talk to them. Pack the wound on his arm."

Carson just nodded and watched her as she disappeared outside with Harry. She was so confident and sure of herself. She had been when he'd first met her, but this was something different. It reminded him of Danielle. Whenever she was on the surgical floor Danielle was a totally different person.

Actually, Carson found most surgeons to be arrogant and so sure of everything they did, but then they'd have to be. Lives were in their hands. Not that lives weren't in his hands, but it was a different scale.

Carson rarely dealt with the traumatic.

He turned to Dave's wound and cleansed it, packing it with gauze to protect it on his journey to the nearest hospital.

Esme rounded the corner and behind her were two paramedics. He could still hear the chopper blades rotating; they were going to pack him and get out fast, before smoke from the forest fires blew back in this direction and inhibited their takeoff.

Esme was still firing off instructions as they carefully loaded Dave onto their stretcher and began to hook up an IV and monitors to him. Carson helped slip on the oxygen mask. They moved quick, and he followed them outside as they ran with the gurney to the waiting chopper.

Esme stood back beside him, her arm protecting her face from the dust kicking up. There was no room on the chopper for them and they weren't needed anymore. The paramedics could handle Dave and he'd soon be in the capable hands of the surgeons at the hospital.

As the door to the chopper slammed it began to lift above the mill, above the thinned forest and south toward the city. Once the helicopter was out of sight, Esme sighed.

"Well, that was more excitement than I was preparing for tonight."

"You were amazing in there," Carson stated. "Was your previous general practice in a large city? I rarely see cardiac tamponades in my clinic. Or did you work at a hospital under a cardio-thoracic surgeon? The way you handled that I'm surprised you didn't become a cardio-thoracic surgeon. You had the steady hand of an experienced surgeon."

Esme's eyes widened and she bit her lip, before shrugging. "Sure, yeah, a cardio-thoracic surgeon mentor. So where's Harry gone? I really want to get back home. It's getting late. I better get my things."

She turned and headed back into the building, her arms wrapped tight around her lithe body.

Carson sighed and followed her and helped her clean up. She didn't engage him in any further discussion about the matter. They just disposed of soiled material and bagged up the rest of their stuff.

"Docs, I have the truck ready. I can take you back to town now," Harry said as he wandered into the room.

"Thanks, Harry." Carson glanced at Esme, who seemed to have relaxed and returned to herself. "You ready to go, Dr. Petersen?"

"Yes. I'm exhausted!" She smiled. "Thanks for taking us back to town, Harry."

Harry shrugged. "It's no problem. I don't stay up here at the camp. I'm local."

"Oh, you're local, all right, Harry," Carson teased as he picked up his bag. Harry just chuckled and they followed him out of the admin building to his pickup truck.

Now that the excitement had died down, workers were headed back to their bunks or back to the mill to work. He could hear the saws starting up again.

Esme climbed into the middle and Carson slid in beside her.

Harry turned the ignition and then rolled down his window, to lean his elbow out the side. "Yeah, the guys are a bit stressed around here. Mr. Draven is coming here tomorrow morning to inspect the mill. It's got the boss Bartholomew on edge. With the Draven contract for his resort that will mean a lot of work. A lot of money."

"What's Mr. Draven's first name?" There was an edge to Esme's voice.

"Silas. He's a big hotel mogul from out east," Harry said.

"East?" There was a bit of relief in her voice.

"Do you know Mr. Draven?" Carson asked.

"N-no. Just heard of him. The name sounded familiar, but I don't know Silas Draven."

Somehow Carson knew that was a lie, just by the nervous tone to Esme's voice and the way she'd sounded so relieved.

"He's never come to the mill before," Harry remarked. "I mean, he's a big rich investor. Doesn't know much about lumber mills other than what his advisors tell him, but I suspect it has something to do with competing. There's untapped tourist resources."

"Another hotel?" Carson asked.

Great.

It was supposed to be a simple resort community. Small and unique. Every time he heard something new about it, it was spiraling out of control. Perhaps it was the competitors that Luke had been taking up into the mountains to do surveying. More change.

Change can be good.

Only he didn't believe that. Change only brought heartache, disaster.

Temptation.

And he glanced over at Esme, sitting beside him in the dark. She was definitely a temptation.

"You okay?" she asked.

"Fine."

"You're scowling."

"I'm not. Besides, how can you tell? It's pitch-black out there."

"There's a moon and the dashboard light."

Indeed, in the flicker of light he could see her smiling at him, her eyes twinkling in the dark, and he couldn't help but smile, even though he didn't feel like it at the moment. Even though he knew nothing about her, being around her tonight had been a bit magical. It had been exciting and he couldn't remember the last time he'd felt such a rush.

Don't think about her like that.

"Do you think Dave will make it?" Harry asked, breaking through his thoughts.

"He should. Once he's in the hands of a capable cardio-thoracic surgeon." Esme leaned against the seat. "Which I'm not."

"You said that with such force," Carson said. "You really want to be clear that you're not a cardio-thoracic surgeon."

Her smile disappeared. "Because I'm not. I'm just lucky enough to have had the chance to perform that a couple of times."

"I thought it was only once?"

Esme stiffened. "Once was an understatement."

"Clearly, because the way you executed that procedure was superb. In fact, it looked like you'd been doing that for quite some time. Especially since you executed it without the use of an ultrasound."

Esme snorted. "I'm just a general practitioner and I did what I had to do to save a man's life. Can we drop the interrogation?"

"I'm not interrogating you."

She shrugged. "I've told you I've done it a couple of times. I guess I was lucky—really there was no other choice. Dave would've died had I not performed it then and there."

"You're right. Let's drop it."

"Good."

Carson turned and looked out the window, not that there was anything to see in the dark, on a logging road, in the middle of the forest, but he didn't feel like engaging in small talk with Esme. She was maddening.

It was clear to Carson by the way she wasn't looking at him and the way her body became tense that she wasn't too keen on discussing the matter further. What was she hiding?

Why do you care?

Perhaps because he'd been duped by a female before.

Working at your dad's practice sounds great! I would love to.

Then of course Danielle's tune had changed.

This is never what I wanted. You didn't give me much of a choice.

Not that he should care if Esme was lying to him. Let her have her secrets. It didn't matter. They weren't involved, they weren't colleagues and they certainly weren't friends. They were just two doctors in the same, sleepy small town.

That was it.

CHAPTER FOUR

ESME MANAGED TO avoid Carson for two weeks after working up on the mountain. She just decided it was in everyone's best interest if she laid low. Less questions to be asked that way. She knew Carson didn't believe her lies.

Great.

Why did that accident have to happen in front of Carson? She was here to be a simple physician. Not a surgeon, but then if she hadn't been there, Dave would've died. He wouldn't have made it to the hospital.

So she'd done the right thing, even if it had meant she'd had to perform a surgical procedure in front of Carson. Something she'd sworn she wasn't going to do when she got to Crater Lake.

The best solution was to avoid Carson for a while.

Which was why Esme was standing in the produce section of a big chain grocery store two towns away, staring at a pile of cantaloupes.

Run.

That was what she was telling herself, or at least the cowardly voice in her head was telling her.

Where?

That she didn't know. She couldn't go home to her

father. He'd made it clear that her running away was not the answer. That was what her mother had done. After Avery's death, she'd packed up and run away.

I've been a wife and mother. It's time for me. I gave up my life for you.

It had broken her father's heart. He'd lost a son and wife in the same year.

Now a daughter.

Ever since she'd left Los Angeles her father had made it clear how disappointed he was in her, so she was the last person her father wanted to see. She was just a big failure.

"Nice melons."

Esme shook her head and looked up to see Carson standing on the other side of the counter of cantaloupes.

"What?" she asked in disbelief.

He grinned and then rubbed the back of his neck. "Sorry, it was just a joke. You were staring so intently at the produce I thought you were trying to see through it."

Esme chuckled when she realized she had been staring at the cantaloupes for a long time. "Sorry, lost in thought. What're you doing here? I thought you went to the co-op in Crater Lake?"

"I usually do, but I was in town visiting a friend and remembered I needed a few things." He walked around the produce counter to stand beside her. "I thought you usually shopped locally? I didn't even know you had a car."

"I don't. I took the bus down here." She picked up a melon and sniffed it, hoping this would be the end of the conversation, that he would get the hint to walk away. Instead he lingered.

Damn. Take a hint.

Carson whistled. "That's a pricey ticket to go grocery shopping."

Esme shrugged. "Didn't have a choice."

"The local co-op is a choice."

"The prices here are better?"

Carson smiled. "Why did you pose that in the form of a question? I doubt they're low enough to justify the price of a bus ticket."

"Are you really going to sit here and lecture me about my shopping habits?"

"No, but I can offer you a ride back to Crater Lake at the very least."

Say no.

Only she couldn't, because she really didn't want to lug all her groceries on the passenger bus back up to Crater Lake. And after this one excursion she knew she'd either have to invest in a car or just pluck up the courage to shop at the co-op, because she obviously couldn't avoid Carson even two towns away.

"Thanks. I appreciate that." She pushed her shopping cart away from the melons and Carson fell into step beside her.

"I haven't seen you around much," Carson remarked.

"I've been busy."

"I saw that Mrs. Fenolio is now one of your patients."

Esme sighed. "Are you going to start on me about stealing your patients again?"

"No. I'm not. Honestly, I'm glad that she's headed over to you. You seem to have more of a grasp of cardiothoracic care."

Her heart skipped a beat.

Oh, God. Had he found out?

"Who told you that?"

"I saw it with my own eyes, Esme. Only someone with cardio-thoracic knowledge would be able to perform that procedure in that kind of situation. I think you've done that more than once or even a couple of times."

He was really persisting about the procedure. He was digging for information, information she didn't want to share. Information she wasn't going to share. It was in her past. She was here to start a new life. She wasn't that person any longer.

"I must have really impressed you."

"Well...yes." And he looked away quickly, rubbing the back of his neck again, as if he was embarrassed. As if he didn't want to give her a compliment.

"It was nothing. Now, about Mrs. Fenolio..."

"She's your patient now and you're the expert."

"I'm not. Not really."

Liar.

"Besides, she's only moved over her cardio care to me. How long has she had that murmur?"

"Do you really want to talk about this in a grocery store?" Carson asked as he picked up a loaf of bread and plunked it into her cart.

"Since when am I buying you groceries?" Esme teased.

"It's my fee for taking you back to Crater Lake. You can buy me my sandwiches for a week."

Esme chuckled. "I'm so disappointed."

"Why?"

"You're a sandwich man."

"What's wrong with liking sandwiches?" he asked.

"Nothing per se, but I'm a bit of a foodie."

Carson snorted. "Right, I forgot you're from Los Angeles."

"You don't have to be from LA to be a foodie. You can be from small towns, too. Not that I expect many people from Crater Lake to have many options."

"What're you talking about?" he asked.

"Oh, come on. Ray's is a fantastic Mom and Pop shop, but it's hardly gourmet."

"We have gourmet in Crater Lake," he said, sounding mildly insulted.

Esme looked skeptical. "Do you?"

"We do, but it's a bit of a secret."

"A secret?"

"Would you be interested in sampling a dinner there? I mean, since you're such a gourmand."

A zing traveled down her spine. Was he asking her out on a date? No. He couldn't be. She should say no, just on the off chance, but then again she couldn't resist a chance at a gourmet experience in Crater Lake.

It was better than sitting at home alone.

Don't do it.

"Okay...but as long as it's not up at the lodge." She didn't want too many people to see her with Carson. She wanted a low profile in town.

"No, it's not up at the lodge. It's been around longer than the lodge."

"Sure, then. Sounds intriguing."

"Good. So perhaps tonight?"

"Tonight?" she asked, trying not to let her voice hitch in her throat. "So soon?"

She thought maybe a day or two so she could get used to the idea.

"Is there something wrong with tonight? Do you have plans?"

Lie. Tell him you're busy.

Of course, if it was tonight she could get it done and out of the way.

"No. Tonight is fine. That's if you can get reservations to such an exclusive posh restaurant."

"Trust me. I can."

"Okay, then, it's a…" She paused because she was going to say *date*, but that was not what it was. At least she wasn't going to admit that was what it was. If she said it was a date, then it was and she couldn't have that. It was like eating a whole cake when no one saw you—the calories didn't count.

You know better than that. The calories do count.

And she might've just bitten off a little bit more than she could chew at the moment.

Carson couldn't believe what he'd just done, but before he could even think logically about what he was doing he was asking her out to a nonexistent restaurant. He was asking her over to his place, for dinner tonight. Carson couldn't help but think that he'd set himself up for failure and he didn't know why he'd asked her out.

Carson hadn't asked out anyone since Danielle.

He'd sworn off women when Danielle left and broke his heart.

He didn't want to get hurt again. It should be a simple matter staying away from Esme, but he couldn't.

He was drawn to her like a moth to a flame and he knew if he kept up this way he was going to get burnt.

Bad.

He was a masochist.

Perhaps she'd only said yes because she wanted to discover this great new restaurant in a very small town. Some hidden gem. Foodies liked to find hidden and new restaurants, especially places that were off the beaten trail, so to speak, and it was all innocent.

Yet the things she stirred deep down inside him were hardly innocent. And it scared him that she stirred desires that he'd buried long ago.

How would she feel when he picked her up and took her to his place, out in the woods? Not that he was that far out in the woods. He had an acre of wood lot and a nice cabin, which Luke had helped him build years ago, when Carson had thought he was building a home for him and Danielle.

There were neighbours within sight, but how would a city girl feel being brought out into the woods by a man she barely knew? He could be a serial killer for all she knew.

You're overthinking things again.

"You've gone positively pale," Esme remarked as they walked side by side through the store.

"What?" he asked.

"Are you okay?"

"I'm fine."

She frowned. "I don't think you are. You totally drifted off there. If it's about tonight, we can make it for another night."

"No, no, it's not that."

Yes, it is. You're setting yourself up for hurt.

"Are you sure?"

"Positive. I was just thinking about one of my files."

"Mrs. Fenolio?"

"Uh, yeah, sure."

Esme bit her lip. "We can talk about it tonight. I get that she's been at your family practice for some time. I understand it's hard to let go of some patients. Boy, do I ever." She mumbled the *Boy, do I ever* and he couldn't help but wonder why. Did she lose a patient that it still affected her so profoundly?

The loss of a patient was something that never sat right with Carson, but then, working in his father's practice, the patients they would lose were elderly. He wasn't a surgeon. Patients rarely died on his table.

When he thought about heading down that path to become a surgeon, he quickly changed his mind because he didn't want to just stitch them up and send them on their way. He wanted a connection with them. He wanted to be their primary caregiver.

It hurt when one of his patients died or became ill, but it wasn't the same as being responsible for someone's death and he couldn't help but wonder if Esme had experienced that.

"You lost a patient in LA?" he asked as they walked slowly down an aisle.

"Why would you ask me that?" She didn't look at him; she pretended to be studying the cans on the shelves.

"Because you're avoiding eye contact with me."

She shrugged and briefly glanced in his direction. "I'm not avoiding eye contact with you."

"You are too. I can tell when patients are lying to me."

She frowned. "I'm not your patient."

"Semantics."

Esme sighed. "I did lose a patient. It was hard, but

I moved on. You can't tell me that when you lost your first patient in your first year it didn't affect you?"

Esme was twisting the subject around back to him. It was a good evasive maneuver that he'd used many times to avoid uncomfortable questions.

Impressive.

"Well?" There was a small smile tugging at the corners of her lips.

"Okay, it affected me. Of course it would affect me. Anyone with any sense of compassion would feel that loss keenly."

"Exactly."

Carson decided he would drop the subject. For now, but he was still going to dig into her cardio-thoracic past. He was convinced that a family physician, just a family physician, wouldn't be able to perform such a procedure with such skill and precision.

She'd been so sure of herself.

So confident.

In that moment Esme had reminded him of a surgeon. A bit of her reminded him of Danielle. The drive, the ambition, and someone with that kind of passion wouldn't want to stay in such a place as Crater Lake.

They didn't talk much about anything else. They finished their grocery shopping and he drove the hour back to Crater Lake. Just chatting politely about nothing really. It was the most uncomfortable car ride Carson had ever taken in his life.

The whole way back to town he tried not to think about Danielle and how her leaving had left a hole in his heart. It had hurt, but he'd moved on. He'd built a solid practice with his father. He was safe and secure.

At least he'd thought his existence was safe and secure. He was comfortable. That was until Esme Petersen had set up shop in town and that had totally rocked the foundation of his safety net. He wasn't sure if he liked it.

Don't you?

He shook his head as he pulled up in front of her clinic.

"So what time will you be picking me up?" Esme asked.

"About seven?"

"Sure. That sounds great." She smiled; it was bright and cheerful. It warmed his heart, made him feel things he hadn't felt in a long time and that scared him.

Back out of the date.

He knew he was playing with fire, but he couldn't help himself. It was just an innocent dinner. He wanted to find out more about her, about her practice and maybe discuss some cases. Things that Luke never wanted to do, things he used to discuss with his father before his parents had upped and moved to Naples, Florida.

"Is there a dress code at this restaurant?" Esme asked, still not getting out of his car.

"No."

She glanced at him. "A gourmet restaurant and no dress code. I think I'm liking this place already."

Carson chuckled. "You'll like it. Trust me."

"And if I don't?" she asked.

"Then I owe you one."

Esme just grinned, but didn't say anything more as she opened the car door. "Pop the trunk for me and I'll see you at seven."

"Seven. I'll be waiting."

Esme climbed out and shut the door, collecting her groceries from the trunk and shutting it. She waved and then headed down the alley toward the back of her clinic.

Carson gripped the steering wheel and sat there for a few moments. What was he doing? He didn't really know. When Danielle had left him, when she'd crushed his heart, his hopes and dreams, he'd sworn he wouldn't let someone in again.

No dating, no nothing.

He was comfortable in his existence.

There were no surprises.

It was nice.

And it was also absolutely and utterly boring.

CHAPTER FIVE

ESME WANTED TO call and cancel the dinner date about three times before seven o'clock. The only problem was she didn't know Carson's phone number. She knew his office number, but the clinic was closed, so she was kind of stuck.

It's just as friends. Colleagues. Nothing more.

That was what she kept telling herself over and over again. The problem was, she wasn't sure if she was able to convince herself of that fact.

This was how it had started with Shane. A dinner with her mentor's son. As a favor to Eli, who hadn't been able to take his son out that night. It had been just a friendly dinner and then it had escalated from there. There was only one difference between Carson and Shane.

The simple fact was Carson Ralston made her nervous and no one made her nervous. Not Shane, not a difficult surgery. Just Carson.

Not even Eli Draven, the surgeon she idolized, made her nervous. He'd yelled and screamed at her before and she didn't care. The only reason she avoided Shane's father was because it reminded her of how she'd hurt Shane.

She was made of stronger mettle than to fold under the pressure of someone like Eli. Of course, Eli was someone else she'd disappointed.

Her father had always taught her to be strong. To stand up for herself and not let anyone walk all over her. Not that Carson was walking all over her. It was just that being around him made her nervous. He made her blood rush, her stomach zing and her body heat.

Carson made her weak in the knees. He made her think of romance and she wasn't a romance type of girl. Love only led to heartache. The only time she'd come close to anything romantic was when she'd almost married Shane on Valentine's Day, and look where that had got her.

Yet, being around Carson made her nervous, made her irrational.

There were times she could feel the heat in her cheeks from blushing and Esme had never blushed in someone's presence before.

Not since she was in the seventh grade and had that crush on Matthew Fenwick.

You do not have a crush on Dr. Ralston.

That was what she kept trying to tell herself over and over again. She didn't have a crush on Carson. She couldn't have a crush on him, she just couldn't, because she didn't deserve it. Men like Carson needed a wife and Esme wasn't wife material. Something that had become quite clear to her when she'd picked up the voluminous skirt of her designer wedding dress and climbed out of the bathroom window of the church, running in the opposite direction to Shane.

He'd demanded so much of her. He'd wanted her by his side constantly, which had taken her away from surgery. She'd forgotten about why she'd become a surgeon. She'd realized all of this when she'd frozen during surgery. How dating Shane had made her off her game.

How could she be the best cardio-thoracic surgeon if she was a society wife and mother? With Shane she couldn't. She couldn't be herself. So Esme had run. *I don't know who you are anymore. I didn't raise a daughter who runs.*

Her father's voice was still so clear in her mind.

She didn't know who she was. Not anymore.

A textbook procedure on a patient and she'd frozen. Not knowing what to do next.

Lost.

And then it had all come back in a rush and despite her best efforts she hadn't been able to save the patient. It hadn't mattered that it hadn't been her fault, that she had done everything she could. All she'd been able to see was her failure in that moment.

That was when she'd walked away from surgery. She was done. Broken. From there things had spiraled and it had led to the collapse of her plans for happy ever after with Shane. If only she could have known her own heart sooner.

That was why she had left Los Angeles. To find herself again. Though that was easier said than done, because her guilty conscience was attacking her at every angle.

She'd run away.

She'd disappointed her father.

Still, there had been no choice in the matter. Here she could live in peace. Here she didn't have to run.

When it came to matters of the heart though, that

was where she was weak. Maybe she should run now?
Go somewhere else until Carson left. Then she wouldn't
have to go out to dinner with him and then she wouldn't
have to feel so nervous around him.

Carson's SUV pulled up in front of her building. He
honked the horn a couple of times. Esme sighed and
grabbed her purse.

No turning back now. She just hoped she was dressed
okay. She didn't want to stick out like a sore thumb.
She'd opted for casual classy. A nice pair of jeans, boots
and a black sweater that was off the shoulders. Also
accessories.

So no matter where he took her, she'd blend in and
that was what it was all about. She just wanted to blend
in. She didn't want to stand out.

She didn't want to be extraordinary, because she
wasn't. Not anymore anyway.

When she walked over to the car Carson got out and
held open the door for her.

"You didn't have to get out," she said.

"My mother taught me good manners." Once she was
in the car he shut the door and then slid back into the
driver's seat, buckling up before he pulled away. "So
this place we're going, it's out in the country. I didn't
want to freak you out or anything."

"Why would I freak out?" she asked.

"You know, a man you barely know is taking you
out into the wilderness."

Esme chuckled. "I assumed it was out of town."

"You did?"

"Main Street, or rather the town of Crater Lake, isn't
that huge. The only eating establishments within the

major downtown core are Ray's, Little Mamma's Bakery and Main Street Deli…which has been closed for repairs for a seemingly long time."

"Twenty years," Carson responded.

"That's a shame. I enjoy a good sandwich." She tried not to laugh. It was so easy to tease him. All the trepidation she'd been feeling seemed to melt away and that was what scared her. It was so easy to be around him.

"What? I thought you had an issue with sandwiches. I mean, that's why I'm taking you to this exclusive spot. You seemed to have a problem with my sandwiches when we were shopping today."

"I like traditional deli sandwiches within moderation. Somehow, though, I think that you're taking bologna sandwiches to work. Two pieces of white bread, mustard, an imitation cheese slice and a piece of bologna. Just like Mom used to pack in school lunches."

"All smooshed down and everything?" Carson asked.

Esme smiled. "Yes, with the crusts cut off."

He shook his head. "You think you know me so well. I'll have you know it's not just bologna in my repertoire. I also enjoy a good salami."

She couldn't help but break out laughing at that and when he realized what he'd said a blush crept up his cheeks and he shot her an exasperated look.

"That's not what I meant at all and you know it."

"Do I? I barely know you," she said. "You could be an axe murderer or something. A doctor who injects his patients with a live virus just so he can test his maniacal cures on them."

"Hardly."

"Whatever you say, Dr. Moreau." Then she laughed.

"Fine, then. Believe what you want." He winked and turned down a gravel drive. She glanced out the window as she saw a beautiful log home in a clearing, built into the side of a foothill.

"What is this place?" she asked.

"The exclusive restaurant. Also known as my house."

Her heart beat a bit faster. *His house?* This was dangerous.

"Your house?" she asked, the words barely getting out.

"I'm sorry for tricking you. I guess I should've explained that it was my place I was taking you to."

"Yeah, you should've."

"Would you have come?"

"No," she said. "I don't think so." And it was true. She wouldn't have. Having dinner with him was temptation enough. She'd thought at least other people would be around. Now they'd be alone, out in the woods in his gorgeous cabin. Suddenly, she was very nervous again.

Dammit.

It was all too seductive for her liking.

"Sorry, but I wanted to prove to you that I'm not just a sandwich guy. Even though I'm not from LA and I don't have exposure to some of the best restaurants in America, I do have experience of some gastronomical delights."

"That remains to be seen."

"You don't believe me?" he asked in mild outrage.

"My expectations were set high," she teased. "You have a lot to live up to, Dr. Ralston."

Carson parked his car. "You can call me Carson. We're not on duty."

Blood rushed to her cheeks and she turned her head away briefly, hoping he wouldn't notice how he was affecting her physically.

Think about something else.

"Okay. You can call me Esme. I mean, no one else is around so no one has to know we've formed this sort of ceasefire."

"Right."

They got out of the car and she followed him up the steps to the front porch. She stopped to take in the breathtaking sight. From the front porch she could see Crater Lake, nestled in the foothills, like in a little valley. The mountains in Glacier National Park rising up to protect the town, as if it were this little sheltered place. Untouched and hidden.

"Wow," she whispered.

"I know. When I have time I like to sit out here at night. It's also beautiful in the morning with the sun rising."

Lucky.

If this was her place she'd do the exact same thing.

Esme walked over to the railing and leaned over, taking in her surroundings. She spotted another house, down the hill in the trees. It looked dark, but lived in. "Whose house is that?"

Carson came up beside her and she was suddenly aware of how close he actually was. His hand so close to her on the wooden railing, they were almost touching. She could smell his cologne. It was subtle, masculine and very woodsy. It made her tremble. It made her weak in the knees.

It turned her on.

So she moved an inch away, trying to put distance between them.

"That's my childhood home. Or rather my parents' house. They come back and visit from time to time. That's where they stay. This land is my family's land. With me nearby I can keep an eye on my parents' house."

"Where are they now?"

"Naples, Florida. They have a condo that backs out onto a golf course. They love it there."

"And I hear you have a brother, right?"

Carson nodded. "Yes. I do."

"Does he live there or here with you?"

"No, he lives up the mountain in a shack."

Esme rolled her eyes. "Are you having me on? He doesn't live in a shack."

"Yes, he does."

"I thought you said he was a doctor."

"He is, but he lives in a shack up the mountain. He's a bit of a mountain man. He doesn't practice traditional medicine. He was an army medic for years in Special Ops and then after he was discharged he liked living in the rough so much he built a shanty out in the woods. He takes surveyors out; he's a first responder. He teaches people how to survive in the hostile environment of a mountain. He will do emergency surgery."

"Emergency surgery in the woods?"

"Sometimes there's no choice."

Esme cringed inwardly at the thought of emergency surgery out in the forest. Hardly ideal, but if you were an ex-army man living rough in a remote community, then it made sense.

"Wow. All the power to him." She moved away from

him. "So are you going to let me inside or are we going to stand here all night?"

Carson grinned and unlocked the front door, stepping aside. "After you."

She tried not to gasp when she stepped inside his house. She was expecting rustic, but on a smaller scale. She was not prepared for the high roof, exposed wooden beams and the massive stone fireplace that dominated the northern wall. All around them were windows, which offered a three-sixty view of the mountains, the town and a lake that seemed to be sunk in, like a hollow. Even in the evening sunlight, you could see its brilliant coral and aquamarine colors. In the center the blue darkened, like a deep hole.

She'd seen the Great Blue Hole in Belize; this wasn't as big, but it was still impressive given the setting. She moved toward the far window to get a better look at the lake. There was no wind outside so the mountains were perfectly reflected in the water. Like a mirror. It was the most beautiful thing she'd ever seen.

Carson came up behind her; she could feel the heat of his body against her back. It made her uncomfortable and she remembered his arm around her when he'd tried to comfort her on the trip up the mountain to the mill. She shifted away, trying to put some distance between the two of them.

Distance was safe.

"What's the name of the lake?"

"That's Crater Lake, what the town was named after."

"I expected something different for Crater Lake."

"Different?"

"Something bigger perhaps." He smiled at her, that smile that made her melt just a little bit. This was why Carson was dangerous.

"I think it's pretty substantial." Carson raked his hand through his hair and then crossed his arms. When he had the blinds in his office windows open, she watched him dictating charts, just like that. His arms crossed, head bent and usually pacing back and forth.

There was something calming about it. Soothing. It made her feel at ease.

She couldn't think about him like that.

"Why is it so blue?" Esme asked, trying not to think about the fact she was standing in Carson's home, that he made her calm and yet nervous at the same time. She couldn't think about him this way. She didn't want to.

This was not what she was here for.

"Mineral water off the glacier in the mountains. When the water is blue like that, it's from the glaciers. If it's more clear, more like a normal lake, it's spring fed." He moved past her to the south end of the house and pointed. "That's Mitchum Lake—see the difference. It's spring fed."

"I think these are better views than where that new resort community was built on the other side of town. I'm surprised that no one made you an offer on this land."

"Who says they didn't?" Carson grinned. "Would you like some wine?"

Esme nodded as he moved past her to the kitchen.

"I'm sure it was a lot of money they must've offered. Most people wouldn't turn that down."

"I'm not most people." He winked and set down two wine glasses on the counter. "Red okay?"

"Perfect." She dropped her purse on an end table. "So what do you plan to cook for me tonight?"

"Bison."

What? "Did I just hear you correctly? Did you say bison?"

"I could cook you elk if you'd prefer?"

"Bison is fine. I have to say I'm disappointed."

Carson cocked an eyebrow and then started to get food ready for dinner. "Why?"

"Isn't Montana famous for beefsteak?"

He flexed and made pointed glances at his biceps, which made her laugh out loud. She couldn't remember the last time she'd laughed like that. It was so easy to laugh with Carson. When the giggles stopped she followed him out onto his deck, which overlooked the lake. He had a stainless-steel barbecue there, where he was grilling the bison steaks.

Esme wandered over to the side and leaned over the railing. She could see the construction off in the distance where the new Draven resort and spa were going to go up. They were going to be an eyesore.

At least that was Esme's opinion.

"What're you thinking about?" Carson asked.

"Pardon?"

Carson glanced over his shoulder at her. "I asked you what you were thinking about. You were staring off into space. You do that a lot."

She couldn't tell him why she had been doing that a lot lately and he was right, she had been drifting off. It was nice and quiet. It was easy enough to do around here.

"I was relaxing and enjoying the view."

"Easy to do," Carson said as he turned back to the

grill and flipped the meat. "I've thought about putting a hot tub out here."

"That would be nice. Especially in the winter, I bet."

"Have you ever experienced winter?" Carson asked.

"Yes, I wasn't born and raised in California. I'm from Ohio."

"So you're used to bitter winters."

Esme nodded. "Yeah, but it's been a long time since I experienced one. I'm honestly not looking forward to it."

He laughed. "I don't doubt it."

"Can I help?"

"You can grab the cobs of corn in the fridge, then I can grill them here on the barbecue."

"Sure thing." Esme set her wine glass down on the patio table and headed inside. She found the shucked corn in the fridge and brought it back to Carson, who threw it on the grill. "Why don't we eat outside?"

"Sure. We can do that."

Esme headed back inside and found plates and cutlery. She brought everything outside and set it all out. Just in time for the meat and corn to be done.

They sat down together.

"I hope you like it. My brother says I'm the best at grilling bison."

"Well, since I have nothing to compare it to." Esme took a bite. It was so tender and absolutely delicious. She'd tried lots of different food before, but never bison.

"What do you think?" Carson asked.

"It's fantastic."

"See, I told you it was the best place in town."

"You were right. Great view, too."

"I always thought so. It's why I built my house here."

Esme was stunned. "You built this house?"

"I did. I like working with my hands. I like building things. I didn't draw up the plans, but I did a lot of the work myself. Luke and my father helped, too."

"That's amazing. Most doctors I know just participate in golf or attend parties at their club."

"Those are surgeons. I can't see a surgeon risking injuring their hands by doing work like this. Well, at least not any surgeons I know."

"I thought you didn't know any surgeons?"

Carson sighed. "Well, I do have to refer my patients who need work to surgeons. Thankfully, most of those surgeons are in Missoula."

"You don't like surgeons very much, do you?"

"Who said that? I have no problems with surgeons. There are some general practitioners I know who are just as goofy as the ones in Missoula."

Esme laughed. "So I take it you don't have many friends?"

"I'm a bit of a loner. I prefer it that way."

"Me, too." And she did, to some extent, but suddenly the idea of going back to her apartment above her clinic made her sad. She had a hard time falling asleep in the quiet.

She wanted to be alone, she didn't deserve happiness, but still. It sucked. And sitting here with Carson made her forget for just a moment that she was lonely. It was amazing being here with him and just talking.

Which was a dangerous thing indeed.

Carson smiled at her; when he smiled like that there was a dimple in his cheek. It was so sexy. She was a sucker for dimples on a man. There were a lot of enticing qualities about Carson. He was so different from

Shane. So down to earth, but she could tell he wasn't the type of guy to be pushed around by anyone.

She was definitely treading on dangerous ground here.

"So Mrs. Fenolio is quite stubborn."

Carson chuckled under his breath. "I thought you didn't want to talk about Mrs. Fenolio?"

"I didn't want to talk about her in the store, but I'm willing to discuss her file with her former physician in this private setting."

She was trying in vain to turn the conversation around. If they talked about work she wouldn't think about how good he looked in the button-down flannel shirt he was wearing, the tight starched jeans and the cowboy boots. Or the fact that he was a fantastic cook.

If they talked about the patient, she wouldn't stare at his slim hips or those muscular forearms or his smiling face with the devious sparkle in his eyes. A sparkle that was promising lots of very bad things that she really wanted to indulge in.

Damn.

He nodded and poured the wine. "You have knowledge in cardio-thoracic surgery."

"A bit."

He looked at her. "Oh, we're going to play this game again."

"I'm not playing any games, Dr. Ralston."

"Carson."

She glared at him. "Carson, then."

"Better."

She sighed. "Okay, I spent some time in a hospital before I decided to open a family practice and that's all you need to know about the matter."

* * *

Carson wanted to press her further, because he felt as if here she was opening up more, but then he didn't want to scare her away either. She might be the competition, but maybe, just maybe, if they were on good terms they could work together and do something more. The town was expanding and it might be nice to have a larger practice. Something his father had never dreamed of.

If it's not broken you don't fix it. That was his father's mantra when it came to business. Thankfully not when it came to medicine.

The Ralston family practice had been the way it was since the town was founded. It was sufficient and efficient.

If a patient required any other kind of care that the practice didn't offer, the hospital was only an hour away. That was the reason why they had air ambulance up in this part of Montana.

The family practice was solid.

It didn't need to be changed and just thinking about that change scared him. He shouldn't be thinking about changing it. What would change do? It could potentially destroy everything his family had built. Did he really want to cause the demise of the Ralston family practice?

He wasn't the one who was going to end that legacy.

Carson wasn't that person. Even if he wanted more, he wasn't going to change a thing.

He turned around and put a stopper in the wine, setting it on the far counter, his back to Esme so she couldn't see him. He didn't want to be thinking about Danielle. Not here, not now. Also it got his mind off the fact Esme was in his home and that his bedroom was just ten feet away. She was so damn sexy and he had to keep reminding himself she was off-limits. He refused to get hurt again.

He had to stop staring at the curve of her neck, her red lips and her bare shoulders.

"I spent some time as a surgical intern, as well," Carson said casually as he handed her the glass of wine.

"Did you?"

"I did. For about three months and I realized that surgery is not my thing."

"Not your thing?" she asked. "Why?"

"I want to save lives."

Her brow furrowed. "You don't think surgeons save lives? They're all about saving lives. They endure grueling training, long hours and sometimes life-threatening situations so they *can* save a life."

There was a fire in her eyes as she passionately defended surgery.

Not a surgeon, my foot.

"How long were you a surgical intern?"

"Ah, a year, and then I decided to open a practice in Los Angeles."

"Huh, I thought you might've gone all the way."

Esme shot him that flinty glare again, the one he was quickly learning to fear. It was the look she seemed to give when someone had pushed her too far. "Why would you assume that?"

"Because you talked so passionately about surgery. Only surgeons talk with such passion and fire about surgery, because those who are meant to be surgeons are married to it. It's their first love."

The glare softened and she smiled. "I just respect them. That's all."

He nodded. "I respect them, too, and I quickly learned in my few months that I was not a surgeon and that was probably for the best for all patients."

She laughed at his joke, the tension melting away. "Well, I tried a new prescription regimen on Mrs. Fenolio, but darned if I can get her to take it."

Carson frowned. "A new prescription regimen? Why?"

"What she was taking for her condition was not working anymore."

"Digoxin wasn't working anymore? Physicians have been using digoxin since the pioneer days."

"Yes, and it did work fine. In Mrs. Fenolio's case it doesn't apply any longer. She's suffering from ventricular tachycardia. In Mrs. Fenolio's case amiodarone works substantially better."

He frowned again. "That's horrible. I'm sorry she's deteriorated. My father was treating her for a decade."

"And he did fantastic. Mrs. Fenolio's disease is progressing rapidly. I've actually added her to the transplant list."

"You...you did what?" Carson was baffled. For a decade his father had treated Mrs. Fenolio and there had been no issues. She had survived and now suddenly Esme was standing here in his kitchen saying that Mrs. Fenolio required a heart transplant. He was having a hard time believing it. Probably because Mrs. Fenolio used to babysit him and Luke. Especially given the fact Esme had only completed her intern year, something she'd just told him. He could believe that a physician who had one year of surgical training could complete the procedure she'd performed up at the mill, but changing Mrs. Fenolio's treatment plan completely and telling the woman she needed a heart transplant? That wasn't someone who did just a year as an intern. It firmed his belief Esme was a surgeon.

"What're you basing your opinion on?" he asked.

"On the tests I ran in my clinic and the fact she wore a Holter monitor for twenty-four hours."

"You admitted yourself that you're not a cardiothoracic specialist. How can you diagnose someone? How can you make that call to put her on the transplant list? You can't. Only a surgeon can do that."

Her eyes widened for a moment as if he'd caught her in a lie and she was trying to think up an excuse.

"Well?" Carson asked impatiently. "Someone who only completed one year of internship of surgery can't diagnose that condition. They wouldn't know and a general practitioner can't put a patient on the transplant waiting list without a surgeon's assessment. Admit you're a surgeon, Dr. Petersen."

"You've lost your mind." She put down her wine glass and grabbed her purse. "I think I'm going to head for home."

Carson stood in front of her, blocking her path. "You're a surgeon, Esme. You have an incredible talent. I've never seen anyone drain a cardiac tamponade or recognize a Beck's Triad that quickly in that kind of situation. I just don't know why you're trying to hide it from me."

She stared up at him. Those blue eyes, so wide. She was afraid to admit it, but why? Why should she be so afraid to admit that she had a gift? Yeah, maybe he didn't want the life of a surgeon. Maybe he'd left something he'd always dreamed about to uphold a family tradition, but why would she throw something extraordinary away?

"I… I don't know what to…"

He gripped her shoulders. "You can tell me. You have skill, Esme. Amazing talent."

"Carson, I don't know you and you don't know me. I shouldn't be having this conversation with you."

"You can trust me."

"Can I?"

"Yes," he whispered as he reached out and brushed back her hair. It was so soft and he fought the urge to kiss her, because that was what he wanted to do. He wanted to kiss her. Badly. "Tell me. You can tell me."

"You might think less of me."

"Doubtful."

Esme smiled, but in a sad way that made his soul ache a bit. "So sure of yourself. I had confidence like that once."

"You still do."

"No, I don't."

"Yes, you do. That was a confident doctor I saw up on that mountain."

She was going to say something else when his door opened and Luke came barging in.

"Carson, I've been looking all over for you." Then he saw Esme. "Sorry, I didn't realize you had company."

Esme pushed out of his embrace. "I was just heading back to town."

"Good, you both need to head back to town," Luke

said. He sounded a bit winded. "I thought you two would be down at the clinic."

"What's going on, Luke?" Carson asked.

"I brought a surveyor down off the mountain. His appendix is going to blow. There's no time to take him to the hospital."

CHAPTER SIX

EVEN IF SHE wanted to hide the fact that she was a surgeon from Carson now, there was no way she could. Not when there was a life on the line.

With this surveyor who was in Carson's exam room in agony, she wasn't going to let the man die from a ruptured appendix because she had something to hide.

Because she was scared.

She was going to operate on him. She might not practice as a surgeon now, but she was a surgeon. Lives were in her hands.

This man's life was in her hands. Luke was examining the surveyor while Carson began to strip off his clothes in the other room. She knew she shouldn't watch, but she couldn't help it. He saw her watching him and her cheeks bloomed with heat as his intense gaze burned into her soul. He pulled out a pair of scrubs and tossed them to her.

"You're not going to want to get your clothes dirty," Carson said. "They look too...nice to get ruined."

"Thanks."

He nodded and turned his back to her as he finished changing. Esme snuck into his office and quickly peeled off her clothes and pulled on the men's scrubs, pulling the drawstring as tight as she could, but they were still large.

As she pulled on her shirt Carson came bursting in, pausing in the doorway. He looked away quickly, rubbing the back of his neck in that awkward way he always did.

"I'm sorry. I thought you were finished."

"It's okay. I'm done. I'm impressed you keep scrubs on hand."

"My father always insisted. I guess in case of emergencies like this."

"I thought he wasn't a surgeon," Esme teased.

Carson smiled. "I never said that. You look nervous. You okay?"

"I'm okay. It's just…"

"It's nothing. You can do this."

"It's a simple surgery."

"Exactly. It'll be easy."

Easy. Right. Though she wasn't sure. The last surgery she'd done was routine. It had been easy and she'd frozen.

"I'll see you in there. Have you performed an appendectomy before?" she asked.

"Once, in the few months I was an intern."

"How about your brother?" she asked.

"He's performed several emergency procedures in extreme situations. He was an army medic. He's a surgeon, but he's not staying. He left the rest of the surveyors up on the mountain."

Esme nodded. "Oh. Well, you'll have to handle the anesthesia."

"Of course."

Esme let him change and entered the exam room

where Luke was pulling down supplies to perform the surgery in this place. The patient had been given morphine and was basically in and out of consciousness.

"Have you performed surgery before, Dr. Petersen?" Luke asked.

"Yes. Many times."

Luke nodded. "Good, I need to get back up the mountain. Carson said you were a surgeon."

"I was. I am." She cursed under her breath as she stumbled over her words. "I've performed more appendectomies than I care to admit."

Luke grinned and nodded. "Fair enough, Dr. Petersen."

She made her way over to the sink and scrubbed the best she could given the situation. Four-minute scrub. Could she even remember the words to the song she sang when she scrubbed? And then it came back to her. She scrubbed and it felt weird to be scrubbing for surgery again, but also it felt good. "Has he been given any antibiotic?"

"Doing that now, Dr. Petersen," Carson said as he was setting up an IV. Carson's brother had left. It was just the two of them here. Alone.

She might have done a ton of appendectomies and emergency appendectomies, but she'd never done one outside of the OR and not in these conditions. Though she was pretty positive if Luke Ralston was a former army medic, he'd probably seen worse. And right now she really didn't need to see worse.

There were no scrub nurses so Esme scurried to lay out the surgical instruments and the supplies she'd need.

"He's under," Carson said over his shoulder as he intubated the man. "I can assist you if you need."

"No, just manage his airway."

Carson nodded. "I'm here if you need me, but you got this."

Esme took a deep breath and palpated the patient's abdomen.

You can do it. You're a surgeon. This guy won't die.

This was just an appendectomy. This was not an open heart. Appendectomies were routine. She could do this.

You used to be able to do open hearts, too.

She *had* to do this. Help was too far away for this man. He wouldn't survive unless she did this. Esme took another deep calming breath, took the ten blade in hand and made the incision over McBurney's point. Once she was cutting down through the layers, everything fell into place. She remembered everything. It was routine. It was easy.

Her hands didn't shake.

Carson watched and then began to assist her while managing the man's airway. As if reading her thoughts he knew what instruments to hand her. The only sound was the rhythmic beat of the manual ventilator.

She found her rhythm as a surgeon again, even though it had been months since she held a scalpel. She'd forgotten what a high it was. How much she loved it. Not that she deserved to love something so much.

Still, it was a thrill. It was amazing.

All too soon she was pulling on the purse strings and inverting the stump into the cecum and closing him up.

"Excellent work, Dr. Petersen," Carson remarked.

"Thank you, Dr. Ralston." She glanced up at him while he continued to manually ventilate the patient. "Has an ambulance been called to take him to the hospital? You may be set up to do emergency surgery, but you're not set up for post-op care. He's going to need a course of antibiotics."

"Yes," Carson said. "I called from my office before we started."

Esme finished stitching and heard the sirens coming closer toward them.

"Speak of the devil," Carson muttered. "Dr. Petersen, can you take over the ventilation and I'll let the paramedics in as I know the surveyor and can give them the information they need."

"Of course." Esme pulled off her gloves, throwing them into the receptacle and putting on a fresh pair. She took over the manual ventilation since she was finished stitching, cleaned the wound and applied the pressure dressing. Carson returned quickly.

"I didn't expect to be doing that again," Esme said.

"You did an amazing job." Then he smiled at her in a way that made her heart melt. "I knew you could."

Why did he have so much faith in her?

She cleared her throat and looked away. "Your clinic was very well prepared for surgery."

"My father and Luke were always insistent on being prepared for any situation. Especially up here in the mountains," Carson said. "First time it has happened under my watch, though."

"Smart move, given the hospital is more than an hour away. This man didn't have an hour in him."

"Accidents and emergencies up here can happen when you least expect it," Carson said, peeling off his gloves. "You did well."

"Thank you." And she blushed again, their gazes locked across the room. She wanted to say more, but couldn't. She just couldn't. She had to keep her distance from Carson.

"There's no need to thank me," Carson said. "I'm just speaking the truth."

"Well, you don't need to say I did well. There's no need. I wasn't going to let him die. I did what needed to be done."

"I know that, but—"

Their conversation ended abruptly as the paramedics entered the exam room. Esme let them take over as they brought in their equipment. In a matter of minutes the paramedics had the surveyor loaded up, leaving Carson and Esme to clean up the clinic. She didn't know what Carson was going to say to her there, but it didn't matter.

Whatever it was, she didn't need to hear it.

They worked side by side in silence. She knew she couldn't really hide who she was. Not after this moment. She admitted it, but she didn't want to tell him why. She didn't want to get into it and she hated that her past was sneaking into her present life.

"So..." He trailed off.

"I was a surgeon in Los Angeles. More than an intern."

Carson smiled. "I figured that."

She laughed uneasily. "I'm not a surgeon anymore."

He stopped his cleaning. "Why?"

Because I froze during a procedure and a patient died on my table. I lost my confidence. I lost myself.

"I wanted a quiet life." Then she laughed at the absurdity of that and he joined in. "I thought Crater Lake would be quiet."

"Well, it usually is. Come to think of it, it was until you came to town."

"Thanks for that." She grinned.

He winked. "Any time."

"I hope it calms down," she said offhandedly.

"With all these new people coming to town I doubt that very much. In fact I can see a hospital being built here."

"You say that like it's a bad thing."

Carson sighed. "No, it's not a bad thing. It's just… change."

"You don't like change, do you?" Esme asked.

"No, I don't. Not really."

"Why?"

Carson didn't say anything. He didn't even look at her and she realized that she must have touched a nerve. Something he was obviously not comfortable talking about. Why didn't he like change? Something had hurt him.

It's not your business.

And it wasn't. Yet he had pushed and pressed her about being a surgeon. Maybe it was tit for tat.

"Change can be good. I mean, I changed…" She trailed off. A lot had changed in her life, but then again maybe it hadn't. She had run away from her career and when she was holding that scalpel it felt so damn good. She felt as if she was at home and for that one brief moment she regretted the fact that she'd left the hospital. That she'd left surgery.

Esme zoned out and Carson couldn't help but wonder what she was thinking. He'd known she was a surgeon, even though she'd denied it. He'd known it the moment she'd stuck that needle into that patient's chest and drained fluid.

She had a gift. Such a tremendous gift.

And he couldn't help but wonder why she would want to give that up.

What is it to you?

It really wasn't his business at all. They were just neighbors, both doctors. Heck, they weren't even friends and even if they were friends it still wouldn't be his business. So why did he care so much?

"Did the change make a difference?" he asked.

"What change?"

"Moving here from LA. You said you changed."

She shrugged. "I think it did…"

"You don't sound certain."

"I haven't been here long enough, but, as they say, a change will do you good." She continued to clean up his exam room as he mulled over her words.

A change will do you good?

He wasn't sure he believed that. Why change something that worked? It was a dangerous thing to do, to ruin one's safety net. He'd tried to once. Tried to make a change in his life and look how that had turned out.

It had left him with a shattered heart, but he'd put away all those feelings in a box. Locked them away because taking over his father's practice had been the right thing to do. It was safe and comfortable. Packing up and moving out of state. Changing professions.

Throwing away a career. One that Carson knew she would've studied long and hard for. Surgeons competed. It was a shark tank and only the fittest survived.

Why would she give that up?

It's not your concern.

Then he realized it wasn't so much that he cared, but he was angry that such a talented surgeon was throwing away her gift. She could be using that education to save lives.

You save lives.

Only not in the same way. He saved people's lives, but not in the same way that she could save lives.

It was a waste and he wanted to tell her that. Berate her. Only he couldn't. That wasn't his place, but he just didn't understand how someone could walk away from talent like that.

One day soon she'd decide that a general practice in a small town in Montana wasn't surgery. She'd close her practice, his former patients would come back and she would go back to the exciting life of a surgical practice.

Just as Danielle had left.

Surgeons wanted more. They needed more.

More than he could offer and he had to distance himself now. He could handle this.

He didn't want to handle this.

He didn't want to be her friend.

He didn't want to be… Carson couldn't even finish that thought, because that thought was dangerous and out of the question.

"Are you okay?" she asked as she tossed the rest of the drapes into the receptacle.

"Fine," he snapped and then he cursed under his breath. "Just tired."

"It's been a long day."

"It has." He couldn't even look at her. Carson just had to get away from her. "Why don't you head home for the night? Like you said, it's been a long day."

"Are you sure you don't want me to stay and help you clean up?"

"Yeah, I'm sure. Just…go."

"Okay." Esme walked out of the room. "Should I leave the scrubs in your office?"

"Yeah, that's fine." Carson could barely look at her, because if he looked at her he might start lecturing her that she was throwing away all that talent that could be used for saving lives.

She nodded. "Okay. Good night, Dr. Ralston."

Carson just nodded as she left the exam room.

He had to keep away from Esme.

If he kept away from her his heart would be safe. If he kept away from her, maybe, just maybe, she'd realize the folly of her mistake and return to surgery where she belonged.

CHAPTER SEVEN

ESME SAW CARSON across the street, walking to his clinic with a cup of coffee, from where she was outside picking up the papers off the front step of her clinic. She hadn't seen him since the night of the emergency appendectomy three weeks ago.

If she saw him, he seemed to turn in the other direction and it was clear that he was avoiding her, which shouldn't bother her, but it did and she was mad at herself that his avoidance bothered her.

This was what she wanted. She wanted to keep her distance from him. She wasn't here to make friends. She wasn't here to find love. She was here to practice medicine.

When she first came to Crater Lake all she wanted was solitude. She wanted her practice and to be alone. She didn't need anyone. She didn't want anyone. That was why she'd left Shane, right, because she didn't want to be tied down to anyone.

She didn't want to chip away pieces of herself to suit someone else. Romance and love weren't for her. She'd proven that to the universe many times. Love only brought pain. Love made her forget who she was. It changed her.

And then she laughed at that thought. Three weeks ago she was telling Carson that change could be good. Yet she was not willing to change herself.

You've done that before, remember?

That was why it was good that he was avoiding her. It was good, so why did it tick her off so much?

Probably because his change after the emergency appendectomy didn't make sense. One moment they were becoming friends. One minute his arms were on her and he was telling her that it was okay if she told him that she was a surgeon, asking her to open up, and now he'd closed her out.

She'd caught him watching her a few times during the surgery and she thought he'd looked impressed or awed. Maybe almost validated in his assessment of her.

Then when they'd been cleaning up, when she'd admitted that she was a surgeon, things had changed. Carson hadn't even been able to look her in the eye. As if he was disgusted with her, as if she was the worst person ever.

So what was his problem? He'd told her it would be okay if she divulged her secret. He'd lied to her. It clearly wasn't okay with him, but he was avoiding her now. She was tired of being ostracized. He had no right to judge her.

Doesn't he?

Esme ignored the voice in her head. Her grip around the flyers tightened and she marched across the road and blocked Carson's path to his clinic.

Carson stopped in midstep, surprised to see her standing there, and she knew by the way his eyes started darting around he was looking for a way to escape, but there was no way to escape. She had him trapped.

"Dr. Petersen," he said.

"Morning, Dr. Ralston. Long time no see."

He rubbed the back of his neck, in that way that he always seemed to do when he seemed to be uncomfortable. She usually found it sexy, but today it annoyed her.

"How can I help you today?"

You could tell me why you're being such a jerk. Only she didn't say out loud what she wanted to say.

Instead she asked, "How is the surveyor? You never updated me after the surgery. I was just wondering how he was doing."

"Mr. Tyner, the surveyor, he's fine. He spent a week in the hospital on IV antibiotics, but other than that he made it through fine. Once he recovers fully in about three more weeks he'll be back to work."

"And the others? Did Luke get them down off the mountain?"

"Yes. He did."

Esme nodded. "Thank you. I was…concerned. I figured the way you were avoiding me that perhaps he didn't make it. That you blamed me for his death, but he made it so…why are you avoiding me?"

"I'm not avoiding you, Esme. I've been busy."

"Busy."

"Yeah."

Awkward tension fell between them. He couldn't look her in the eyes. Something she was used to after she'd frozen during that surgery. Other surgeons had avoided her. They'd avoided working with her; her name had disappeared from the OR board numerous times. It was the same look on her father's face when she'd run out on Shane.

No one trusted her. She didn't trust herself either.

She was used to it, but she was getting tired of it.

Just turn around and walk away. Let him ignore you. It doesn't matter.

Only it did matter. It annoyed her. She didn't deserve this.

Don't you?

"Well, I'll let you get back to your busy day." Esme turned around to head back to her clinic, dumping the flyers into a recycling bin.

"Esme, wait up."

She glanced round to see Carson heading toward her.

Just ignore him.

Only she couldn't. Even though she kept reminding herself over and over again that she didn't need anyone. That she was here in Crater Lake to just find herself again. She was lonely. She hadn't realized how much she enjoyed Carson's company until he was no longer talking to her.

So she waited for Carson, because, even though she didn't deserve to have friendship or companionship, she was lonely and she couldn't help herself. She couldn't help herself and that made her weak.

She was so weak. Especially when it came to him.

"I'm…not ignoring you. I mean I was, but… I'm sorry," Carson said. "It got intense in there and…look, I'm not used to intense situations."

"Fair enough."

"I should've told you about Mr. Tyner's recovery earlier. For that I'm sorry." And he smiled at her, those blue eyes of his twinkling.

Esme nodded. "Yeah, you should've. I mean, I may have been a surgeon and done quite a few appendectomies in my past, but that was the first time in a long time I've performed one in that kind of situation and not known the outcome. I was worried."

"I bet you were. I'm sorry."

"Thanks for telling me. I'm sorry if I attacked you there. Especially on a Sunday morning."

"You had every right to. I should've known better, but…well, it was my first time ever. I did a few months of a surgical internship, but I never did perform an appendectomy on my own."

"You never did a solo surgery?"

Carson shrugged. "What can I say? I wasn't a surgeon. I'm not a surgeon."

"I would ask you if you were fired, but that's a bit too much information for a street conversation." They both laughed.

"Yeah, I haven't told anyone beyond my family that I was an intern."

Esme winked. "Got it. I'll leave you to your clinic." She turned to leave again, at least satisfied with the answers he'd given her. At least knowing she wasn't totally being ostracized in this town. She remembered when she'd left Shane standing at the altar on Valentine's Day when she'd played runaway bride. How most of her so-called friends had dumped her.

When the press had been hounding the hospital, when she'd been called into the board meeting in front of Dr. Eli Draven to be questioned about how she'd frozen during surgery and her resident had thrown her under the bus because that resident had wanted to take her place as Dr. Draven's new protégé.

That was when she'd noticed the pointed stares, the whispers and seeing her name disappear from the OR boards. When patients she'd been treating for months had moved to other doctors and hadn't even been able to tell her why other than it "fit their schedule better" or "they wanted a second opinion" because maybe she was a bit emotionally scarred.

It was cutthroat. All of it, and once she'd been like that and that thought made her sick.

She'd deserved that punishment. She deserved to be alone.

But then Carson had reached out to her, handing her an olive branch. Even though it was dangerous to accept it, she hadn't been able to help herself. Loneliness had made her weak.

Ever since she'd started interacting with Carson she'd done two surgical procedures in her short time in Crater Lake. Something she had promised herself she wouldn't do. Yet she had.

He brought out something in her. Something she'd thought was long gone. Something that scared her.

It didn't have to mean anything. She could be his friend, even if she did want a bit more, but that bit more was out of the question. She didn't deserve that bit more.

She didn't deserve any of it.

"Esme, wait."

She turned around again. "Dr. Ralston?"

"It's Sunday. I just have to fax off a referral and then I was planning to take a hike around Crater Lake later. Would you like to come? You seemed to enjoy the view from my place. I thought you might want to check it out firsthand."

Say no. Say no.

But another part of her said, *You can be his friend.* And she did want to see around the area. It was Sunday, the clinic was closed and her plans for the day involved cleaning and possibly binge-watching some reality shows she'd been recording. Nothing that exciting.

Do it.

"I'd like that. What do you think, an hour?"

"Two. Wear a good pair of shoes and pants...there's ticks in the woods." He winked and grinned, before turning and heading back toward his clinic.

"Ticks?" Esme called out, but he just waved and disappeared into his clinic.

She chuckled and headed back to her own clinic. Apparently she had to find a clean pair of yoga pants and socks that went up to her waist, maybe a turtleneck, too, and she shuddered at the thought of ticks.

There were a couple of times that Carson seriously thought about calling Esme up and canceling the hike. After he wrote up and faxed in his referral, he just sat there letting it all sink in that he'd actually asked Esme to go on a hike with him today.

He hadn't planned on going on a hike today. He hadn't planned on seeing her. Yeah, he had been avoiding her, which was a hard thing to do when she lived and worked across the street from where he worked. Even though he hadn't spoken to her, he'd seen her and it had killed him just a bit not to go out and talk to her. To kiss her.

Kissing would lead to more and he wasn't sure he could give more. He was whole again and he couldn't risk his heart again.

So Carson had kept his distance.

Then he'd seen her, blocking the way to his clinic, and all those reasons for avoiding her had melted away. He'd missed her. Missed her feistiness. Missed her smile, her laugh. He hadn't realize how lonely he'd been without her around to annoy him.

The invitation for the hike had not been on the agenda at all. It just had been a spur-of-the-moment decision really. Everything was spur-of-the-moment when it came to her. He planned things. He liked the familiarity of it. Being around Esme changed all that. He didn't plan or prepare, he just did and that was far out of his comfort zone.

Why he'd chosen a hike today, he had no idea. He didn't particularly like hiking around in the woods. He liked living in the woods, he liked working with his hands and working on his house, but he didn't like traipsing around in bear country. He liked the comforts of home. His brother and he were totally opposite in that way. His brother liked living in a shanty up the mountain and using an outhouse. Carson liked plumbing.

Live a little.

Instead of canceling on her, he pulled his hiking gear out of his office closet and got changed. If only Luke could see him now.

Luke would probably laugh over the predicament he'd got himself into.

And as he stood out in front of her clinic, waiting for her to come down, he was really fighting the urge to turn around and head back to his office, call her up and cancel.

Avoiding her was better for him. Inviting her to join him in the woods was not avoiding her. It was the complete opposite. And that was dangerous.

If he didn't see her, he wouldn't be tempted by her,

but he was made of stronger stuff than that. He could be her friend. Couldn't he?

Carson could be around her, he just had to keep his distance when he was in her presence. He had to resist the urge to touch her or get too close and be caught up in the scent of her hair, her skin and he definitely had to fight the urge to reach out and kiss her.

Turn around. Just turn around and run. Don't go on a hike with her. Don't be alone in the woods with her.

He shook his head and stood his ground. He had to do this. He was the one who had invited her and he wanted to be on good terms with the only other doctor with a clinic in town. He wanted to be on good terms with the competition, even if he wasn't really even thinking of her as competition at the moment.

Esme walked out of her clinic, locking the door behind her. She'd changed and was wearing what looked like yoga attire.

"I'm ready. I think." She spun around, waiting for his approval on her outfit. At least that was what he assumed she was doing. He tried not to stare at her. It looked okay.

Actually it looked better than okay. She looked damn good.

Carson looked her up and down. The yoga pants and jacket hugged her curves and made his blood heat.

She looked so good.

Think about something else. Don't think about how tight her clothes are. Don't think about pulling her into your arms and squeezing her butt.

He was doomed.

"Well? What do you think? Is it okay for the hike today? You kind of freaked me out about the ticks."

"Well, it's an interesting choice for a hike in the mountains."

"Yoga is all I had. Sorry, I'm not really outfitted for mountain living." Esme's eyes sparkled.

"Not kitted for mountain living? Aren't there mountains in California? Isn't Mammoth Mountain in California?"

"Yes, it is, but I've never been to it."

"Doesn't Hollywood have hills as in Beverly Hills?" He winked at her.

"You're teasing me now, Carson. Los Angeles mountains hardly compare with Montana mountains. Besides, there's more comfortable amenities in Beverly Hills."

"You're right on that," he said. "Okay, I'm sure it's fine. To be honest, I really am not the mountain man I make myself out to be."

"What? Don't you live up in that cabin in the woods? I thought you were a regular Davy Crockett. King-of-the-wild-frontier type of guy."

Carson chuckled as he headed toward his SUV. "That would be Luke."

"So you're more refined?" she asked, falling into step behind him.

"Most certainly. He's a Neanderthal."

Esme laughed. "Here I thought you two had a loving relationship."

"We do most definitely, but like all brothers we have our differences, as well. I still haven't forgiven him for scaring me numerous times when we were playing in the woods. To tell you the truth Luke was a bit of a butt head when we were growing up."

Esme laughed again and he held open the door, closing it once she'd climbed up into the SUV. When he slid into the driver's side she was still laughing.

"It must've been nice growing up with a brother," she said wistfully, but there was a touch of sadness to her voice.

"I take it you don't have any siblings?"

"I did, but he died." There was hesitation.

"I'm sorry," he said.

She shrugged. "It was a long time ago. I was raised by my father and stepmother."

"What happened to your mother?" Carson asked.

Her smile disappeared. In the short time he'd known her he'd discovered when she didn't want to talk about something she clammed up and avoided the topic.

So he was bracing himself for the fact she was going to go silent again.

Instead she sighed. "My mom left me and my dad when I was little. It's no big deal—she just didn't want to be a wife and mother."

"I'm sorry." Carson couldn't imagine not having his mom around. He'd had a good childhood, a stable childhood. His dad had worked late a lot of the time, but it had never been detrimental to him or his brother.

His father had still been there taking them fishing and camping.

He'd been there to play baseball with them and teach them how to build things.

Carson's dad was dedicated and had had a sense of pride in his work. He was a good father.

As a child he'd felt safe, secure.

"There's nothing to be sorry about. I saw my mother from time to time when she came through town. My father remarried and I had an awesome stepmother. So don't feel sorry for me. I had a great childhood." Only the hint of sadness remained as she stared out the window, as if she had gone far away.

"Sorry. Are you okay?"

Esme smiled. "I'm okay. When I say my mom left me I know the look it gets. I see the sad, forlorn look thinking that I had this horrible childhood and that's why I became a cold-hearted surgeon."

"Well, isn't that the reason?"

They both laughed at that. Then silence fell between them as they headed out of town. Only it wasn't an awkward silence. It was companionable. It was nice. As he glanced over a few times to look at her, she was looking out the window with a smile on her face as she took in the scenery around her. She was seeing it through new eyes and he envied her, but he also enjoyed it.

The look of wonder at the place where he grew up.

He never got over its sense of beauty and majesty.

Yeah, he liked the modern conveniences like plumbing, but he was glad he wasn't living in a city surrounded by concrete and fumes.

He turned into the gravel parking lot that was at the head of about three different hikes that you could take around Crater Lake. Carson parked the car. There was only one other car in the lot and he recognized it as Mrs. Murphy's. She was a seventy-year-old voracious hiker and dog walker. Her St. Bernard, Tiny, was a slobber hound and he really hoped they didn't run into them.

"Wow, three paths to choose from!" Esme slung her knapsack over her shoulder.

"I think we'll stick with the easiest one for your first time out."

"Are you afraid I can't handle the challenge?" she teased.

"No. See that truck there?" he said, pointing toward Mrs. Murphy's orange truck.

"Yeah, what of it?"

"That's Mrs. Murphy's truck."

"So?" Esme was looking at him as if he were a crazy person.

"She has a very large dog that is overly friendly and overly smelly."

Esme laughed. "Are you serious?"

"Very."

Her eyes widened. "Okay then, we'll take the path you suggested."

Carson chuckled. "Good choice."

"Lead the way, Macduff."

"Mac…what?"

"Something my father always used to say. Some Shakespeare thing."

"Is your dad an English major?"

"No. Not at all. He just really likes Shakespeare."

"I think the actual quote is, 'Lay on, Macduff, and damned be him who first cries, "Hold, enough!"'"

Esme looked impressed. "Now who's the English major?"

Carson nodded. "I liked English. I also like Shakespeare."

They started walking up the gravel path to the easiest hiking trail. One that wrapped around the lake and took the path of least resistance. It was littered with lots of benches and scenic lookouts. Lots of opportunities to stop for a picnic and take in the glorious sight of Crater Lake.

Not that many people knew about it. Crater Lake barely made a Montana map. Of course that was all going to change with this grand hotel and spa, set to open Valentine's Day.

Soon Mrs. Murphy's dog Tiny was going to have a lot more people to slobber on and it concerned him about the fragility of the ecosystem around here.

Now I sound like Luke.

They didn't really talk too much as they took the first half a mile together. There wasn't really a need to talk. It was just nice.

When they came to the first scenic lookout Esme stopped and took in the sight.

"Wow, it's much bluer up close."

"The sun is overhead." Carson set down his rucksack on a bench to stretch his back.

"How long is the trail?"

"Two miles."

Esme nodded. "It's beautiful and peaceful here. Though I suspect that won't be for too much longer."

"Very true." He pointed to the far ridge, which you could see from this vantage point. "See that clear cut up there where all the dust from the road is kicking up? That's where they're going to build his hotel and spa."

Esme looked worried.

"Is something wrong?" he asked in concern.

"No, why?"

"You looked like you were going to be sick there for a moment."

"No, I'm fine. Not sick." Then she sighed. "It's just such a waste. Such a waste of trees and beauty. I guess it's a good thing we're out here enjoying the quiet solitude of this place before the parking lot is jam-packed with city folks and more dogs like Mrs. Murphy's."

"Yeah, but it's good for the town. It'll be good for our practice. Well, that's until Silas Draven brings in his own doctor for his hotel."

"He's bringing in a new doctor?"

"Yeah. A private doctor to deal with his clientele. I heard that the timeshare community that's already up and running will be bringing in their own on-staff doctor, too, but then again that's just a rumor."

Esme crossed her arms and looked a bit shaken. "I hope it's a rumor."

"Me, too."

"You just said Mr. Draven's venture would be good for the town. I thought you rebuffed change."

"Certain changes I do, but I'm realizing the benefits."

"You don't sound too convinced."

"It'll be good."

Change had brought Esme here. Maybe, just maybe, change wasn't all that bad. Carson picked up his rucksack; he needed to start moving again. If he kept thinking this way he'd kiss her. "Let's keep going," he suggested.

The sun was shining, it was warm and it was Sunday. He was going to make the most of his day off. "You ready to make it to the other side of the lake?"

She nodded. "Let's go. I'll lead the way, try to keep up."

Carson laughed under his breath. She was teasing him and he liked it. There were so many things he liked about her.

He liked the fact that even though she had lost her

mother, she didn't resent it. She didn't use it as an emotional crutch and she didn't seem dark and twisted inside. He liked her willingness to try new things. She was bright and shiny, but there was still something beneath the surface she was hiding.

Something she didn't want to share with him.

Something he shouldn't care about knowing because she wasn't his, but the more he got to know her, the more he did care.

The more he wanted to know.

CHAPTER EIGHT

"FAVORITE HOLIDAY?"

Esme rolled her eyes, but smiled. She didn't mind the fifty questions game at this moment because she was stretched out on the grass listening to the gentle waves lap against the shore of Crater Lake. She was staring up at the blue, blue sky and white-capped mountains. Only a few puffs of white clouds dragging over the peaks.

It was like a slice of heaven. Sitting here she felt small and unseen. Hidden. It was exactly what she wanted.

Do you?

Avery would've loved this place. He always dreamed of the west. Montana, Wyoming, South Dakota. Avery had wanted to be a bush pilot and work in remote areas. It was why she'd chosen Crater Lake. It would've been just the place Avery would've chosen.

A hand waved in front of her face and she glanced over at Carson, who was lying beside her in the grass.

"Hey, you agreed to fifty questions. Actually, you were the one who suggested it. Especially in light of the fact you want us to be friends."

"Sorry." She rolled over. "So what was the question?"

"Favorite holiday?"

"Independence Day."

Carson cocked an eyebrow. "July the Fourth?"

"What's wrong with that? I love fireworks, barbecues, summer. Oh, and red, white and blue."

"Most people like Christmas and most ladies like Valentine's Day."

Esme's stomach knotted when he brought up Valentine's Day. She'd used to like February fourteenth. She liked the hearts, the chocolates and the cupids. Even though she wasn't a romance girl at heart, she liked the campy fun of Valentine's. Only Avery had died on Valentine's Day. His heart had stopped right under her hands. She'd avoided the day for as long as she could until she'd met Shane.

Shane loved Valentine's Day.

It was why she'd agreed to the wedding on that day. She'd foolishly hoped she could replace a sad memory with a happy one. That was until she'd realized she didn't want to be Shane Draven's wife. They were too different. They were from different worlds.

So then Valentine's Day had become jilting day. A day of guilt.

A day she'd broken a man's heart.

So no, she didn't like Valentine's Day.

"I don't like Valentine's Day."

"Why? Most women do. I mean, such pressure for us guys."

"Well, I don't. I don't care for it."

Esme wanted to tell him how much she hated it. How she now hated the pressure, the hearts, the flowers and the romance. How it reminded her of pain and loss, only she couldn't.

She hated Valentine's Day, but she wasn't going to tell Carson why.

No one needed to know her secret shame. No one needed to know about the ghosts of her past.

"Isn't it my turn to ask a question?" Esme asked, changing the subject.

"Right."

"Your favorite holiday."

"Such an unoriginal question," he teased.

Esme chuckled. "Shut up and answer it. What's your favorite holiday?"

Carson grinned. A devious smile. "Valentine's Day."

She sat up and punched him in the arm. "It is not!"

"It is. I swear it is."

"I don't believe you."

"Okay, fine. It isn't. I'm not a romantic. I like Thanksgiving the best. All that turkey. Does that make you happy?" Carson asked.

"Yes," she said. "As a matter of fact it does."

He snorted. "This is a dumb game."

"One question in and you're ready to give up? Pathetic."

They both laughed at that. It was easy to laugh with him. She couldn't remember the last time she'd laughed like this. Shane wasn't much of a joker. He definitely didn't do PDA in public. Shane owned a successful company. He was a public figure and public figures couldn't show much affection out in the open. When they would go out, they'd always have to dress up to the nines. She would've never spent a day with him like this, playing fifty questions in her yoga clothes. Any displays of affection had been done in the privacy of her apartment or his, because he hadn't wanted the press snapping pictures.

At the time she'd got that and respected it.

She'd understood his position, that he had an appearance to keep up. There was a facade he had when he was out in public. Shane would barely touch her.

Every step they'd taken there had been press there. Photographers, paparazzi. Shane Draven was a rich, handsome, powerful man. And he needed a woman by his side. But she wasn't that woman. She didn't want to be that woman and that was why she didn't marry him.

Esme sighed and lay back down in the grass, tucking her arms behind her head and crossing her ankles to watch the water. The mirror, blue water.

"You're pretty relaxed," Carson remarked.

"I am. Is that okay?"

"Yeah, it's nice. Since I've known you, you've been on edge. Skulking in the shadows of the town trying to stay unnoticed."

"Apparently me keeping a low profile hasn't been working very effectively, then."

"No. It hasn't." His eyes twinkled. "I see you, Esme. I see you."

Their gazes locked and her heart began to beat a bit faster as he smiled at her. A smile that sent a zing of anticipation through her and she fought the urge to kiss him.

She'd thought about it before, in passing, but she'd never had the urge to just reach over and kiss him passionately. And that was what she wanted to do right now.

Desperately.

She looked away and cleared her throat. "Maybe we should head back."

"Right. You're right." Carson stood and held out his hand. "Milady."

Esme snorted and took his hand as he helped her up. As soon as she was back on her feet she let go of his hand, so she wouldn't be tempted to hold it. To pull his body closer, to let him kiss her.

That was not what friends did.

And they were just friends.

Right?

For one moment he thought Esme was going to kiss him. And for one moment he thought he was going to reach out and kiss her himself. It was hard to not reach out and touch her, to press her against the grass and capture her lips with his own, tasting her sweetness.

And he had no doubt she tasted so, so sweet.

Don't think about it.

So he didn't try. Instead he helped her up and then they continued on their hike around Crater Lake. Not that he minded the hike; it was just his mind and body wanted to take part in other activities. Activities he hadn't thought about in a long time.

Don't think about it.

"How are you enjoying the lake?"

"It's beautiful. So how did Crater Lake get its name? I would assume maybe a meteor long ago?" Esme asked.

"Well, that's one of the theories. Though no one knows for sure. They can't find a bottom at the center of the lake."

"For real?" She sounded intrigued.

Carson nodded. "They've tried and it seems almost bottomless. A local tribe, long ago, felt the lake was the gateway to another world. Of course I believe under the lake is a dormant volcano. This whole time just waiting to erupt. There are a few volcanoes slumbering in these mountains on the west coast."

"Volcanoes? I thought earthquakes in California were bad enough."

"I've never been through an earthquake." And Carson planned to keep it that way if he could help it.

"Well, I've never been through a volcanic eruption."

"Neither have I, but we have evacuation plans in town. I mean, after Mount Saint Helen's went, most towns near dormant volcanoes implemented some sort of evacuation plan."

Esme looked toward the lake. "Can you swim in the lake?"

"You can, but it's only June. It would be cold."

"Oh, that's too bad. It would be amazing to swim in. A picture-perfect lake with mountains surrounding it… it would be amazing."

"Luke told me once a monster lived in there. In the deep part in the center."

She smiled up at him. "It sounds like you and your brother had some good times."

"Yeah. We did. He was always the headstrong one. It was his way or no way."

Luke hadn't wanted the family practice. He'd wanted to be an army medic. So, his parents had let him enlist after he'd completed his residency in surgery, while Carson had taken up the family practice, not even completing his first year as an intern, to keep the legacy alive.

When Luke had been discharged after two tours of duty he was supposed to join Carson so their father could retire early. Only Luke had wanted to live up on the mountains. So their father had put off his retirement.

Carson had taken up the slack so their father would feel confident enough to leave. So that he could retire early. He worked so many long hours, nights of charting and researching. House visits and hospital visits, too, when his patients were in there.

The only life he'd known was work. He wasn't even sure what he really wanted, except he wanted to stay in Crater Lake. That much he was certain of. He wanted to live here.

It was safe.

He knew what to expect. Day in and day out it had been the same thing, that was until Esme had walked into town.

She'd shaken things up.

Now he wasn't sure how he felt. He wasn't sure of anything.

And he found he wanted a bit more.

Of what, he didn't know, but he wanted something else and it scared him.

While he was contemplating this there was a rumble in the distance. The earth shuddered beneath his feet. Just minor, though.

"Earthquake?" he wondered out loud.

"No. Doesn't feel like one. I *hope* it's not your volcano."

"Doubt that, too." Then his cell rang. He pulled it out of his pocket and recognized Luke's number immediately.

"Luke, what's up?"

"Where are you?" Luke asked. It sounded as if he was far away and out of breath.

"Hiking around Crater Lake with Dr. Petersen. Did you feel the rumble?"

"Yeah. I was right at the epicenter."

"Epicenter?" Carson asked.

"Landslide up on the mountain near the build site of Draven's hotel."

Carson felt the bottom of his stomach drop to the soles of his feet. "Landslide? Is anyone hurt?"

"Yeah. Lots of people. Some are missing. Can you and Dr. Petersen gather as many medical supplies as you can from your clinics? And can you contact as many local search-and-rescue teams from nearby towns? Other doctors. I'm trying to contact as many people up here as I can…"

"No, don't worry. I'll handle it. Preserve your cell phone battery."

"Thanks. See you soon."

Carson hung up his phone and cursed under his breath.

"What is it? What's wrong?" Esme asked.

"Landslide. We have to get back to town, gather supplies. There's a lot injured, a lot missing. We have to help."

Esme nodded. "Okay. Let's go."

Carson glanced at her. "Thanks."

"For what?" Esme asked, falling into step beside him as they all but jogged the last half mile to the parking lot.

"For jumping into the fray. I swear, it's not usually like this in Crater Lake."

"No, it's okay. Of course I'll help. Why wouldn't I?"

Why wouldn't you, indeed?

Esme had given up an extraordinary skill. She had given up an amazing talent, walked away from the hospital setting. It was something he didn't quite understand, but right now he didn't care too much about that. About her reason for running away, because she was here now.

She was here and she was willing to help and that was all that mattered.

They didn't say much on the way back to town. There wasn't much to say. Carson was trying to keep his eyes on the road and trying to think about all the supplies that he had in his clinic. What he could pack and how he could get it up to the landslide site.

When he glanced over at Esme he could see her muttering to herself and heard the word *syringes*, so he knew she was doing the exact same thing he was.

Carson parked the car in front of his clinic.

"I'll grab what I can and meet you back here in ten minutes?" she asked.

Carson nodded. "Ten. Yeah."

Esme dashed across the road. Other people were rushing around, gathering supplies, needing to go up to the accident site. Carson glanced to the south and saw dust rising from the distance and he saw smoke. He couldn't even imagine what was going on up there.

And he didn't have time to think about it.

Not right now.

Right now he had a job to do.

People's lives were at stake.

CHAPTER NINE

"HOLY…" THE CURSE word she was thinking of at the time died on her lips before it could even form. She'd been through a couple of larger earthquakes living in California, but they hadn't been anything compared to this, she thought as she stepped out of Carson's SUV.

There was dust still rising. A brown dusty cloud against the brilliant blue sky. They were still far from the accident site, but she could see the landslide from the base-camp point.

Tarps were going up as makeshift shelters and then she saw that people were being brought in. People who looked hurt, injured, broken, and it was evident to her that it was a triage area.

That was when every bit of fear she'd been feeling about this situation melted away and the surgeon in her took over. She couldn't let people suffer. She had to help.

Carson was already running toward the triage area, toward his brother, who was directing people and assessing the injured, but he was clearly overwhelmed by the sheer volume. Esme followed Carson to the first makeshift shelter. More and more paramedics and first responders were arriving, but clearly they needed help.

Luke barely glanced at them.

"Thank God you two are here." Luke scrubbed a hand over his face. "It's bad. Really bad."

"Where do you want me?" Esme asked.

"Over there, help Carson on that group of injured. I have to head back to the site and try to get out as many people as I can." Luke jammed a bunch of colored toe tags into her hand. "Tag the emergency patients with green for go. The helicopters and ambulances will take the greens to the nearest hospital in Missoula."

"Don't worry," Esme said. "Go. We got this."

Esme headed over to Carson. He was examining a head wound on a man. He was encouraging the man, telling him that it was going to be okay. He had so much empathy and compassion. An excellent bedside manner. The compassion he showed was the sign of a good doctor.

Carson was an excellent doctor. He was gentle, good and he was devoted to helping people. Just as she was devoted to medicine.

She moved to the next patient. A woman who was lying on her side, moaning.

"Ma'am, can you tell me where it hurts?" Esme bent down and the woman rolled over. Her breath caught in her throat when she saw who the woman was.

She might have run out on Shane Draven on Valentine's Day last year, but that didn't mean he'd stayed heartbroken for very long.

Six months later she'd seen in the paper that he'd married a woman from a wealthy family. A member of the Manhattan glitterati. A bit of an "it" girl.

And that was who was lying on this tarp now, moaning in pain with scratches on her face. Manuela Draven.

Esme couldn't help but scan the immediate area for Shane, because that was definitely the last person she wanted to see. Manuela Draven didn't know her from a hole in the ground. She was a self-centered person, full of herself.

Perfect for the Draven family. She looked good on Shane's arm, but Esme seriously doubted that Manuela was a good fit for Shane. Shane might have resented her time spent in surgery, they might have come from different worlds, but he was compassionate. Kind.

He's not your concern. Assess Manuela's ABCs and move on.

"My stomach hurts," the woman moaned, not looking at her. "Do something."

"Hold on, ma'am." Esme rolled Manuela onto her back and lifted her shirt. There was visible bruising on her left side.

Crap.

Bruising that fast could be an internal bleed. Esme began to palpate the abdomen and it was rigid.

Dammit.

"Ow, you're hurting me," Manuela whimpered.

"I'm sorry, but I think you have internal bleeding. We have to get you to the hospital as soon as possible." Esme grabbed the green tag, marking Manuela as priority. Where the bruising was forming, and the fact it was happening so fast, indicated that the spleen was probably involved. She would most likely need surgery.

Esme might have been able to pull off an emergency appendectomy in the clinic, but there was no way she would be able to remove this woman's spleen if needed. Not up here. Especially not since this was Shane's wife.

She didn't want to be the surgeon responsible for operating on Shane's wife.

So, Manuela had to get down off the mountain, but it made Esme wonder if Shane was here in Crater Lake—did they have one of those timeshare villas? Was she now going to run into Shane regularly?

Dammit.

It was hard to breathe and her head pounded as if a migraine was forming. That was the last thing she needed in the middle of a medical emergency.

Why Crater Lake? Why did it have to be the one place she'd settled? Couldn't she shake off the ghosts of her past?

"What're you doing?" Manuela whined.

"You're going to the hospital." Esme waved to the paramedics who had just landed helicopters at the base camp.

Manuela opened her eyes and stared at her. Hard, and there was a faint glimmer of recognition. Esme turned away quickly and rattled off instructions to the paramedics, letting them take Manuela away so that she could get the proper help she needed.

Esme kept her back to Manuela while they transferred her to the stretcher to load her onto the helicopter. There had been that faint recognition in Manuela's eyes, which scared Esme to her core, and she couldn't let Manuela recognize her.

That was why she'd come here. So no one would recognize her.

Not even herself. She didn't recognize herself anymore.

She was angry at herself, but really what could she

expect? She had to live with herself. She'd made her bed and she had to lie in it.

Esme glanced back once to see them load Manuela on the helicopter, ready to take her to the hospital as another helicopter flew over a ridge toward the base camp. Her head hurt and her stomach was doing backflips, as if she was going to be sick. Who was she? She didn't know. Not anymore.

Focus. You have a job to do.

She watched Carson, who was bent over patients, triaging them with expert care. He didn't have anything to worry about. No one would ruin his career and question his medical decisions. Esme envied him.

No one questioned him. No one would question him about his right to be here. She wanted that. She wanted to love medicine again. She wanted to feel passion about her work again. Only, she'd never have that. And she had to live with that for the rest of her life.

He glanced over his shoulder. "Dr. Petersen, can you come assist me here?"

"Sure." Esme rolled her shoulders and tried to ignore that panicky voice in her head and the oncoming headache. Right now she didn't have time for self-doubt. Right now she had to be a doctor. Esme knelt beside Carson.

"What do you need?"

"Could you look at the woman next to this man while I suture up his scalp wound?" Carson leaned over and whispered, "I think she has a concussion. She was fine when I first triaged her."

"Of course."

"Are you okay?" Carson asked. "You're pale and squinting."

"Fine," Esme said.

She moved over to the next patient. Examining her pupillary reaction and then examining her head and asking the woman questions, which she could not really answer clearly. It appeared to be a concussion, by the woman's confusion and the complaints of nausea. Esme pulled out a green tag and assured the woman she was going to get help as soon as possible.

She then moved on to the next patient and did another assessment.

It continued like that for the next thirty minutes as more injured people came into the tent. As more people came down off the mountain.

When the people stopped coming in, Esme counted up how many people she had seen and fifteen seemed like a lot for such a remote area. She stretched her back and made a round over her patients who were yellow. Patients who weren't seriously injured, patients who could wait.

All of her green patients had gone.

Including Manuela.

Which was a relief. Now she was exhausted. She was bone tired and it was hard to breathe.

Carson ducked back under the shelter, having assisted the last medevac with the last green patient out of base camp. He headed over to her.

"How many did you see?" he asked.

"Fifteen. Five of them were green. I've seen trauma, but I've never triaged in this kind of situation before."

Carson nodded. "We've had landslides up here before, but nothing like this."

"Any word from your brother?" Esme asked.

Carson shook his head. "He'll come back once he knows that everyone is accounted for."

"Do you know how many people were around the site?"

"No. Why?"

Esme shrugged. "Just curious."

She thought of Manuela Draven and found it really hard to believe that she would be up here without Shane. She was actually surprised that she was here. She didn't think the Dravens of Los Angeles would have anything to do with Silas Draven the developer.

Carson's cell went off. "Hello? What do you need? I'll be right there."

"What's wrong?"

"It's Luke. He found a man trapped under some rock. We need to take a team up there and try and extract him."

"Do you need me to come?" Esme asked.

"Yeah, if you don't mind. We have first responders here now to deal with the patients who are injured, but this man sounds like he's in a bad way. Luke will need all the hands he can get."

"Of course." Esme began to gather supplies to refresh the bag she had filled down in town. Once she had the equipment Carson took her hand and led her away from base camp and along the trail, up around the side of a cliff. It was a ten-minute hike and during that Carson was extra vigilant and withdrawn.

Esme couldn't help but keep her eyes trained on the mountain above her, watching and waiting to see if more rocks and mud would come raining down on them. It was tiring. One thing she had learned when she had been triaging a surveyor who was used to working in mountainous regions was that landslide sites were always dangerous, even after the landslide had happened. There was a high percentage risk of it occurring again if some of the debris had been caught up by trees or larger boulders.

There was still a chance that another landslide could happen and it terrified Esme beyond reason. She'd thought earthquakes were bad, but then mudslides and landslides had happened in California before.

As did wildfires.

She'd lived in California longer than Crater Lake and already she was seeing a lot of natural disasters. All she wanted was a quiet life.

When they rounded the corner, Esme whispered a curse under her breath when she saw the devastation the landslide had caused. She could see part of the new hotel and spa was being built and it had been so close to being destroyed.

Trees up the mountainside were snapped in half or simply gone. All she could see was rubble. And then she caught sight of Luke, kneeling near the edge of the path of destruction. He didn't call out to them. Any loud sounds could start another slide.

Carson and Esme quickly headed over.

"He's in bad shape and I didn't have enough of the proper supplies to help him." Luke moved out of the way. "Carson, we have to get him out of here. He has blunt force trauma to the chest and God knows how many other fractures or crush injuries. I hope you brought a chest tube kit, Dr. Petersen."

"I did." Esme knelt down beside Luke and then glanced at the patient. "Can you tell me…?" She couldn't even form coherent words as she stared down at the half-unconscious man buried under the rock.

At least she now had her answer as to Manuela's presence.

His face was bloodied, but she would recognize him anywhere. You couldn't forget the man you left standing at the altar. A man she'd thought she'd once loved.

Shane Draven was her patient.

Carson stepped beside Luke and started to help his brother try and remove some of the smaller rocks off the injured man. They could start small until Esme had him more stabilized, then they could move the larger rocks. Moving the larger rocks would mean that they would have to be ready to get him off the mountain, because if this man had crush injuries he was going to bleed out right here.

That much Carson knew.

He glanced over at Esme, who was staring in disbelief and horror at the man's face. As if she couldn't believe this man was in this kind of situation. Then she shook her head and started pulling out supplies.

It was odd for her, because they had been in multiple different emergency situations and she didn't seem to get this distracted when it came to patients. He'd noticed her withdraw earlier, when they'd first arrived at base camp. When she'd been getting her first green patient onto the helicopter. Esme had barely been able to make eye contact with the woman. She'd looked visibly ill.

He couldn't help but wonder what was going on with her.

"Luke, please tell me a medevac has been ordered here," Esme said in a barely audible whisper.

"No. The sound and blades of the chopper could cause another landslide. We need to get him stabilized and on a stretcher. Then we can get him away from the slide zone. Once we're around that bend, then we're home free."

"That's nothing more than a trail. There's no place for a helicopter to land," she said.

"The helicopter won't land," Carson said. "We'll have to hook him up to a hoist and fly him out off the trail."

"He could bleed out." Esme glanced back down at the patient, her face getting paler. "We can't let him die."

"I don't have any intention of letting him die, Esme," Carson said.

"My team is coming with a gurney. We'll have as many men carrying him out of here and to a safe, clear spot a helicopter can send down a hoist. Right now, you have to triage him," Luke snapped.

Esme nodded and pulled out her stethoscope, quickly going over the ABCs. Airway, breathing, consciousness. Carson watched her bend and listen to the man's chest. Or what she could get of his chest.

"There's muffled sounds in his chest. I suspect a definite crush injury. I'm going to have to insert a chest tube. Just like you said, Dr. Ralston."

Luke nodded. "Let us know when you get it in and it starts draining, then we'll start lifting these larger rocks to get him free."

"Was he conscious when you found him, Luke?" Carson asked. "Do you know who he is?"

Luke snorted. "Everyone knows who he is. He's Shane Draven. One of the richest bachelors on the West Coast."

"He's not a bachelor anymore," Esme remarked as she set up the instruments she needed to insert a chest tube.

Carson wondered why she sounded a touch bitter about it and he wasn't even sure that it was a bitter tone. It was just odd the way she said it.

It's nothing.

"I'm about to insert the chest tube. If he regains consciousness he's going to scream and scream loudly."

"I'll take care of it." Carson moved to sit by the man's head. Ready to hold him down, cover his mouth so that his screams wouldn't dislodge debris, so that they wouldn't all be buried under a metric ton of rock.

Esme worked fast and as she inserted the tube Shane Draven's eyes flew open and he screamed. In agony.

"Hold him!" Esme shouted. "He may be buried under the rocks, but half his chest is free and if he moves I'm liable to puncture a lung and kill him."

Carson lay across the man's body as Esme made one last twist and the tube was in place in the intercostal space. She taped it down so it wouldn't jar. The man was still screaming, but not as loud as Carson held him.

The moment the chest tube was in, bright red blood drained from his chest.

"We have to get him out of here now." Esme jumped up and began to help Luke and Carson as they pulled debris and rocks off the man.

"Oh, God, what the hell happened?" Shane screamed.

"You were in a landslide, sir. You're going to be okay," Carson said, trying to reassure him.

The man stared up at him and then past him, to Esme. His eyes widened for a moment, as if he recognized her, but it was only for a moment until his eyes rolled back into his head and he was unconscious again.

"God." Esme moved past Carson and checked his pupillary responses. "We have to get him down off the mountains and fast. He'll die."

"Last rock," Carson said, tossing it.

The first-responder team came around the bend with the stretcher and in the distance Carson could hear the whirring chopper blades as the medevac made its way to the rendezvous point. They worked together quickly, getting Shane Draven onto the stretcher, covering him and strapping him down.

Luke and his team ran with the patient down the path toward the helicopter. Carson and Esme followed them. Carson could see the thick cable drop down from the chopper as they hooked the stretcher up and secured him.

It wasn't too long until Shane Draven was secure and hoisted up; Luke had harnessed himself in to ride with Shane off the mountain. Carson watched them as they left. He turned back to Esme.

"We have to get away from this site. It's dangerous."

Esme nodded. She looked a bit green, but it only lasted for a moment before she ducked behind a bush and was sick.

"Esme?" Carson tried to touch her, but she slapped his hand away.

"Don't look at me," she whimpered.

He looked away for a few moments, until she finished being sick. When it was over she was leaning against a tree. Her breath shallow, as if she was working hard to breathe. She started retching again.

"Are you okay?" he asked again. He was worried the

trauma was too much for her, but then again she was a surgeon. A full-blooded surgeon. She shouldn't shy away from situations like this.

Esme nodded weakly. "Just get me off this damn mountain."

CHAPTER TEN

CARSON WAS WORRIED about Esme. She hadn't said much since he'd got her back to the triage area, where she was able to get some water into her and rest for a moment. He was wondering if she had a touch of heatstroke, or too much exposure from the sun. They had been working outside for a while and running on adrenaline. She'd been a trooper through it all, but they'd started working after a two-mile hike. They both had been out of breath sprinting that last half a mile before going up the mountain.

What if it was mountain sickness?

With Esme being from Los Angeles, he knew that she wouldn't be used to the higher altitude and, working as they had been on injured people, that could be the reason why she was ill. He didn't know if she'd been this far up the mountain before. They were higher up than his place or the mill.

After he'd got her settled another shallow quake rocked the ground and they heard a pop as more debris was carried down the side. She gripped his arm and buried her face in his chest as the second landslide hit. Carson held her close to him. Soothing her, and it felt so good.

So right.

When the shaking ended he reluctantly let her go and went to see if anyone else was injured.

At least this time no one was in the path, but it was clear to them they had to get down off the mountain, even if they were relatively safe on the lee side.

Only they couldn't leave. Not until all the injured were taken down first.

Esme refused to lie down, but at least he had her sitting down, picking at the label of an empty water bottle as the last of the injured was taken down the mountain in an ambulance. Carson headed over to her.

"Here." He held out another bottle of water.

"No, thanks. I just finished one."

Carson took the empty bottle from her. "You need to drink a lot of water. I think you have altitude sickness."

Esme sighed and took the water from him. "I don't have altitude sickness. I'm just tired and have a headache."

"Something is up with you. You were sick after we got Mr. Draven off the mountain."

Her eyes widened for a moment at the mention of Mr. Draven's name, but then she shrugged and looked away quickly. "You know what? You're right—it's altitude sickness."

Only Carson didn't really believe it was only altitude sickness suddenly. She was hiding something again.

It's not your concern. How can you trust her when she clearly hides the truth from you? You're just going to get hurt again.

The sting of Danielle's departure hurt, but somehow the idea of Esme hurting him made him ill, because if she broke his heart like Danielle he'd never recover and that scared him.

Only he couldn't walk away, because he cared about her.

She was going to be his downfall.

He sat down beside her and began to pull instruments out of his rucksack.

"What're you doing?" Esme asked.

"I'm going to examine you. You could have heat-stroke or heat exhaustion. I want to make sure you're okay. You know that acute mountain sickness can be serious and if it's that we need to get you down off this mountain."

Esme sighed. "Fine. Do your exam, but I'm perfectly okay."

"Right. A seasoned trauma surgeon throws up after inserting a chest tube." Carson snorted and then peeled off his fleece sweater, wrapping it around her shoulders to keep her warm.

Esme pulled his sweater tighter around her. Even though it was hot out and it was summer, being up on the mountain was a lot colder than being down in town and if she was suffering from acute mountain sickness she could get hypothermia quite quickly. That was something Carson didn't want for her.

Not after all the work she'd been doing.

Three traumatic events since she'd pretty much set foot in Crater Lake and each time she'd thrown herself into the fray without hesitation. He admired that about her. Danielle wasn't the kind of doctor who jumped into the fray.

Danielle wasn't a trauma surgeon. She was a neurosurgeon and, last he'd heard, was working on a big research project somewhere in the South.

The woman who didn't want to stay in Crater Lake because she wanted to be a surgeon was now working on a research project somewhere. Danielle wouldn't have gone up to the mill to save Jenkins's life. She wouldn't have operated on that surveyor and she would've come up the mountain, but only grudgingly.

Luke detested Danielle. That should've been a big clue to him. Only he'd been blinded by what he'd thought was love. He wanted a family. When his father had taken over the family practice from Carson's grandfather, he had brought Carson's mother to Crater Lake and they had started a family soon after.

Carson was following in his father's footsteps. Or maybe he tried, but didn't realize that he didn't have to follow the same footsteps as his father.

"You know, you're wrong," Esme said, shaking him from his thoughts.

"About what?" Carson asked as he pulled out his stethoscope.

"You keep calling me a trauma surgeon."

"I assumed you were. You said you were a surgeon."

"I am... I mean I was, but your first instinct was right. I was a cardio-thoracic surgeon."

Carson was stunned. "Why did you feel the need to hide that from me?"

Esme shrugged. "I honestly don't know anymore. Like the specialty of surgery I practiced makes a difference."

Carson chuckled. "I knew it was more than trauma the way you worked at the mill. Now take a deep breath."

He placed the stethoscope on her chest and then realized what he was doing, how close he was to her and that his hand was basically on her chest. He could hear her heart beating fast. She took a deep breath, inhaling and exhaling for him.

"Good." He packed his stethoscope away and tried not to think about touching her. He was performing a medical exam. Just because he was attracted to her, didn't mean he had to do anything about it.

He cleared his throat and took her hand to examine it. Her hand was so small in his. Those delicate long fingers. Talented. How many lives had she saved with those hands? How many intricate surgeries?

"What're you doing?" she asked.

"Looking to see if your nail beds are blue. It's a sign of acute mountain sickness." Then he tipped her head back to look at her lips. The last time he'd stared at her lips, all he'd wanted to do was kiss them.

Focus.

Her skin was so soft. So, so soft.

"What's the verdict, Doc?" she asked.

"You have cyanosis starting in your nail beds and I'm sorry, but your breathing sounds labored."

Her brow furrowed. "Acute mountain sickness? Are you sure?"

"Positive. I've seen it often enough in newcomers to the area. You exerted yourself on the mountain. It was too much."

Esme sighed. "So the solution is descend?"

Carson nodded and got to his feet. "Descend, descend, descend. And water. We have to get you down before it progresses. I would hate for you to end up with high-altitude cerebral edema."

"Coma?"

He helped Esme to her feet. "You got it."

"I clearly need to do more research on acute mountain sickness. I thought it only affected people out of shape."

Carson chuckled. "No, it can happen to anyone not used to the altitude. Come on, I'll drive you back down."

"Can we leave?"

"I'll let the leader of the first responders know. You head over to the car."

Esme nodded and huddled into his sweater as she slowly walked over to his SUV. Carson watched her, to make sure she didn't fall over. Since she had a bit of cyanosis, he was positive that she was experiencing some vertigo and dizziness.

His case of weak knees, however, had nothing to do with acute mountain sickness. It all had to do with Esme. Once she was safely in his SUV, he found the team leader of the first responders who were still at the base-camp site.

"Dr. Ralston, how can I help you?"

"Dr. Petersen is suffering from ACM. I have to get her down off the mountain. If you need me to come back, I'll return when I make sure she's stable and resting."

"I don't think we'll need you back, Dr. Ralston. All missing have been accounted for and all injured are being taken down off the mountain. If there are any other issues I'll contact the other Dr. Ralston."

"Well, he traveled with an emergency patient off the mountain. So if you need someone, page me."

"Will do. Thanks, Doctor."

Carson nodded and walked to his SUV. When he sat

down he could see Esme was shivering, trying to keep the fleece around her tight.

"Sorry for throwing up out there," she said through chattering teeth. "I've heard of altitude sickness. I just didn't think that it would happen to me. I thought..." She trailed off and shook her head. "Sorry."

"No one expects it to. Don't worry about it. Just don't do that in my car." He winked at her and Esme laughed.

"That was a pretty big landslide," she remarked.

"It wasn't. I've seen worse. Way worse." He drove the car slowly down the mountain road. He didn't want to descend with her too fast.

Esme shuddered. "Worse. That's a scary thought."

"It was. I was ten. My father spent the night on the mountain with Luke when a landslide hit a smaller town just west of Whitefish. It almost buried the entire town. Luke was fifteen and was able to help Dad. They searched for survivors. So many were lost. I just remember being terrified. Left at home with Mom, not knowing if Luke and Dad would come back and worrying that it would happen in Crater Lake."

"I'm sure your mom probably felt the same," Esme said.

"I'm sure she did." Carson smiled, seeing she could barely keep her eyes open. "You look exhausted."

"I am. I feel so exhausted. I haven't been sleeping well at night." Esme yawned. "It's so quiet here. I'm used to the sounds of the city outside my apartment. It's too quiet here."

"Lay your head back and sleep. It's okay. It's going to take us forty minutes to get back to town."

Esme nodded. It didn't take much convincing for her to lean back against the seat and fall fast asleep. She looked so peaceful sleeping that when he got close to town he didn't head for town. She needed rest and he wasn't going to try and find her key and wake her up so she could sleep alone in her apartment above her clinic.

It was better that he took her home, so he could watch over her while she slept.

Is it really a better idea?

From a medical standpoint it was. She had experienced the symptoms of acute mountain sickness. He couldn't leave her alone—what if she didn't improve? What if her cyanosis worsened?

It has nothing to do with acute mountain sickness.

Why was he torturing himself like this? He couldn't have her. He wasn't willing to put his heart at risk.

He wasn't a fool. She'd leave. She'd miss surgery and head far from Crater Lake and he couldn't follow. He had a family practice to run. He wouldn't disappoint his father or grandfather, who'd left him this legacy.

Carson turned off the main road, to his property.

Esme was pretty out of it. She barely even acknowledged him as he helped her out of the SUV and into his house. The closest bedroom was his on the main floor, so he scooped her up and carried her into his bedroom, setting her down on his bed. The sun was in the west and flooded his room with light, so he closed the blinds slightly, to darken the room.

He picked up her hand one more time to check her cyanosis and the pink was returning. The blue disappearing.

The cure was working.

Thank God.

She didn't deserve to suffer from acute mountain sickness. Not after helping all those people today. He felt bad; she was probably suffering so much the entire time they were up there on the mountain. And their hike hadn't helped much. She was probably worn right out.

At least he'd got her off the mountain.

Descend, descend, descend.

Something his father and brother always reiterated. Especially Luke during his survival classes that he taught to people so they could survive in extreme conditions if they found themselves trapped up on a mountain.

She looked so peaceful sleeping on his bed.

He wished for moment that he could join her and the second that thought crossed his mind, he knew he had to get out of the room as fast as he could or he might do something he regretted.

She could see Shane's broken face looking down the aisle at her as she stopped midway. His sad, bloodied, broken face and as she glanced down it wasn't her wedding dress that she was wearing. It was the stained clothing from the mountain, her hands were turning blue and she couldn't breathe.

Esme woke with a start. It was dark and she had no idea where she was. It was someone's bedroom, but whose? The last thing she remembered was sitting in Carson's SUV and he was telling her to go to sleep as he slowly drove down the mountain.

So she must be in Carson's house. She got up slowly, her head pounding as if she had a hangover. It must've had something to do with the acute mountain sickness. At least she didn't feel as dizzy anymore. She didn't feel as if she was going to throw up.

Oh, God.

Esme sank back down on the bed, mortified that she had been ill in front of Carson. He was a doctor, so therefore he was used to seeing stuff like that, but it was him.

It was her.

If it had been anyone else she wouldn't be so embarrassed, but it was Carson. He'd been the one to see her at her most vulnerable on that mountain and she didn't like that one bit. No one saw her vulnerable. She was a dedicated surgeon.

That's what I love about you, Esme. You don't care. You're cool as a cucumber and have a great public image.

Of course after the jilting those endearing sentiments had changed in tone.

You have no heart. You're a cold, heartless woman.

Maybe it was true, but then why had it hurt so much when Avery died? When she'd lost her nerve in that surgery? If she had no heart why did it beat so fast around Carson? She hadn't realized how numb she'd been. And he'd seen her at her most vulnerable up on the mountain.

Granted he thought it was acute mountain sickness, it made sense, but she had a feeling it was something more.

Yeah, she had been feeling exhausted, her breathing had been harder to come by, but she could work through all that. She had been working through all of that. Her stomach hadn't turned until Shane had looked at her. When their gazes had connected and she'd seen the recognition, followed by anger or hurt.

Of course, it was hard to tell if it was because she had been there. When she'd run out on him the day of their wedding he'd told her, or rather his father had told her in no uncertain terms, that he didn't want to see her ever again.

That Shane loathed her.

Hated her. *You have no heart. You're a cold, heartless woman. You could have been great, but now you're nothing. Not a surgeon. Nothing but a shadow.*

And she didn't blame him. She hated herself for it.

Of course it was hard to tell if it had been loathing or the fact she'd been shoving a chest tube in between the intercostal spaces of his ribs, saving his life. And even then she wasn't sure if she'd saved it. He was so injured. Maybe he didn't make it down off the mountain. If he died…she didn't want to think about how that would make her feel. How it would end her career here in Crater Lake. A place she was falling in love with.

She was tired of running.

She didn't want to leave.

Shake it off.

Her eyes adjusted to the dim light of the unfamiliar room. She could see from the digital clock on the nightstand it was almost 10:00 p.m., and as she padded over to the window and peered through the blinds the sun was going down finally.

Even though she'd been here since April, she still wasn't used to extended daylight hours. At least it would still be daylight out when she found her cell phone, purse and called herself a cab, because she couldn't stay here at Carson's house.

That was unacceptable.

Her purse was at the end of the bed. She grabbed it and then opened the door as quietly as she could, peering out. The main room was dark, except for the flickering of the television. Esme could see Carson in the light and he was asleep. Flat-out on his back asleep.

Good.

She would quietly leave his house and then call a cab from outside so she wouldn't disturb him; that was the last thing she wanted to do. He needed his rest. He'd given up his bed for her. The couch was long, but it couldn't be too comfortable. Especially since Carson was over six feet tall and his legs were propped up over the edge of the sofa, his arms crossed and his head at an odd angle. It didn't look at all comfortable.

Esme's heart melted. He was such a generous person. She'd seen the way he was with his patients. No matter what the Johnstone twins thought of him, he was kind, caring. A little closed off. There was a hurt buried under there, but she didn't know what.

And she couldn't believe anyone would hurt him. She never wanted to hurt him. Which was why he was off-limits. So whatever secrets he had were his. Carson had the right to his secrets, just as she had the right to hers. As she wanted to keep her hurt private, because she didn't deserve absolution. It was her private hurt to keep.

Even if she was done carrying it.

She had to fight the urge to join him on the couch, to curl up beside him and watch a movie with him. To just feel safe in his arms, but she didn't deserve that because she wasn't sure that she could give that to a man.

She'd panicked about her marriage to Shane.

That was different.

And it was.

Shane didn't understand her. Carson did, but she

wasn't sure of that. Maybe he'd resent her eventually, as Shane did.

Esme sighed. Why couldn't she have some happiness? She deserved some happiness.

No. She didn't. She had to stop having this same argument with herself over and over again. She didn't deserve Carson. She couldn't have Carson.

He was off-limits.

I broke Shane's heart. I froze in surgery. I let everyone down.

Esme let out a sigh. Maybe she should leave him a note. Thank him for taking care of her because she didn't have anyone to care for her. She didn't have anyone to sit with her or visit her, but that was par for the course.

She turned around and headed for the door. It was best that she get out of here as fast as she could. She grabbed the doorknob. A light flicked on.

"Going somewhere?"

Esme cursed under her breath and turned around. "You're awake."

Carson was sitting up, staring at her with that goofy grin on his face. One that melted her heart. Damn him.

"And you were trying to sneak out of here."

"I wasn't trying to sneak out of here. You were asleep and I was going to call a cab."

He raised an eyebrow. "You were going to call Bob?"

"Who's Bob?"

"The only cab guy in Crater Lake. You would've been standing out there all night. He's not the most reliable."

Esme groaned. "Are you kidding me?"

He chuckled. "I wish I was."

"He's going to have to up his game when that big resort opens up."

"Maybe someone else will move into town and give him a run for his money." Carson winked at her.

Esme shook her head. "Thanks for that dig."

"It wasn't meant as a dig. It was meant as a compliment." He got off the couch and walked over to her and her pulse began to race as he came closer to her. She needed to get out of here fast. She took a step back from him.

"I should go. Tomorrow is Monday. I have to open my clinic. Patients to see."

Carson planted himself in front of the door, barring her exit. "You had more than a mild case of acute mountain sickness. You need your rest."

"I had my rest. I slept for several hours on your bed. I'm fine."

He grabbed her hand and checked her nail beds. "Well, you're not cyanotic anymore. Your hypoxia is gone."

Esme tried not to gasp at his touch. He just held her hand, his thumb brushing over her knuckles causing a zing of excitement to course down her spine.

She wanted to pull her hand back, but she couldn't. So, like a fool, she just stood there and let him hold it.

Snap out of it.

"Yes. I told you, I'm fine."

"You still need to rest. You should call your nurse and reschedule your patients. Besides, after that landslide and all the press heading into town Crater Lake will be a bit overrun tomorrow." Carson let go of her hand and moved away from the door.

Which was a good thing, because if he didn't he'd feel how badly her hand was shaking.

Press? Did he just say press?

"What?" she asked, hoping that the nervousness in her voice didn't give her away. "Why would the press be coming here?"

"It was a major landslide and among the injured was some actress by the name of Manuela Draven, who happens to be married to the head of some big internet company and nephew of Silas Draven and he's currently the guy that Luke is operating on now in Missoula."

Silas Draven's nephew?

Well, that explained why Shane was on the mountain. Then it clicked in that Luke was still operating on Shane.

"Is Sha… Is our chest-tube guy okay?"

"It's touch and go, but Luke's fairly confident he'll pull through."

"Good." She tried to take a deep calming breath, but everything began to spin and Esme gripped the door handle to steady herself and for ease of access when she bolted out of here.

It was like some kind of nightmare that she just couldn't get away from. Was her jilting of Shane going to haunt her for the rest of her life?

It would be only a matter of time before someone mentioned her name and they tracked her down. Wouldn't that be a juicy story?

"Runaway Bride of Shane Draven saves his life on top of a mountain. Is a reunion in the air? Did Manuela break Shane Draven's heart like Dr. Petersen did?"

And she felt the nausea begin to rise in her again.

Without saying a word she dashed across Carson's

house and found the guest bathroom, slamming the door and locking herself inside. She knelt beside the toilet, expecting to be ill, but nothing happened.

The only thing she could hear was the pounding of her blood, like an incessant drum in her ears as her heart raced. Her stomach twisted, threatening to heave, and she could feel sweat on her palms.

She couldn't believe this was happening.

Not again.

And the only thing she could think about at that moment was to run. Run as far away and as fast as she could.

There was a gentle knock on the door. "Esme, are you okay?"

"No," she said through chattering teeth.

"Can I come in?"

"No."

He sighed on the other side of the door. "I'm worried that it's the acute mountain sickness again. If it is we have to get you to a hospital."

Esme got up and unlocked the door. He opened it as she sat on the floor. "It's not the mountain sickness. I'm breathing fine."

"All the same…"

"It's not that. It's the press and the landslide and the Dravens."

Carson looked confused. "What's wrong? Why does that scare you?"

"Oh, God," Esme moaned and buried her head in her knees, the tears threatening to come. She felt his hand on her shoulder. His strong, strong hand.

"Tell me and maybe I can help."

"You can't help me."

"Try me. What can I do?" His eyes were full of concern, his hand so warm and reassuring as he gently stroked her cheek. "Please, let me help you, Esme."

She wanted his help. She wanted much more than that, only she couldn't have what she really wanted, but she could have tonight. One night with him, lying in his arms, and he could help chase away the ghosts that were haunting her at this moment.

Esme leaned forward and then kissed him. Just as she'd pictured a thousand times before, as she'd wanted to do the moment he'd stood outside her clinic demanding that she hand over the patients she'd stolen. She kissed him the way she'd wanted to when he'd invited her over to dinner, when he'd wrapped his arm around her on the pitch-black ride up to the mill, when he'd worked side by side with her, saving lives.

It was sweeter than she'd ever expected.

It was healing, but she wanted so much more for tonight. She wanted all of him, even if it was just for now.

She could have now.

She could forget who she was for just a few dark hours.

And maybe, just for once, she'd remember the woman she used to be.

CHAPTER ELEVEN

CARSON WAS A lost man.

He hadn't been expecting that kiss to happen. He'd wanted it to happen so many times, but, of all the ways he'd fantasized about his first kiss with Esme, never once had he imagined it would happen in his guest bathroom.

It would've bothered him before, because she was off-limits. Right now he didn't care. Right now all he could think about was her hands cupping his face and the taste of her honeyed lips on his.

And then the kiss ended, leaving him wanting more.

So much more. For once he didn't care if she was going to hurt him or that she was off-limits. He just wanted her.

"Carson, I want you. Please let me in tonight." She kissed him again and there was no way he could argue with that. It had been so long since he'd connected with someone. He avoided that for a reason, because it wasn't just sex to him. Sex to him let people in. Let them see a side of him that he shared with no one.

He'd been hurt, burned, and he didn't want to let someone in, but with Esme it was different. She made him forget about what had happened to him, about when his heart had been broken so long ago.

"Please, Carson," she said, stroking his face. "Please. Just for tonight."

"Esme, when you kiss me like that…I don't want to stop. I can't stop."

"Then don't. You don't have to promise me anything. I don't need a promise of something that I can't give."

It was a way out. She was offering him a way out. He wasn't sure how he felt about it. It should be a simple matter, only with her so close to him it wasn't a simple matter. He couldn't think rationally with her so close.

It was complicated.

Why did everything have to be so complicated?

This didn't have to be. This could just be the moment.

He could have this exquisite moment with her.

For once he could have what he wanted, even if it didn't mean anything permanent. He could have this moment with her.

All he wanted was just this moment.

She tried to kiss him again, but he stopped her. "No."

"I thought you…"

"I do. It's just we're not doing this here. There's only one place we're going to do this tonight."

Esme grinned and Carson helped her to her feet, leading her out of the tiny powder room. Once they were out of the bathroom he picked her up in his arms. He'd been wanting to sweep her off her feet since he first saw her, but he'd fought against it for so long. Right now he didn't have any fight left in him.

Right now he was going to forget everything and be with her as he wanted to, even if it meant putting his heart on the line.

He just wanted to feel again.

He just wanted to be close to someone again.

Carson carried her straight to his bathroom. A much larger room, with a large shower, because he wanted to kiss every inch of her and maybe the water would wash away some of the past.

"You read my mind," she whispered against his ear, nibbling it.

"I thought after a day on the mountain that you might enjoy a nice hot shower." He sat her down on the floor. He turned on the shower; the steam felt good. "I'll have one after you."

"Or you could have one with me."

His blood heated at her suggestion. The thought of her wet and naked made him burn with desire.

"Are you sure?" he asked.

She didn't answer him; she just smiled and took off her shirt. She was wearing a pink lace bra. It was hot pink. And though he'd never really cared for that color before the fact it was on her made him hot. Then she undid her pants, slipped them down and kicked them away, revealing a matching pair of panties.

"I'm sure."

Carson couldn't have looked away if he'd wanted to. He was entranced by her. She unhooked her bra and then slipped down her panties until she was naked. Standing there, completely naked.

"So beautiful," he murmured.

She walked over to him and started to unbutton his shirt. He reached down and ran his fingers over her bare shoulders. Her skin was so soft.

Esme slid her fingers inside his open shirt and peeled it away, touching his chest. He sucked in a deep breath.

It had been so long since he'd let a woman touch him like that. He'd forgotten what a rush it was.

Only this was different than anything he'd experienced before. It scared and thrilled him all the same. He wanted Esme to continue touching him. Her hands trailed down his chest and she undid his belt, slowing, driving him wild with need.

When her fingers broached the top of his jeans, he stopped her, grabbing her wrists and holding her back.

"I think you need to get in that shower, because I'm liable to take you right here on this bathroom floor and even though our first kiss was in a bathroom I would rather our first time be in my bed."

Pink tinged her cheeks, her eyes sparkling as she stepped away from him and walked into the glass shower.

It didn't take him long to remove his jeans and underwear. He only hesitated for a moment because he didn't lie. He didn't want their first time to be in the shower. Carson didn't want to take her up against the tiled wall. When he made love to Esme for the first time he wanted it to be in his bed. Her underneath him as he thrust into her with her legs wrapped around his waist.

He wanted her to spend the night in his arms.

He didn't want a quickie in the shower. Carson wanted to explore her body, take his time and make sure that he remembered every single moment of this time together, because it could only be this one time.

The water hit him, but his body was already heated so it felt cold instead of hot. He leaned down and kissed her the best he could. She was so much shorter than him.

"I want you," she whispered, running her hands over his chest.

"I want you, too, but not here. Not against this hard surface. I want to do it properly. I want to make love to you properly."

Something flickered across her face when he said the words *make love*. As if she was changing her mind for a moment, or maybe shock, but whatever it was it was just a flicker.

So instead he kissed her as she washed his body.

When he couldn't take the touching and teasing any longer he turned off the shower and wrapped her up in the largest fuzzy towel he had.

It might have been summer, but he wasn't taking any chances of her getting cold and catching her death. Especially not after today on the mountain.

He carried her through his en suite to his room, the room where she had spent the past few hours napping, and set her down on the bed. She tried to pull him down, but he moved away.

"I have a surprise for you." He walked over to the gas fireplace and flicked it on. He rarely had it on in the summer, but tonight was special. He didn't want her shivering while he made her come.

She was grinning, lying against the bed seductively. "Gas? I thought a rugged mountain man like you would build your own fire."

He chuckled. "I'm not that rugged of a mountain man."

"I think you are."

He came back to the bed and gathered her up in his arms. "Do you now?"

"Oh, yes," she said, nuzzling his neck. This time when she pulled him down, he didn't fight her, because whatever fight he had left in him when it came to her was gone.

He was a lost man.

It felt so good to have him pressed against her. It had been a long time since she'd been with anyone. Not since Shane and even then she was never all that interested in sex. She'd rather be in the OR, elbow deep in someone's chest, than having a night of hot sex.

Now that Carson was here with her, kissing her lips, her neck, her collarbone while his hands slipped under the thick terry-cloth towel to cup her breasts, she realized what she'd been missing. It had never been like this with anyone before.

No man had fired her senses so completely.

She'd never wanted anyone as badly as she wanted Carson now.

Esme wanted him to possess her. To take her.

Hard.

This was what she'd wanted when she'd kissed him. She wanted Carson to help her remember who she was. She just wanted to escape the world for a little while, because when the press came, and found out that she was in town and was the one who'd put the chest tube in Shane, she'd never know peace again. She'd be *that* person again. The runaway bride, the runaway surgeon, and she'd sworn to herself she'd never be that person again.

She had to leave Crater Lake. She had to go somewhere new. Someplace where no one knew her name. She didn't want to leave but she had no choice.

It was for the best, but until she had to leave she was going to cling to this moment. She wanted something to remember Carson by. Just one stolen moment that she could treasure for a long time.

Something that no one had to know about.

Something that could never be exposed and ruined.

Esme sighed, she couldn't help it. His lips were tracing a path slowly down her body. She arched her back, her body tingling. Every nerve ending standing up and paying attention.

"Do you want me to stop?" he asked, his lips hovering just above her collarbone, his breath like a brand of fire on her skin.

"God. No."

"Good." He leaned over her and a shiver of anticipation coursed through her.

So good. Just so, so good.

She didn't deserve this, but right now she didn't care. All she wanted to do was feel and she wanted to feel with him. She'd been numb for so long. He opened the towel, his eyes dark and seeming to devour her. It sent a tingle of excitement through her.

He pressed another kiss against her lips, light at first and then more urgent, as if he couldn't get enough of her. She opened her legs wider, wrapping her legs around his waist, trying to pull him closer.

"Oh, God," Carson moaned. "Oh, God, I want you. I want you so bad."

"I want you, too," she whispered and then arched her back. "Feel how much I want you."

Carson kissed her again, his tongue pushed past her lips, entwining with hers, making her blood sing with need. He ran his hands over her body, his hands on her bare flesh.

"I can't resist you," Carson whispered against her neck. "I can't. I'm so weak."

"I want you, too."

She did. Badly. Right now they weren't competing doctors in town. They were just two people about to become one. Two lovely people who needed this moment of release.

"Please," she begged.

His lips captured hers in a kiss, silencing any more words between them.

"So beautiful," he murmured. His fingers found their way up to her breast, circling around her nipple, teasing.

She ran her fingers through his hair as he began to kiss her again, but just light kisses starting at the lips and trailing lower, down over her neck, lingering at her breasts. He used his tongue to tease her and she gasped as pleasure shot through her again.

His hand moved between her legs and he began to stroke her. Esme cried out. She'd never been touched there before like that and then when his hand was replaced by his mouth and tongue, it made her topple over the edge. She tried to stop herself from coming, but she couldn't. It was too much. It had been so long.

As she came down off her climax Carson moved away and pulled a condom out. "Now, where were we?"

"I think I remember," Esme teased. She took the condom packet from his hand.

"What're you doing?" he asked.

She pushed him down and straddled his legs. "I'm just helping you out."

"Oh, God…" He trailed off as she opened the wrapper and rolled the condom down over his shaft. He was mumbling incoherent words as she stroked him.

"Now you're under me. I like it when you're under me," she murmured, leaning over him and nibbling on his earlobe.

"No. You need to be under me."

"And what're you going to do about it?"

"This." Carson flipped her over, grabbing her wrists and holding her down as he entered her. It felt so good that he was filling her completely. She dug her nails into his shoulder as he stretched her.

"Make love to me," she begged.

He moaned. "I can't say no to you."

Carson moved slow at first, taking his time, but she wanted so much more of him, she urged him to go faster until he lost control and was thrusting against her hard and fast. Soon another coil of heat unfurled deep within her. Pleasure overtaking her as he brought her to another climax.

She wrapped her legs around him, holding him tight against her, urging him on as he reached his own climax. She wanted Carson. She wanted him to make her forget about all her mistakes. Of how she'd run from surgery.

She wanted to feel again. To remember who she was.

She wished they could stay like this forever, but they couldn't. Right now she just wanted to savor the moment of being with him. That she was lying in his arms as she'd wanted, as she'd dreamed.

Carson kissed her gently on the lips, his fingers stroking her face as she ran her hands down over his back. He rolled away from her and propped himself up on one elbow, his eyes twinkling with tenderness.

"I don't want to go home," she whispered. She didn't mean to say that thought out loud. It just came out, because she didn't want to leave the safe, happy, warm bubble. She didn't want to go home to the empty apartment above her clinic and think about packing it all up and leaving.

A sly smile played on his lips. "You don't have to leave if you don't want to. I wouldn't mind you staying here for the night."

"Are you sure about that?"

"Positive. Stay. I want you to stay here." He leaned over and kissed her again. "You taste so good."

"I'll stay."

"Good." He got up to leave.

"Where are you going?"

He leaned back over and kissed her again. "I'll be right back. Just get under the duvet and relax."

Carson took the discarded towel and wrapped it around his waist. He opened the blinds and finally the sun had gone down. The inky black sky was lit by a full moon and a thousand stars.

She'd never seen so many stars.

"Amazing," she whispered.

Carson nodded and then climbed into bed beside her. "You can see it through the skylight, as well."

Esme leaned back against the pillow and stared up at the sky thick with stars. "It's like we're under the Milky Way."

"Almost."

"What would make this perfect is the aurora borealis."

Carson chuckled. "Don't push your luck. Fall is a better time to see them. You'll see one then for sure."

Will I?

Esme rolled over on her side and touched his face.

She didn't want to leave, but she couldn't stay. A man like Carson deserved so much more than her.

"I want you again, Carson." She couldn't believe she was uttering those words, but she did. She wanted him again.

He grinned lazily. "I'm happy to oblige."

She cocked an eyebrow. "Oh, yes?"

"Yes, because I'm not done with you yet. We have all night."

A zing coursed through her. Oh, yes. This was going to be her undoing.

It was going to kill her to leave Crater Lake.

It was going to kill her to leave him.

CHAPTER TWELVE

CARSON REACHED OUT the next morning, but she was gone. The spot on her side of the bed was empty and cold.

Her spot.

He'd never thought of it as anyone's spot before. It was just his bed, somewhere he slept. Now he missed her and she'd only been in his bed one night.

One night and he was hooked on her as if she were a drug. This was exactly why he couldn't be with someone.

The morning light flooded into his bedroom. It was blinding and he realized that he'd slept through his alarm.

Dammit.

At least he didn't have a patient until the afternoon. Besides, if he had a patient in the morning Louise would've called him by now, berating him for being late.

He glanced over to where Esme had been, to the spot where he'd made love to her under a sky of stars, but now she was gone. His bed felt empty.

Only your bed?

Why had he thought it was going to be any different? Why had he expected her to stay with him?

They always left.

Danielle had left and now Esme. Even though he knew logically it was just for a night, that they hadn't made promises to each other, it still was like a knife to the gut. He'd wanted to wake up next to her. He wanted to make love to her again, in the morning light. Only she was gone.

His bed was empty.

It had never felt empty before.

Not even when Danielle had left. He didn't like the way Esme affected him. He was fine before she'd come to town, but now that he'd had her, he wanted her all the more.

Dammit.

His cell phone went off and he reached over and grabbed it. It was Luke's cell.

"Hello?" Carson answered.

"I called the office but Louise said you hadn't shown up for work yet."

"I overslept."

"I haven't slept yet," Luke remarked.

"Where are you?" Carson asked.

"I'm still in Missoula. The guy we pulled off the mountain is in bad shape."

"It looked like he was."

"I had a bit of a fight with a surgeon here," Luke said and then snorted. "I won out in the end. I always do."

"Did he survive?" Luke asked.

"Of course he did. Didn't you hear me say I always win out in the end?"

Carson rolled his eyes. "Do you need me to cancel my afternoon appointments and come get you in Missoula or are you catching a flight back?"

"Can you come get me? I have to get back up on the mountain and assess the damage. Plus Eli Draven is demanding a personal status update on his son."

"You mean the surgeon Dr. Eli Draven, the cardio-thoracic surgeon?"

"Yeah. That man we saved was his son."

"Why doesn't he just go to Missoula?"

"Dr. Draven was in Great Falls with his daughter-in-law. She had a splenectomy."

"They didn't fly her to Missoula?"

"No. Missoula was slammed and Great Falls had a bed. Shane Draven got in here only because it was dire."

"Why was Missoula slammed?"

Luke sighed. "Another landslide south of Whitefish."

"So how is Dr. Draven's daughter-in-law?"

"Apparently she's on the mend and he's back in Crater Lake demanding blood."

"For what?" Carson asked. "It was an act of God."

"You know that and I know that. There's no talking to these guys sometimes. He wants to speak with Dr. Petersen. I told him that Dr. Petersen is the one who probably saved his son's life. He didn't seem thrilled that it was Dr. Petersen and not you or me."

"Whatever, his son is alive thanks to Esme."

"I know that. And Esme, eh?" Luke asked, teasing. "I didn't know you were on a first-name basis."

"Mind your own business."

"Fine. So can you come and get me?"

"Okay," Carson said. "I'll shower and come get you in Missoula."

"Thanks, Carson. Oh, and bring coffee."

Luke hung up and Carson set his phone back down on his nightstand. He'd rather just spend the morning in bed where Esme's scent still lingered on the pillow, but he couldn't do that. He couldn't leave Luke stranded in Missoula.

The bubble had burst and he had to head back out into the real world, as much as he hated to do so.

"Who called?"

Carson nearly jumped out of his skin as Esme padded into his bedroom with a tray that had what looked like breakfast on it. Though he wasn't sure.

"What?" Esme asked, confused. "You look like you've seen a ghost or something."

"I thought you left." He sat up and scrubbed a hand over his face.

"I almost did, but then realized that probably Bob's taxi service wouldn't be up and running at six in the morning when I woke up."

Carson chuckled. "You're probably right, but it's ten in the morning."

"Do you want me to leave?"

"No, it's not that…"

Esme grinned. "Good, 'cause now you can get your coffee."

He moved over and she sat down on the bed next to him, placing the tray on the bed. "I didn't know I had one of those."

"What?" she asked, glancing around.

"This tray thing." He took the mug and sipped the coffee. It was good, but as he eyed the black and yellow stuff on the tray he wasn't so sure. "So, what do we have here?"

"Eggs," she said as if he should've known what the burnt gelatinous mess was.

"Ah, can I pass? I have to get up and drive to Missoula today."

"Missoula?"

"Luke needs a ride back to Crater Lake. He has to get back on the mountain. He was in Missoula operating on Shane Draven all night, the guy we pulled out from under the landslide. Did you know he's Dr. Eli Draven's son? His father is a surgical legend."

The moment he said the name Shane Draven again her demeanor changed completely. She set down her almost-empty mug on the tray and then picked the tray up. She wasn't making eye contact with him. And then things started to piece together. He just didn't know the connection yet.

"Well, then, you better get going."

"What's wrong?" Carson asked.

"What do you mean?"

"What is it about Shane and Eli Draven that made you tense? You totally changed and, come to think about it, it happened at the mill. As soon as they mentioned Silas Draven was a client, but then you realized it was someone else. It's Shane and Eli who make you nervous. Why?"

Esme shook her head. "I—I don't know what you're…" She trailed off and then set the tray down on his dresser to cross her arms.

Carson got out of bed and pulled on his jeans and then came around the other side. "I think you know exactly what I'm talking about. Don't you? Luke said Dr. Draven didn't seem too pleased you worked on his son."

"Is that so?" Her voice was shaking so bad. As if she was terrified. Come to think of it, he was pretty terrified, too.

He was terrified about how he was feeling about her.

Last night when he'd taken her in his arms it had changed. It had all changed. After Danielle had left him and broken his heart he'd never wanted to feel anything for anybody again. He wasn't sure what he was feeling at the moment.

All he knew was he wanted to console her.

Tell her that it was all going to be okay.

Only, he wasn't sure if it would be, because he wasn't sure if he was okay.

"Tell me. It'll be all right. Tell me."

Esme shook her head. "I can't. You wouldn't understand."

"Try me."

"Right," she snorted. "Look, you wouldn't understand. You can't understand."

"I think I might. I've seen hurt before. I've seen heartache."

"Really? You've seen heartache?" she snapped. "Well, was that heartache spread all over the national newspapers? First when you froze during a surgery that cost a patient his life and then leaving your fiancé, who happened to be your mentor and boss's son, on Valentine's Day? Did you have the press hounding you constantly, camped outside the hospital you worked at? Having patients suddenly changing their minds because they had no faith in the surgeon who froze? Your mentor turning on you? Your family disappointed in you?"

Esme's lip trembled, her eyes filling with tears. "Shane Draven was my fiancé and I ran. Dr. Eli Draven was my mentor. He taught me everything. I was his star pupil. After my reputation was shattered by the press, I gave it all up. I gave up surgery, the one thing I loved more than anything, because I didn't deserve it. I don't deserve happiness. I hurt Shane. Me. It was me. All me."

Carson took her in his arms. She tried to fight him, but he held her still. "I was engaged."

Esme stopped and looked up at him. "What?"

"I was engaged. She left me, because I wanted to stay in Crater Lake and she wanted to take a job as a surgeon across the country. It was my fault that she left. So I understand heartache. I get the pain."

Only she didn't look convinced and Carson didn't think that she believed him.

That was okay, because he hated himself for being the cause of his own heartache. Just as she was the cause of her own.

Esme sighed inwardly. She wanted to tell him that he didn't understand, because he wasn't the one that left, but she didn't. Carson wouldn't understand what she was feeling and she got that. No one would understand.

It was her pain to bear alone. She'd lost herself and her career. It was all her fault.

She didn't expect anyone to take it on, to understand it.

Carson and she had shared that one night together, but that was all it had to be. It didn't have to be anything else and it couldn't be, because she was leaving Crater Lake.

As soon as she was able to, she'd send her patients back over to Carson and find some other small town where she could disappear. Where she wouldn't get involved with anyone, because that was all she deserved.

When it came to Carson she'd been so weak. She'd let her loneliness dictate her actions. She'd been so isolated in Los Angeles; people she'd thought were friends had cut her out of their lives. Her father had been disappointed with her giving up surgery and then leaving Shane at the altar, and then her job had been taken away from her. It had taken her a long time to even pluck up the courage to pick up the remnants of her life and find somewhere to start fresh.

Only, her past had caught up with her up on that mountain. Everything she cared about. Everything she loved was taken away from her in the end. She couldn't lose Carson. She wouldn't even risk it.

She had to leave and when she started over, she wasn't going to make the same mistakes that she'd made in Crater Lake.

"I need to go home now," she said, hoping her voice didn't crack too much as she tried to control the tears threatening to spill. "Besides, you have to pick up your brother in Missoula."

"Come with me to Missoula. The drive will do you good."

She shook her head. "No, thanks. I have some patients to see this afternoon. If you could just take me back into town."

Which was a lie. She didn't have any patients.

Not today.

Carson looked disappointed. If it were to anywhere else, if the landslide hadn't happened, if he hadn't discovered her secret, she might've gone with him because she liked car rides. She'd driven to Montana, her car giving out on her when she'd rolled into Crater Lake.

But now she just needed to get back to the place she called home. Two days before the landslide she had unpacked the last box, thinking that she had found a permanent home. Now she realized that was just a myth.

There could be no permanent home for her.

There was no safe place for her.

"Okay, just let me get dressed and I'll take you back into town."

Esme picked up the tray and nodded. "Thank you."

She left him to get dressed as she headed into the kitchen. She rinsed the dishes and put them into his dishwasher for him, cleaning up the mess she'd made trying to make him breakfast. Totally oblivious for a moment that her past had caught up with her.

She'd let her guard down and she hated herself for that.

Esme wandered over to the window and looked down at Crater Lake, smiling as she remembered that short stolen moment down on the shore of the lake that she'd had with Carson. When she'd forgotten who she was.

She'd forgotten she was a disgraced doctor.

She'd forgotten that she'd broken Shane's heart.

She'd forgotten that she'd disappointed her father and she'd forgotten about why she became a surgeon.

"You ready to go?" Carson asked.

Esme turned and he was fully dressed again, which was a shame.

No. You can't think that way.

"Yeah."

They didn't say anything to each other as they went out to his truck. The trip to town was awkward, too. She wanted to tell him how much last night had meant to her, because it had, but Esme thought it would just make things worse.

It wouldn't be good for either one of them.

Carson was frowning as he drove, his hands gripping the steering wheel. It was as if he was holding back things to say to her.

Things, if her circumstances were different, she'd want to hear.

He pulled up in front of her building and sat there.

"Thanks for last night," she said, breaking the awkward silence that descended between them.

It meant so much to me.

Only she didn't say those thoughts out loud and she didn't think the other three words that she really wanted to say, because if she thought about it then it would hurt all the more when she left.

"It meant a lot to me, too," Carson said. Then he turned to look at her. "We didn't make any promises, I know that, but..."

She touched his lips. "No. We didn't and that's okay."

He took her hand. "It's not, though. It wasn't your fault. Patients die all the time and you shouldn't let that inhibit your career. You're a brilliant surgeon. We all make mistakes. You shouldn't leave that talent on a shelf, rusting away."

Only she had and that inhibition had cost her her career in the end.

She smiled and then kissed him gently on the lips. "Thanks again."

Carson nodded. "Are you sure you don't want to come to Missoula with me?"

"Positive. Go get your brother. I have patients."

He nodded. "Right. I'll call you when I get back from Missoula."

"Sure." Only she wasn't going to answer her phone and by the time he realized she was leaving she was hoping to be packed up, in the new car she'd have to buy, and be on the road. If they weren't making any promises to each other, then he shouldn't worry that she didn't answer her phone.

"Do you want to have dinner when I get back?" Carson asked.

"No. Like I said, I'll be really busy with patients this afternoon and I think I'll try to head to bed early tonight. Give me a call in a couple of days. I have a lot of stuff to get caught up on."

It was a lie. She hated lying, but it was for the best.

"Okay. I'll see you later."

Esme nodded and got out of the car. "Goodbye, Carson."

And before he could say anything else she shut the door and ran into her building. Only glancing back once to watch his SUV head off on the main road out of town. Tears stung her eyes, but she wouldn't let them out. She brushed them away, because she didn't deserve to cry for him. She didn't deserve to have him.

She was going to hurt him as his former fiancée had. She was breaking another man's heart.

Even if it was the best for him.

And the worst for her.

CHAPTER THIRTEEN

"LOUISE, MAKE SURE that my afternoon is clear. I have to go get Luke in Missoula."

"Of course, Dr. Ralston."

Carson rubbed his forehead. He'd been supposed to get Luke on Monday after the landslide, but he'd got as far as Whitefish, Montana, when he'd got a text from Luke asking Carson to call him.

Carson had pulled off the road at a rest stop and called his brother back.

Apparently Shane Draven had taken a turn for the worse and Luke had wanted to stay in Missoula to monitor Shane's progress. Dr. Eli Draven had been insisting on it as Luke was the one who had saved Shane's life and Eli had made it clear Esme was not to go near Missoula.

Ungrateful jerk.

Luke knew the chief of surgery at the hospital and was getting special privileges to stay and work there. His brother had also had a few choice words about the annoying female trauma attending who was working on Shane's case with him, which had made Carson chuckle.

So Carson had returned to Crater Lake. He'd tried to call Esme, but she hadn't answered his phone or his knocks on her door and he was worried about her. She'd probably been avoiding the press that had come to town. He didn't blame her for keeping a low profile with the media circling.

Of course now the press was leaving. There was nothing new to report in Crater Lake.

Why are you so worried?

When they'd decided to sleep together, they had both made it quite clear that nothing could happen between them. He should be relieved or happy that she was now giving him the cold shoulder.

She'd been hurt.

Just as he'd been hurt.

This was for the best. It would make it easier. No awkwardness. No expectations.

Was it really the best?

It wasn't. He didn't like it one bit. It had been three days since he'd dropped her off at her clinic. Three days since he'd seen her.

Three days since he'd last kissed her.

He wanted so much more from her. He wanted it all; he just wasn't sure if he could trust her. There was a greatness in her, something she had suppressed because she had been scared. Esme would soon discover that and she'd move on.

Carson couldn't move on.

Crater Lake was his home.

He glanced out the window at her clinic. It had been closed today, which was odd. He hadn't even seen her nurse head to work.

Is it really your concern?

It wasn't and he had to keep reminding himself that it wasn't his business at all. They were just friends, just colleagues. That was all they were. He couldn't give her more and she couldn't give him more.

Why not?

Carson cursed under his breath and tried to concentrate on the chart in his hand. He was supposed to be going over his patient's file. He was supposed to be analyzing tests so that he could tell his patient tomorrow what was going on with him. All he should focus on now was his patients and the fact he had to drive about three and a half hours to Missoula to get Luke.

He shouldn't be worrying about Esme Petersen.

Only he couldn't help himself. She'd gotten under his skin, into his blood. She was in his veins like a drug.

Dammit.

There was a knock at the door and Louise opened it. "Dr. Ralston, Mrs. Fenolio is hoping that you could fit her in tomorrow. Can I fit her in?"

Carson was confused. "Mrs. Fenolio is not my patient. She's Dr. Petersen's."

"Not anymore according to Mrs. Fenolio. Apparently Dr. Petersen is selling her practice and leaving town."

Carson's world began to spin off-kilter.

I'm leaving, Carson. I've been offered a job as Head of Neurosurgery in New York. I'm going.

Are you asking me to go?

No, Carson. I'm not. You won't leave Crater Lake and that's why I'm leaving you.

That's it? You never even gave me the chance to say yes or no.

Well?

I can't leave my father's practice.

See, what was the point of asking? Goodbye, Carson.

"Pardon?" he asked, shaking the memories away.

"Actually, Mrs. Fenolio is not the first former patient to call and ask to come back. The Johnstone twins have an appointment at the end of the week. I also have a pile of patients from that timeshare community who are looking for a new doctor now that Dr. Petersen is closing up shop. So what do I tell them?"

He didn't give Louise an answer. Instead he pushed past her and ran out of the office, crossing the street to bang on Esme's clinic door.

"Esme, open up. I know you're in there."

He continued to pound his fist against the door until she answered. There were dark circles under her eyes when she opened the door just a crack.

"Carson, I don't have time—"

"You're leaving town?" Carson cut her off.

Esme sighed. "I don't have time to talk to you about this."

"I think you can make time for me."

"Go back to your clinic." She tried to shut the door, but he stuck his foot in the gap and forced his way in. "Get out of here, Carson. Go home."

"No." He shut the door behind him and stood in front of it. "You're giving up your practice?"

She crossed her arms. "Yes."

"Why?" he demanded.

She shook her head, annoyed with him. "It's none of your concern."

"You're running away from ghosts. Aren't you? I mean, that's what you did when you left Los Angeles and that's what you're doing here."

Her eyes went positively flinty. He'd hit a nerve and he didn't care. She was running away. She was running out. Just as Danielle had and it hurt. He should've known better, but he was a fool and he was blinded by love.

He'd been blinded by her.

"It's not any of your business."

Carson shook his head. "Why? Why are you running away?"

"As I said. It's not any of your business why I'm leaving. People leave towns. They grow, they change and they forge new trails for themselves. Of course, you wouldn't know anything about that, would you? Since you refuse to leave Crater Lake. I mean, that's why your last relationship failed, wasn't it?"

It was like a slap to the face. It was the truth, but it stung all the same. He should've known better. He'd opened his heart and it was being thrown back in his face. Torn asunder again. Only this one hurt worse than when Danielle had discarded him.

"Go, then. I don't care. At least I'm not a coward. I can face what I'm afraid of. I don't run away from my problems."

A tear slid down her cheek and he knew that he'd hurt her, just as she'd hurt him.

"No, you just let your problems run away for you."

He didn't say anything as he opened the door to her clinic and slammed it behind him. It was good she was leaving.

Was it?

Carson didn't know.

He didn't know what he was feeling. Only that he

was angry at himself for opening up to someone again. For letting someone in.

For letting Esme absolutely shatter his heart.

Esme wanted to go after him, even if he had hurt her, because he was right. She was running away from the ghosts of her past again, but it was for the best. She cared for Carson. She loved Carson and she didn't want to drag him into her mess.

It was in Carson's best interests that she left. He didn't need to be associated with her; he wouldn't want to be associated with her. She was a failure.

What would that do to his practice, being associated with her? It was an old practice that had been in his family for so long. She couldn't destroy that, because she loved Carson.

It was better to get out now before she got in too deep. Before she totally destroyed Carson's career or ran out on their wedding.

Who says you'll run? a little voice inside her asked.

She didn't know that for certain, but any time any relationship in her past had gotten serious she'd run.

The only problem with running was that she was so alone.

And she was getting tired of running even if it was for the best. Even if it was mandatory. She was a coward. Carson was right. She was too afraid to love. Too afraid to lose someone she loved.

It hurt that he'd called her a coward, but it was true.

She'd run away from surgery. She'd run from Shane and now she was running away from Carson. She wasn't even giving him the choice or the chance to be with her.

You didn't run from Avery. You stayed with him.

Stayed and tried to keep him from bleeding out, even though you'd been alone, young and terrified.

Esme crumpled up in a ball and began to sob.

When had her life become such a failure?

There was a knock at her door. She wanted to ignore it. Worried that Carson had come back, because she didn't want him to see her like this. She didn't want him to see her again. She didn't deserve any kind of absolution or pity from him.

The knocking was incessant and then she heard a voice. One that she hadn't heard in a long time.

"Esme, it's your father. Can I come in?"

Dad?

She hadn't seen him since she'd disappointed him so badly, when she'd given up on surgery and run out on Shane.

She leaped up and ran to the door, flinging it open. "Dad? What're you doing here?"

Before he answered he hugged her, pulling her close into an embrace that made tears well in her eyes, but she didn't return the hug, too shocked that he was standing here.

"I can't believe you're here," she murmured as the hug ended.

"Well, I saw on the news that there was a massive landslide in Crater Lake. Your mother mentioned to me that was where you were moving to. Can I come in?"

"Sure." Esme stepped to the side and let him in her clinic. She shut the door and locked it. "I don't understand. I didn't tell Mom where I was going. I haven't talked to either of you since Valentine's Day, the day I...the day I ran from Shane."

"Not your stepmother. Your biological mother."

"Ah, yes, I did tell her." She ran her hand through her hair. "I called her for the first time in a long time when I was leaving Los Angeles. She'd lived up this way for some time and she helped me make a decision about where I was going to set up shop."

Her father glanced around the waiting room. "It looks nice, except for all the boxes. You've been here a few months—I thought you would be further along with setting up than this."

"I'm not setting up. I'm packing up." She couldn't look him in the eyes. She was worried she'd see the same disappointment. When she glanced over, when she dared to look at him, she was surprised it was concern not disappointment etched in his face.

"What? Why?"

Esme sighed. "It's complicated."

"Esme Petersen, what is going on?"

She threw her hands up in the air and collapsed in a waiting-room chair. "I don't know."

Her father gave her that look. The one that struck fear in her heart and usually terrified most criminals when he was working the beat. "I don't believe that for a second. You know, I did watch the news reports. I know that two of the victims in that landslide happen to be Shane Draven and his wife."

Esme nodded. "Yeah."

"Did you see him up there?"

She nodded. "I did. In fact, I saved his life. At least, I think I did. He was airlifted off the mountain. I put in his chest tube."

Her dad made a face, as he always did when she talked medicine, but then she noticed the worry in the lines of his face and the dark circles under his eyes.

"I was worried about you. When I heard there was a landslide... You haven't spoken to me in a long time. I wanted to see for myself that you were okay. I couldn't lose another child."

A tear slid down Esme's face. "I'm sorry."

"You should've called. I've been so worried."

"I would've called, but when I walked out on Shane you made it pretty clear that you were disappointed with me. I could tell that you saw Mom in me and that I was a disappointment to you and Sharon. I know how hard you both worked to give me an education and I let you both down."

"Esme," her father whispered and he took a seat next to her. "I might've been concerned, but disappointed in you leaving Shane? Never, but I was disappointed you walked away from surgery. You walked away from your gift."

"I froze during a surgery I knew. I froze and the patient died. I don't have a gift, not anymore."

"Yes, you do...you're a damn good surgeon. I don't know how you do it, dealing with all the blood and vein things."

Esme chuckled, her dad breaking the tension that had fallen between them. "Vein things?"

"You know what I'm talking about. Point is you ran. You should've held your ground. You're stronger than that."

She nodded. "Am I?"

"You are."

"That's kind of you to say, Dad, but I don't think my surgery career would've survived. I became a surgeon for Avery. I dedicated my life to it and then... I don't even know who I am."

surgeon in her own right and her career would only be defined by one person.

Her.

Her dad had made her see that she was being foolish. She'd run scared too many times and she was letting people's judgments of her rule her life.

She wouldn't run from Carson. She might have run from Shane, but she understood why she had now. She hadn't loved him. Shane had wanted her to be someone she wasn't. Carson loved her for who she really was. Carson wanted her to be a surgeon.

She loved Carson.

He brought out the best in her, encouraging her when she was scared of picking up that scalpel again.

Until that day at the mill she hadn't performed a surgical procedure in so long but he'd encouraged her. He thought her skill was a gift she was squandering and he was right. It was.

Of course, she'd ruined things with Carson now, but even if she had she wasn't going to run from that pain. She was going to stay now. Hopefully in time Carson would trust her again and maybe if she was lucky he'd open his heart.

And when he did, she wasn't going to let him go.

"So?" her father said, interrupting her chain of thoughts. "Have I got through that thick, stubborn shell of yours? Are you going to stay and finish the job you started here? Because Sharon and I didn't raise a quitter."

"No, you guys didn't." She kissed her father on the cheek. "Yeah, I'm going to stay here. Even if the residents find out about my past. I'm going to stay and face it. I'm tired of running away."

"Good." Her father stood up. "Now, are you going to make me stay in that little motel until I leave tomorrow night or are you going to put up your old man?"

"I think I'll put up my old man. Of course you can stay here."

"Good. Do you want to go get some lunch and then I'll grab my stuff from the motel?" he asked.

"That sounds good, Dad, but I have to do one more thing. Can you wait?"

"Sure."

Esme gave him a quick peck on the cheek and then ran out of her clinic. She ran across the street to Carson's clinic. She needed to talk to him. She needed to tell him how she felt and she needed to apologize for the things she'd said to him. Even if he wouldn't listen to her.

She ran into his clinic.

Louise, his nurse, came to the front from the back. "Dr. Petersen? How can I help you?"

"Is Dr. Ralston in? I need to speak with him."

"No, I'm sorry. He went to Missoula to pick up his brother."

"I thought he did that three days ago?" Esme asked, confused.

"He was supposed to, but the other Dr. Ralston had to stay and monitor Mr. Draven's health. It took a turn for the worse."

Oh, God.

"Did Mr. Draven pull through?"

Louise shrugged. "I really don't know. I'm sorry. Anyways, Dr. Ralston has gone to Missoula today. I don't think he'll be back until later tonight."

"Thank you, Louise."

"Can I take a message for him?"

Tell him I love him. Tell him I'm staying. Only she didn't want to leave that message with his nurse. She wanted to tell him herself.

"No. It's okay. I'll talk to him another time." Esme left the office and headed back to her clinic, hoping that it wasn't too late for her and Carson.

She prayed it wasn't too late.

CHAPTER FOURTEEN

CARSON WAS SURPRISED that he got to Missoula in one piece. He actually didn't remember the drive to the hospital because all he could think about was Esme and that she was leaving. It was a blow. He was hurt.

His heart hurt.

He should've known better. This was why he didn't put his heart on the line. It was his fault. Everything he was feeling, it was his fault. He shouldn't have cared about her. He shouldn't have let her in.

He shouldn't have fallen in love with her, because, try not to as he might, he was absolutely in love with Esme and once again his heart was breaking. Only this time it was much, much worse.

When he got to the hospital he noticed all the press vehicles around. Not surprising as Shane Draven was president of a big corporation and son of a prominent surgeon.

Shane Draven.

That was who Esme had been engaged to. He'd read interviews about Shane and his father and he had a hard time picturing someone like Esme with Shane. Then again, Luke always said he'd had a hard time picturing Danielle and Carson together.

Still, it explained her behavior when they'd been up at the mill and when she'd jammed that chest tube into Shane Draven's chest.

If she had run away from Shane, and because she was a gentle person, she probably blamed herself. Felt as if she didn't deserve love.

Boy, do I understand that.

Maybe that was why she'd pushed him away.

Still, she's running away.

While another voice inside him said, *You could go with her.*

And it scared him to think of leaving the safety net of Crater Lake, the only home he'd known, of giving up the family practice, of changing for Esme.

Could he? Could he really pack up his whole life on the possibility that she'd still be with him in the future? How could he leave Crater Lake? It would mean that the family practice, which had been open for over a century, would close.

How could he let his family down?

How could you let yourself down?

He got out of his car and headed into the hospital. At the front desk they told him where he could find Luke, who was still on the CCU floor.

Carson couldn't even think straight. He didn't know what to think. When Danielle had left it had hurt him, but he'd got over it. The prospect of Esme leaving left a gnawing hole in him. It ticked him off that she was giving up.

Why was she giving up?

Aren't you giving up?

"Carson?"

The familiar voice dragged him out of his reverie

and he stopped in his tracks. He turned around and behind him was Danielle.

She'd changed. He barely recognized her, but it had been several years. He'd thought that he'd never forget Danielle's face. He'd thought it was so burned in his brain, reminding him of the hurt as a warning to him, but now, compared to Esme, Danielle was a dim memory.

"Danielle, how are you?" He held out his hand, but she gave him a quick awkward hug.

"Good. Luke said you were arriving today."

Carson cursed under his breath. "Did he?"

"Yeah, he hasn't left Shane Draven's side in the CCU. There were several times we weren't sure he'd pull through."

"Well, when Luke saves someone on the mountain, he likes to see a job to the end."

"Did he put in that chest tube?" Danielle asked.

"No...he didn't."

She raised her eyebrows. "Did you?"

"No. Another doctor did."

"Ah," Danielle said. "Well, whoever did did an amazing job. Dr. Ledet, the other surgeon on the case, said the chest tube probably saved Shane's life. Wish I could meet that doctor, to insert a chest tube in the emergent situation like that, in conditions like that."

"Yes, she's a brilliant doctor. We're going to miss her."

A strange look passed over Danielle's face. "She's leaving Crater Lake."

"You say that like it's inevitable."

Danielle rolled her eyes. "Come on, Carson. Even with all these new hotels and resorts going up on the outskirts of town, it's still a small town. Nothing changes. Nothing. Not even you."

It hit him hard, because it was true.

He couldn't change for Danielle, but could he change for Esme?

"Some things do change, Danielle. I'm glad you found your place. I'm happy for you."

Danielle was stunned. "Thanks."

Carson nodded and then continued on his way to CCU. He had been so angry with Danielle for so long, he hadn't realized how angry he had been and, because he'd been angry at her, he hadn't been able to move past it. He hadn't been able to forgive himself.

When he got up on the CCU floor, he found Luke at the charge station, charting and wearing... "Scrubs?" Carson teased.

Luke glanced over at him. "It's about time you showed up."

"It's a three-hour drive. I had to finish some of my own charting this morning."

Luke nodded. "You're so tied to Dad's practice."

"My practice, you mean. It could be yours, as well."

Luke shut the chart and grinned. "You know it's not for me."

"Who says it's for me?"

Luke arched his eyebrows. "Do tell."

"Never mind. You ready to go?"

He nodded, handed the chart back and grabbed his rucksack from behind the counter. "Let's go."

They walked in silence back through the hospital. Carson wasn't saying much. He was trying to process everything, process his feelings, his future. He didn't know what to think.

"So you're in a mood," Luke commented as they walked out of the hospital toward the parking lot.

"Am I?"

"I take it you saw Danielle?"

"I did, but that's not really bothering me."

"What is?" Luke asked, tossing his rucksack into the backseat.

"You are."

"What?"

"You. Why won't you take over Dad's practice? Why does it have to be me?"

Luke crossed his arms. "Who said it has to be you? I didn't force you to take the practice."

"You kind of did," Carson snapped. "You went off to the army and then decided you didn't want to work in Dad's clinic. I had to step up. Dad wanted to retire and there have been Ralstons in Crater Lake forever. What else was I supposed to do?"

"Follow your own path," Luke said. "It's obvious."

Carson cursed under his breath. "It's not obvious."

"It is." Luke scrubbed a hand over his face. "Ever since you were a kid you've had this great sense of duty. You were a good kid. I was a bit of a screwup, but you've had this sense of keeping our family's practice alive. Of not changing and it's been nothing but detrimental to you. Painful. How many dreams have you given up for the sake of family heritage?"

"You need to back off, Luke."

He snorted. "No. I think you need to realize that you're never going to have what you want unless you change. Do something for yourself for once."

Carson shook his head. "I can't."

Why not?

Why did he have to stay in Crater Lake? Another doctor would set up shop. He could sell off the practice.

"She'll walk away, she's going to walk away and you know who I'm talking about," Luke said.

It was his now. His dad had said he could do whatever he wanted with it. Even though he loved his hometown, the house he'd built, it just wasn't enough when you had no one to share it with.

As much as he loved Crater Lake, his job, he loved Esme more.

"Forgive yourself," Luke said. "And for once follow your heart. Do what *you* want to do. Live!"

Carson didn't say anything as he slid into the car to drive back home. He was kicking himself now for the way he'd left it with Esme.

She was going to leave and she was going to leave hating him.

He needed to tell her how he felt.

And he needed to tell her now.

Esme couldn't believe that she'd broken into Carson's home. She'd told her father what she had to do and he'd understood. He'd encouraged her to go with a promise that they would catch up later. She wasn't even sure if he'd be happy to see her. The way they'd left things, the way she'd broken his heart, it might be too late. The person she once was screamed in her head to run away, to not face the hurt, but she couldn't run away.

Not now.

Even if he rejected her. Even if he couldn't forgive or care for her, that was okay. She deserved it, but she wasn't running. She wasn't leaving Crater Lake.

She had plans. She was going to set down roots again

and the prospect of setting down roots and not running away was something she'd always wanted.

Even if the press came pounding at her door about Shane, she didn't care. She wasn't going anywhere. She deserved the life she wanted and she was going to do everything in her power to keep that.

She was going to be a surgeon again. She was going to make her father proud, but, more importantly, she was going to be proud of herself. No more hiding in shadows, keeping her head down.

Esme wandered over to the window. It was dark out and the stars were out again. It made her think of Carson. Of being in his arms, in his bed.

And as she watched the celestial display the aurora borealis erupted across the sky. Beautiful greens, just dancing above the lake. It made her catch her breath in the beauty of it all.

Yeah, she was doing the right thing.

If Carson didn't want her anymore, then that was something she could live with, but she couldn't live with herself if she didn't tell him how she felt.

The sound of his key in the door made her heart skip a beat and she turned around, waiting for him.

He came in and flicked on the lights. He startled to see her standing there.

"Esme?" he asked in confusion. "What're you doing here? I thought you were leaving?"

"I was, but I've changed my mind."

Carson dragged his hand through his hair and then shut his door, dropping his keys on the side table by the door.

"You've changed your mind?"

"Yes."

"Why?" he asked. "You were pretty clear today about your reasons for leaving."

"I know. My reasons have changed." She sighed. "Look, I'm not a girl who ever believed in romance. I thought I wasn't the girl for you. I mean, I ruined the most romantic holiday in the world by jilting my former fiancé. Romance and love have never been my priority."

"So what is?" he asked, crossing his arms and taking a step toward her.

"Surgery." She took a deep breath. "When my brother died I dedicated my life to surgery and when I got together with Shane I forgot who I was. I thought love complicated things and I lost focus."

Carson looked confused. "Why?"

"I don't know."

His expression softened. "I'm sorry. How did your brother die? You never told me."

"I was ten and he was twenty-two. We were in an accident on Valentine's Day. I had to put my hands in his chest to stop the bleeding. His heart stopped under my hands. When he died my mother left. I was scared to love. Scared to lose. It hurt too much, but I swore I would be a surgeon. To save lives so no one had to hurt the way I did."

"So that's why you chose cardio thoracic as your specialty and why you hate Valentine's Day. Why did you choose to almost marry Shane on Valentine's Day?"

"He insisted."

"And you agreed because you thought it might make you forget that day?"

She nodded. "Yes. I did it to please him. It's what Shane wanted. I ran from that wedding because I was tired of not being me. I lost myself. Still, I hurt him. I had closed myself off for too long."

"And now?"

She nodded. "I came here to find myself. To forget surgery, because I didn't deserve happiness, but…"

"But?" he asked.

"Then you walked into my life and my priorities have changed because I didn't take into account something that's very important."

"I love you," he said, surprising her.

"What?"

Carson grinned. "I love you. I figured that's what you were going to say, too."

Esme grinned. "Y-yes, I was."

Carson smiled. "Say it, then."

"I love you." Esme took a step toward him. "I used to run. Afraid of facing my inner demons, afraid of facing rejection, pain. Afraid of facing my own failures, but you changed all that. You changed it the moment you asked me to go up that mountain during that mill accident. No one has ever been able to change my mind once it's set. A drawback of being a cardio-thoracic surgeon."

"I thought you weren't a surgeon?" he asked.

"I'm a surgeon and I'm going to stay here. I'm going to keep practicing as a surgeon."

Carson nodded. "Well, I guess I'm not selling my practice after all."

Esme cocked an eyebrow. "What?"

Carson closed the gap between them. "I was going to sell my practice and go with you. I had been so afraid of forging my own path for so long. So unbending. I couldn't change for anyone. It's cost me in more ways than I care to admit. I used different excuses to keep me here, but when you said you were leaving it… I couldn't bear to live without you. I will change for you. I'd give up anything to be with you. Without you, this isn't my home. You're my home."

Esme couldn't hold back the tears. No apologies were needed. Nothing further needed to be said. She wrapped her arms around him and he held her, but only for a moment until he picked her up, kissing her. Kissing away the tears that were not tears of sadness, but joy.

"I love you, Esme. I love you and I can't live without you. You're my everything." Carson brushed away a tear with his thumb.

"I love you, too. I'm tired of running. I don't want to run. I'm in this for the long haul."

Carson kissed her again, making her weak in the knees, making her melt into his arms. He scooped her up in his arms and carried her into his bedroom.

And she was never going to let him go.

She was done running. She was done hiding.

This was her home.

She was home.

EPILOGUE

February 13th

"THIS BETTER NOT be a Valentine's Day thing," Esme said as Carson covered her eyes and led her into the house. "I don't like Valentine's Day."

"I know. I know, but it's not Valentine's Day. It's the thirteenth and it's a Friday. Does Friday the thirteenth hold any kind of dark secrets for you?" Carson asked.

"Well, this one time at this summer camp…" she teased.

"Ha-ha. Don't tease about that. That movie scared the living daylights out of me."

"Hey, you're the one who is leading a surprise on a Friday the thirteenth. Not me. And how did I not know that you didn't like horror movies? I'm shocked."

"You do?" Carson asked.

"I do. Does that change things?" She tried to suppress the laughing.

"Well." He removed his hands and Esme gasped when she saw the spread laid out for them. They were at home and there was a new dining-room table set up, overlooking the floor-to-ceiling windows at the back of the house.

The fire was snapping and crackling in the large central fireplace, and there were candles and roses everywhere.

"Oh, my gosh," she gasped.

"So, you see, the love of horror movies might just change my mind." There was a twinkle in his eyes.

Esme laughed. "Oh, come on. It's just a minor thing."

"Well, maybe this will change your mind with associating February thirteenth as an unlucky day or a day that has to do with axe-wielding, hockey-mask-wearing monsters."

"A nice dinner? For sure." Then she gasped as he dropped to one knee. "What're you doing?"

"Giving you a good memory, I hope." He pulled out a ring. "Will you marry me, Esme?"

Tears filled her eyes. She'd never expected to get engaged again. She hadn't planned on it, but that had all changed the moment she'd met Dr. Carson Ralston. And since the summer, she'd been patiently waiting for him to ask her.

Actually, she'd planned to ask him tomorrow. On Valentine's Day. Only this time she wasn't trying to bury a painful memory with something that *could* be happy. She knew that Carson was the one. She knew that their lifetime together *would* be happy.

Esme had only been certain about surgery in her life, never in matters of the heart, but when she'd foolishly almost walked away from Carson last summer, she'd known that he held her heart. He was meant for her.

She'd found herself and her place was in his arms. The thought of losing him was more than she could bear. She wanted to be his wife more than anything, to share her life with him and only him.

She'd just thought that she would have to do the proposing. And she was okay with that, but this was so much better.

This was almost too much for her heart to handle and she thought she was going to burst. She wiped away the tears and didn't care if they smudged her mascara. She wanted a clearer look at Carson, down on one knee holding out a diamond ring, which sparkled in the firelight.

How could she ever have contemplated leaving Crater Lake? Leaving him?

"Well? Your silence is kind of worrying me." His brow furrowed. "Was this too much?"

"Yes," she whispered.

"Yes, too much, or yes...?"

Esme sobbed happily, dropping to her knees to kiss him. "Yes. I'll marry you."

He cupped her face in his hands and kissed her. "You had me worried there."

"I'm sorry. I couldn't believe you were actually asking me there for a moment."

"Can't you?"

Esme laughed. "I'm sorry, but I have to say you've ruined Valentine's Day for me."

"What?" he asked. "How could I have ruined Valentine's Day for you? This isn't even Valentine's Day. I didn't even buy a single rose."

"I was planning to propose to you at the Valentine's gala tomorrow night. I even had a dress and everything."

Carson threw his head back and laughed. "For real?"

She nodded. "Your brother was in on it."

"What? How did you manage to pull that off? He's not one for romance either."

Esme shrugged. "I have my ways."

"So what did the dress look like?" he asked huskily.

"Would you like me to model it later for you?" Her pulse began to race and she wrapped her arms around his neck, nibbling on that sensitive spot by his earlobe that she had discovered soon after they'd moved in together.

"You can model for me later, but not the dress. I couldn't care less about the dress."

She laughed. "Can I have my ring now?"

"Hmm, I don't know. Maybe I do want you to get down on one knee and propose to me," he said, teasing her.

"Do you want me to slug you?" She kissed him quickly on the lips. "Will you marry me, Dr. Ralston?"

"Let me think…" Esme punched him on the arm and he laughed. "Of course, you foolish girl."

"You had me worried there for a fraction of a second." She winked.

"Well, I want to make you work for it." Carson slipped the ring on her finger and kissed her, a kiss that melted her down to her very core. "I love you, Esme Petersen. With all my heart. There isn't anyone else in this world that's meant for me. It's you I want. Only you."

"Even if I spend countless hours in an OR a couple hours from home?"

"Even then. I love you."

"And I love you, too, Carson." She kissed him again

and then whispered against his neck, "With all my heart, too."

And she did. Absolutely and completely love him. Only him.

* * * * *

CRAVING HER
EX-ARMY DOC

BY
AMY RUTTAN

Published in Great Britain 2016
By Mills & Boon, an imprint of HarperCollins*Publishers*
1 London Bridge Street, London, SE1 9GF

ISBN: 978-0-263-25428-0

Our policy is to use papers that are natural, renewable and recyclable
products and made from wood grown in sustainable forests.
The logging and manufacturing processes conform to the legal
environmental regulations of the country of origin.

Printed and bound in Spain
by CPI, Barcelona

For my boys. For the times you have fun together
and the times you drive each other crazy.
Remember this, Aidan, James *will* grow bigger than you.

Love you both.

PROLOGUE

"GET OUT OF my OR!"

"Not on your life." Luke stood his ground. He wasn't about to be pushed out of the OR by the arrogant upstart trauma surgeon at the hospital. "I got him off the mountain and I'm not going to let him die on my watch. So if you want me out of your OR you're going to have to physically remove me."

Those blue-green eyes behind the surgical mask glittered with barely concealed rage and Luke smiled behind his own mask, knowing he'd pushed the surgeon's buttons. She was some hotshot surgeon from out east. One who had been teaching a workshop in Missoula and got called in when Shane was brought in, because Missoula was slammed.

There had been several landslides after a small earthquake rocked the area. All hospitals in a hundred-mile radius were overflowing with the injured. If Luke had the supplies he could've set up a mobile OR in Crater Lake. He'd worked in worse conditions in Afghanistan.

Only, he hadn't practiced surgery since his honorable discharge and he certainly wasn't going to start on Shane Draven. He did surgery when needed, but he preferred practicing in the wilderness. So in this situation he'd rather this trauma surgeon work on Shane.

Still, she needed to know he was just as capable as her. He would have done the surgery another way. That was why he was questioning her.

She was cocky and full of herself. She definitely needed to be taken down a peg or two and he was just the guy to do it.

He might not practice as a traditional doctor, but he was just as much a surgeon as this woman. He had spent time on the front line, patching up soldiers in the midst of fire. How many lives had he saved? He wasn't sure, because he didn't keep score. All that mattered was saving lives. That was why he'd joined the army, it was what he'd wanted for so long, but he'd given it up for another.

Don't think about that now.

This surgeon had sized him up the moment he'd rushed in with Shane Draven's stretcher. She thought he was nothing but a first responder or a paramedic. Obviously a surgeon who didn't know any better. Paramedics were on the front line.

Usually he wouldn't question another surgeon in the OR, unless the patient was at serious risk, but the moment he walked into the OR with Shane she'd been treating him like a second-class citizen. Which was why he decided two could play at that game. So he questioned her every move.

She wanted a fight? Oh, he'd give her a fight.

"I will physically remove you," she snapped.

"I'd prefer you focus on my patient, Doctor, rather than argue over my presence here."

Her angry gaze met his. "You're questioning my skill, Mr...."

Luke grinned smugly. "It's Dr. Ralston."

Her eyes widened in obvious surprise. "Doctor? I thought you were a paramedic."

"Looks can be deceiving, I guess, but I am a doctor. Though I'm not insulted you thought I was a paramedic, but I suppose that's the reason why you feel I should be kicked out of your OR."

She cursed under her breath. "Doctor or paramedic, it doesn't matter. I won't have you undermining my authority in my OR."

"This isn't your OR. You're not from around here."

"When I'm operating it's my OR, whether or not I'm from here."

Luke had to admire her spunk. And she was right. Perhaps he'd been undermining her a touch, but this was a man he'd pulled off the mountain and Dr. Eli Draven was this patient's father. He had made it clear that he was going to hold Luke responsible if Shane died, because Luke had allowed Dr. Petersen to place the chest tube.

Luke didn't know what Dr. Draven had against Dr. Petersen and he didn't really care. He'd pulled Shane down off the mountain. He was responsible for Shane's life. Dr. Draven had been throwing his weight around in the Missoula hospital, because the chief of surgery was one of his former students.

Besides, Shane was also the nephew of Silas Draven, who was sending Luke the most work up on the mountain, and Silas Draven was someone he didn't want to mess with. Luke appreciated all the work, but still he felt responsible for taking care of Shane. Luke, his brother,

Carson, and Dr. Petersen were all instrumental in getting Shane Draven to Missoula alive.

Luke hadn't left Shane's side since they were airlifted off the mountain and he wasn't going to leave him now.

No man gets left behind. Every life gets saved.

Luke's commanding officer's words rang true to the credo he lived by and it wasn't going to change now. He'd served two tours of duty as an army medic. Even when he couldn't live by that credo, when life couldn't be saved, it still drove him.

Don't think about losing patients now. Not with Shane on the table.

He shook those thoughts away. There was no place for them here.

"I got this man down off the mountain. He's my patient whether this is *your* OR or not."

"If you stay, Doctor, keep your opinions to yourself, then." She looked away and continued to work on Shane. A true hardened trauma surgeon, as he'd been once.

Damn, she's a spitfire.

He admired that about her and if circumstances had been different, meaning if he had any interest in pursuing a relationship again, he'd go after a strong-willed spitfire woman like her, but she was off-limits.

All women were.

He wanted to say more, but he knew when it was best to keep his mouth shut. As long as Shane's life was saved, and then he could get Eli Draven off his back, but he still watched the surgeon like a hawk.

"Yes, Doctor." And he gave her a little salute.

The surgeon mumbled a few choice words under her breath, but continued working on Shane.

Luke tried not to move toward the side of the table, where the lead surgeon stood, because if he did that then she would have grounds to throw him out of her OR.

He might be a bit of a control freak when it came to his patients, but there was no way he'd push it any further. He wasn't leaving this OR. He wasn't going to leave Shane Draven behind.

He didn't even know her name and he didn't care; she seemed to be competent. That was all that mattered.

When the surgery was over and they were wheeling Shane to the ICU, Luke gave up his perch in the OR. He planned to be on that ICU floor and personally monitoring Shane until he came out of the woods, as it were.

Dr. Ralston is a fine surgeon and a heck of an officer.

Only that wasn't entirely true. Not anymore. He wasn't an officer anymore. He'd given it all up. He didn't renew his commission because his wife was done being an army wife, but then Christine had left him. He did it all for her and for nothing.

Luke shook that thought from his head. Nope. He wasn't going there, because he wasn't going to let that happen again.

No one was going to dictate how his life should be again. Which was why he wouldn't settle down into a practice with Carson. It had been Christine's wish after he finished his tours of duty. He'd partner with Carson, raise a family with Christine and do what he loved, practicing medicine. He'd been planning to do that. Luke was going to give up the army for his wife to make her happy. At least that had been the plan.

Then it all went to hell in a handbasket.

Christine left him when he finished his second tour, for his best friend, Anthony.

He cursed under his breath as he walked down the hall to the ICU. He was angry at himself for allowing those thoughts to creep into his head again. To let her creep into his thoughts again. It was because he was in a hospital again.

Surrounded by people.

On his mountain it was just the sky, the wind, the trees and the majestic behemoths rising from the earth toward the clouds.

On his mountain he was himself and he had no one to answer to. No one but him controlled his life, his fate, his destiny.

"Hey!"

Luke spun around and saw a woman in surgical scrubs and cap approach him. The physical attraction was immediate. Full red lips, which were slightly pouty. White-blond hair peeked out from under the scrub cap and big blue-green eyes sparkled with annoyance.

Oh. No.

It was the spitfire surgeon. He'd only seen her over the surgical mask. Now seeing that she was a gorgeous woman with a strong personality to boot, well, that was a dangerous combination for Luke.

"Can I help you?" he asked.

She crossed her arms and sized him up. "I'm looking for a Dr. Ralston. Do you happen to know where he is?"

Luke took a step back, in case she started swinging, but then the words sank in and he realized she didn't know who he was. But then, he'd been wearing a surgical mask, cap and gown when he'd been in the OR with Shane. And this surgeon wasn't a local surgeon. She was visiting. She wouldn't recognize one person from another behind a surgical mask, because not being at this hospital every day he certainly didn't.

This could be fun, one part of him thought. While the other part told him to walk away and not entangle himself with her, because he knew she spelled danger.

"Why do you need him?"

She huffed. "If you see him tell him Dr. Ledet is looking for him." She turned to walk away and for a brief moment, one fraction of a second, he saw himself grabbing Dr. Ledet and pulling her into his arms, kissing her. Forcing the image away, he overcame the urge to taste those soft, moist lips, running his hands through her blond hair.

Maybe doing a little bit more than that.

Definitely dangerous.

"Where can he find you?" Luke asked.

She glanced at her watch. "After eight he can't. I'm flying back to New York."

"New York?"

"Yeah, I was here on business and decided to lend a hand for an old teacher. A fat lot of good that did me when I had to deal with an arrogant jerk like Dr. Ralston."

"Well, if I see him before eight I'll tell him."

She didn't thank him, just nodded curtly and walked away.

A New York surgeon, eh? Well, that was too bad, but it was for the best.

He'd never see her again.

It would've never worked anyway and not because of the distance, but because he would never let it.

CHAPTER ONE

Six months later, mid-January,
Crater Lake, Montana

I HATE THE COLD. I hate the cold.

Sarah thought coming from New York she'd be used to the frigid temperatures of northwest Montana. New York State bordered Canada, too; it should be the same, but it wasn't. Not at all. This was a different kind of cold. There was no moisture in the air and as she tried to shake the remnants of bone-chilling frigidity from her brand-new office, she couldn't remember why she'd decided to take this job in Crater Lake, Montana.

Dr. Draven.

Right. Her teacher from medical school. Dr. Eli Draven. She didn't study under him, because she didn't have an interest in becoming a cardio-thoracic surgeon, but she remembered him clearly from her days at Stanford.

He was a good teacher, if not a bit full of himself. He'd taken a shine to her until she'd decided not to pursue cardio; then she was no longer his star, but he still spoke highly of her and when this job was offered to her by Dr. Draven's brother, she couldn't pass up the opportunity, because she was more than ready to get out of New York and out of her father's iron grip.

No matter what she did, nothing was good enough for her parents.

They still saw her as their baby.

And they wouldn't be happy until she was living a pampered life in a Central Park West penthouse, married to an investment banker or a lawyer or even a doctor.

She couldn't be the doctor, however.

That was unacceptable.

Why do you need to work, pumpkin? Your husband, if you marry well, can take care of you.

Her mother's archaic way of thinking made her shake her head. Sarah peeled off the thick parka she'd bought when she moved out to Montana and hung it on the coat rack in her office. There were no cabs in Crater Lake, unless you counted the very unreliable Bob's Taxi, and she didn't.

At least she'd bought a car when she first landed in Missoula and had snow tires put on it. She was well versed in the rugged country living she was immersing herself in, even if she did complain about the cold just a bit.

Why do you want to go work out in the wilderness?

Sarah's sister, who was married to a very prominent surgeon and occupied one of those coveted penthouse suites on Central Park West, couldn't understand what was driving her to do this.

Sometimes Sarah wasn't even sure herself.

Because your dad got you your prestigious appointment in that Manhattan hospital. It wasn't you.

Sarah sighed when she remembered. After a summer

of touring around different hospitals in each state, presenting her Attending's research and teaching different surgeons on using the newest model of robotic surgery, she came home to New York to accept one of the most prestigious positions offered to a trauma surgeon at Manhattan Grace, only to find out that the only reason she was chosen to tour the country and work with Dr. Carroll was that her father was friends with Dr. Carroll. They played a few rounds of golf in the Hamptons. Even her brother-in-law pulled strings for her as if she couldn't make it on her own.

It just shook the foundation of everything Sarah had thought she knew.

It had knocked her confidence completely. Perhaps she wasn't the surgeon that she'd thought she was? So she'd turned down the position, much to her father's chagrin.

This was why she distanced herself from people. So many people trying to control the course of her life. She just couldn't trust anyone.

Not even herself.

Do you know how many strings I've had to pull for you over the years? Just so you can play doctor? Come to your senses, Sarah.

Sarah came to her senses all right. She threw the job back in her father's face, sold her apartment on the Upper West Side and took the job offer from Silas Draven to be the general practitioner and general surgeon at his newly opened ski lodge.

The ski lodge was set to open in one month, on Valentine's Day, and Sarah couldn't wait to get started. It would be a slower pace of life, but at least she would be able to help people here. She could be a doctor and not worry that her father was pulling strings to get her whatever she wanted. She was burned-out and really didn't know who she was or what she wanted anymore. She didn't even know if she wanted to be a surgeon and that thought terrified her, because for so long surgery had been her life.

For now a general practitioner sounded good. She could practice medicine and figure out where to go next. It sounded almost too good to be true.

Yeah. She could do this.

She smiled to herself and picked up her diploma from Stanford, in its frame, which was looking so forlorn on her desk. In fact her whole office was a complete disaster, with boxes and supplies scattered everywhere.

This was not an office yet. She couldn't see patients in a place that looked as if a storage unit had exploded. It wasn't very professional.

"Time to make this place my own." She spied the stepladder that had been left by the painters in the corner. She grabbed a hammer and a nail. She'd never hammered anything in her life, but there was always a first time for everything.

"I can do this," she said, as if trying to reassure herself. How hard could it be to hammer a nail into a wall? She had this. Except where she wanted to put the nail in was a little out of her reach for the stepladder. So she climbed to the very top of the ladder and held the wall for a bit of balance. Her perch was precarious, but all she was doing was hammering in one nail and it wasn't that big of a drop down to the carpet.

She lined up the nail and held the hammer, ready to drive the nail home.

"Did you check for a stud?" a male voice asked from behind.

"What...?" Sarah turned, surprised that someone had snuck into her office and she hadn't heard them, but in the process of turning around she forgot what a precarious perch she had on the top of the stepladder and lost her footing.

Sarah closed her eyes and waited for her backside to hit the floor, but instead she found herself landing in two very strong arms and being held against a broad, muscular chest.

"You shouldn't stand on the top of a..." He trailed off.

"Who are you to tell me...?" Sarah opened her eyes and bit back a gasp as she stared up at the most stunningly handsome man she'd ever seen. Brown hair, with just a bit of curl, deep blue eyes and a neat beard, which just added to the ruggedness of his face.

Those blue eyes of his were wide with surprise and then she had the niggling sensation that she'd seen this face before, but couldn't recall when or where.

"What in the name of all that's good and holy were you doing up there with a hammer?" he demanded as he quickly set her down on her feet and took a step back from her as if she were on fire.

"Excuse me?" she asked. Who did this guy think he was?

"I'm telling you that wasn't a smart move climbing up on that ladder. You could've killed yourself if I hadn't showed up."

"Why did you show up? Who are you?"

His blue eyes flashed and he crossed his arms, fixing

her with a stare that was meant to frighten her. Well, it didn't scare her.

"I'm here to take you out."

"Out? I don't believe I made any dates with anyone since I arrived in town."

He smirked. "Not on a date, darling. Though if I were to go on a date with someone, you're quite the fetching thing."

"Fetching? Darling?"

He held up his hands. "Look, I was teasing. I'm not interested in dating coworkers, let alone headstrong doctors from out east. I'm to take you out on the skis to show you some of the private residences being built and how to access them."

"Oh." She was slightly disappointed. Not that she had any interest in dating a mountain man, but a fling might've been fun. Especially since this mountain man was deliciously handsome.

Don't think like that. You're here to prove yourself, not date.

Sarah didn't date.

Her parents had tried over and over, setting her up with the *right* sort of man. Well, in their eyes anyway. It was just easier to concentrate on work and not bother with dating, romance or sex.

All the right kind of men Sarah had dated briefly in her early twenties were all wrong. It never felt right. There was never that spark or connection one was supposed to feel when falling in love with someone, but then again, since she'd never experienced it, maybe it was just a myth.

Men seemed to gravitate to her because she was a socialite and came from money. It was all about status for them, and as she was too focused on her career, she never pursued a man on her own and she never made the time to look for a man beyond her parents' circles.

Single life was so much easier.

And lonely.

"Do you know how to ski?" he asked disparagingly, breaking her chain of thoughts.

"No." Then she groaned inwardly at the thought of going back outside in the cold.

"I thought as much," he said condescendingly. "Well, I'll give you a few minutes to suit up so we can head out."

It was the tone that sparked a vivid memory for her suddenly. She could see those dark blue eyes glittering above a surgical mask. Defying her.

Get out of my OR!

Not on your life.

No way. It couldn't be him. It just couldn't be him.

"What's wrong?" he asked. "Don't like the cold?"

"It's not that. I think I know you."

He smiled. "Do you?"

"What's your name?" she asked.

Don't be him. Don't be him.

Then he grinned like the cat who'd got the cream. "Dr. Luke Ralston."

Damn, but then she was ticked. She'd put that memory of her time in Missoula far from her mind, not giving it much of a second thought because, really, what did it matter? She was in New York, let Luke Ralston have Montana.

Besides, Shane Draven had pulled through.

It was all trivial. Except now she was in Montana, working on their patient's uncle's resort and Dr. Luke

Ralston was her coworker? This was a totally messed-up situation. Something she was not comfortable with.

"You knew exactly who I was."

Luke shrugged. "Not at first, but when you fell into my arms it all came back to me."

"And you didn't say anything? Like, maybe, 'Hey, we know each other, we've worked together before' or something like that?"

He shrugged again and then hooked his thumbs into the belt loops on the waist of his tight, tight jeans. "What does it matter?"

"It matters a lot. You're a jerk!"

"Why am I a jerk? I mean, I did save you from probably concussing yourself or something."

"You were the guy I talked to in the hallway in Missoula. When I asked who Dr. Ralston was, you said you didn't know where he was. You lied to me."

"I didn't really want to argue with you in the hallway. I was on my way to the ICU to check on my patient. To make sure he pulled through surgery."

"He was my patient."

He grinned, smugly. "I brought him down off that mountain. He was my patient. You were just a locum surgeon. You didn't stay to make sure he made it through the night. You headed back east, to wherever you came from. I knew nothing about you and I didn't trust you. Of course, now you're going to be a regular here in town."

"Had I known there was a Ralston in Crater Lake I would've turned the job down."

Luke chuckled. "You must've taken this job on an impulse, then."

"Why do you say that?"

"If you'd researched Crater Lake you'd realize the

family practice in town is run by a Ralston. I wasn't really hiding my identity. Not in my town."

Damn. He was right. She hadn't really looked to see what physicians were in town. She'd taken the job so quickly. She'd just been so eager to get out of New York City and away from her father's control. Crater Lake had sounded like a nice small town, and a job catering to the rich and famous in a resort had sounded perfect. It was a chance to prove herself to those who moved in her parents' circles.

Then maybe she could step out of her father's shadow. She wouldn't be Sarah Ledet, New York heiress and daughter of Vin Ledet, one of the wealthiest men on the eastern seaboard. She'd be Dr. Ledet, physician.

"You're regretting your decision to take this job, aren't you?" Luke asked. "I can see it on your face. You look absolutely horrified."

"Not the job, just who I have to work with."

He grinned and then laughed. "You're still a spitfire."

"Spitfire?"

"It's a compliment."

Sarah tried not to smile. She didn't want to smile. He was the jerk who'd disrupted her OR, given her a hard time and then lied to her. He was the one who'd questioned her surgical procedure and every move she'd made on that patient until she'd snapped. Only his smile had been infectious and she couldn't remember the last time she'd laughed, even though she was ticked off that it was him. The thorn in her side from last summer, standing right there in her office.

She should just throw him out. As she should have done from her OR.

When she glanced back up at him the lighthearted

mood had changed. He looked annoyed and uncomfortable.

"What?" she asked.

"Nothing."

"Something changed. Just a moment ago you were complimenting me and joking. Now you look annoyed."

"I'm annoyed we're wasting the light standing around pointing fingers."

"Okay, you're right. I'm sorry."

"Well, I would gear up. I don't have all day to wait around for you." He walked out of her office leaving her standing there absolutely confused.

What had just happened?

Sarah wasn't sure, but she knew it would be best to keep her distance from Luke Ralston, though that was going to be tricky seeing how she was about to be dragged out on the mountain in the bitter cold with a man who was a little bit dangerous.

Not just a little bit dangerous.

A lot.

CHAPTER TWO

DAMN. IT HAD to be the spitfire.

Luke had forgotten all about her when he'd returned to Crater Lake after Shane Draven had pulled through. For a while he'd thought of that trauma surgeon he'd butted heads with in Missoula, but as he'd dealt with the last messy stages of his divorce, he'd put her from his mind.

Dealing with his ex just reminded him of all the reasons why he didn't trust women or romantic entanglements.

It hurt too much, but Christine wasn't the only reason. Hurt went both ways. He liked his life too much and part of that was doing risky things to save lives up on the mountain.

He'd given up his life in the army for a woman he loved and look how that turned out.

To live the life he'd made for himself since leaving the army, he couldn't have love. He wouldn't give up his life for anyone.

He threw himself completely into his work and avoided hanging around the town of Crater Lake as much as possible. It was bad enough being divorced, but having your ex-wife and former best friend, who was now your ex's husband, living and working in the town you grew up in was a little too much for him.

The problem was, his former best friend was the town sheriff. That was why they were staying in Crater Lake, but Luke wouldn't be driven out of town.

He'd grown up here. He was going to stay here.

And an injury to his leg during an avalanche last winter prevented him from returning to active duty, even after giving up his commission.

Besides, he preferred being up on the mountain.

He liked being alone in his cabin. He liked the work; though he missed surgery and envied Carson just a bit for seeing patients every day, there was no way he could've chained himself to a desk, to an office or a hospital. He would suffocate, but he'd been willing to do it for Christine.

Maybe if you hadn't joined the army Christine wouldn't have left. Maybe you could've been happy.

Only his call of duty had been strong. He'd always wanted to serve and further his medical education in the army. And Christine had known that when they'd got together.

Luke cursed under his breath.

No, she would've left. Just as he hadn't wanted to change the course of his career, Christine hadn't wanted to be his wife. Of course now he wasn't a soldier, but by the time his career in the army was over Christine was over him.

No, he wasn't going to think about her. She'd broken his heart and he wouldn't let her or anyone else make him feel that way again.

Why did it have to be her? Why did it have to be the spitfire?

Silas hadn't told him the name of the physician who would be working at the resort. All he'd said was that she was from out east and had asked if Luke could train her on mountain survival and survival medicine.

She's from money, Ralston. I'm sure she's been on skis, but probably not in a way that would satisfy your sensibilities.

Which was why Luke was here. It was just fate was a bit sick and twisted by making that physician Dr. Ledet, the surgeon he'd butted heads with.

As if dealing with her in the summer wasn't enough? Maybe it was karma? He'd teased Carson when Esme Petersen had come to town. Perhaps this was retribution?

The only difference was Carson had found love with Esme and Luke was not looking for that at all.

Carson hadn't been looking, either.

"Is this okay?"

Luke shook that little voice from his head and glanced over at Sarah. She had a good parka on, waterproof mitts, a hat with ear flaps, boots, but nothing on her legs except black stretchy pants that fit her curves like a glove. His blood heated.

Think about something else.

"Where are your snow pants?" Luke asked, tearing his gaze away from her. He didn't want to look at her at the moment. He had to regain control.

"Snow pants?"

"Don't you ski?"

"I told you before, no. I've never skied."

"Doesn't every eastern WASP rich girl ski? Isn't that what the Poconos are for?"

Her stare was icy cold and she put her hands on those

curvy hips. Hips he'd thought about touching himself. "Excuse me?"

Luke groaned. He wasn't going to get in an argument with her. "You need snow pants. If you fall out there and your pants get wet there's no way we're turning around so you can change. I'm here to teach you survival skills. If you were out there on your own, there would be no option to change. You'd freeze to death."

Sarah still looked as if she were going to skewer him alive. "Fine. I'll find some snow pants, but, really, stereotyping me, that was so not cool."

"If the shoe fits."

She cocked her eyebrows and smirked. "Oh, really? Didn't we have this argument in the summer? I seem to recall bits and pieces of it…"

He groaned. "Fine. You're right. I did accuse you of stereotyping me. I apologize, but, really, put on some snow pants before we lose the light."

"Fine and, for your information, not all of us 'rich girls' ski. Some of us prefer yachts and sailing." She winked and then disappeared into her office again.

Luke rolled his eyes, but couldn't help but laugh to himself. He still admired her spunk.

When she came out of her office again, she was properly attired.

"Good, now let's get down to the ski shack and get geared up. I'm going to take you up the first of the four main trails at this resort."

Sarah fell into step behind him; the only sound was the swishing of the nylon fabric rubbing together as they walked down the hall and outside. Luke tried not to laugh, because just under that sound was some muttering. And maybe some bad words, but he couldn't quite tell.

"I feel like a marshmallow," she mumbled. "Do I look like one?"

"Yes. You do, but it will keep you warm." He helped open the door to outside. "Ms. Marshmallow."

With a huff Sarah pushed past him out into the snow. "You're a bit of a jerk. Has anyone ever told you that?"

"Several people."

There was a twinkle to her eye and she smiled slightly. "Good."

"Well, now that's all settled. Let's get the skis on and head out." He led the way to the ski shack, which was closed up. It would open on more regular hours when the resort had its official grand opening on Valentine's Day. Right now, Luke had full run of it and of all the equipment.

It was one of the perks he liked about working for Silas Draven. He wasn't a huge fan of skiing, but cross-country skiing on the mountain trails was the only way to access some of the remote residents of Crater Lake. His horse just couldn't handle the deep snow that collected on the side of the mountain in the winter.

And he would never put his horse in the way of a possible avalanche.

He glanced over to the southern peak, to the forest that was thick, before it disappeared into the alpine zone of the mountain. Old Nestor lived up in that dense forest.

Nestor was a hermit. He liked to live off the grid and away from everyone else. Luke admired him and went to check on him often. Nestor was the one who'd taught him many things about surviving on the mountain, since Nestor had been living up on the mountain for as long as Luke could remember and before that.

Only, Nestor was getting old and in the winter the cold bothered him something fierce. So Luke was thankful for access to skis and snowshoes. It made checking on Nestor that much easier.

He unlocked the door and headed over to the rack.

"Oh, cool! Snowshoes," Sarah remarked. "I've always wanted to try them."

"Really?" he asked, surprised.

She nodded. "Anything to make walking on snow easier."

"Snowshoeing is just as much work as skiing. Skis can move you faster."

"Yeah, but cross-country skis don't go uphill. You said you wanted me to learn how to access trails and stuff. Shouldn't I be snowshoeing?"

She's got a point. Skiing will only get you so far.

"You're right," Luke admitted. "Okay. We'll add snowshoes to our pack."

"Pack?"

Luke picked up the large rucksack that he'd stuffed full of emergency and survival gear. The pack was probably half the size of Sarah and when he held it up to her, her eyes widened and her mouth opened for a moment in surprise.

Then she shrugged. "Sure. That's reasonable. Just out of curiosity, though, what's in it?"

"Don't you know?"

She glared at him. "Really?"

"You should know."

"I don't. I've never lived near a mountain. I'm from Manhattan."

Luke shook his head. "Hey, I was trying not to stereotype you."

"I ought to slug you."

He laughed at that. He couldn't help himself; it was easy to tease her. He was enjoying the banter. "I'm sorry. I'll stop."

She crossed her arms. "Fine or I could start talking about mountain men."

"What do you know about mountain men?" he asked.

Sarah shook her head. "Tell me what's in the bag."

Luke knelt down and unzipped it. "This is a standard pack to help you survive in a winter climate on the mountain."

"So I'll only need to carry around this stuff in the winter?"

"No," Luke said. "Some things can be left behind, but if you're working up near the Alpine zone or higher, you'd be surprised how cold it can get even in the heat of summer."

"Okay, so always be prepared for snow?"

He nodded. "Yep. So in this pack you have your essentials like first-aid kit. The only thing I haven't packed in here is a change of clothes for you so I just packed some of my old clothes. If worse comes to worst you can always wear those."

Her cheeks reddened slightly, as if she was blushing, but Luke could've been wrong. It could've been the wind.

She cleared her throat. "Go on."

"Canteen for water."

"What about melting snow?"

Luke cocked an eyebrow. "You're going to need something to carry it in. I also have a pot, ice pick, rope, matches, GPS, topographical map of the area, one day's worth of rations, sleeping bag and an axe."

"It's like you're camping."

"If you get lost out there, yeah, you'll be 'camping' until help arrives." Then he held out something he was sure she'd never seen before. "This is one of the most important things."

"A compass?"

"Close. It's an altimeter."

"A what?" she asked.

"It's a barometric altimeter. It measures changes in atmosphere. The higher you go, the lower the pressure is. If your GPS or compass isn't working, this can be used along with the map to determine where you are. I'll show you how to use it."

"Good, because seriously my eyes were glazing over there for a second." She laughed nervously and he handed her the altimeter to look at. "Though, really, won't you know if you're at the top of the mountain? How can you get lost if you're up there?"

"You can get lost all right and if you're not used to high altitude you can get acute mountain sickness. Dr. Petersen in town suffered from it last year. Just ask her."

"Dr. Petersen? There's a female doctor in town? I thought the other doctor was your brother."

"Dr. Petersen is a cardio surgeon. She's opened a clinic in partnership with my brother. She sees a lot of heart patients from around this area."

"Huh, I wonder what would make a cardio-thoracic surgeon settle down in a place like this," Sarah wondered out loud. "I mean, the nearest hospital is quite a bit away."

"Why did you?" Luke asked.

The question caught her off guard, because she blushed again and quickly started examining the altimeter.

Did it really matter?

It shouldn't matter to him, but he couldn't help but wonder why. There weren't many single people in Crater Lake. It was small. When they'd first got together, Christine had wanted to stay in Crater Lake, and when he got his posting to Germany she wouldn't go with him. She didn't want to live on a base. She didn't want to be an army wife. So she'd decided to stay and start a family with Anthony.

A family he wanted so desperately.

A family he was never going to have.

Don't think about it.

"Come on, I'll pack the snowshoes, as well. We have some distance to travel and some more stuff I have to show you before it gets too dark, and it gets dark here early." He took the altimeter back from her and packed it in the knapsack.

He didn't have time to focus on the past. To focus on his past hurts or the things he would never have.

He was here to do a job and that was to show Dr. Sarah Ledet how to survive on the mountain. That was all. Once he'd done that, he never had to see her again and he was going to make sure that happened.

Sarah thought her lungs were going to burst. She was sweaty and exhausted. Parts of her that she hadn't even known existed ached and each breath was harder to take.

At least I'm not cold.

She just shook her head and leaned up against a tree as Luke set their skis against a fence line that ran on one side of the trail. He glanced over at her.

"You okay? You look tired."

Of course I'm tired, but she wasn't going to tell him that. All her life she'd been labelled and she'd had enough of it.

"I'm fine. Just catching my breath."

He frowned. "If you get a headache or feel ill, let me know right away. That's a sign of mountain sickness."

"Will do." She didn't feel sick and didn't have a headache. All she was was sweaty and tired. "You said Dr. Petersen had this? How did she get over it?"

"You get off the mountain."

"I live on the mountain."

Luke chuckled. "You don't live that far up the mountain, though."

"I thought it was pretty high up, considering I used to live pretty close to sea level."

"Never thought about it that way." Luke pulled out the snowshoes that had been strapped to the back of the enormous pack Sarah had had on her back, which was now resting under a fir tree on a bed of needles so as not to get wet.

Maybe she was picking up mountain survival a bit.

"You ready for snowshoeing?"

Sarah groaned. "How about we head for home? I'm sure it will be faster downhill on our skis."

Luke chuckled. "We'll head down soon enough. I

want to see you practice on these. Just up the trail the snow gets pretty deep. Too deep for skis."

"No one lives up that trail."

"Right, not now, but when this trail is groomed regularly and a lone cross-country skier or snowshoer gets injured or lost up there, you're going to have to know how to get to them."

Sarah sighed, but then took the snowshoes and strapped them on. They were quite easy and didn't look like she'd expected them to. They were made of aluminum and nylon.

"Take a step and tell me what you think," he said as he moved back and then clamped his on.

Sarah began to walk up the trail and it took her a few times to really find her stride, but it wasn't all that bad.

"I think this is easier than the skiing, to be honest." She bounced in her step. "I could get used to these."

"Just be careful," Luke called out over his shoulder.

"Of wha…?" She spoke too soon as she lost her footing and toppled face-first into a large snowdrift. Snow shot up her nose and into her mouth, burning.

I hate winter. I hate winter.

"Are you okay?" Luke was beside her and she could hear the amusement in his voice.

"Fine," she said as she wiped her face. "I really wasn't expecting to do a face-plant with snowshoes on. Skis for sure, but snowshoes. I know I'm klutzy."

"Well, at least this time I didn't have to catch you." He rubbed some of the snow from her face and a rush of butterflies invaded her stomach as she looked up into his eyes. He was smiling at her, but it was tender, as if he really cared that she'd done a horrible face-plant in the snow.

Of course the butterflies could be from that mountain sickness, but somehow she didn't think so.

"Thanks," she said, looking away and glad the snow had made her cheeks red, because if it hadn't he would surely see her blush.

"You should've been wearing your goggles to protect your eyes. Goggles don't belong on your forehead."

"I forgot to put them back on after my break. I was wearing them when we were skiing."

Luke helped her to her feet, his strong arms around her waist as he righted her. She liked the feeling of his arms around her, steadying her. It was comforting.

You don't date. You can't date.

Her mother would set her up on the occasional date, but those were all with men who would take care of her. Who just wanted her to be this pretty, well-dressed society wife. None of them were really interested in her and she'd been burned too many times.

And she never had time to find men on her own, because she was working so darn hard to show her parents that she could have it all, that she didn't need a man to take care of her. That she was old enough to take care of herself.

Men were off-limits.

Of course, her father admitting that he'd had a hand in almost every aspect of her career made her think that all that hard work, all those hours she'd put in weren't worth it. Maybe she should've been out there partying, being seen in all the right places with all the right people, just like her older sister.

Really?

She shook her head. That was all in the past, though. She was in Crater Lake now. In a job of her own choosing and she planned to make the most of it. Even if it meant traipsing around in the snow with the sexiest mountain man she'd ever laid eyes on.

A man that also drove her a bit crazy.

"You ready to try again?" Luke asked.

"Sure. The sooner we get this done, the sooner I can head back to my apartment in the resort and curl up in front of a fire."

"Glad to see you're on board." Luke went over and picked up the knapsack. "You're going to need this."

Sarah moaned as it was placed over her shoulders again. "Thanks. I almost forgot."

"It's your lifeline up here. You can't forget. We'll do a half-mile hike up this trail through the snow, we'll triage a fake patient I have up there and then head back down to the resort. That's after we build a makeshift stretcher."

"You have a patient up there?" Sarah asked. "Who in their right mind would wait out in the cold for hours for you?"

Luke winked. "It's a dummy."

"Clearly."

He rolled his eyes. "It's a simulation. A mannequin. It's not a real person, but it's simulating a very real situation."

Sarah sighed. "Okay. Lead on."

Luke nodded and pulled on his own pack. She watched him for a few moments as he broke a path ahead of her. Even though he was wearing thick snow pants you could still make out the outline of his strong, muscular thighs and his tight butt.

Sarah shook her head. It was apparent she was suffering from altitude sickness, because she was thinking about the strangest things.

Dr. Luke Ralston was off-limits.

He worked for Silas Draven as well, so that meant it was a no go for her. She didn't mix business with pleasure.

So she couldn't think about Luke that way.

She just couldn't.

CHAPTER THREE

IT HAD BEEN three days since she last saw Dr. Luke Ralston and that was a good thing after the torment he'd put her through up on that high mountain trail. He hadn't been kidding about a simulation. When they'd got to the mannequin, it had been half-buried in ice and under a tree trunk. There had been broken skis and fake blood.

Sarah had never picked up an axe before, but she did that day. She had the blister and the splinters to prove it.

Even though she'd wanted to tell Luke his simulation was cracked, she hadn't backed down. She knew that he thought of her as some kind of spoiled rich girl and that was far from the truth. So she'd learned quite quickly how to use an axe. She'd shown him a thing or two.

She'd also learned how to make a makeshift gurney out of broken skis, rope, a tarp and duct tape. After assessing the mannequin's ABCs, they'd got him on their gurney and down off the mountain.

There had been quite a few stares as she'd come down to the lodge with a mannequin on a stretcher splattered with craft-store paint. Still, she'd done it and he'd grudgingly admitted that she'd done a good job and that was the last she'd seen of him.

She thought she was going to be put through some more training, but so far she hadn't seen him. She should be happy about that and she was, but she wasn't totally. She looked for him everywhere, as if he were going to pop out of the shadows and frighten her. The thought of seeing him actually made her excited, as if she were some young girl with a crush.

There was no denying Luke was handsome. She'd thought that the first moment she saw him. But there was something else about him. A lone wolf quality. He was a man who didn't want or need anyone else. The kind of man who was completely untamed.

He was a challenge, and she'd always liked a challenge.

Focus.

She couldn't think about him that way. Distance. That was what she needed. Right now this time was about her. Career was her life.

If she got together with someone, her parents would never believe she could function on her own. That she was a surgeon.

Even then, she wasn't sure of anything. Everything she'd thought she earned had really come because she was Vin Ledet's daughter. Her father knew people on the admissions board at college. She'd fought so hard for her MCAT scores, achieving one of the highest that year, which should've been enough to get her into medical school, but apparently not enough for her father. Then her residency and her fellowship, her father had had a hand in that. Everything she'd pursued in her medical career her father had had a hand in.

No wonder her belief in herself was fleeting.

Except this place.

She'd earned this on her own by saving Silas Draven's nephew Shane in Missoula.

Silas and her father moved in the same circles and never saw eye to eye.

Sarah knew it wasn't because of who her father was. This job was because of her own merit.

Someone believed in her abilities and she wasn't going to let them down.

She could do this.

This was her focus and she was going to prove to everyone she was up to the task. This clinic was going to be her pride and joy.

Her clinic had opened a bit earlier than she'd planned, but Silas Draven had had a large party of tourists coming in and he'd wanted to make sure that it was up and running. He wanted his resort to be all-inclusive, and didn't want his guests having to go into town and wait at the local clinic.

Even though the resort hadn't officially opened, the large party of skiers was certainly giving her a run for her money. Her clinic had been full the two days she'd been open. It was usually just minor stuff, cuts and sunburns, but she was enjoying the work and, the best part, it was honest work. Though, she missed surgery, the rush of the hospital, but this job she'd got on her own.

Her parents didn't have a hand in it.

Really, Sarah? Sunburns? The only sun you should think about is evening out your tan.

She cursed under her breath, trying to shake away her sister's annoying voice. Her sister had never said those exact words, but she could almost picture her, standing in the waiting room and saying them, because her sister had nagged her about similar things before.

"Patient ten?" Sarah briefly looked up from her chart, to the busy waiting room at her clinic. "Patient number ten?"

A man with a very red face stood up and walked toward her. He nodded and winced. "I am Mr. Fontblanc."

Sarah smiled. "I know, we just use a numbering system here to keep anonymity."

"Ah, oui. Merci beaucoup."

"You can have a seat in exam room one. I'll be with you momentarily."

Mr. Fontblanc nodded again, shuffling off down the hall. She looked at her chart one more time and was about to call the next victim of a really bad sunburn when the door to her clinic burst open. Luke strode into her pristine clinic, dirty and breathless.

"What're you doing?" he asked.

"I'm seeing patients," Sarah said, trying not to look at him. Distance was the key.

"Good, I have a patient for you."

"What? Where?"

"He's in the lobby."

"In the lobby? Why is he in the lobby?"

Luke rolled his eyes and crossed his arms. "Would you stop giving me the third degree and just come to the lobby?"

"I have a patient waiting in my exam room. I can't leave him there."

"Is your patient bleeding profusely with a head injury?"

"That's confidential."

Luke shook his head and pushed past her into the exam room.

"Dr. Ralston!" Sarah tried to stop him, but he was in the exam room. Mr. Fontblanc looked a bit stunned.

"Sorry to keep you waiting..." Luke peered at the man. "Too much sun?"

"*Oui*...uh, yes."

"*Vous êtes Français?*" Luke inquired in perfect French.

"*Oui.*"

Sarah stood back, stunned. She didn't know French at all. Spanish, she knew quite a bit, but French, she was at a loss. Luke seemed to know it. He questioned the man briefly and then pulled out a tube of topical cream from her medicine cupboard, handing it to her patient and then patting him on the back.

The patient still seemed shell-shocked, but overall was happy.

"*Merci.*"

"*Pas de problème,*" Luke said.

The patient left the room and Luke turned back to her. "You ready to go and help the patient in the lobby now?"

"What just happened here?" She watched as Luke began to grab suturing trays, gauze and a bolus for an IV. "What's going on? Why are you stealing my supplies?"

He groaned and grabbed her hand. "Come on. I need another doctor's help with this."

Sarah didn't really have much of a choice as she was dragged from her clinic. The other patients watched her leave, just as confused as she was at the moment.

"If this patient needs another doctor, why didn't you get your brother to help you?" Sarah asked.

"There was no time to take this man to town." Luke pushed the button on the elevator, not looking at her, but watching for the door to light up and open.

"What's wrong with the patient?" she asked.

"Have you ever seen a mauling?"

Sarah gasped. "Did you just say a mauling? By what?"

Luke glanced at her. "A bear."

She shook her head. She'd seen pictures in textbooks when she was a resident. As a trauma surgeon you had to be prepared for everything, but she'd never actually encountered one personally. She was aware of the damage that could be done. Her stomach twisted in a knot at the very idea, but they were in bear country. It was to be expected.

The elevator arrived and they got on. It was a quick ride down to the lobby. When the doors opened everything was in chaos and Sarah could see a trail of blood from the door to a boardroom down a darkened hall.

"I don't get it," Sarah remarked as she fell into step beside Luke.

"What don't you get?" he asked.

"Bears hibernate. It's January."

Luke sighed. "No, not really. It's called torpor. It's like hibernation—they can be woken. This idiot was fool enough to stumble on a bear's den and, instead of leaving the bear well enough alone, he crawled inside to get a picture. Thankfully, people were with him."

"Idiot is right."

He nodded. "If you haven't seen a mauling before, prepare yourself."

She nodded. "I've seen worse stuff in the ER."

"Possible disembowelment and bite marks?"

"Yeah. A car can do damage to a patient, too. I'm ready."

A small smile played on his lips, but just briefly. It was almost as if he was impressed that she didn't shy away or that she wasn't squeamish at the prospect. It scared her. It was something she was completely unfamiliar with. It was something she was a little terrified about herself since moving from Manhattan to a remote town in northwest Montana, but this was her job. She was going to help Luke any way that she could. It was the trauma surgeon in her.

"Did you bring enough supplies down?" she asked.

"We've got enough supplies in here. We have to get him stabilized before the air ambulance gets here."

Sarah nodded. "Okay."

She walked into the room and tried not to gasp. The man was in bad shape. There were deep lacerations to his arm, his legs and torso, but his face was really bad. She could see teeth marks, deep gouging all over; she could see bone on his arm and the bandages on his abdomen were already soaked through, which tipped Sarah off that this guy would need packing if he was going to survive the trip to the nearest hospital. The way his abdomen was distended, she knew from her trained eye he would suffer from compartment syndrome sooner rather than later and that could be fatal if not controlled.

"Buddy, I've brought another doctor here to help me." Luke spoke to the man. "Just take it easy."

The man just moaned.

"I'm surprised he's lucid."

"Me, too," Luke said. "I did give him a shot of morphine in the field when I found him, but he's lost a lot of blood."

Sarah nodded and pulled off her white lab coat. "Gloves?"

Luke gestured in the direction of the sideboard, where a box of rubber gloves was waiting. She slipped on a pair and then grabbed a pack of gauze.

"I need you to hold him down—I'm going to put in a central line," Luke told her.

"You're going to put in a central line here?"

He nodded. "No choice. Look at his arms, and his veins are chunky. The bear did damage. Lots of damage."

"Sure." Sarah leaned over and held the man down. She looked down into his dark eyes, full of confusion and fear. "Don't worry, sir. We're going to get you patched up in no time. Soon you won't be in so much pain. I promise."

"Hold him now for me," Luke said.

"I've got him. Just do it."

Luke inserted the central line quickly and efficiently. She couldn't remember the last time she'd seen someone put in a central line so fast before. She was impressed. The patient barely flinched, but that could be because maybe some of the fight had gone out of him, or it could've been the morphine.

Once he was hooked up to a drip, he passed out and Luke went about stitching what they could to help control the bleeding. Sarah packed his face and set a broken bone in his arm. They didn't say much to each other; there wasn't much to say, really. They were both totally focused on their patient.

The last time they'd worked on a patient together,

they were at each other's throats. This was different. It was nice. Comforting almost, as if she'd been doing this with him for a long, long time, and she couldn't remember the last time she'd felt such a familiarity with another surgeon before.

"He has extensive damage to his abdomen. There is nothing I can do here."

"Pack him?" Luke asked.

She nodded. "No choice. If I start poking around to find the source of the bleeders I could do more damage. His body needs to rest before repairs. Does bear saliva have an envenomation? You know, like the wolverine or Komodo dragon?"

"No, but the saliva often carries staph or strep, which can lead to infections and organ shutdown." He frowned and seemed upset for a brief moment. "Either way he'll need a good course of antibiotics, tetanus and rabies. Though rabies from bear bites are rare."

"Why is that?"

"The injury rate from bear attacks in North America is like one person per couple million. Of course, that report by S. Herrero is from 1970. It could be different now."

"Wow."

"The more we encroach on their territory, the worse it gets. I read a lot on animal attacks for obvious reasons."

"Makes sense."

She would have never thought about reading medical papers on animal attacks before coming here. It wasn't something that happened a lot in Manhattan. She'd dealt with dog, cat and human bites in the city.

It was time to broaden her reading if she was going to stay here.

Luke impressed her with his knowledge and that was a hard thing to do. She liked working with him. They could work on the patient seamlessly and still chat easily. She'd never had that kind of rapport with another surgeon before.

It felt so right working with him. It was just sad that this poor man had to suffer and Sarah decided right then and there: she didn't want to mess with a bear in any way, shape or form.

When they had done all they could do, they just monitored him and waited for the air ambulance to come. Nothing but the sound of the portable monitors between them.

"How long do you think it will be before the air ambulance comes?" Sarah asked, breaking the silence.

"Should be here soon, though there was a storm rolling in from the southwest. I hope that didn't hinder the flight in from Missoula."

"If it does?" she asked.

"Great Falls will send one. Missoula is bigger, though."

She nodded and there was a knock at the door. A paramedic stood there. "Someone call an air ambulance?"

They worked with the paramedics to get the patient onto the stretcher and then out into the cold to the waiting ambulance, which would take him down to the airport. The ambulance had landed on Silas Draven's private airstrip.

Once the patient was loaded up the ambulance flicked on its sirens and headed down the long windy road to Crater Lake. Sarah didn't stand outside for too long because it was cold and she didn't have her coat on.

Luke followed her back inside.

"I hope he makes it," Sarah remarked.

"He will. Death is rare. Although compartment syndrome worries me."

"Me, too," Sarah said. "Glad you caught that, as well."

"I've seen compartment syndrome many a time as an army medic. The bowels inflating, then the liver and kidneys begin to shut down. It's a domino effect."

"It is. I thought you would've followed him. Didn't you get him down off the mountain?" she teased, as that had been the reason why he'd stood in her OR last summer questioning her every move.

"I usually would, but he woke a bear up. The bear just didn't go back to sleep. I have to track it and…" He trailed off.

"What?"

"I have to make sure it goes back to its den, but, since the bear has been fully woken up from its torpor, it's going to be looking for food. I don't want to have to destroy it."

She frowned. "Oh. I hope you don't have to do that."

"Me, too. It's not the bear's fault that moron decided it would be a good selfie. Me with a bear."

Sarah chuckled. "A tourist?"

"Close, a surveyor. A new one. The surveyors I train to work up in these mountains know better than that."

"I'm sure they do, but I didn't see his pack."

Luke chuckled. "I think he left it up there on the mountain."

"How are his friends?"

"Shaken up. I should go talk to them."

"Do you want me to?"

"No. It's okay. I can. Thanks for helping me," he said.

"I really didn't have a choice." She smiled at him.

"I'm sorry about that. I overstep my boundaries in emergency situations."

"It's no problem. That's what I'm here for. To help patients."

And then it hit her.

Oh. No.

"Darn it," she cursed out loud. "Darn it."

"What?" he asked.

"My patients in the clinic. How long was I gone for?"

Luke glanced at his wrist. "About forty minutes."

Sarah groaned. "If they complain to Mr. Draven…"

"If they complain I will tell him you helped one of his employees who was dumb enough to stick his face in a bear's den."

"I think Mr. Draven will be more ticked about the patients in my clinic, though."

Luke frowned. "Come on. We'll tell them why."

"Are you serious? We have to protect privacy rights."

"They won't know him. These are tourists. Tourists like bear stories."

Sarah looked at him as if he were crazy. Maybe he was. Maybe he'd spent too many winters up on that mountain and he'd lost his mind. Her patients were going to be mad that she'd left them up there for that long.

Mr. Draven had made it pretty clear that he wanted patients to be seen within twenty minutes of their arrival and registration at the clinic. Not forty.

"I don't know. I don't think that's a good idea."

Luke rolled his eyes and then took her hand. It shocked her. It was calloused, warm and strong. It sent a tingle of electricity through her and she could feel the heat flooding her cheeks at just the simple act of a touch from him, but then she wasn't used to physical intimacy. It had been so long and her parents weren't exactly huggers. So that simple touch threw her for a loop.

"Come on, we don't have to tell the particulars, but you can bet when I warn that group of European tourists off the mountain trails because of a bear being at large, that will get them talking."

"Or send them packing." Sarah grudgingly let him lead her back to her clinic. "If it were me and I heard that about a bear, I would be packing my bags and leaving the general vicinity. Bears are beautiful animals, but I never want to encounter one in the wild."

He shook his head. "That's because you haven't been properly trained on how to deal with a bear in the wild."

"Please don't show me."

He laughed and pushed the button to the elevator, the doors opening instantly. "If you're living in bear country, Sarah, you really don't have a choice in the matter. Everyone in Crater Lake needs to know what to do in case of a bear. Do you have bear deterrent?"

Sarah shook her head and pinched the bridge of her nose. "Oh, God."

"I take it you don't."

Sarah glanced up at him and could see he was enjoying her torment. "I have a spray can of something in my office, but I didn't buy it. It was just there when I took over."

"I know. I bought it and put it there. Most offices of the permanent staff have a can. It's better to be prepared and, since most of you aren't from Montana, I thought it would be the best."

"You're really enjoying this, aren't you?"

"Enjoying what?" A small smile played across his lips. It was a devious smile, even if it was partially hidden behind his beard. It was the kind that made her a bit weak in the knees and she fought the urge to kiss him. Even though she couldn't remember the last time she'd kissed a man. She resisted the urge to kiss him and gave him a playful shove instead.

"Hey, what was that for?"

"For enjoying my torment and for teasing me." Sarah shook her head. "What am I going to say?"

"Sorry would be a start."

"Not to you. The patients."

"I'll handle it. Besides you don't speak French."

She chuckled. "This is true."

The elevator dinged open and her stomach knotted. She hoped word wouldn't get back to Silas Draven that she'd left a big group of VIP tourists by themselves. She didn't need him to think she couldn't handle her job and she definitely didn't want this to get back to her father.

"Don't be nervous. It will be fine." Luke took her hand and she tried not to gasp at his familiarity. "Come on, you have to face the music."

She took her hand back and marched ahead of him, trying to put some distance between them. "Okay, we can do this."

Facing all those tourists was better than having him touch her. Not exactly better, but safer. Actually she'd rather face a bear over being alone with Luke. Luke was dangerous. He was the kind of dangerous she secretly yearned for. It was electric, intense and was, oh, so wrong.

The patients left in the waiting room were pacing and looked none too pleased when she walked in.

"I'm sorry," she began, but as the words came out the din of French was overwhelming.

Luke stepped into the fray and shouted over the noise. A few choice words and the noise ebbed and the patients sat down again.

"Do you have enough exam rooms for five people?" Luke asked out of the corner of his mouth.

"No, I have two."

Luke made a face. "I guess Mr. Draven didn't really think you'd be this busy on any given day."

"Or maybe he thought two would be enough. I'm sure he didn't expect me to be called away for a mauling."

"I'd call your next patient. I'll help you. We'll get them in and out fast.

"Really? You're going to help me."

"Of course."

Sarah nodded and picked up the discarded patient charts, handing Luke three and keeping two for herself.

"Hey, how come I get the majority?"

"You speak the language." She winked at him and then walked away. Pleased that she was tormenting him just as much as he was her, but most importantly she had to put distance between them.

"Patient eleven?" she called out.

Luke put the last of the files on Sarah's desk. She was typing away on her computer and didn't even bother to look up at him.

"There. All done. Two more sunburns. The French have mountains, don't they? Surely they ski."

"These guests are from an island in the Caribbean called Marie-Galante. It's tropical."

"That doesn't explain sunburns. They should know how to use sunblock."

"Snow sunburns. One of them told me they'd never seen snow before—they didn't think they could get a sunburn in the winter. Actually, I'm glad they spoke French and not Creole."

Luke grinned. "Me, too. I knew a Cajun man once in my unit."

"Right, you were a medic in the army."

"Yeah. Right." Luke should leave, the conversation was turning in a direction he wasn't comfortable with, but he couldn't pry himself away from her and he didn't know why. He was drawn to her. This was why he'd gone out into the woods for a few days.

He'd had to get out of temptation's way.

"Thanks again for helping me," she said. "It's been a while since I've been in a clinic."

"No problem. You helped me with the mauling, but honestly I'm surprised you're in a clinic. I thought you were a surgeon."

"I am a surgeon."

"So why did you leave the OR?"

Sarah's lips pursed together and he was wondering if maybe now he was making her uncomfortable, just as he'd felt moments ago when he'd unthinkingly mentioned his time in the army. Something he was not ready to talk about, because he did miss it and it reminded him of his failed marriage, which was something he wanted to forget.

So what had made Sarah leave surgery?

None of your business.

Only he couldn't help himself. She'd been such a bulldog in the OR last summer. Surgeons with that kind of drive and passion didn't just walk away.

You did.

"I wanted a change of pace," she said.

"A change of pace?"

She shrugged. "Sure, why not? The city was getting to me."

"Somehow I don't believe that."

"You want to talk about truths? Why did you leave the army?"

Luke's spine stiffened. "My tour of duty ended. Well, I better go. Thanks again."

"You're welcome."

He left her office, without so much as a look back. It was for the best. If he looked back, he might stay. The way that she'd looked at him, he knew that she didn't believe him. Heck, he wasn't even sure if he had convinced himself of that fact. This was why Sarah was dangerous. She affected him like no one else had. Not even Christine. Sarah got under his skin. She actually made him yearn for things he used to want. Things that he'd thought were long gone.

He didn't need that.

He didn't want that.

Didn't he?

CHAPTER FOUR

"SHE DID WHAT?"

"She signed out a pair of snowshoes and headed up the lake trail," said the equipment-rental guy. He looked a bit scared, which was good. Luke wanted to strike fear into the guy's heart. Didn't they know there was a bear loose? A bear that had mauled a guy two days ago. A bear that hadn't been tracked down yet.

What was she thinking? Clearly she wasn't. He had to find her before the bear did.

"What trail did she take?"

"The Lakeview trail."

"When did she leave?"

The rental guy looked confused and shrugged. "Like twenty minutes ago?"

"Why did you let her go out?"

The young man just stuttered. "I didn't know I wasn't supposed to. Besides, I just started my shift. She was heading out just as I came in."

Luke cursed under his breath. "Don't let anyone else out. There's a bear on the loose."

"Aren't bears supposed to be hibernating?"

Luke just shook his head and walked away from the

rental guy. He couldn't believe she'd gone out there. Why would she head out on her own?

You haven't seen her for a couple days. Maybe she thinks the bear has gone by now.

It was a foolish assumption. Anyone from around here would know to wait for the all-clear, or at least find out the areas the bear had been seen in.

She's not from around here. It was his fault. He should have explained it to her. Instead he'd kept his distance.

He'd avoided her because she was getting too close for him. Since he'd come home expecting to start a life with his wife and realized his life wasn't going to be how he'd pictured it, he'd been keeping people at a distance.

Less chance of getting hurt that way.

Except, he enjoyed being around Sarah. The back and forth with her was refreshing and it totally caught him off guard. He couldn't be around her, yet here he was, worried about her.

She most likely would be fine on the Lakeview trail as the bear's den was nowhere near that, but, still, she didn't know anything about the mountains.

Luke returned to the rental chalet. "Give me a pair of snowshoes, please."

Once he had the snowshoes secured to his knapsack, he climbed on his snowmobile and headed up to the Lakeview trail. When he got to the edge of the trail, he parked his snowmobile, strapped on his snowshoes, pulled on his rucksack and unstrapped the tranquilizer gun.

He could see Sarah's fresh tracks in the snow. She couldn't be too far off. He'd taken her out once; she was good, but she wasn't that good. He was confident that he could catch up with her in no time.

As he headed up the path, he soon saw her. She had stopped not that far into the trail, at a lookout. She was holding her camera and was taking pictures.

Luke watched her for a few moments. She had a really fancy camera. He didn't know much about cameras, but it looked high-tech. Sarah was completely immersed in what she was doing. She was very unaware of everything around her.

Her cheeks were flushed from the cold and the exercise, but she was smiling as she held up her camera and then he couldn't help but smile, too, watching her. It was enchanting.

She's so beautiful.

And he shook his head, because he couldn't think about her like that. She was off-limits to him. It was a beautiful vista; he couldn't really blame her for that. Crater Lake was a beautiful place. This was home.

There had been so many times when he was serving overseas, in the heat and the desert, trying to patch up wounded soldiers who were flown in from the front lines, that all he'd been able to think about was the mountain with the snow cap. The blue, blue water.

And of Christine. Only she'd never seemed to miss him. Maybe that should have been an indicator that rushing into marriage with her hadn't been the best idea. That was her reasoning when he'd come home and found out that she wanted a divorce.

We were too young, Luke. You were going to medical school and you were my first. You were safe. Anthony understands me. We don't have anything in common,

Luke. When you were gone he was here. He was always here. I can rely on him...

His smile instantly vanished. Just thinking about Christine and the heartache that she and Anthony caused him ruined the moment.

This was why he couldn't get involved with someone. This was why he was single and kept people at a distance. You couldn't trust people. It was too painful.

"You know, there's a bear on the loose still and you're on a trail that is an avalanche risk."

Sarah lowered her camera and stared at him in shock and there was a touch of annoyance there, as well.

"What're you doing here?" she asked.

"Didn't you hear me? There's a bear out there on the loose."

She paled. "Wait, I thought you caught it."

"Who told you that?"

"The woman at the rental chalet. She said, and I quote, 'I think he caught him or something. Yeah, yeah, he caught it.'"

Luke rolled his eyes. "Well, that explains it. I spoke to a clueless guy. He really doesn't know much."

"Apparently so. I would've never come out here had I known. I really thought the bear issue was a moot point. I figured since I hadn't seen you for a couple days that you'd dealt with it. I thought you'd gone back up into the woods like you do all the time."

"I understand the woods. I'm used to them. I live in the woods."

She cocked an eyebrow. "Really?"

He nodded. "I have a cabin in the woods. It's on the edge of my parents' property. I built it myself."

"Wow, I'm impressed. I mean, I figured you were a

bit of a hands-on guy, but I had no idea that you could build a home with your own hands. That's amazing."

"Thanks. Well, when I got back from my tour of duty I had a bit of free time." Then he cursed inwardly, because again just a simple twist in the conversation and he was opening up to her again. How did she manage to do that? He was worried that she would try to turn the conversation back to his time overseas. Something that was off-limits.

"Well, it's quite impressive. Most surgeons I know wouldn't risk damaging their hands by doing something like that."

"I'm not like most surgeons. I'm not traditional in any sense of the word." Besides, he didn't practice much surgery anymore. He missed it, but he loved this more. He loved what he did in Crater Lake.

"That's for sure." She smiled and then looked away, aiming her camera at the mountains.

"Didn't you hear me say there's a bear on the loose?"

"I did, but I just want a couple more shots."

A couple more shots? The woman was infuriating.

"So why are you up here?"

"Taking pictures."

"I thought you didn't like the cold?" Luke asked.

"I don't, but it was a beautiful day."

"So what do you do with the pictures?"

She grinned. "I paint a bit."

She paints?

Now it was his turn to be impressed. He hadn't thought she had any hobbies beyond what he'd seen, and that hadn't been much. He'd thought she was a career-focused surgeon. Usually young surgeons didn't have the time for much else—they were too focused on honing their craft.

It pleasantly surprised him.

"Paint?"

Sarah nodded. "I have hidden depths, too."

Luke laughed. "I guess you do. I build homes and you paint."

"I wouldn't mind seeing it sometime."

His blood heated at her suggestion. The thought of her in his home was definitely a dangerous idea, but not all that unpleasant. Luke cleared his throat. "Maybe sometime, but really we have to get down off the trail. Until I find that bear, I really can't authorize people being out here alone and unarmed."

"I brought that can of deterrent."

He smiled at her briefly. "That won't be enough to dissuade a hungry bear just fresh out of torpor."

Sarah sighed. "You're right."

"Come on, I brought my snowmobile, so at least you don't have to hike the entire way back. Even if it would be good practice for you."

She glared at him as she packed her camera carefully back in its case and into her knapsack. "Ha-ha."

"Glad to see you were taking my advice about the backpack."

"Good advice is good advice. Though I'm a bit worried about avalanches. Do those happen a lot up here?"

Luke nodded. "They do. We can do a little simulation if you'd like?"

Sarah groaned. "Fine, but as long as it's inside."

"I promise. I wouldn't want to risk causing an avalanche out here."

* * *

Sarah had been surprised to hear Luke's voice from behind her. She hadn't seen him in a couple of days since the mauling. Every time she seemed to get a little bit closer to him, he turned tail and ran into the woods. Of course, she didn't mind. It was better they had that separation.

She barely knew anything about him and really she shouldn't care all that much, but she wanted to get to know him. Maybe because she was alone here in Crater Lake. She didn't know anyone apart from Luke and a few employees that she greeted in passing at the resort. Then again, when had she really had any friends?

Her whole medical career, heck, her whole life, she hadn't had much time to form any interactions or friendships. And that was the way she wanted it. Her parents had tried to put Sarah into the same activities as her sister. It was just Sarah never really was social. She'd preferred science camp or painting class over tennis camp. She'd been so focused trying to prove to her parents she could do the things she wanted to do, she hadn't made many friends.

Or at least friends who were interested in the same things as she was.

The last date she'd been on the previous year had been so unremarkable. The guy had been handsome, well-to-do, but boring and very full of himself.

Luke was cocky, confident, but there was a difference. He didn't think he was a god. He didn't think he was better than anyone else. He actually tried to help people around him, even if he didn't want people to know that he cared, which she didn't get.

And most of all, he didn't date her because of who her father was.

"You ready?" Luke asked as he straddled the snow-mobile.

"I don't have a helmet."

He reached into his knapsack and tossed her one. "There you go. Now get on."

"Do you have furniture in there? Is it like a bottom-less bag?"

He chuckled. "Perhaps. You know my motto is be ready for anything."

Sarah laughed and put on her helmet, climbing on the snowmobile behind him. Suddenly she was very nervous about being so close to Luke. Which was ridiculous. They were just coworkers. They weren't even friends.

He's the closest thing you have to a friend.

Which was true and that thought scared her.

"You need to hold on," Luke said over his shoulder.

"Right." Her heart was pounding and she was very aware about how close she was to him. Though she couldn't feel his skin, she was pressed against him enough to feel the hard muscles under all the thick layers of his snowsuit.

At least that was something. There was a wall of protection between the two of them, but for one brief moment she wished there weren't and she couldn't help but wonder what it would be like to be wrapped up in his arms.

Where did that come from?

She shook that thought away, because she couldn't think like that.

Luke was off-limits.

She just held on tight and tried not to think about it. She had to shake the idea of Luke out of her mind. This was her chance to prove to her parents that she didn't need their help to survive. She didn't need anyone's help. She was here because of her own merit. She'd earned the right to be here and she was going to prove to everyone she had the right to be here.

Nothing was going to get in her way.

This was her chance and she had to focus on making this clinic the best. She had to be the best, so there was no time to think about Luke or what might be.

She didn't have time for romance. She couldn't lose her focus and if she got involved with Luke, she probably would. He was so gorgeous, so delicious and so very distracting.

This job was too important to her. Her parents had scoffed when she'd turned down the job her father had got for her and taken this one. They believed she would fail and come back to them with her proverbial tail between her legs.

This job won't wait for you, Sarah. I pulled a lot of strings for you.

She couldn't let them think that way. They might not think she could handle this, but she could.

Luke was not for her, even if she wished she could indulge. She had to be strong around him, keep him at a distance and remember why she was here.

She wasn't here to fall in love. That wasn't in the cards for her.

She was here to be a doctor. She was here to run the most prestigious private clinic in northwest Montana.

This job was her chance, because, even though everything about her medical career had been handed to her, according to her father she was a damn good doctor.

She was a damn good surgeon.

Are you sure about that?

They pulled up to the resort and Luke parked his snowmobile away from the main entrance. When the engine was off, Sarah clambered off the snowmobile, her legs shaking from the ride.

"That was my first and last snowmobile ride, I think," she said, trying to make light of the situation. She handed Luke back the helmet. "Thanks for being prepared."

"No problem. Now, no going back out onto the trails until that bear has been subdued."

"I hope you don't have to kill it."

Luke frowned. "I hope the bear returns to its den, but I doubt it. The game warden is combing the mountains, as well."

"Thanks again for coming to get me. I hope I didn't ruin your day."

"You didn't ruin it, but you put a serious dent in my plans." He winked at her.

"You're an idiot."

Luke was going to say something more, but they were interrupted when a front-desk person came running out of the side door.

"Thank goodness I found you both," she said. "There's an emergency up in Suite 501."

"What's wrong?" Sarah asked.

"A guest has gone into labor."

Luke's eyes widened. "Well, that's something I've never dealt with."

"Really?"

"Not many pregnant soldiers on the front line."

"Well, perhaps I can teach you something." Sarah turned to the front-desk woman. "Get her comfortable, call the air ambulance and tell them we'll be there in ten minutes."

The woman nodded and disappeared back inside.

"You've seriously delivered a baby before?" Luke asked with a hint of admiration in his voice.

"I'm a surgeon and part of the training was a rotation on the obstetrical rounds. I can do this."

"I'm sure you can. Not sure I can."

She grinned. "After today you will. Come on."

Luke nodded and they headed inside.

Sarah didn't want to tell him that she was nervous, too. She hadn't delivered that many babies, but right now she didn't have a choice. She couldn't be nervous. There was a job to do.

There were two lives to save.

CHAPTER FIVE

"COME ON, ONE more push," Sarah urged. "You can do it."

It had been a long time since she'd delivered a baby. She had been nervous for a moment, hoping she'd remember how.

As a trauma surgeon she didn't see many births. When a pregnant woman came into the ER Sarah would look at them briefly before an OB/GYN was called, but the moment she'd checked on the mother at the hotel everything she'd learned had come back to her.

Which was a good thing. This patient needed her.

Luke was behind the mother, holding her up, helping her. The air ambulance had arrived, but by the time they arrived there was no way they could move the mother. The baby was on the way out and moving the mother would put the baby at risk.

"You're doing great," Luke reassured the woman.

Sarah smiled up at him, but he wasn't looking at her. Instead he was focused on helping their patient and it warmed her heart. He could've stood back because he admitted that he didn't know anything about childbirth, but instead he threw himself into the work.

He was gentle. Kind.

For a man that was referred to around the hotel as a lone wolf, keeping people at bay, disappearing into his cabin up in the woods, Luke had a large amount of tenderness to him. It made her chest tighten just a little bit.

There was something about a rough, tough exterior and a gentle hand. It made him endearing.

The mother let out a loud yell and Sarah gently helped the baby girl into the world. Sarah rubbed the baby's back and soon the newborn was crying lustily.

"Good job," Sarah encouraged.

The mom laid back and Luke came over to help her. He was grinning ear to ear as he handed her sterile scissors.

"Good job, Doctor," he whispered in her ear. It sent a tingle down her spine.

She didn't say anything as she cut the umbilical cord and then wrapped the baby up in a blanket and handed her to Luke so he could give her to the mother.

"Congratulations, Mom," Luke said as he carefully transferred the baby to her mother's arms. He glanced down at the tiny girl as he did so, those blue eyes twinkling as he gently cradled her. So little in his big hands. It made Sarah's heart skip a beat.

Having a family had never been on her radar. Maybe because she'd had such a lonely childhood, even with a sister. They were raised by nannies in the old archaic "children should be seen and not heard" style.

How could she even contemplate raising a family when she didn't even know how one was supposed to function?

So she'd never entertained the idea, but in this moment, watching the joy on the mother's face, she yearned for something more.

"She's beautiful," Luke said.

The mother cried tears of joy and exhaustion as she took the small bundle from Luke. It was this moment that Sarah had always enjoyed when she'd been a resident and worked the obstetrical round. The moment of pure joy and elation. The moment when mother and child met. It could warm even the coldest hearts.

And watching Luke hold that small child melted hers completely.

What was it about him?

Most of the time he drove her completely around the bend, but there were times like this, when he was dealing with patients, that made her soften toward him. She wanted to get to know him and she never wanted to get to know anyone. What was it about him?

He's a mystery.

And maybe that was why she was so drawn to him. He was a challenge and she'd never backed down from a challenge before.

You need to back down from this one.

Sarah tore her gaze away from Luke and turned back to the patient. The paramedics stood at the ready. Even though the birth had been simple, mother and baby still had to be taken to the nearest hospital to be checked out.

Once she was finished the paramedics stepped in and started to get ready to transfer the patients. Her job was done. She cleaned up the mess and put it in a trash bag that she would take down to her medical-waste receptacle in her clinic.

Now you're picking up trash? Sarah, you weren't raised to do that.

You can't be an obstetrician. I didn't pay for your medical schooling so you can do obstetrics.

She hated the way her parents' voices were always in her head, trying to control her. For a long time she'd managed to tune them out, right up until she'd discovered what her father had done.

Now they were constantly there, questioning her every move.

Sarah would've liked to have been an OB/GYN surgeon, but her father didn't think it was dignified enough. Of course, he hadn't been too pleased when she gave up training to be a cardio-thoracic surgeon under Dr. Eli Draven, but Sarah preferred general surgery. She preferred trauma surgery.

Most people thought that general and trauma surgery was boring, but it wasn't. It was exciting. She got to work on so much with general surgery, and as a trauma surgeon she saw everything, but still she'd kind of missed her chance on working with mothers and babies.

Even though she'd always stressed that she didn't want to get married, that she wanted to focus on her career, there had always been a part of her that wanted the family she hadn't had as a child.

Sarah had grown up in wealth and privilege. She'd wanted for nothing except love and admiration from her parents. Maybe even to spend some time with them.

Watching this mother dote on her new baby made her wonder if her own mother had ever looked at her that way before, and seeing Luke smile so tenderly at them made her yearn.

In this moment she longed for something more.

She just didn't think that was possible.

Not in the near future anyway. Probably never.

Luke came over and peeled off his gloves and threw them in the bag, interrupting her train of thought.

"Good job, Dr. Ledet."

She chuckled. "I really didn't do much. The mother did all the work."

He smiled at her. "Still, you did a good job nonetheless. I would've been totally lost."

"What about your brother? He's the town doctor, doesn't he deliver babies?"

"He does, but he lives in town. That's at least a twenty-minute drive in this weather. He wouldn't have made it in time."

"No," she agreed. "That baby was coming quickly."

They moved out of the way as the paramedics passed them.

"Thank you, Doctors," the mother said, grinning ear to ear.

"Congratulations," Sarah said. "Everything will be okay."

Sarah watched as they wheeled her patient and the baby out of the suite. It had been so wonderful being a part of that moment, watching a family being formed. Being part of their love. She was sad to watch them go.

She sighed. "Well, that was certainly exciting."

"It was, but I don't understand it."

"What don't you understand?"

"I don't understand why a woman so close to delivering decided to come up here on a ski trip," Luke said as he moved away from her.

"I think it was a family trip. Perhaps she would've been left home alone. I think it was a good thing she was here."

He nodded. "Yeah. You're probably right."

Sarah knotted the trash bag and glanced around the suite. "I feel bad for Housekeeping, but honestly I think that mattress is no good anymore."

"That's the first birth I've attended. I mean, besides my own."

"You've never attended one in medical school?"

He shook his head. "I did most of my training in the army. My residency was in Germany at a hospital there. So not only do I speak fluent French, I speak fluent German, too."

"You're a man of many trades, Dr. Ralston."

"I have a lot of secrets." Then he grinned and winked at her in a way that made her heart skip a beat. She had to get out of the room. She had to put some distance between them.

"I'm sure you do, but I have to take this to the clinic." She held up the garbage bag.

"When are you going to show me your paintings?"

The question caught her off guard. Any time anything had ever gotten too personal between them, he'd disappeared into the woods. So when he asked about her paintings, it shocked her.

No one had ever asked to see her paintings before. And she never told anyone about them. If he hadn't caught her taking photographs, she wouldn't have told him. Most people thought her art and pursuing it was silly.

Again, another dream her parents quashed really fast.

They're called starving artists for a reason, Sarah.

Her mother hadn't wanted her to be an artist, and yet her mother had supported the local arts scene in New York City. Bought paintings, attended galas and gallery openings. Then again, that was what women like her mother did. It was *the* thing to do in her parents' circles.

"You want to see my paintings?"

"Sure. You said you take pictures and then do paintings. I'm interested. I've never met a doctor who painted landscapes or drew or anything for that matter."

Sarah chuckled. "It's good for the hands. Especially surgeon hands. Keeps them strong."

"So, when do I get to see them?"

"I don't know. When do I get to see the house you built?" Then the blood drained away from her face when she realized what she'd just done. This was not keeping him at a distance. This was inviting him in.

"How about tonight?" he asked, surprising her.

"Tonight?"

"You have plans tonight?"

"No."

He nodded then, those blue eyes twinkling with something she wasn't sure of, but it made her heart beat a bit faster.

"Okay, then, so you'll come to my place tonight. I'll see some of your paintings and you can see my handiwork."

"Okay." Sarah looked away and hoped that she wasn't blushing. "I better get this to medical waste."

"I'll pick you up at seven."

She nodded and didn't look back at him. She couldn't, because if she did then he would see how he was affecting her.

Damn him.

And then she cursed herself a bit, wondering what the heck she'd just gotten herself into.

* * *

What have I done?

Luke had repeatedly asked himself that since he'd invited Sarah over to his house. He didn't have anyone at his house. Ever.

Only Carson and that was rare. Usually when Luke got together with Carson he went to Carson's place.

It was larger.

Luke went for the understated. An open-concept cabin. Carson referred to it as a shack, as if Luke were some kind of prospector up in Alaska on a gold claim.

Everything in the cabin he'd made. Well, the furniture anyway. So what if he preferred to live off the grid a bit? He wasn't totally off the grid. He had electricity and running water. No, he didn't have a phone or cable, but he had a radio if he ever got into trouble or if someone wanted to reach him.

There wasn't any cell phone reception where his cabin was and he still hadn't quite figured out why. Probably all the pine trees around it.

Christine had hated this cabin when he'd planned it. Even though it did have creature comforts like a sauna out back and a nice bathroom. Everything was too "rough" for her.

When he picked Sarah up at the hotel, he was actually hoping that she would make up an excuse and cop out, but she didn't. She was waiting for him at the front in her coat with a black portfolio slung over her shoulder.

He had no choice but to live up to his end of the bargain and take her to his home. The truck ride over was tense, because he didn't know what to say to her. All he could think about on the journey was how he was going to get out of this situation. A situation that was his fault. He only had himself to blame.

When he'd told Carson what he'd done, he'd thought his brother had witnessed a miracle healing the way his mouth had dropped open.

"You don't date. You said so yourself and you repeatedly made fun of me when I got together with Esme."

"It's not a date. She's a coworker."

Carson had grinned, smugly. "You keep telling yourself that, my friend. You're not fooling me."

Luke had decided he didn't need Carson's advice, called his brother a few choice names and left. Carson was certainly making him eat crow and maybe he deserved it just a bit, because he'd certainly given Carson a run for his money when Esme had started coming around more often.

Still, that was a completely different situation.

Carson was in love with Esme.

Luke wasn't interested in Sarah. Not in that way.

Liar.

This was a dangerous situation. They were in his cabin, in the woods and they were alone. That wasn't a good combo. His self-control was going to be tested tonight, because any time he was around her it was tested.

All he wanted to do was kiss those pink lips, to run his hands through her blond hair and hold her in his arms, to feel her body pressed against his.

Don't think about her like that. She's not yours. She can't be yours. That's not what you want.

Only the more he tried to convince himself of that the harder it was for him to believe it.

"Wow, so this is it?" Sarah asked as he parked his truck in front of his cabin.

"Yes, this is my shack, as my brother calls it."

"Well, at least it'll be warm. I can see you left the home fires burning."

"Yes, I have electricity, but my house is heated by my wood stove. I live a bit off the grid, as much as I can. I like to rough it."

"Do you grow your own food, too?" She was teasing him.

"No, I don't really have a green thumb. I forage mostly. Our dinner tonight will be moss and various pine needles."

She laughed. "Well, can we go inside? I'd like to see this old shack you built."

"Ha-ha." They climbed out of the truck and he opened the door for her. She stepped in first and stood in the small mudroom of his cabin. She was silent and he found himself starting to sweat, waiting for her approval.

Probably because the last time he'd shown a woman his place it had been Christine and she'd hated it and then it had been only the schematics and blueprints.

You expect me to live here?

You wanted a house when I was done with my tours. I'm building this for us.

Don't think about her.

She wasn't going to intrude into his thoughts. Not tonight.

"Well?" he asked, trying not to seem too anxious. "What do you think?"

"It's beautiful. I'm pretty impressed that you built this place." She took off her coat and hung it on the hooks that he had in the entranceway and then kicked off her boots and stepped on the thick Berber area rug that he had in the living-cum-bedroom area of his home. "The furniture seems to match the house perfectly."

"It should, I made it."

She cocked her eyebrows. "You made the furniture, too?"

He nodded. "Everything. Even the mattress."

Why did I say that?

Pink stained her cheeks when he said mattress, but she wouldn't look in the direction of the king-size bed that he'd built in the far corner. Seeing how he affected her made his own blood heat. Since she'd dropped into his arms in her office a couple weeks back, there had been countless times that he'd pictured her naked in his bed, her legs wrapped around his waist.

What he wouldn't give to peel that pale pink boat-neck sweater and those tight blue jeans from her body, to run his hands over her soft skin.

Get a grip on yourself.

He cleared his throat and ran his hand through his hair nervously.

"Yeah, I made the mattress out of feathers I'd collected over time. It used to be a straw tick, but that was quite uncomfortable."

"This isn't *Little House on the Prairie*, Pa."

He laughed with her and it defused the tension. He headed into the kitchen. "Would you like a glass of wine?"

"Did you press the grapes yourself?" she teased, setting her portfolio down on his coffee table.

"No. I do go to the grocery store from time to time. I'm not Davy Crockett."

"Could've fooled me." There was a twinkle in her eyes and she leaned over his counter. "I didn't expect dinner or drinks. I thought you were showing me your handiwork and I was going to show you some of mine."

He shrugged. "I rarely have dinner guests. I'm a bit of a Grinch around these parts."

"So I've heard."

"Who did you hear that from?" he asked.

"I went into town on my first week. Met a woman with these two twins and they mentioned how cantankerous you were. I had to agree with them at the time."

Luke groaned. "The Johnstone twins. Yes, they're not fond of me and I'm not too fond of them."

"Why? They looked like innocent enough children."

Luke snorted. "They delight in spooking my horse."

"You have a horse?"

He nodded. "I board her in a stable close to town in the winter. In the summer I have a pad out back that I keep her in. She can't handle the deep snow up here in the winter. She is getting on in years, sadly."

"You have hidden depths, Dr. Ralston."

You have no idea.

Only he didn't say that out loud. Instead he pulled down two wineglasses from where they were hanging on the wall and set them down before her.

"I'm afraid I only have white, but I think white will do well with the salmon I'm making."

"Salmon?"

"I smoked it myself."

She grinned. "I should've known. White is fine."

He pulled the only bottle he had in his house and uncorked it, pouring it into her glass and then his. He wasn't much of a wine drinker, but Esme really liked wine and so he figured Sarah would, too, but she took a sip and made a face.

"What's wrong?" he asked. "Did it go bad?"

"No, it's fine. It's just… I'm not much of a wine drinker. I like beer instead."

Now it was his turn to be shocked. "Who has hidden depths?"

She laughed. "My mother would be horrified if she knew that I was telling a man this. I was brought up to be prim and proper. I was not brought up to be a roughneck."

"A what?" he asked.

"My mother is from a very proper British family. A roughneck is someone who works offshore in oil or gas. Tough, rugged, dirty. I was meant to be refined and graceful."

"You're a bit of a klutz. I don't think you're all that graceful. I have seen you face-first in a snowdrift."

She laughed again and it warmed his heart to hear it. She had an infectious laugh and he couldn't remember the last time he'd felt so at ease around a woman before. Usually he was hiding behind his wall, but not at this moment. He was exposed and he didn't like that one bit.

What was she doing to him?

Sarah didn't know what she was expecting when Luke brought her out to his cabin. She must've been thinking more of a barren shack. Even though his home was rustic, it wasn't barren. It was cozy. It was homey.

It was the kind of place people from the city rented when they went on ski trips. The only difference was it would probably be larger. It was a little too small for most people, but she kind of liked it.

She was shocked that he made most of the furniture in the home, though she seriously doubted he made the leather L-shaped couch that was in the living room adorned with pillows and a polar fleece throw.

Then her gaze drifted off to the bed in the far corner of the open-concept cabin. It was a large wooden four-poster bed with a thick, down-and-feather-filled mattress. Well, according to him it was.

He made his own mattress?

She shook her head. Stop thinking about the bed.

He was in the kitchen checking on the salmon, his back to her. He'd handed her a beer a few moments ago and then gone about cooking the rest of dinner, leaving her to her own devices and the naughty thoughts that were running through her mind.

She sat down on the couch and tried to ignore the large bed, which felt like an elephant in the room at the moment.

Don't think about it. This is just dinner as friends.

Luke came out of the kitchen, holding a bottle of beer. "Just a little bit longer. Sorry about that."

She shrugged. "I didn't expect dinner tonight. It's a nice surprise."

"After all your hard work today, it was the least I could do."

"I just did my job."

"Yeah and you did a good job." Luke picked up her portfolio. "Do you mind if I look?"

"Go ahead. I am at your mercy." Blood rushed to her cheeks.

Luke grinned at her, that devious grin that made her insides turn to goo. "Well, let's see your artistic abilities."

Sarah's pulse thundered in her ears as he thumbed

through her very small portfolio. It was something she'd never shown anyone before. It was something she'd always felt she couldn't share with someone, but Luke had caught her in the act.

And she couldn't lie to him.

Or she didn't want to lie to him, but now she was regretting it because he wasn't saying much. What if he hated it? What if she sucked at it?

Who cares?

Only she did care. She cared if he hated it. What he thought mattered to her and that scared her.

"These are great. Where was this one done?" He held up a picture of the Black Hills. She'd spent some time around Mount Rushmore when she was a kid. That picture was something that she'd painted from memory, because that trip to Mount Rushmore with her parents was one of her last happy memories. They weren't this socialite family, they were just like everyone else. Except her father had rented a massive cabin on the outskirts of Keystone on this huge ranch that had horses and tennis courts, but still it was a happy time in her life.

"The Black Hills."

Luke glanced at it again. "South Dakota?"

She nodded. "Yes. Keystone, South Dakota."

"Yes, now I see it. I like South Dakota."

"You've been there?"

"Who hasn't? It's like Mecca for American families of our generation. Plus, it's not too far away for a family doctor to take his family for a summer vacation. My father was the only town physician in Crater Lake for a long time, so any vacation had to be taken in a drivable radius to home. Where did your family vacation, other than Mount Rushmore?"

"Jamaica, Brazil...India."

He raised an eyebrow. "Have you been around the world?"

"Pretty much." She took a swig of her beer. "My last job, teaching at different hospitals, took me to a lot of places, too. That's why I was in Missoula that day."

"Teaching?"

She nodded. "I worked with a surgeon who was developing a new technique in robotic trauma surgery. It was a good job."

"Why did you give it up?"

Her stomach twisted as she thought about those last moments. About when she'd found out that the job she'd been working on so hard hadn't really been something she'd earned.

It still made her angry.

"You look tense."

"I don't like to talk about the past too much." She set her beer down on the table. "Maybe I should head back to the hotel. I'm not that hungry."

"You're staying. I'm sorry, I won't pry." He set the portfolio down on the table. "Besides, I think it's done."

She watched as he walked into the kitchen. Why did he have to pry into her history? He didn't share his.

What was she doing here?

You're lonely.

She should just leave. It would be better if she left, only she couldn't.

She was a bit of a masochist.

"Have a seat at the table and I'll bring you dinner."

Sarah picked up her beer and headed over to the dining-room table, sitting down at the end. "Don't tell me you made this too?"

"Yep. I told you. I made most of the furniture here."
He came out of the kitchen with two plates and set down
in front of her a perfectly cooked filet of salmon, as-
paragus and new potatoes. It smelled delicious. "For a
long time since I returned from the army, I didn't practice medicine and all I wanted to do was build stuff for
my home."

"Why?" she asked.

He frowned and she knew she was treading on that
dangerous ground. That moment when he would clam
up. "I needed time."

"I get that."

He shrugged, but he didn't say anything else and an
awkward silence fell between them. She wished that he
would open up and share with her, but then again she
wasn't exactly sharing much with him either.

So they were at a standstill.

And maybe that was for the best.

After dinner, she helped him clean up, though he insisted that wasn't necessary. Then they returned to the
couch in his living room, where he continued to look
at her paintings and drawings. As he was skimming
through he found one that absolutely captivated him.
It was a self-portrait she'd done and by the date on the
bottom it was a few years ago. It took his breath away.
The details in the drawing. It was just a pencil sketch,
but there was so much life to it.

The kissable lips, heart-shaped face, nose that turned
up again, thinly arched brows and beautiful eyes that
captured him. In the portrait her hair hung loose over
bare shoulders, like wisps. Usually she wore it back in
a braid and tonight it was done up in a bun. He resisted

the urge to undo that bun and let her hair cascade down all over her shoulders. So he could kiss and hold that woman in the picture. It was as if the drawing showed a hidden part of her.

The true Sarah.

And he longed to know the true Sarah, which scared him.

"Which one are you looking at so intently?"

Luke quickly flicked the page. "Uh, this one. The horse on the plains. It's beautiful."

She smiled. "You can have it if you want."

"Thanks."

The horse one was good. It actually reminded him of his own horse, who he hadn't seen in a couple of days, but he'd rather keep the pencil-drawn self-portrait she'd done.

Why torture yourself?

"You said you have a horse?"

"Yeah. I do."

"What's its name?"

"Her name is Adele."

"That's an interesting choice."

"Well, I didn't really choose it. When I bought her that was her name. I didn't see a point in changing it."

"I love horseback riding." Sarah sighed. "I miss it."

"You know how to horseback ride?"

She nodded. "Regular lessons. One thing I didn't mind my parents pressuring me into."

"Your parents have a large impact on your life?" he asked.

She frowned and then shrugged. "What parents don't?"

"True," Luke agreed, but there was something more

to what she'd said about her parents. He wanted to press her further, but decided against it.

He didn't mind this friendly chatter or when they worked so well together when faced with a medical emergency. Anything else was risky and he didn't want her to find a way in. He set down his glass.

"You know, I haven't seen her in a long time. I've been so busy. I should go check on her. Would you like to come?"

Her eyes lit up, as if he were offering her a thousand dollars.

"Really?"

He nodded. "Really."

"I would love that."

"Grab your coat." He handed her back the portfolio. "After I check on her I'll take you back to the hotel."

It was a short drive to the stable where he kept Adele. The owner of the stable was used to Luke keeping odd hours and didn't mind that Luke was here to visit his horse at eleven in the evening.

As they got out of the car a brilliant set of northern lights erupted across the sky, because the cloud cover that had been hovering over Crater Lake the past few days had dissipated.

"Oh, my God!" Sarah said, a cloud of breath escaping past her lips. "Look at that."

"Pretty spectacular, isn't it?"

"I've never seen one. Too much light pollution."

"I can imagine that. Cities are so ugly."

She shook her head. "New York isn't ugly. The lights are beautiful. Especially around the holidays like Christmas and Valentine's Day. They light up the Empire State

Building and then at Christmas there's this large tree at Rockefeller Square."

Luke wrinkled his nose. "Christmas sounds fine. Valentine's, why even bother? Besides, light pollution has nothing on this. Look straight up."

Sarah leaned back and he watched as her expression turned from amusement to awe. Now that the cloud cover was gone there were millions of stars splattered across the sky. As if Van Gogh's *Starry Night* were painted across the inky black sky.

"Amazing."

He smiled at her as he watched her stare up in amazement at the star-filled sky. He remembered so many times, after working on soldiers for countless hours, walking out of the OR and standing in the dark, staring up at the sky in Afghanistan and wishing for this.

The night sky was different.

And there was no aurora borealis.

Afghanistan's sky was beautiful, silent and cold at night, but nothing beat Montana, the mountains. Nothing beat home.

And in this moment, he wanted to take Sarah in his arms and kiss her. The urge was undeniable and he had to regain control before he did something he would regret.

Who said you'd regret it?

"Come on, I don't want you to catch your death out here. Adele won't like it too much if your teeth are chattering the whole time."

They walked into the stable and as soon as he did Adele stuck her head out of the stall, watching him.

"She knows you're here."

Luke grinned. "I know, but really she's just looking for treats."

"I don't know about that."

Luke's blood heated at her teasing tone, but he didn't acknowledge it; instead he cleared his throat and pulled out Adele's carrot treat.

"Hey, girl," he whispered against her muzzle. "How have they been treating you?"

"I'd love to paint her. She's beautiful."

"Come pet her. She doesn't mind. What she minds is people spooking her."

"Can you blame her?" Sarah asked and then she approached Adele slowly. Adele moved her head slightly, not used to the stranger who was about to touch her.

"It's okay, Adele. This is a friend. Another doctor."

Adele nickered and Sarah was able to stroke her muzzle.

"You're so beautiful, Adele," Sarah whispered.

Luke watched Sarah stroke and touch his horse, and his heart, which he'd thought was safely encased in ice, began to melt for her. She was like no other woman he'd ever met and his blood burned with the need to possess her. To have her for his own.

You can't have her.

"She's beautiful, Luke. So beautiful. I would love to ride her one day, if you'd let me."

Luke cleared his throat. "We'll see. I better get you back to your hotel. It's getting late."

"Sure." Sarah leaned forward and kissed Adele. "Good night, beauty."

And at that moment Luke knew he'd have to put

some serious distance between the two of them, or he was liable to carry her off and make love to her.

Right now.

CHAPTER SIX

"You're a sadist—you know that, right?"

Luke just grinned at her, as he stood over her in the snow. Gone was the gentle soul of a man she'd seen last night in that horse stable, the gentle giant cradling that fragile infant. That man made her ache with need. She craved him like air, but this guy, torturing her with endless simulations, this guy she wanted to club upside the head.

He'd taken her outside to where the snow plows had been piling the snow from the parking lot. The large snowbank was littered with CPR dummies, half-buried. It was a simulation massacre.

Only he'd dubbed this as avalanche training.

"I thought we were going to do avalanche training inside?"

"How would that work?" he asked.

"We could pretend. Use our imagination."

"We were, until I found this snow pile. It's perfect."

"Great," she mumbled.

"You need to work harder to dig this man out."

Sarah rolled her eyes. "I'm just a hotel doctor. I'm not going to be the first line of defense called for this.

You are, your brother probably and every other first responder up here on this mountain."

"You'll be called, too. In situations like this, everyone with medical training will be called into action. That's how it works up in these remote communities. Are you saying that you're not going to come to an avalanche site because you're just a hotel doctor?"

Damn.

He was right. She wouldn't walk away from an emergency situation. She was a doctor and she was trained in trauma, just as he was.

"Fine." She kept digging away at the snow.

"Use your ice axe, too. Chip away at the hard stuff. Just don't hit the patient."

Sarah made a face at him and he just laughed.

"Do you think you can insert a chest tube in below-zero temps?"

"You're not serious, are you?"

"You said you worked in an ER. Haven't you inserted chest tubes before?"

"Of course," Sarah said. "But not in the bitter cold. Usually when I insert a chest tube it's in a trauma pod, sheltered and indoors."

Not negative eighty with a windchill.

"Ah, but sometimes there's no time to get the man down off the mountain and you have to do it in the field." Luke reached into his knapsack and pulled out a chest-tube kit. "Insert a chest tube. The patient's lungs are filling with blood—he needs a chest tube."

Sarah pulled off her mitts and fumbled with the chest-tube tray. She hadn't realized how cold her fingers actually were, but then she remembered that they'd been out here for an hour already while he went through avalanche drills with her.

The mitts were warm, but, after a while digging in the snow, their protective lining couldn't keep out the bitter cold forever. She cursed under her breath, as she prepared the chest tube and inserted it perfectly the first time.

She had always been pretty good at it.

"Good job," Luke remarked. "Now put on your gloves and keep digging."

"I need a break."

"You don't get a break on the mountain."

"This isn't a mountain. It's the snow from the main parking lot and as you can see we're the current entertainment." She pointed to the window where staff and a few guests were watching them cavorting on top of the dirty snowbank, with mannequins strewn everywhere.

"It's mandatory training, but I suppose you can have a break. You were up late last night."

Sarah smiled and tried not to blush as she thought about it. She actually hadn't wanted the night to end, though it had been for the best. If it hadn't ended she might have done something foolish, like kiss him, and maybe that one foolish kiss would have led to something more.

So it was good that the night had ended when it had.

Still, she couldn't remember when she'd had such a good time. "Yes, thanks for the fantastic dinner and the conversation. I enjoyed it."

"Me, too," he said, but then the small smile that he had for her quickly disappeared and he got up, to walk slowly down the side of the snowbank.

For a while after their awkward conversation it was

pretty quiet, but then he started asking about her art and her photographs, then the tension melted away. Still, at the mention of last night the atmosphere changed and put distance between them. Maybe he was regretting last night. She certainly hoped not.

He was the closest thing she had to a friend in Crater Lake. Loneliness had never bothered her before, but that was probably because she'd been busier as a surgeon. There were guests at the hotel, but not many as the grand opening was only a couple of weeks away on Valentine's Day and, even then, guests weren't always getting sick.

So far, since her arrival in Crater Lake, she'd treated about eight sunburns, three cases of some gastroenteritis, a bear mauling and a birth of a baby. And because she wasn't as busy as she was in her previous job, she had a lot more free time. A lot more time to remind her that she was alone.

Of course, she didn't really think that if she followed her mother and sister in their footsteps that she would feel any different. Her society friends weren't really friends at all.

None of them had called her since she'd decided to cut ties with New York and move to Montana. Actually, they'd been quite horrified when she'd told them she'd given up the prestigious job and was moving to Crater Lake.

Who cares if your father pulled strings? My father did, too. It doesn't matter.

It matters to me, Nikki. My father doesn't think I can do anything. He's thinks I'm this baby. He thinks I'm helpless. I need to do this on my own.

Thinking about that last conversation with her so-called best friend made her blood pressure rise. It made her angry. It made her remember that she wasn't sure if anything in her life was her own. She wasn't sure if she'd earned anything.

It was humiliating.

Don't think about it. Don't give them the time of day.

"Do you have avalanches here every year?" she asked, hoping that the conversation could turn in another direction and distract her. It would keep her mind off her parents, her so-called friends and Luke.

"Pretty much."

"To this extent?"

Luke shook his head. "No, thankfully we haven't had a major disaster like this in a long, long time, but being in a mountainous region there are always avalanches. Always. That's why we have avalanche zones."

"How do you determine what an avalanche zone is?"

Luke clambered back up the snowbank to stand beside her. He pointed toward the mountain. "You see that part of the mountain? You see how it's on a forty-five-degree angle? It's considered an avalanche zone. In fact we had a landslide on that slope last year."

"The landslide that almost killed Shane Draven?"

He nodded. "Yes, Dr. Petersen, my brother and I extracted him and got him down."

"All-hands-on-deck type of situation, then?"

He nodded. "You got it."

"So only steep slopes are considered dangerous."

"No, gradual slopes are at risk, too. And shady slopes can pose a threat."

"Why?" she asked. "Wouldn't the snow harden there as opposed to being in the sun?"

"No, the sun actually hardens the snow better. It

melts it and then at night ice forms and seals the snow-cap better. Shady slopes don't have that chance—it's just powder."

Sarah shuddered. "I hope we never have a bad avalanche, then. I wouldn't know what to do."

"As long as you're aware of the avalanche zones, you'll be fine, but that's why I'm training you. So you know what to do in an emergency. You can get seriously hurt. I broke my leg during an avalanche last winter. Avalanches are a mighty force. You need to learn how to survive." Luke moved behind her and she was very aware that he was close to her. He touched her arms and, even through all those thick layers, it was electric the way he affected her.

"What're you doing?" she asked, her voice hitching because he was touching her.

He leaned over her shoulder, his hot breath fanning the exposed skin of her neck. "I'm teaching you how to survive if you're ever caught in one. This is Special Forces training now."

"Oh," she said. "How can you fight fast-moving snow?"

"Swim." Then he took her arms and moved them gently in a breaststroke. "If you're ever caught in fast-moving snow, drop your gear because it will weigh you down, open your arms wide and swim to the side of the snow pack. Even if you can't make it across, the movement will help keep your head above the snow so you can breathe."

"Swim through snow?" Sarah smiled. "I've never heard of that before. And what happens if I'm covered with snow?"

"Bring your arms and hands to the front of your face

and wiggle back and forth. It will create an air pocket and you'll be able to breathe until help arrives."

"Have you ever been trapped in an avalanche?"

"No, never trapped and never been standing at the edge of an active one. The avalanche I was injured in was because I was rescuing someone. I jumped from a helicopter and landed the wrong way, losing my footing. I've never been trapped, thank God, and I hope I never am."

"I hope so, too." Sarah looked up at him, but his face was unreadable because his sunglasses were covering his eyes, protecting them from snow blindness.

"Thanks." He cleared his throat and moved away from her. "We should get back to freeing these victims."

"Good, 'cause I have big plans this afternoon." She was teasing, but his brow furrowed.

"What kind of plans?"

"I'm going to Crater Lake. I haven't been in town since I first arrived. I have the rest of the day off and I thought I would explore."

"I don't go to town this time of year," Luke remarked.

"Why not?"

"Valentine's Day is coming." He shuddered. "The town is going a little bit crazy about it because of the hotel's grand opening that day. There's going to be a big gala or ball or something."

"I know. Silas Draven is insisting all his employees go, but it sounds kind of fun."

Luke grunted.

"You're not a fan of Valentine's Day?"

"Nope. It's pointless."

"Love is pointless?" she asked.

"No, not pointless just…there's no need to celebrate Valentine's Day with such vigor."

"Why do you hate it so much?" she asked.

He just grunted again, but avoided her question and she wondered why Luke thought love was pointless. She didn't know many guys who actually liked Valentine's Day, but Luke was acting a bit like a Grinch about it.

Why should you care?

And really she shouldn't. When did she ever give two hoots about Valentine's Day before? Usually she was in the hospital, doing surgery and stealing candy from the nurses' station as she went from OR to OR.

She'd never had a Valentine before. Still, the idea of a town getting all decked out and celebrating it sounded as if it could be fun.

"I think it will be fun to see what the town is doing," she said, trying to change the subject before Luke shut down on her again and didn't say anything else.

"Well, have fun. I have to take a group of surveyors out on a trail for some training."

"More surveyors?"

Luke nodded as he headed down the snowbank to their next patient. "I guess some more people are trying to cash in on Silas Draven's bright idea to turn Crater Lake into the next Whitefish."

"I thought you worked exclusively for Silas Draven?" she asked.

He grinned. "No, I'm a free agent. Now come on, get down here so we can save this patient and then we can call it quits for the day."

Sarah groaned but climbed down the snow pile to-ward him, because she was tired of being in the snow. She was cold and, really, what was the point?

Luke was a closed book.

And that was all there was to it.

Luke had lost his mind. Well, he had for a brief moment there when he'd stepped behind Sarah and touched her. He didn't know what he'd been thinking about at that moment. Clearly, he was suffering from the cold.

He'd shown other people how to swim out of fast-moving snow and he did that without touching them. He just told them to open their arms wide and mimic swimming, but with Sarah he'd reached out and guided her arms.

And he had no idea why he'd felt the need to do that.

Probably because he liked to torture himself?

Or maybe it was because he couldn't resist her. When he was around her, he wasn't himself. He didn't guard his walls as carefully as he used to. She made him weak. As if she was his Achilles' heel or something.

Yet, like a masochist he kept going back to her. Kept reaching out to her.

She'll hurt you just like Christine did.

He'd done so much for Christine when they were newly married. She'd known he was going to serve in the army, but she hadn't cared. She hadn't wanted to accompany him to Germany, but their marriage had survived. And it had survived his first tour of duty, too.

It was only when she'd demanded he end his career, that he return home to start a family with his wife, that he'd learned she didn't want him.

She didn't want to be his wife.

She'd rather be Anthony's wife, because he'd always been there for her. Unlike him.

I gave up my commission in the army for you.

It was too late for me then, Luke. It was just too late.
You could've come to Germany with me.

You never asked if I wanted to go to Germany. You just said we were moving there and, no, I didn't want to go live in Germany. I didn't want to stay here in Crater Lake either, but it was better than Germany. Of course, my dreams don't matter to you at all. Why couldn't you just open a practice with your father? What was wrong with that? Why couldn't you bend your plans for me or at least ask me if I shared them?

You want me to practice with my father and Carson. Fine. I will.

It's too late, Luke. You were selfish. My desires and wishes never mattered. I'm sorry, but I can't be with you anymore.

This was why he couldn't be near anyone. Why he thought love was pointless. For him anyway. What was the point of falling in love when it could be taken away in an instant?

Carson found love again.

He shook that thought away. That was a different situation. Carson never married Danielle. Carson was never betrayed as Luke was.

There was no room in his heart anymore. He couldn't let there be.

"So what's wrong with this patient?" Sarah used air quotes.

Luke groaned. "Why are you using air quotes? This is a serious situation."

Sarah laughed behind her hand and he couldn't help but smile.

Darn her.

Why was it so easy to be around her?

"Okay, so what is wrong with the patient?"

"Do you know how to perform a surgical cricothyrotomy?"

"Yes. I have done one before, but not when the patient is buried in a snowdrift."

"Peel off your mitts, because you're about to do one on this mannequin. It's better to perfect it here in this simulation rather than on someone who is actually buried under snow." He tossed her a cricothyrotomy kit. "I'll time you."

"Do you want me to go through the steps as I'm doing it?" she asked as she pulled off her mitts.

"If you want."

She peeled back the cover on the kit and began to work. "Damn, my fingers are already going numb. This is going to be more difficult than I thought."

"Which is why we're practicing out here."

Sarah nodded. "Cricothyroid membrane detected and trachea grasped. Making incision."

Luke squatted down and watched her. "You're doing good."

She cursed under her breath. "My fingers are already numb."

"I know, but you can do it."

"Okay, making incision."

Luke watched as she made a beautiful incision in the skin. "Now expose the membrane with the handle of the scalpel."

"Got it." She set the scalpel down and finished the rest of the surgical cricothyrotomy. As she was suturing she cursed again. "My fingers are frozen."

"I know, but that's what happens."

Once it was finished, he handed her the mitts, which she hurriedly put on.

"You did a good job." Luke moved away from her quickly. "Well, I have to get ready and take those surveyors up the mountain. I'll see you later."

"Okay. Thanks." She scurried down off the snow pile and headed back inside. He didn't mind that. It was for the best, because she was stirring up things inside him that weren't welcome. Things that he'd thought were buried deep down.

He admired her. He had fun with her and he was highly attracted to her.

He wanted her and that was not good.

That was unacceptable.

CHAPTER SEVEN

AFTER THE TRAINING SESSION, Sarah had a shower and changed her clothes before heading into town. Her hands were still a little bit numb from performing that surgical cricothyrotomy out on the snow pile.

When she got to town she couldn't help but smile to see all the decorations going up. Hearts on the lampposts. Hearts in store windows. It was a small-town feel, like something straight from the movies, and it made her smile, even though she'd never felt so alone.

That was the thing about small towns. Everyone knew everyone. Or at least it seemed that way. Sarah was a stranger. All she knew was Luke and a couple people up at the hotel, but were they really her friends?

None of them were here with her. Really, she had no friends and it had never really bothered her before. She'd spent so many years distancing herself from her parents' world, she'd put up a wall to keep out everyone.

It hadn't bothered her until now. Even then she didn't know what she wanted. She wasn't sure that she could bring down those walls that were safe.

That were comfortable.

Sarah headed into the coffee shop that was on the corner of the main street. She was still shivering from the cold. When she entered the coffee shop, a few people stopped their conversation and looked in her direction, but only briefly. Being new in town generated some interest, but not enough for someone to come up and talk to her. And Sarah wasn't the kind to go up and start up a conversation with a stranger either.

If they were in a hospital or her clinic, then it would be no problem. She'd be able to talk to them quite easily.

Here, not a chance.

She made her way to the counter and sat down. It was like something out of the fifties. The coffee shop was a mishmash of retro and bohemian, but as long as they served good coffee she didn't care too much.

"What'll you have?" the girl behind the counter asked.

"A large black coffee with a shot of espresso, please."

"Will do." The girl moved away and Sarah undid her jacket and glanced around at all the people chatting. She envied them a bit.

"You're the new doctor in town, aren't you?"

Sarah turned to see a short, blonde woman slip into the seat next to her. It shocked her. In Manhattan this would've never happened. People she encountered in coffee shops there were always in a rush or kept to themselves, just as she did.

"I am," Sarah said. "I'm Dr. Ledet."

"I know." She grinned, her blue eyes twinkling. "I'm Dr. Esme Petersen."

"You're the cardio-thoracic surgeon."

Esme nodded. "I am. Luke mentioned that there was a new doctor up at the hotel. He also mentioned that you briefly worked with Dr. Eli Draven."

"I did. Do you know Dr. Draven?"

Esme nodded. "He trained me."

"I'm impressed. Dr. Draven is a world-class surgeon. Wait, Dr. Petersen, weren't you the one who inserted that chest tube into Shane Draven last summer?"

"I was," Esme said. "How did you know about that?"

"I was the surgeon in Missoula that operated on him."

Esme frowned slightly. "I thought you were from New York?"

"I was training some surgeons on a new technique when I was asked to help with incoming."

"What will you have, Dr. Petersen?" the girl asked as she set down Sarah's coffee in front of her.

"Cappuccino, please, Mary. Thanks."

"Sure thing." Mary walked away again.

"How are you enjoying Crater Lake?" Esme asked.

"It's been great." Sarah took a sip of her coffee. "It's quiet, though."

"Oh, no," Esme said. "You didn't just say that, did you?"

"What?"

"Quiet. I thought you were a trauma surgeon?" Esme said teasingly.

Sarah laughed. "How do you know so much about me?"

"It's a small town and you're new and shiny." Esme winked. "I was new and shiny last summer. I remember clearly."

Mary set down the cappuccino in front of Esme and disappeared again. Sarah could see that a heart was made in the foam.

"Aww, that's sweet," Sarah remarked.

Esme made a face. "I don't like Valentine's Day."

"What? I thought a heart surgeon would love Valentine's Day."

Esme took a swizzle stick and stabbed at the foam heart. "You'd think that, right?"

Sarah laughed. "You're the second person I've met in this town that hates Valentine's Day."

"Really? Who is the other person? Perhaps I should befriend them."

"Dr. Luke Ralston."

Esme laughed. "Luke? Oh, yeah, I forgot. He's such a grouch. I'm surprised he's talking to you, though."

"Why is that?"

"Well, he had a serious hate on for the surgeon who argued with him in Missoula."

Sarah started to laugh. "Yes. We didn't exactly get off on the right foot and I think I've been a thorn in his side."

"That doesn't surprise me. Although, it could work both ways. I think he might be a thorn in your side, too. He is in mine."

"Is he?"

"I'm dating Luke's brother, Carson. So, yeah, he's a bit of a pain in my butt."

"Has he ever dragged you out in the woods and forced you to train for emergency situations in minus-forty weather?" Sarah asked.

"Oh, he made you do that? What a jerk."

They both laughed at that. It was nice to chat with someone. It was nice to talk to someone and feel as if it wasn't superficial. She'd never had an easy chat with another woman before and certainly not another surgeon. She was used to being one of many sharks in a shark pond.

Once the coffee was done, Esme insisted on paying for both and they walked back out into the cold together and stood on the street.

"Thanks for having coffee with me. I was feeling a bit isolated up there," Sarah said.

Esme nodded and wound her knitted infinity scarf around, making a pretty knot in it. "I get it. I was once the new kid in town. Some people around here don't really like change. A few resent the resort community up there and the fact that there are a couple more that will be built, but most are coming around to the idea. It brings more business."

"How do you feel about a fourth doctor in town?" Sarah asked. "Is your practice suffering or is the other Dr. Ralston's?"

"No. It's steady. I get a lot of people from the outlying towns as I'm the closest cardio doctor. Were you worried?"

"Yeah, I didn't want to see an old family practice collapse."

"It won't." Esme reached out and squeezed her arm. "We should have coffee again or maybe even dinner. Carson's not a bad cook. Maybe we can even convince Luke to come down off that mountain."

Blood heated her cheeks and Sarah shook her head. "I seriously doubt that. He's up there now gallivanting around with surveyors."

Esme smiled. "Well, we'd still like to have you over sometime. Have a good day. Watch out for falling hearts."

"What?"

Esme pointed to the lamppost. "They tend to fall in a

strong wind. It happened at Christmas. A Santa landed butt-first on a woman. It wasn't pretty."

Sarah nodded. "Thanks."

Esme walked down Main Street toward the clinic. Sarah glanced up at the glittery, tinsel hearts that were hanging off the lampposts. It made her smile. She jammed her hands in her pockets and headed back to her truck, but as she was walking back to the parking lot there was a rumble. A deep hollow sound followed by a large crack, like thunder, and then a roar like a jet plane was flying overhead. Sarah spun around and watched in horror as a cloud of snow spiraled up into the sky and moved like a wave down the side of the mountain.

It was an avalanche. She could hear screams from other residents of the town as the avalanche wiped away everything in its path.

It was close to home. It was large and it made Sarah's heart stop in her throat.

At least it was on the peak opposite the hotel. The peak was a remote site that could potentially be another hotel.

Then it hit her. That was the Lakeview trail that she'd been on only a couple of days ago. It was the trail that Luke was planning to take a group of surveyors up to.

Luke.

He was up there somewhere on that mountain and could be trapped.

Esme came rushing back up behind her. "Oh, my God. We have to get up that mountain."

"I drove the hotel's truck down."

Esme nodded. "Come help me grab supplies. Carson is already on his way from our place, but we need to get up there and see if anyone's been injured. Do you know where Luke is?"

"He was up there." Sarah pointed at the peak. "He was with surveyors."

Esme cursed under her breath. "I'm sure he's fine. He knows the danger signs. He wouldn't take them somewhere unsafe. Come on."

Sarah nodded, but she felt numb.

As if this weren't happening.

They just did a practice run of an avalanche emergency and now one had actually happened? She'd thought that Crater Lake would be a little bit more laidback, but a bear mauling, a birth and now an avalanche? This place was just as busy as any city.

And last summer there was a landslide?

She'd thought living in the mountains would be peaceful, but she was beginning to realize just how isolated and dangerous it could be and she prayed that Luke had had the sense to see that taking the surveyors up on the Lakeview trail was dangerous and that he'd got out of the way of the avalanche.

"Luke, you're okay?"

Luke turned around to see his brother approaching the hotel. He was out of breath, as if he'd been running.

"I'm fine," Luke said.

Carson nodded and gave him a hug. "When I heard that crack I feared the worst. I knew you were going out on the trails today."

Luke nodded. "I saw the break in the cap before I set out. So I kept the surveyors at bay. I really thought, though, for a while that it wouldn't go and that they would be ticked off at me for wasting their time."

"Was anyone else on the mountain?" Carson asked.

"No. I shut the trails down to everyone else until that bear was caught. The game warden hadn't given me the okay to reopen them since the bear was subdued. We've had some mild temperatures at night and I knew we were due for an avalanche. I'm glad it was contained somewhat, though I'm still waiting to see how far it reached. There are some remote cabins in the way. I'm hoping it didn't get as far as Nestor's place."

Carson nodded. "Me, too. I'm glad you're okay."

Luke was going to say something further when he saw the resort truck driven by Sarah pull up and in the passenger side he saw Esme.

Great. Just great.

"Who's that with Esme?"

"Dr. Ledet," Luke mumbled.

Carson grinned. "No wonder I haven't seen you for a while. I thought you were spending too much time up at the hotel."

"What's that supposed to mean?" Luke asked, glaring at his brother.

Carson nodded in Sarah's direction. "I've seen her. I'm not blind. Isn't that similar to what you said to me in the summer when Esme came to town?"

"Ha-ha. Your witty humor amuses me."

Carson laughed out loud. "This explains a lot."

"It explains nothing," Luke snapped. "And you better remember that. I do have a large hank of rope in my truck. I still know how to set snares that entangle animals bigger than you."

"Dad said you weren't allowed to snare me anymore, remember?"

"No. I don't." Luke turned his back on his brother,

giving Carson the hint he was done with this conversation and not to push him further. He looked back as Carson headed toward the truck to greet Esme and tell her that no one was hurt. Esme looked relieved and Carson kissed her.

Darn him.

Just for a moment Luke was jealous that his brother had that. Then he saw Sarah with a knapsack walking through the snow toward him and he smiled. She had a knapsack with her. She was learning and it made his heart melt, just a bit.

Don't let her in.

"I thought you were in town?" Luke asked gruffly as she set her bag down on the roof of Carson's truck.

"I was and then an avalanche hit. Was anyone hurt?"

"No. You are safe from performing any surgical cricothyrotomies for the moment."

She smiled. "That's great news. It looked so large I thought for sure someone was going to end up injured or worse."

"That actually wasn't too big. That was a medium."

Her eyes widened. "You're joking, right?"

"I don't joke."

"Right. I forgot. You're Mr. Serious all the time."

Luke grinned. "How did you know to bring up Dr. Petersen? I didn't know you knew each other."

"I didn't know her until today. We had coffee together."

Luke's stomach twisted. *Crap.* "What did you two talk about?"

"Wouldn't you like to know?" Her smile stretched from ear to ear.

Oh, Lord.

"Dr. Ralston?"

Luke turned to see one of the rangers coming toward him. "What's wrong, Officer Kyc?"

"The avalanche's zone has extended past Nestor's place. You're the most trained individual to go out and get him. If he was ten years younger and not suffering from cancer he'd be fine up there on his own, but…"

Luke nodded. "I'll get my gear together and go get him."

"Thanks, Dr. Ralston."

"Who's Nestor?" Sarah asked.

"He's a hermit. He likes to keep to himself. He really lives off the grid, taught me everything I know about surviving on the mountain. As much as the army did, but he's getting on in age and I'm not going to leave him up there to die."

"I'll go with you."

"Are you crazy?"

Sarah glared at him. "He might be injured. How are you going to get him down yourself?"

She had a point.

Carson wasn't equipped at the moment to go with him to get Nestor. It would take him over half an hour to get back home and change. There wasn't time. Luke wanted to get to Nestor before nightfall.

"Fine. Hurry up and get changed."

Sarah nodded and headed into the hotel. Luke scrubbed a hand over his face. What was he getting into?

She's just going to help me. Nestor needs help.

That was all there was to it. They were doing their job. That was it. They would go up and get Nestor and bring him back down to the hotel until they could clear a safe path for him to get to and from town. Luke had been giving him heck since the snow started to fly that he should move to town because of his cancer treatments, but Nestor wouldn't leave the mountain.

And really he couldn't blame him.

The mountain might be a harsh, cold and hard mistress, but she stood the test of time. She was more reliable than a heart.

CHAPTER EIGHT

THE SNOWSHOE WALK up to Nestor's cabin was brutal. Sarah knew it was going to be a long haul, but she really didn't have any idea until they were trudging through the snow, roped together for protection. Just in case one of them was swept away.

It terrified her, but she wouldn't back down.

She could do this. She was doing this.

At least Luke didn't treat her as if she were incapable of helping. In fact, he was the first person in a long time who actually appreciated her help. Instead of doing stuff for her, he taught her how. He pushed her to her limits. Made her work and feel things that she'd thought were buried deep inside her.

She hadn't thought that he would let her, to be honest. She knew that he was wary about letting her accompany him, she could see that plainly on his face, but one thing she'd learned about Luke Ralston was he wasn't an idiot.

Sarah knew, just as much as he did, that it would be faster for her to get suited up and assist him than it would for his brother, Carson. She knew that she would be traversing into dangerous territory, but a life was at stake.

She wasn't going to pass up on that. That wasn't the kind of doctor she was.

So without complaint she'd strapped on the heavy rucksack laden with supplies, strapped on the snowshoes and had let Carson tie a rope between Luke and her. It was a lifeline, just in case she slipped and fell. Or just in case the snowcap decided it would crack again and sweep them away.

When she finally saw the cabin in a small clearing she let out an inward sigh of relief at the sight of it and she quickened her pace to keep up with Luke.

Luke stopped in a small copse of trees and set down his rucksack, but he didn't make a move to untie it.

"Why are we stopping?" Sarah asked, though secretly she was glad. She was in pretty good shape, but she wasn't used to the strenuous pace that Luke had kept, or to how much of a sweat she'd worked up under all her winter gear.

"We need a break. Just five minutes to catch our breath and have some water. You okay with that?"

"Perfectly." Sarah dropped her backpack next to Luke's and pulled out her canteen, taking a big swig of water.

"I'm impressed you brought a backpack," he said.

"Of course. I wouldn't have heard the end of it if I hadn't."

He chuckled. "This is true."

"So, if this Nestor guy is a hermit how do you know him? Don't hermits usually keep to themselves?"

"*Hermit* is probably the wrong word. Nestor just likes to live off the land. He's a pioneer man."

"And how do you know him?"

"He taught me everything I know about survival. I

could make up a brilliant story about how he saved my life, or something, but really it was just because my father and he were friends. I always took a real interest in what he had to say. He's like a second father to me. Since my dad moved away and my brother, Carson, started dating Dr. Petersen I've been hanging around Nestor quite a bit." Luke smiled. "He's the only one who ever believed in me when I went to the army."

"Your father didn't approve?"

Luke snorted. "Not really. He wanted me to go to the same medical school as my brother and then to train in the same hospital. My father wanted Carson and I to be partners, but that's not what I wanted. I never wanted that." Luke frowned. "Anyway, Nestor was the only one who told me to follow my dreams."

Sarah was a bit taken aback. It was the first time Luke had ever really talked, opening up warmly about someone else. She'd thought he kept everyone out. That he was cold and closed-off. But underneath that hard surface there was something more about him.

Something warm and loving.

"Is he the one who taught you how to build a log cabin?"

Luke grinned. "He is. He helped me quite a bit. He would like me to live more off the grid, but I do like some modern conveniences."

"Are you sure about that, Pa?" Sarah teased. "You did make all your furniture."

"Yeah, but I like electricity and running water too much." Luke stood up. "We'd better get going. Night falls fast, and we don't want to be trying to bring Nestor down off the mountain in the dark."

Sarah nodded. "Okay."

They packed their canteens back in their bags and headed out on their journey again. Now she understood why Luke was so concerned about getting up there to see if Nestor was okay. It wasn't just the first responder training in him. Luke *cared* about Nestor.

He was worried, and she couldn't even begin to imagine what he must be feeling.

Can't you?

Then she remembered how panicked she'd been when the avalanche had first hit and she'd thought Luke was up there in its path. That was probably nothing compared to worrying about someone who meant something to you.

Luke means something to you, though, doesn't he?

Sarah shook that thought away. There was no time to think about things like that. She had to stay focused on the task at hand. She wouldn't be the one to slow Luke down from getting to his friend in an emergency situation.

When they were at the house, they dropped their knapsacks, undid the rope and took off their snowshoes, propping them inside the lean-to.

"If you think I'm rustic, Nestor is worse," Luke said, kicking the snow off his boots. Then he pounded on the door. "Nestor, it's Ralston. There's been an avalanche."

There was no response.

Luke knocked again. "Nestor, open up."

"It's awfully dark in there and there's no smoke coming from the chimney," Sarah said.

Luke grinned. "I'm impressed you noticed that. Most people from the city don't think about a chimney or smoke from a fire. I'm going to check in the back window."

Sarah nodded while Luke put his snowshoes back on and walked to the back of the house. Sarah stood there waiting. The only sound was her breaths. There was no wind howling in the natural wind break where Nestor's cabin was nestled. There were no birds, no rustling of evergreen needles. It was deadly calm, like right before a storm.

It was a nice spot, but as she glanced through the forest she could see a wall of snow from where the avalanche had barely missed his cabin. It was at least six feet high, with broken and snapped trees everywhere.

She shuddered. It was eerie. Something was not right. She didn't know what, but she could feel it in her bones that something was wrong.

"He's gone," Luke said as he came back into the lean-to.

"You mean he's dead?"

"No, I mean there was a note that he got down before the avalanche hit. He left for Missoula two days ago for his chemo treatment."

"For a hermit who lives off the grid on the side of the mountain I'm surprised he's undertaking chemo."

Luke chuckled. "Well, that might be my doing and his son's, too. Greg came up here last summer and gave his father a stern talking-to. He tried to convince him to move to Missoula with him permanently, but he refused. They struck this bargain. Well, the rangers will be glad to hear that he's not in harm's way. Though I wish he'd checked in with them or me at least."

"So we can head back to the hotel?"

He nodded. "Yep. Sorry, I know you're a bit bushed. Though I'm glad you came, and I'm glad you came prepared and were able to keep up with me. I know I move faster on snowshoes than you're used to."

"It's no problem. I had a good teacher."

Luke's easygoing smile disappeared. "Yes...well, I'm glad you came. Had he been injured, two sets of medically trained hands would have been better than one. Especially when both sets are trained in trauma."

She had obviously made him uncomfortable, which had not been her intention. She'd meant every word she'd said about him being a good teacher. A month ago she wouldn't have had a clue what to do.

She shrugged. "It's no big deal. I'm just glad he's not injured and we don't have to drag him back down."

"Me, too. Let's go before it gets too dark."

Sarah nodded and put on her snowshoes and slung on her knapsack. Luke led the way out of the lean-to and retied the rope between them. That was when she noticed that it was getting dark. Fast. The clouds were low, thick and full of snow. She might not be native to Montana, but, after living in New York and now here, she could recognize snow clouds.

"Do you think a storm is coming?" she asked when they were through the trees back out into the clearing, following the same path they'd taken before.

Luke stopped and looked around. "Yeah, I think so, but we'll beat it."

"You sure?"

"Positive, but we..." He trailed off as he looked up the slope. She looked where he was looking and saw a crack, spreading across a huge chunk of snow.

Oh, my God.

The horror dawned on her fast, because they were right in its path.

"Throw your pack and kick off your snowshoes. Now!" Luke shouted.

Sarah's pulse thundered in her ears and she heaved her knapsack as far as she could, before kicking off her snowshoes. She sank into the deep snow as a loud crack thundered across the slope. The rumbling struck dread in her, right down to her very core, as she tried to run back to the cabin. If the cabin was buried, at least it would be some kind of shelter. Nestor had been smart and built it into the slope, but running through the snow toward salvation was like trying to move through deep sand. It was heavy and it felt as if her limbs weighed a hundred pounds.

"Remember to swim, Sarah. Swim!"

Luke was close to her. All Sarah wanted to do was cling to him, but survival instincts kicked in and as that wave of snow hit she used her arms to swim, fighting the current of snow that tried to drive her down the mountain. Her body screamed in agony as she swam, the rope between Luke and her taut. She didn't even know if he was still there.

All she had to do was keep swimming. She had to keep her head above the snow. She had to breathe.

There was a yank on her arm and she was pulled out of the torrent of snow and fell on top of Luke, who was gasping for breath. One arm tightened around her as the snow roared and thundered past them.

She buried her face in his chest and tried not to cry. She just clung to him. He was her lifeline in this moment. When the roar stopped, only then did she lift her head up and see that their path was cut off and the snow swirling around them was a storm just getting started.

She didn't know how long they had been fighting

the avalanche. It felt like hours the way her body ached. Snow had crept through every crack of her snowsuit.

"You okay?" Luke asked. There was a deep cut to his forehead, by his hairline. It was bleeding profusely.

"I'm fine," she whispered and then she got off him and stood up, her legs weak and her head spinning. "You're bleeding."

"It's a scalp laceration. I'm okay. We need to get to shelter." Luke got up and winced. "At least we have Nestor's place."

Sarah saw that they had been pushed farther down quite a bit, but at least Nestor's cabin had only been partially buried. The lean-to was uncovered and they had access to the door. It was a way inside.

"Come on," Luke said. "We'll get inside and start a fire. Once the storm dies down, they'll send for help."

Sarah nodded and then she spied the backpacks a few feet down at the edge of the pile. "Look, the backpacks made it."

"Good. The snowshoes didn't. I'll break the path. You follow."

Sarah stayed close behind Luke as he broke a path down to the backpacks. Her legs were like jelly, but the storm was getting worse and they had to seek shelter. Once they retrieved their backpacks they headed up to Nestor's cabin.

Luke managed to force the door and they were out of the wind. It was cold in the cabin, but Sarah didn't care. At least they were safe in here. It was shelter.

"Can you tape some gauze to my lac?" Luke asked.

"You'll need more than a dressing. You'll need stitches."

"I know, but first you'll need some boiling water to

clean it out and sterilize and to do that I need to start a fire. It's hard to operate with blood dripping in my eye."

"Sure." Sarah pulled out the first-aid kit and did a quick patchwork on Luke's laceration. Then she helped him bring in a lot of wood. While he started the fire in the fireplace, she grabbed a large pot and filled it with snow from outside the lean-to so they could boil it. Nestor had an old-fashioned water pump, but it was frozen.

It didn't take Luke long to get a fire started, which began to heat up the small cabin in no time. Sarah pulled out their sleeping bags from the bottom of their knapsacks.

"Zip them together," Luke said, wincing slightly.

"What?" she asked.

"Body heat in the night. Nestor only has one small bunk over there. We won't both fit and he's shorter than I am. I know I won't fit on that bunk."

Sarah nodded and zipped the bags together. "I should really take a look at that laceration. Get it cleaned and stitched up. The blood is soaking through the gauze."

Luke agreed, his face pale as he sat down in front of the fire. Sarah found an oil lamp and lit it so she could see a little bit better. She carefully peeled off the bandage and inspected the wound and his head.

"I don't feel a fracture."

"I know," he said. "It's just a laceration. I'm fine."

Sarah glared at him. "Don't play brave with me. It's a deep lac. I'm the one with the needle. I'm sorry I don't have any anesthetic. I do have some morphine for after, though."

He shook his head. "It's okay. I'm not playing brave. I've been stitched up before like this. Just do it."

"Okay. At least it won't need a lot of stitches."

He didn't say much, just looked off into the distance over her shoulder as she got ready to suture. There were a few winces, but mostly he didn't make a peep as she threw four stitches into his forehead, disinfected and then bandaged up the wound. She threw the bloody gauze into the fire and then used the antibacterial foam to clean her hands.

Luke got up and started rummaging around in Nestor's cupboards.

"What're you looking for?" she asked.

"Something to numb the pain," he said.

"I have morphine."

"Ah ha!" Luke pulled out a bottle of amber liquid. "Whiskey. Much better than morphine."

She laughed. "Much better, but won't Nestor be angry that we're rifling through his cupboards?"

"Nah, he'll know this is an emergency. I'll replace everything we have to use."

Sarah began to shiver again. "I think my socks are wet."

"Mine, too. We have to get out of these damp, cold clothes and into the sleeping bag to preserve body heat."

What?

Only she couldn't say that out loud, because her mouth dropped open and she felt a bit dumbstruck at the moment.

Luke moved past her and started to strip off his outer gear and then took off his flannel shirt, exposing his chest and back. Sarah didn't need a fire at that moment, because she realized that he was expecting her to climb naked into a double sleeping bag with him.

"I can't get naked."

He glanced around, hanging up his clothes. The only thing on him was his trousers and she couldn't help but notice how incredibly ripped and tanned Luke was under all those flannel shirts he wore. Her body was very aware that she was going to see all of him in a matter of moments and that he would see her.

She'd never undressed in front of a man before.

The last time she made love to a man, she didn't undress in front of him. It was done in dignity with the lights out and, even then, she really couldn't remember much about that encounter because, like the rest of her past romantic life, it hadn't been overly memorable.

Who says you're going to have sex?

The cabin was heating up and it wasn't just the fire.

"What's wrong? Why can't you get undressed?"

She crossed her arms. "I don't get naked in front of strange men."

"I'm not a stranger. Besides, if you don't you'll most likely get hypothermia. Okay, I'll close my eyes until you get into the sleeping bag. I swear to you, nothing untoward will happen."

"What about the extra clothes in the knapsack?" she asked. "You told me to always pack extra clothes."

"They'll be too cold and we've been exposed outside too long. This is the fastest way to get our temperature back up. Besides, we're doctors. It's not like we haven't seen naked bodies before."

Dammit.

He had a point. The only difference was, she hadn't seen him naked before and vice versa. There was a difference between seeing a patient for an exam and seeing a man you were highly attracted to, naked.

"Okay." She began to peel off her clothes and hung

them near the fire so they could dry and just as she did that Luke peeled off his pants and her breath caught in her throat at the sight of his very muscular, well-defined backside.

She tried not to look, because she didn't want him to see the blush that she knew was slowly creeping up her neck into her cheeks.

This was going to be a very long night.

CHAPTER NINE

LUKE WAS TRYING very hard to ignore the fact that in a few moments he was going to be inches away from Sarah and that she was going to be naked. He'd fantasized about having her naked in his bed before, but this was not how he'd pictured it.

When he glanced over at her, her pale cheeks were flaming red and she was looking away. He felt bad for her, so he walked across the room to Nestor's bed and wrapped a blanket around his waist. Then grabbed another quilt and walked back over to her.

"I'm respectable."

She opened her eyes and he held out the blanket. "Where did you get these?"

"Nestor's bed. Besides, the extra blankets will help keep us warm."

She nodded. "Thanks."

He moved away from her and tried not to look at her as he climbed into the sleeping bag. He poured himself a shot of whiskey and swigged it down quickly, trying to numb the pain of his throbbing head and also to try and distract himself from the fact that Sarah was undressing a few feet away from him.

How many times had he thought about this? Too

many times. His pulse was racing, his blood had heated and he was fighting to control his yearning for her.

The only trouble was being in Sarah's presence did that to him.

When he was in her presence he lost all control.

He wished he could just take her in his arms and make love to her like he desperately wanted to.

Don't think about it.

Only he couldn't help it and he stifled a groan.

"You okay?" she asked as she wrapped the blanket around her and then climbed into the sleeping bag beside him.

"My head hurts, just a bit." He didn't want to admit to her that the groan he'd been trying to get under control had nothing to do with the injury to his head.

"Well, that's to be expected. I can get the morphine."

"Stop pushing drugs on me." He winked at her and she laughed, but she still seemed nervous.

She's not the only one.

"Fine. Have another shot of whiskey, then."

"I will," Luke said and he poured her a cup, handing it to her. "First you. It'll warm you up."

"Thanks." She took a sip. "That does help."

He nodded. "I told you it would. You did really good out there today."

"You taught me well." She took another sip of whiskey. "You told me to swim and I did, but that…"

"I know. When that avalanche hit us and I started to swim, it was powerful. More powerful than any current I've swam in, in water. Being in that avalanche was like nothing I've ever felt before. I'm glad we weren't swept away down the side of the mountain. It was a minor one."

"That was minor? I thought you'd experienced an avalanche before?"

"I've seen them, I've helped those injured, but never have I experienced almost being swept away by one."

"At least we weren't trapped." Sarah shivered; he could hear her teeth chattering. So he moved closer, wrapping his arm around her. His blood pounding between his ears, because he was touching her.

You're just keeping her warm. That's all.

Her breath hitched in her throat the moment he pulled her close. Her skin was so soft, the flowery scent of her silken, blond hair surrounding him and he wanted to pull it out of the braid she'd put it in and run his fingers through it.

"No, we weren't trapped. That's a good thing." Only right now in this cabin they were trapped by the storm. Being here with her, with nothing between them, was more dangerous to him than being trapped in that snowstorm.

He was nervous, but he couldn't pull himself away.

You're just warming her, he told himself again.

"That feels good," she whispered.

"What does?" he asked.

"Your arm around me." Then she moved in closer to him and touched his face. Her fingers lightly brushing over his skin, which made him feel as if he were on fire. Her lips so close to his. Then her fingers touched his lips and he closed his eyes, trying to regain control of his senses, but before he could maintain that control, before he could stop what was happening her lips pressed against his in a feather-light kiss. He tried not to cup her face and drag her tight against his body, as he wanted to. He'd forgotten what a woman's kiss felt like.

He'd forgotten what passion tasted like. It had been far too long and he was caught off guard by it. It rocked him to his very core and he didn't want it to end. He wanted more.

Oh, God.

Luke needed to put an end to this before he got carried away and forgot himself. Before he forgot why he distanced himself from women, about why he distanced himself from her.

"Why did you do that?" he asked.

"I wanted to. I've wanted to for some time." Her blue eyes sparkled in the dim flickering light thrown from the fire. "I want to kiss you again, Luke."

"I don't think that's wise," he said, though his body screamed yes, yes, yes.

"I don't think it's particularly wise either," she whispered, but then her hands ran through his hair and she was kissing him urgently.

He should push her away, but the moment she sighed and melted against him he was a lost man.

He was completely lost to her.

Luke undid the braid in her hair and gently ran his fingers through it. It was as soft as he'd imagined. Like silk. It fanned over her bare shoulder and he couldn't help but brush it away. Ever since he'd first met her, he'd dreamed of touching her skin, her hair, and now he was.

He'd forgotten what it was like.

Christine had hurt him so bad with her betrayal and he'd buried these feelings deep inside. He didn't ever want to feel like that again, but in this moment he was reveling in being with Sarah and he was worried that if he indulged then he wouldn't ever be able to stop.

That he'd want more.

And he couldn't have more.

He wouldn't put his heart at risk again. When Christine left him, he'd promised himself he wouldn't let another woman affect him like that. Love just brought pain.

Who said anything about love?

He moved away. He couldn't do this even though he desperately wanted to.

"What's wrong?" Sarah asked.

"I don't know if we should be doing this."

"Doing what?" she asked.

"Kissing."

"I think we should be." Sarah touched his face again and then kissed him. "I don't think we should stop."

"Sarah, I can't promise you anything."

She smiled at him. "I'm not asking for promises. I just want you. Here and now."

"I want you, too. I can't help myself, but I do."

And it was true. When it came to Sarah, he couldn't help himself.

Sarah wasn't sure what made her reach out and kiss Luke. It wasn't the whiskey, that was for certain. She could hold her drink better than most. No, she was sure it was due to the fact that moments ago she'd almost died.

Working in the ER Sarah had seen countless people face death, sometimes because of the simplest reasons, like a reaction to a medication or food and sometimes because of something more complicated that damaged their body. She'd wrestled with death in the OR, saving patients while she operated on them and, though they could never remember that moment when they came so close to losing the battle because they'd been under general anesthesia, she always wondered what it might be like.

Did they feel anything?

Did they see their life flash before their eyes, even in a dreamless sleep?

Did they understand how close they came and how hard they fought, how hard she fought for them? Overcoming death for her patients was a high. The lives she saved meant more to her than all the money her parents had.

It was why she did what she did.

So when her moment came it was surreal. When the snow came roaring down the hill toward her, there was a clarity.

Live or die.

And she chose life. She fought hard. She swam and when she came through it, it hit her how many chances she'd passed on. Not when it came to her career, but her life. She'd been fighting her whole life to prove to her parents she was her own person, to the point that she didn't know when to stop fighting. Maybe life didn't always have to be such a fight? Maybe she hadn't really been living her life, because she was so busy trying to show everyone that she was capable of doing things on her own that life was passing her by. She wasn't even sure anymore.

When she thought she had been living her own life, she hadn't. Her father had made that painfully clear. She'd spent so long building up walls that now she wanted Luke on the other side with her.

She wanted to live her life. Take chances, take risks, because even though that avalanche had been the most terrifying thing she'd ever experienced, surviving after the fact was equally scary.

Right now, in this moment with Luke, she just wanted to feel. She chose this and she wanted it.

Really she shouldn't but she couldn't fight it anymore. She wanted Luke as she'd never wanted another man before. It was something fierce. Primal, even. It scared her and thrilled her.

She wanted to feel again.

"Sarah, I'll ask again. Are you sure?"

"I'm sure."

Luke rolled over, pressing her against the floor and laying kisses against her lips, her neck and lower. He brushed his knuckles down the side of her face and kissed where her pulse raced under her skin.

"You make me feel," he whispered. Then he leaned down and brushed another kiss against her lips, light and then urgent. His body was pressed against hers. It made her feel right and she loosened the extra blanket he'd given her so they could be skin to skin. She opened her legs to let him settle between her thighs. Sarah arched her hips. She wanted him.

She craved him.

"I have to stop," Luke moaned.

"Why?"

"I don't have protection. One thing I didn't pack for."

Sarah grinned. "It's okay. I'm on birth control and I'm clean."

"So am I. Are you sure you want to, though?"

"Yes. I want to. The question is do you want me?" She bucked her hips and he groaned.

"Oh, I want you."

"How much?"

Luke kissed her again, his tongue pushing past her lips, entwining with hers, showing her just how much he wanted her.

"I want you so much." He ran his hands over her body, his hands hot, branding her skin as he touched her.

"I've tried hard to resist you," Sarah whispered against his neck. "You drive me crazy."

He grinned. "I want you, too, Sarah."

Luke's lips captured hers in a kiss, silencing any more words between them. Sarah pulled him closer and wrapped her legs against his waist. His hands slipped down her sides.

"So beautiful," he murmured.

His hand slid between them and he began to stroke her. Sarah bit her lip to stop from crying out. She wanted so much more. She wanted Luke inside her. She wanted him to take her and make her feel again.

Sarah wanted Luke to remind her of who she was, because she couldn't remember. She just wanted to forget it all and get lost in this one moment with him.

"I love having you under me," Luke whispered against her neck. "I want to be inside you."

"I want you, too."

He pushed her down, covering her body with his and thrusting into her. Sarah cried out then. She couldn't help herself. Being joined with him was overwhelming, but it was what she wanted. It was what she needed.

"You feel so good," he moaned. "Damn."

She moved her hips, urging him to move, but he wouldn't. He just held her still, buried deep inside her.

"You're evil," she gasped.

"I know."

Luke moved slowly at first, taking his time, and it drove her crazy. She wanted him hard and fast. She wanted to feel him moving inside her. She urged him to go faster until he lost all control and was thrusting against her hard and fast. Then she could feel her body succumbing to the sweet release she was searching for. Pleasure overtook her and she cried out again, digging her nails into his back, making him hiss in pain, but it didn't stop him. He kept going until his own release came a moment later.

He rolled away onto his back and she curled up on his chest, just listening to his heart race. It was soothing and reassuring. She'd always liked the sound of the heart. It meant life. Then tears started to roll down her face.

"Sarah, are you okay?"

She sat up, trying to brush the tears away. "I'm fine."

"Do you regret what happened?"

"No," she said quickly. "No. I wanted that to happen. What happened here tonight was a long time coming. It's just...we could've died today."

He smiled softly. "But we didn't."

"I know. You know, it was in that moment on the slope that I couldn't recall if the life I've been living has been my own."

Luke's brow furrowed. "How do you mean?"

"Everything I've accomplished is because my father has had a hand in it."

"What?"

"You want to know why I came here? I came here because my father got my last job for me. Just like every other job. So I came here, without his help. I'm tired of being labelled as his helpless daughter."

Luke nodded. "Stepping out of a parent's shadow can be hard. And you're far from helpless."

Sarah sighed. "I'm not sure if I know myself anymore."

"I understand that."

She frowned. "Do you? You're living out your dream here."

Luke shrugged. "I love the mountains, but it wasn't my dream to be a lone wolf. I was married before."

"You were?"

He nodded. "She left me for my best friend while I was overseas."

"No wonder you have trust issues."

"Yeah. I suppose I do."

Luke turned from her, withdrawing from her once more. But for a moment she had seen a little piece of himself that he kept hidden from the world.

Sarah had been absolutely shocked to learn that he'd been married before. He just didn't seem the type to settle down with a wife, and she couldn't help but wonder what he'd been like before he'd become this walled-off man.

And no wonder, when his wife had left him for his best friend. Two people he'd trusted completely had betrayed him.

It explained so much, but Sarah had a feeling there was more to it than that. There was something else he wasn't saying.

"It's hard to trust when you trust no one."

Luke turned back around. "What?"

"At least you have a family to turn to. I don't. I can't rely on my parents."

"Why?"

"They were never around."

"I'm sorry."

Sarah shrugged. "My mother preferred the company of her friends over her children and my dad was too involved with his businesses. Money drives him."

"Must've been a lonely childhood."

She nodded. The words, though the truth, stung. Her whole life had been lonely up until now. She had just never realized it.

How could she trust a man who guarded his heart so? He'd never open up fully. His ex-wife had hurt him terribly, and in the short time Sarah had known him she'd learned that he didn't give people a second chance.

He was stubborn that way.

Which was a shame.

"It was. I sometimes felt invisible," she said. She hadn't intended to say that thought out loud, but she had.

He moved toward her and touched her face briefly "I get not knowing who you are anymore. I get it, but I want you to know. I see you."

She wanted to believe him. She really did, but she didn't think anyone could see her, especially when she couldn't even see herself. So long she'd been under her family's thumb, she didn't even know it. How could she believe him, when she couldn't even believe in herself?

"You don't believe me," Luke said.

"What?"

"Your expression. I can read you like a book."

She glared at him. "Thanks."

"It's something I've learned to do as an army medic."

"Why did you leave the army?"

His demeanor changed almost instantly. "What?"

"What made you change your mind about the army?"

"I thought I had a wife waiting for me."

"I'm sorry."

Luke shrugged and then unzipped his side of the sleeping bag. "Are you hungry?"

"Sure." She watched him as he dug in his knapsack for his dry pair of pants and slipped them on. "Hey, I thought you said we shouldn't wear our extra clothes?"

He grinned. "That was when we were still damp and cold. I bet you're warm now."

She blushed and then grabbed her knapsack, pulling out the dry set of clothes and pulling on the pants, shirt and socks. There was a definite draught on the floor. She got up and padded toward the window. It was dark, but that was about all she knew. She couldn't see a thing. All she could hear was the howling from the wind.

"Still storming?" Luke asked as he pulled down some cans from Nestor's cupboard and set them down on the counter.

"It looks that way. How long do you think it will last?"

Luke shrugged. "I don't know. Probably not that long. Usually when a bad blizzard is about to whip up, they warn us. The only warning I heard for today was a squall."

"I think that's more than a squall out there."

Luke nodded. "Nestor has beans. I hope you don't mind."

"Yes. I totally mind." She walked over to him. "I don't think those hearts will survive."

"What?" he asked as she rifled through drawers.

"I was in town and they were decorating for Valentine's Day."

Luke snorted. "Of course. They're probably going overboard, too, because of the big party that's going to happen on Valentine's Day at the hotel. Just the idea of the town covered in all that paraphernalia makes me a bit queasy."

"Well, the resident party planners have been working around the clock since I arrived in Crater Lake. I think it's going to be a big party."

Luke snorted again. "Pointless."

"Why?"

"Darn it, do you think Nestor could keep things in a logical spot?" Luke cursed again and bent down to rummage under the counter.

Sarah rolled her eyes. There was no getting through to him. At least not about this or why he left the army. His ex-wife really did a number on him and she felt bad that he'd been hurt. He'd been betrayed by the woman he loved and she'd been betrayed by her parents in a way.

Though really it wasn't the same thing.

They were both damaged souls and she hadn't made any promise to him, just as he had never made any to her. She didn't regret what had happened between them here tonight. She was glad it had happened.

Even if it could never happen again, because she couldn't let it happen again. Luke was her friend and she wouldn't hurt him the way his ex-wife had hurt him and she doubted very much Luke would even let her in if she tried.

His heart was guarded, just as much as she had her own walls of protection up. At least he'd let her in just briefly, even for a moment.

It was better they remained friends. Just friends and coworkers. That was all they could be, but that made her sad and for one brief moment she wished for something more.

CHAPTER TEN

AFTER THEY HAD something to eat they curled up together by the fire to spend the night and even though Luke wanted something to happen again, he wouldn't allow it. If it were warmer in Nestor's cabin he would've had her sleep on Nestor's bunk and he would've stayed on the floor.

Sarah fell asleep almost instantly after they had something to eat, but Luke couldn't sleep. Which ticked him off. If the storm subsided they were going to have to hike out of here. He knew that Nestor had snowshoes and skis in the lean-to, but in order to hike back down to the resort he would need his energy and that required sleep.

Especially after the strenuous activity that they'd engaged in a couple hours ago.

Don't think about it.

He didn't want to let Sarah in and risk his heart. The trouble was, she was already digging her way in there. He couldn't fall in love again. It was too much of a risk.

And living up on a mountain tracking bears and rescuing stranded people isn't?

What if Sarah decided to head back to New York?

What if she wanted him to give up his life here and when he couldn't she'd leave him?

He wouldn't be hurt again. He wouldn't put his heart in that kind of danger again. It wasn't worth it. It was pointless.

Luke cursed under his breath and slowly climbed out of the sleeping bag, making sure that he didn't disturb Sarah. He wandered over to the window and peered outside. The snowstorm was beginning to subside. He could see black instead of just a wall of white.

He glanced back over at her, sleeping so peacefully, her blond hair fanned out around her head, and he desperately wanted to go back and join her. If he'd been in a different place.

If he'd never married Christine.

When Christine had left it hurt, but it also relieved him because he was beginning to see that they weren't meant for each other.

It was a clean break.

Still, it hurt. The betrayal stung.

Trust was not something he gave easily or freely.

So yeah, risking his life on the mountain was not playing it safe, but the only one who was affected by the choices he made was him. There was no wife to think about. No kids. He was free.

Really?

He sighed. Yeah, he was free, but the cost of his freedom was loneliness. He hadn't realized how lonely he had been until Sarah ended up in Crater Lake. When he'd started working with her, he'd been dreading it at first, because all he'd remembered was the surgeon from the summer. The one who'd rankled him and had fire in her eyes.

This Sarah was different from that surgeon from the summer.

She still was a spitfire, but something had changed in her.

The fire was diminished. He shouldn't really care why, but he did. And he discovered that he looked forward to all their training sessions. Although, she didn't know that those sessions weren't Silas Draven's idea, but his.

At first he was supposed to show her a bit of emergency first aid and tell her about some of the common injuries that could occur on the mountain, especially injuries that would happen to guests, but, after taking her out that first time and seeing how she threw herself into everything she did, he wanted to show her more.

And he soon found that he liked spending the time with her. Which was bad, because the more time he spent with her, the more his walls came down and he didn't like that.

Those walls were there for a reason. Those walls protected him.

Those walls would protect her.

He didn't want to stop being a first responder. He didn't want to stop doing what he was doing, because it mattered and because of that he wouldn't leave a widow or children behind. A life of solitude was the only answer.

It was the only way. That way no one got hurt.

I need to put some distance between us.

As soon as they were back at the resort, Luke was going to sever ties with Sarah for a while. She'd move on and find someone else. He had no doubt. She was beautiful, kind, funny. Of course, thinking about someone else kissing her made him angry.

She can't be yours.

And he had to keep reminding himself of that fact. The squalling stopped, almost as suddenly as it had started, which was good. He just hoped another system wasn't about to start up again. He didn't want to eat all of Nestor's rations.

Just as he was about to turn away, he saw lights coming up off the trail. Several lights and he realized they were snowmobiles.

"Sarah, wake up!" he shouted.

She bolted upright. "What's wrong?"

"Our rescue team has arrived."

She was confused. "What?"

"The squall ended and there's a pack of snowmobiles headed this way."

She got up and ran over to the window. "Oh, thank goodness. At least we don't have to hike down the mountain tomorrow. I'll start packing up."

Luke nodded and then grabbed his dry flannel shirt, quickly pulling it on as well as his socks and boots. If he didn't know any better, his brother or Esme would be on one of those snowmobiles and he wasn't going to have them catch him half-naked in a cabin with Sarah. He wasn't going to be subjected to their constant questioning for the next few weeks.

As soon as his boots were on there was a knock at the door.

"Luke?"

It was Carson. Luke opened the door and his brother let out a sigh of relief and pulled him into a bear hug.

"You're freezing and I just got warm. Get in here."

The rescue team shuffled into the small entrance way of Nestor's cabin. Carson and two other first responders had come up the mountain.

"We were about to call off the search," Carson said. "Then I saw smoke coming from Nestor's cabin. We found out about twenty minutes after you and Sarah left that Nestor was in Missoula with his family getting chemotherapy. And then the avalanche. I'm glad you're okay. I'm glad you're both okay."

"Yeah, we learned he was gone when we got here. We were heading back when the avalanche struck, but we got out of it."

"We swam," Sarah said.

Carson and the first responders looked at her in shock. "You swam? You mean you were hit by the avalanche?"

"Yeah, but it was minor. Then the squall hit, so we got back to Nestor's and broke in. I owe him some provisions and some firewood."

"I don't think he'll mind," Carson said. "We should get back down the mountain before another squall hits. Last check on radar was another one was brewing to the northwest of here."

Luke nodded. "We'll pack our things and get our gear on."

Carson and the other two men stepped outside into the lean-to.

Sarah was shoving the last of her things into her knapsack. The zipped-together bags were undone and the blankets had been folded and put back on Nestor's bed. It was as if what had happened between them had been swept away.

It's for the best.

"I'll be glad to get back to my own bed. Maybe even a hot shower," she remarked as she zipped up her coat.

"Yeah. Me, too." Which was a lie. Even though he knew it was for the best this was happening, deep down he secretly wished he could spend the night with her, but he shook that thought away as he finished packing his things and putting out the fire.

Sarah was already outside, by the time the fire had been extinguished and the oil lamp turned off. The cabin was so dark and lonely. The small window panes illuminated by the headlights from the snowmobiles.

He wished they could stay, just for a bit longer, but this was better.

Luke was getting the distance he needed from her.

And if he did that, he would have a chance for his walls to rebuild.

Yeah. Right.

It was the fastest ride she'd ever been on. One of the responders, named Lee, had said that there was another squall brewing and they were trying to beat it back to the resort.

Sarah didn't care at that moment. All she wanted to do was get back to her bed, electricity and a hot shower. She didn't want to be stuck in another squall, in a shack and eating beans. Although, the company was fine.

She didn't mind that in the least.

Luke was on the snowmobile with his brother and Sarah wished that he were driving one of the machines and that she were riding with him.

Something had changed up there and she didn't know what it was, other than he was more closed off than

before. He barely looked her in the eye and it fright-
ened her.

*Who cares? You both were consenting adults and
didn't make any promises.*

Only, when it was all over with, she found herself
craving more. She wanted him again, but that was not
possible. If she took up with Luke, her mother would be
somewhat happy that she'd found a doctor to settle down
with, but then her father would say to her again that
she couldn't handle the job in Crater Lake on her own.

*You try too hard, pumpkin. You don't need to try
so hard.*

She hated when her father talked down to her like
that. As if she were still four years old. She was the baby
and therefore couldn't make it on her own.

As much as she wanted to be with Luke, maybe a
little distance was a good thing. Besides, he wasn't telling her something. There was some hurt still buried
there. How could she trust him if he couldn't trust her?

He didn't seem to take much stock in love. As was
evident by his hatred for Valentine's Day and intimacy.

She didn't understand why he felt this way, other
than his failed marriage, but there had to be something
more to it than that. How could someone have so much
hate for an emotion that also brought joy? Yeah, love
did hurt, but in the end wasn't it worth it?

Of course, she wouldn't know anything about love.

She'd never been in it. She'd had crushes or relationships, but love? That was something she'd never
experienced. It was scary and messy. She just didn't
have time for it.

Why not?

She shook that thought from her head as the snowmobiles slowed down and came to a stop in front of the hotel. Sarah's legs were shaking, but she held her ground and walked toward the entranceway.

There were still people milling around from earlier, but she didn't linger. She just wanted to get back to her room and forget about what had happened between Luke and her.

"Sarah!"

She turned and Luke was headed toward her.

Just say good-night. Turn around and walk away.

Only she couldn't. She was so weak.

"Yeah?" she asked.

"Thank you for stitching up my head."

She nodded. "You should get that checked out later by Carson. Try not to get it wet. You probably know the drill when it comes to stitches."

He smiled. "I do, but thanks."

Turn around. Walk away.

"Will I see you tomorrow?"

You fool.

"Probably not. I have to get back up to Nestor's place and restock some stuff. I actually might rest for a couple of days."

"Of course. Take it easy and thanks for saving my life up there."

"I didn't save your life. You saved your own."

"If you hadn't shown me, I wouldn't have known what to do."

"If I hadn't shown you, you would've never been allowed to come up there with me," Luke said, and she realized his tone had changed. "You shouldn't have been up there with me."

"What are you talking about?" Sarah asked, confused. She'd thought he was happy that she'd gone up the mountain with him. He'd said so. What had changed? Why did he look so guilt-ridden?

Luke grabbed her by the arms, giving her a little shake. "You could've died in that avalanche."

"You could've, too."

He shook his head. "You could've died and it would've been my fault. I couldn't have borne that."

"I wanted to go with you."

Luke pushed her away and cursed under his breath. But she wasn't going to let him run away so she stood in front of him, blocking his path.

"I wanted to go with you," she stated again. "You said you were glad I was up there. You were glad to have the extra set of medically trained hands. You didn't force me up that mountain. It was my choice. Just like you couldn't have forced me down the mountain. You wanted me up there and I wanted to be there."

"What I wanted doesn't matter. It doesn't matter when it comes to your life. I won't be responsible for that."

And before she could say anything else to him he turned and walked away. She wanted to go after him, but she recognized that look.

He was going to retreat back up into the mountains. When he was ready, she'd see him again, but only when she was ready.

Right now, she wasn't ready to see him for a long time.

CHAPTER ELEVEN

SARAH HADN'T SEEN Luke in the week since they had spent the night together up in the cabin caught between a snowstorm and an avalanche. She'd been expecting it. Any time she got too close to Luke, he hid in the forest for a while.

It was the same with her.

Only she hid in her clinic.

She didn't regret what had happened between them. She'd wanted it. And she'd meant what she'd said about not promising anything to him. It had been only about the moment that night.

Only now she missed him and she wished they'd promised each other that it wouldn't be weird after. That they could still be friends. And she wished he didn't feel so guilty about putting her into a dangerous situation. It had been her choice. He had nothing to feel guilty about, but there had been no telling him that.

She'd gotten so used to him being around, his absence made her heart ache. Loneliness had never bothered her before, until now.

Though she didn't have much time to dwell on it. The hotel was busier than ever. As Valentine's Day and its grand opening approached more and more guests were coming to Crater Lake. Including a lot of wealthy A-listers. The population of Crater Lake went from just under six hundred people to more than a thousand overnight.

And it wasn't just Silas Draven's hotel that was selling out.

All the guest accommodations in town were full. Even privately owned rental cabins, which had never been rented during the winter season before, were full. Crater Lake was turning into a winter hotspot.

Sarah had been go, go, go since she came down off the mountain. Her clinic was busy with superficial stuff, stomach bugs and someone requesting a bikini wax and Botox, which she didn't do and promptly sent them to the on-site spa. She hadn't a moment to think for herself. So when she finally did get a break she headed to town to grab a cup of coffee and some peace and quiet.

As she walked down the street she spotted Esme in a stationery store and headed in to visit her. Esme was standing beside a large rack of Valentine's Day cards, mumbling to herself and frowning.

"You look like you're going to be sick," Sarah teased, coming up behind her.

"Oh, hey!" Esme laughed then. "I might. Did I mention that I hate Valentine's Day?"

"Yes. You mentioned something about that the first time we met. If you hate it so much, then why are you standing here in a shop that's overflowing with abomination?"

"Because my boyfriend likes Valentine's Day." She wrinkled her nose. "So I thought I would be nice and get him a card that I can shove in his face when he forces me to go to that Valentine's ball gala thing next week and makes me dress up like a princess or something very fluffy."

Sarah chuckled. "Not really romantic to shove something in someone's face and dressing up can be fun."

Esme grinned. "It depends on the dressing up, though."

"I don't know you well enough to talk about that." And they both laughed.

"He knows how much I hate it. He bought tickets just to annoy me." Esme pulled out a card. "This one is perfect. What do you think?"

The card in question had a large chimpanzee on it, making a kiss face. There was also faux fur glued to the outside. It was tacky and hideous, but Esme seemed so pleased with her find.

"That's an interesting choice. What does it say?"

"It says 'It's no monkey business, because I'm bananas for you.'" Esme grinned. "Yes, this is the one."

"That's a terrible card," Sarah said between chuckles. "It makes me cringe. Besides, that's clearly a chimpanzee and not a monkey, so really it's false advertising."

"Which is why it's so perfect. So, how are things with you?" Esme winked and Sarah groaned inwardly. What had she learned? Did Luke say anything and if so what did he say?

Just play it cool. Pretend as if nothing happened.

"I'm good."

"Good, huh? I hear your clinic has been busy."

"It has. More and more guests are arriving every day. A lot of big names."

Esme's expression hardened. "Hollywood A-listers?"

"Yeah, why?"

Esme sighed. "I used to run in that crowd before I came here. It's not my favorite crowd. You know I was engaged to Dr. Draven's son."

"No. I didn't. Wait, you were engaged to Shane Draven? When?"

"A couple of years ago. I ended it and I fell out of grace with that group of people. I don't miss it at all."

Sarah nodded. She didn't miss the glitterati of Manhattan or the so-called friends she'd made in the circles of society her parents traveled in, because once you weren't in that circle anymore you became a ghost. Just a memory that was briefly touched upon during lulls in conversation.

"I couldn't agree more." Sarah picked up a card with a red heart. One thing she did miss about this time of year was when they would light up the Empire State Building with pink or red, sometimes even a heart.

"Have you seen the other Dr. Ralston lately?" Esme asked.

"Luke?"

"Yeah." There was a twinkle in her eye.

"Why?"

"No reason. I didn't mean to put you on the defensive. Carson told me what happened up there."

Sarah groaned. "Oh, he did?"

"Yeah. I can't even begin to imagine being caught in an avalanche. You were so lucky that you weren't swept away. Why, Glacier National Park had several avalanche-related deaths last year. It's scary. I never really thought about snow as a threat."

"You wouldn't—you come from California."

"I'm actually from Ohio originally. I have a respect for winter, but never seen an avalanche. Heck, until last summer I'd never really seen a landslide and apparently there's a dormant volcano around here."

Sarah laughed. "Guess we really did move to a danger zone."

Esme shrugged. "It's beautiful here, though. I love my life here. I wouldn't change it for anything."

Sarah nodded. "Well, I better head back to the hotel. I only had a small break and I'm sure there's another group of people wanting me to laser off their hair or inject them with silicone or something."

"I hope you're kidding?"

"I wish I was. Why they come to me instead of heading to the spa I can't understand."

She missed being a surgeon. She loved living in Crater Lake and the opportunity to work in Silas Draven's hotel was fantastic, but she missed the ER. For the first time in a long time, she actually missed the hustle and bustle of the ER.

She hadn't thought that she would when she'd first left active trauma surgery, when she'd taken on that job and started touring the country and training doctors. Despite what her father had done, she'd really enjoyed the travel and connections she'd made working with some of the finest surgeons in the world.

Returning back to the ER as a trauma surgeon had seemed like a step back, but now she realized that really this job was a step back. The only thing that really excited her was working with Luke. The bear mauling, the birth, even operating on Shane Draven last summer, all of those instances when she was called in to help in an emergency situation were when she felt like herself.

When she felt free.

And she missed it; she just hadn't realized how much she had until now. She'd leave, but she had a contract to fulfill and she wouldn't back down. She finished things she started. On the other hand she didn't want to leave Crater Lake.

She didn't want to leave Luke.

"Well," Sarah said. "It was nice to see you again, but I have to head back."

Esme nodded and then reached out and squeezed her arm. "It was nice talking with you, too. Will I see you at the Valentine's ball?"

"Yes. I have to go. Silas Draven's orders. I would skip it since I have no one to go with and I'll probably be too busy the next day dealing with hangovers. It would be nice to get the extra sleep."

They both laughed at that. Sarah waved goodbye and headed back in the cold. If she could only remain in Crater Lake, but as an independent doctor, then she wouldn't mind that too much, but how many doctors did a small town need?

If she wanted to return to surgery, she'd have to leave Crater Lake.

It was as simple as that, but she might be persuaded to stay if Luke wanted her to. Even though that was very unlikely.

Luke was not ready for love and she doubted he would ever be.

She couldn't put her career on hold on the off chance Luke might want her. That was no way to live a life, so, as much as she hated the thought, once her year was up at Crater Lake she was going to find a hospital and go back to her first love of trauma surgery.

Even if it meant breaking her own heart in the process.

Then she thought of that painting he loved. The watercolor she'd done of the horse on the plains. She'd told him to take it, but he hadn't. Maybe she could give that to him as a peace offering.

If they couldn't be anything else, she wanted them to be friends. When she got back to the hotel she grabbed the painting and scrawled *For Adele* on the back before slipping it into an envelope.

Then she headed back to her clinic.

When she arrived she was surprised to find Luke pacing outside her office. The sight of him made her pulse quicken and she could recall every kiss of his lips on her skin, the weight of his body on her and the warmth. It had been over a week since she'd seen him, but looking at him now it felt as if it were just yesterday and that moment in the cabin came flooding back to her.

She both hated and loved the effect he had on her, but she was glad he was here. She'd missed him.

The only telltale sign that time had passed was that he'd had the stitches removed, but the gash had healed nicely, only leaving a small red mark barely visible at his hairline.

"Luke, what a surprise." And she held out the envelope ready to give it to him, but he didn't look at her.

"Where were you?" he snapped.

"In town. It was my morning off."

"I thought you would be here." He was clearly agitated.

"I'm here now. What're you so worked up about?"

Luke didn't say anything; he opened her clinic door, which she'd thought was locked, and dragged her inside, shutting the door behind them and locking it.

"What is up with you?" She tried to touch his laceration. "Do you want me to check your head?"

He grabbed her hand by the wrist and stopped her, shocking her, and then he let go of her hand, but didn't offer up an apology.

"It's not me," he said. "It's Nestor."

"Nestor?" She understood why he was so upset.

He's like a second father to me.

"Where is he? I'll see him right away."

Luke nodded and took her to one of the exam rooms, where Nestor was lying on a bed, pale and barely moving, cocooned in blankets. You could see the effects of chemotherapy. His face was gaunt, yellowish and there wasn't a hair on his face or head.

"What happened?" Sarah asked, setting the envelope down on the counter.

"I found him in a snowbank when I went up to cut some more wood for him. I don't know how long he's been out there. It's hypothermia—I think it's moderate. I knew I had to get him here. I would have administered warm IV fluids, but the cabinet is locked."

Sarah didn't question the fact he'd broken into her clinic and tried to break into her medicine cabinet. He was trying to save his friend's life. There was no time for arguments as she tossed Luke the key from her pocket.

"Not lactated Ringer's. With the chemo I don't know

how well his liver is functioning and if he has hypothermia his liver might not be able to metabolize the lactate."

"I know," Luke called over his shoulder.

Sarah pulled out her stethoscope and the moment she touched him, he was cold, but, as she was taught in medical school, the patient was not dead until he was warm and dead. His temperature when she took it was twenty seven. Which was another reason she didn't want lactated Ringer's solution. He was too cold. He was heading toward profound hypothermia.

She tried to listen to the heart, but couldn't hear anything.

"Asystole!" Sarah shouted, then she felt the carotid artery; there was a faint thready pulse. "No, there's a pulse."

The heart was moving, but barely.

Luke came running back with bags of warmed IV fluid. "There's a pulse?"

"It's weak, so no CPR. Let's get the warm bolus into him."

Luke set up the IV and she grabbed warmers. Right now the most important thing was to heat his core; limbs could wait. The best way though to warm up a body that was this cold was cardiopulmonary bypass, but she was not equipped to do that here. Esme might be in town, but Nestor was here and they couldn't move him.

They could lose him if they took him out.

Hopefully the warmed IV would help, but given the state of Nestor's body, which had been ravaged by the chemotherapy, he didn't have much of a shot.

"Come on, Nestor," Luke whispered to the old man.

"Come on. You're not going to go out like this. You said you wanted to go out riding a bear like a horse off the side of a cliff. This is not the way to go."

Sarah's heart broke as she watched Luke gingerly touch the old man's face. She knew Nestor was important to Luke, because Nestor had taught him how to survive in the mountains. It pained Sarah to see Luke like this, but there was not a lot she could do here with severe hypothermia.

Watching Luke beg his friend to keep fighting brought tears to her eyes. Here, in this moment, Luke was so raw, so real.

This was the genuine Luke Ralston. Not the lone wolf everyone else saw. This tender, concerned Luke, begging the man he admired so much to hang on, was the man she longed to know.

The man who could feel.

The man who could teach her how to feel.

As she watched the two of them she knew that she didn't have that kind of parent-child relationship with her parents and probably never would.

It made her sad to watch Luke suffer so much. She didn't have the heart to tell him that Nestor might not make it. Though she probably didn't have to tell him that. He probably already knew.

"Did you call the air ambulance?" Sarah asked.

"I did, but we have to warm him up before we can get him out to meet the ambulance."

She nodded, but didn't say anything.

When a patient's core temperatures were below thirty, they required to be rewarmed internally through cardiopulmonary bypass, gastric lavage and other means. Ways that Sarah couldn't provide for him in this private clinic.

Usually people that severe were taken straight to the hospital where aggressive rewarming could start instantly. All they could do with what she had was blankets, heaters and the IV. She took Nestor's temperature again, but it was dropping fast.

She knew what was going to happen next. His heart would stop completely and if they rewarmed him too fast, his heart could collapse, but she couldn't use CPR to keep the brain alive until after he was asystole.

"What's his temperature?"

Sarah sighed. "Twenty-five. Luke, the lowest someone has come back from such a severe hypothermia is thirteen point seven."

"He'll make it."

She listened for cardiac activity, but there was none that she could make out. She felt for the carotid artery and the pulse was gone. He wasn't warm enough to start CPR, but she had no choice.

"Starting CPR. Get the AED."

Luke nodded as she began CPR.

Come on, Nestor. Don't die here. Don't die on me.

Luke got the AED ready and Sarah stopped CPR while Luke shocked Nestor. There was no response. Sarah continued with the CPR and they alternated.

"Nestor, come on," Luke urged.

When she looked at the clock, she could see that they'd been doing CPR for far too long. The ambulance had still not arrived.

"Take his temperature," Sarah said as she continued CPR.

"Dammit, it's fourteen."

Come on, Nestor.

"I can't pronounce him but..."

"Don't say it," Luke begged. "Don't. People survive hypothermia all the time. Cancer kills, but hypothermia can be cured."

Sarah sighed, and continued, but there wasn't much hope. Luke turned his back on the scene. His fists clenched as she worked on. He obviously couldn't stand to watch his friend slip away.

She didn't have any hope...and then Nestor's heart came back under her hand and he groaned, before coughing.

"Oh, my God," she whispered.

Nestor opened one eye, groaned, and passed out again. But the point was, he was alive.

"What?" Luke asked, then leaned over. His eyes widened in shock. "You got him back?"

Sarah had never brought back a person with such severe hypothermia, with a body already so weakened by chemo, from the brink of death. Tears of joy stung her eyes and she laughed out loud because she couldn't contain herself.

Luke smiled at her briefly before turning back to his friend.

She was so relieved. She hadn't wanted to be the one responsible for not saving Nestor's life. She hadn't wanted to hurt Luke like that, and she hadn't wanted him to be reminded of Nestor's death every time he saw her.

She didn't want Luke to remember her like that.

"You brought him back," Luke said, stunned. "I've never seen that."

"I've never done it in this situation before. And especially not outside a hospital."

"I can't believe you did it."

Nestor was still unconscious, but he was stable, and when she took a temperature again it was rising. He had a good shot at making it now.

The paramedics came then and took over, Sarah gave an update about Nestor's temperature and how long he'd been down. They were going to take Nestor to the hospital and continue to warm him up, but Nestor wasn't out of the woods yet. Chemo took its toll. As did Nestor's age.

She followed the paramedics down out of her clinic and made sure Nestor was in the air ambulance and on his way.

Luke stood beside her, his expression unreadable and his gaze trained on the ambulance as it disappeared from view and on to the nearest hospital. There they could work on him. They walked back up to the clinic to clean up the mess.

Luke cursed under his breath as he picked up Nestor's hat, which had fallen on the floor of the exam room. His eyes were wild, but he wasn't about to cry. It was rage she saw there.

That brief moment of tenderness and joy after she'd saved Nestor's life had faded away. Luke's walls had gone back up again. Like armor.

She wanted to tell him that he didn't need to guard himself in front of her.

He could be himself.

How can he be himself when you can't be yourself?

Sarah touched Luke's arm. "I'm so sorry that happened to him. I wonder what caused him to collapse in the snow."

He shrugged it off. "People don't die from hypothermia and he won't either."

"They do, Luke. You don't know how long he was in the snow for. Or how he even got there. He's alive, but with chemo…his body's been through a trauma."

He scrubbed a hand over his face. "What I meant was that people don't die of hypothermia on my watch. They don't. No man gets left behind. Every life gets saved. Nestor has fought cancer, he can fight this."

"Is that what you would tell yourself in the army?"

His gaze was positively flinty. "What?"

"Why did you leave the army, Luke? It's clear to me you're so passionate about it, why would you leave it?"

Luke snorted and tried to push past her. "I don't have time for this."

"Of course you don't. You never do."

"What's that supposed to mean?"

Sarah shook her head. "It means you'll disappear off into the forest, like you always do, and when you're done sulking you'll come back and pretend like nothing happened. I can't deal with that kind of hot and cold, Luke. I won't deal with that."

"How do you expect me to act, Sarah? A friend of mine almost died. Never leave a man behind, that's the way I've always lived and yet…" He trailed off and then shook his head. "I'm done. I can't deal with this. This is why I keep to myself. This is pointless."

He turned and started to walk away.

"It is. You're a coward, Luke."

He spun around. "I'm the coward? How do you figure that?"

"You're a coward because you won't let anyone in. You won't let anyone help you. I'm sorry you were burned before by people you care about. I'm sorry that you've lost people important to you, but you can't run away from your fears. You have to face them."

"Is that a fact?" He crossed his arms. "And what do you think you're doing here?"

Honestly, she didn't know. She didn't know why she was bothering with him. He clearly didn't want her involved in his life. She should know better.

She was better off alone. Then she only had to answer to herself for her own actions and mistakes. Maybe Luke had it right.

"Working and trying to save lives."

"I mean why are you in Crater Lake? You gave up a prominent job because you were afraid you weren't good enough. You were afraid that everyone would think you were just riding on Daddy's coattails. You ran away from your talent. You're just as much a coward as I am."

"You're a jerk." She threw the envelope at him. "This was for you, because I thought we were friends. Clearly, I was wrong."

Luke touched his face where the envelope had hit him, snickered and then walked away from her. His words had stung, as if he'd cut her open with a scalpel, but then the truth did hurt. It hurt all the more that it came from him.

Someone she'd thought she could trust enough to tell

her darkest fear to. She'd never told anyone else that she'd given up the job because her father had gotten it for her. That was her shame to bear. She'd thought Luke would understand, but she was wrong.

Then again, she was wrong about a lot of other things.

This was no different.

CHAPTER TWELVE

"Luke, I know you're in there. I can see you."

Luke looked over at the window to see his brother peering through. He'd thought that if he retreated to Nestor's cabin, to clean up a bit and close it up until Nestor could come and claim it, it would help get his mind off the fact that he'd probably broken the heart of the woman he loved.

When he'd said those things to Sarah, the moment they'd slipped from his lips he'd realized what a mistake he'd made. That this time, he'd hurt someone he cared about, but she would move on. Like Christine had and he would be the only one with a broken heart.

It served him right.

Sarah hadn't made any promises the night they made love. That was what he'd thought he wanted; that was what he always wanted. He didn't want any commitments. He didn't want anyone to love, but the problem was she'd gotten underneath his skin.

When she was working so hard to save Nestor's life, when she thought it was completely hopeless, she still fought and she was doing it for him. And she'd brought him back. He knew that. Sarah did the best she could with what she had. She could've turned him away, but she hadn't. She wasn't that kind of person and he admired her for it, but Sarah was not meant to be his.

She deserved so much more. He'd hurt her, dragged her into dangerous situations and he demanded so much of her.

Sarah was better off without him.

He didn't deserve love.

Luke didn't know anything about love. He hadn't been able to keep Christine happy when they were married. He'd chosen his career over her. She hadn't wanted to live in Germany. She hadn't wanted to live in a cabin in the woods, yet he'd been selfish and tried to have it his way.

No wonder Christine had left him.

How could he have love, deserve love, if he couldn't change or bend, too? It was too hard, too painful. The problem was, Sarah had somehow snuck in and captured his heart. He didn't know how, but she had.

Of course, that was all ruined now.

He'd taken that piece of her, the one she'd shared with him, and thrown it back in her face. He'd used it to hurt her. To drive her away. So, no, he didn't deserve love. She'd given him that horse painting, as well. Another piece of her she'd shared with him that he'd tossed back at her like garbage.

He hated himself for it.

He'd made his bed and he was going to lie in it.

Of course, coming back to Nestor's cabin was a huge mistake. Not only because it made him emotional, thinking about the friend he'd almost lost, but also because it reminded him of being in her arms. When she kissed him, when she opened herself up to him. The night they became one. That night he was lost to her because she entrusted him with a piece of her.

Now he'd shattered her heart.

Her words might have stung him, but he'd deserved it because the unseen wound he'd inflicted on her was a thousand times worse.

He'd seen her once in town. He'd wanted to tell her that Nestor had pulled through, that they had managed to warm him with lavage, but she hadn't looked at him. She hadn't said anything to him. She had been silent, which was odd for her. Since they first met she'd always been frank about what she thought about him.

The cold shoulder had been too much for him to bear. Even though he'd deserved it. So he'd retreated back to the mountains, under the guise that he was cleaning up Nestor's cabin for the family, but really he just wanted to be alone and mend the broken heart he'd caused himself because he let Sarah in and then pushed her away.

You don't know if she loved you back.

Which was true, but it didn't make the pain better and was pointless now, because he'd completely ruined it. Then he glanced at the painting on the mantel where he'd placed it when he came up here. The horse that looked like Adele. Something she'd painted herself; he could see her slender, graceful hand in each delicate brush stroke. Detailed and precise, as a brilliant surgeon should be. It was a piece of her and just knowing that hurt all the more.

"Luke, it's cold out here. Let me in." Carson's shouting from outside interrupted his train of thought.

Luke groaned and got up to open the door. Carson burst past him and stomped his feet at the door.

"What're you doing here, Carson?"

"Looking for you. After Nestor's accident, you disappeared."

Luke shrugged. "I came up here to clean it up. Nestor's son Greg won't be back up here until spring, possibly summer. I wanted to make sure nothing would go bad. I wanted to make sure everything was squared away. Nestor's lucky to be alive. He'll be in the hospital for a while."

Carson nodded. "Right."

"What's that supposed to mean?"

"Exactly what you think it means."

Luke cursed. "I don't have time for this."

"Why? Because you're so busy up here moping?"

Luke glared at Carson, but his little brother was holding his ground and looking quite smug about it.

"What are you grinning about?"

"I'm thinking back to a conversation we had this summer. Do you remember that particular conversation?"

"No."

Which was a lie. Luke vaguely remembered it. He remembered his brother coming to get him in Missoula, struggling with the fact that he was in love with Esme and was scared of getting a broken heart. Scared of possibly walking away from a family practice, because Carson had put it on himself to carry on the family legacy in Crater Lake.

Luke had told him, in a nutshell, to snap out of it and live.

And now the jerk was throwing it back in his face. Typical.

"I believe you said to me, and I quote, 'Forgive yourself. And for once follow your heart. Do what you want to do. Live.' Wasn't that the line you fed me?"

"It sounds vaguely familiar."

"You're an idiot. You also told me, 'She'll walk away, she's going to walk away and you know who I'm talking about,' and now it applies to you."

"Do you have an eidetic memory or something?"

"No. I just stored those particular lines away for future blackmail and use."

Luke rolled his eyes. "I said those words to you because you deserved Esme. She loved you and you love her."

"Sarah loves you and you're an idiot if you think any different."

Luke shook his head. "You don't know what you're talking about."

"And I'll say it again, you're an idiot."

"I don't deserve love. I blew my first marriage because I was too selfish. And this time around I shut her out because I didn't want to get hurt. It was selfish. I threw it away. For me, love is pointless."

Carson sighed. "Luke, you gave up the army for her. That doesn't sound like someone who is selfish."

"I should've given it up earlier."

"Why? Christine knew your passion for the army before you were married to her. She was just as selfish as you. You gave up the army for her, you tried for her. She ruined it. She found happiness, why can't you? You deserve happiness."

"No. I don't. Maybe it was all me. I can't take the risk again. I don't want to take the risk again. It's better that she leaves. It's better she walks."

Carson took him by the shoulders and shook him. "I love you, but you're an idiot."

"So you've said."

"I'll say it again, like you said it to me. Forgive yourself. Take a chance and live. You love her. You may not admit it, but I can see it as plain as day."

Luke walked away from his brother and sat down on the edge of Nestor's bunk, running his hands through his hair. His hand brushing over the tender scar from the laceration Sarah had stitched up.

That was one of the scariest moments of his life, when he saw that avalanche raging down the side of the mountain toward them and saw the look of horror on her face. All he could do was tell her to do what he'd taught her. In that moment he didn't care much about his life. Only hers, because he couldn't bear it if he lost her.

Yet, he had lost her.

He'd driven her away.

Carson was right. He was an idiot.

"You've realized what a moron you are now." Carson was grinning ear to ear.

"I thought I was an idiot?"

Carson shrugged. "Both, I think."

Luke laughed. "Yeah, you're right."

"I know what happened between you and Christine was bad and the fact that she ran off with Anthony sucks. It does, but you said so yourself, you wanted different things. I think you and Sarah want the same things."

"And what would that be?"

"She's a trauma surgeon and so are you. You're a great first responder, Luke, but you have to get off the mountain and become a surgeon again. Don't you remember what it was like in the OR? I know you loved it. I remember the emails. You were born to be a surgeon. You are a surgeon, you just stopped practicing."

"I don't think she wants to be a surgeon anymore. She left that life behind her."

"She thinks she has. She's a surgeon. Just go live. Do you think that soldier who died would want you mourning his death for the rest of your life? No. Go live your life, Luke."

The words sank in slowly.

He'd been blaming himself so long for his heartache that he didn't realize he'd given up the thing he'd loved the most and that was surgery. He was so busy trying to rescue everyone that he didn't see that he was the one who needed rescuing. He was going to make it up to Sarah. He was going to win her back, even if he didn't know how exactly or if he ever would, but he was going to try.

He couldn't live without her. Of that he was certain.

Luke got up and clapped Carson on the back. "Thanks."

"No problem. I just hope she forgives you." Carson winked. "Now, are you coming down off this mountain? Tomorrow is Valentine's Day. I think that's a perfect time to make up."

"I don't have tickets to that dance," Luke said.

Carson reached in his pocket. "You can have mine. Esme and I aren't going to that dance. I suspect tomorrow we'll have more important things to celebrate."

Luke cocked an eyebrow. "Like what?"

"I'm proposing to Esme tonight. She has no idea."

He grinned. "It's Friday the thirteenth. You know that, right?"

Carson chuckled. "I know, but she really hates Valentine's Day. I mean really hates it. I found a card with a chimp on it."

Luke shook his head. "Would you get out of here? I'll come down off the mountain in time for tomorrow."

"Good." Carson punched him on the shoulder. "Good luck."

"You, too. It's about time you did that, by the way."

"What?"

"Propose to Esme."

Carson snorted. "Look who's talking."

Sarah's heart hurt. It had been a few days since she'd last seen Luke in town briefly. It had looked as if he'd wanted to talk to her, but he'd turned away. He'd looked pale and emotionless. Several times she'd talked herself out of going over to him and comforting him, because really what good would it do?

He would just push her away.

You need to fight harder.

She let out another sigh, because she was all out of fight. How could she fight for the man she was in love with when she couldn't even stand up to her parents? Luke had been right, she should've stayed in that job she'd thought she earned and proven to them she was more than a name.

Even though she'd saved Nestor's life, she'd done so much good here and she wanted more.

She missed the OR.

She missed the chaos of a busy emergency room, the beauty of an OR being prepped by scrub nurses, the feel of the water on her arms as she scrubbed in and the calm she felt as she waited for the patient to go under and the magic of saving a life.

Being around Luke reminded her of that.

How long had she just been walking through the paces of life and not living it?

A long time.

With Luke, she mattered and working with him made her realize she was a damn good surgeon in her own right. As soon as her yearlong contract was up, she was going to find an ER job again. Even if it meant she wasn't running the ER, she still wanted to be where she belonged. She'd known the moment she'd picked up her first scalpel that she didn't belong in her parents' penthouse on the Upper West Side.

Just as she didn't belong in a clinic treating minor injuries.

She belonged down on the front lines and on the surgical floor.

Just as she and Luke belonged together, even if he didn't think they did. She'd never fallen in love before, but, with him, she fell hard and the answer was simple. He brought out the best in her. He made her work harder than she'd ever worked before.

Around him, she felt like herself and she hadn't felt like herself in a very long time. She was so busy distancing herself from her parents, trying to step out of their shadows to prove that she didn't need them, that she didn't realize she'd blocked out everyone.

Including herself.

"Excuse me, are you still open? I know it's four o'clock on Friday and your clinic states you're only open until four, but I'm hoping you can see me."

Sarah looked up from her chart and saw a middle-aged woman, guarding her side, standing in the doorway. She seemed vaguely familiar, but perhaps she'd treated her earlier.

"Of course. Come in."

The woman looked relieved and followed Sarah into an exam room.

"Why don't you have a seat, Ms...?"

"It's Mrs. Vargas, but I can't sit, I'm afraid. I fell while I was skiing and I'm terrified I broke a rib."

Sarah smiled. "It must've been a nasty fall."

"It was. I've never skied before, but my husband insisted we come here for a romantic Valentine's weekend, when really I should be back in Great Falls and working."

"What do you do, Mrs. Vargas?"

"I'm the head of a board of directors for a hospital. We've scouted an area just outside of Crater Lake to build a small hospital that deals mostly with trauma. There's a serious lag around here. Missoula and Great Falls sees most of the trauma, but those locations are too far away to do any help."

"So you're going to build a hospital that only deals with trauma?"

She nodded and then winced. "I'm sorry for boring you, but I thought you might be interested in that seeing how you're a doctor and everything."

"You're not boring me. I totally agree this area is seriously lacking in a trauma center. I can only do so much here."

"Well, I know there's a cardiac surgeon in town and we've offered her use of our operating rooms. It's just a matter of finding a trauma surgeon for next year."

"Well, Mrs. Vargas, you don't have a broken rib."

"Are you sure?"

Sarah nodded. "Positive. If you had a fracture in your ribs you wouldn't be talking to me so easily. You're guarding, but I suspect you've given yourself a nasty bruise. Inhale deeply for me."

Mrs. Vargas did that.

"Did it hurt or was it hard to do?"

"No."

"I'll prescribe you some painkillers, but rest now and put some ice on it."

Mrs. Vargas nodded as she filled out the prescription and handed it to her. Mrs. Vargas stared at it. "Ledet? Are you related to Vin Ledet from New York?"

Sarah groaned inwardly. "Yes. He's my father. Do you know him?"

"No, I just remember someone telling me that Vin Ledet's daughter was a brilliant trauma surgeon. They said you saved their life last summer. Who was it? Oh, yes, Shane Draven. His uncle owns this hotel."

"I really can't say brilliant, but I was that trauma surgeon. I did work on Shane, but he came to me in stable condition thanks to both Dr. Ralstons and Dr. Petersen, who tended to him in the field. I just happened to be a locum surgeon in Missoula, throwing in a hand during a busy stint."

"Well, you're not blowing your own horn. Shane Draven spoke very highly of your skills." Mrs. Vargas pulled out a business card. "If you're interested in returning to an ER and running it as chief of surgery, please do call me."

Chief?

"I think you'd want someone more experienced?"

"The way Shane talks about you I'd say you're experienced enough. I did do a quick background check on you, before realizing you were here. Everyone speaks highly of you as a surgeon."

Sarah blushed. "Thank you, Mrs. Vargas."

"Will I see you tomorrow at the Valentine's Day dance? I would like to introduce you to some members of the board."

"*I* will be at the dance. Silas Draven wants all his staff there, but I don't want to see *you* at that dance. Are we clear?"

Mrs. Vargas winked. "Very well. Please do think about my offer. I would love to have a surgeon of your caliber in charge of this project."

Sarah walked Mrs. Vargas out and when she'd left, Sarah stared at the card for a long time. The offer came because of Shane Draven, not her father. Mrs. Vargas was aware of who her father was, but it was her own merit that preceded her. Not her father pulling strings.

She would take the job to stay in Crater Lake. She loved it here.

She was making friends here.

She was finding her place in this world, when for so long she'd felt as if she was drifting.

Here she wasn't Vin Ledet's daughter. Here she was a surgeon, a doctor. She'd found herself and she'd been foolish not to look sooner. She'd been so busy trying to show her parents who she wasn't that she couldn't show them who she was.

She didn't have to prove anything to them, because there was nothing to prove. Their opinion of her was never going to change and, for the first time in a long time, she was okay with that.

Chief of surgery sounded like a dream job. And she could stay in Crater Lake.

What's keeping you in Crater Lake?

And that realization made her sad.

Luke had made it clear how he felt about love. He thought it was pointless and he'd shut her out. She didn't want to remain in a town where he was.

She loved him too much and it was clear that he didn't return those feelings. So the best thing to do after her contract was up was make a clean break, for both of them.

Even though a clean break was the last thing she wanted, because all she wanted was to be his. To be by his side and in his arms.

She was in love with him and she doubted that feeling would disappear anytime soon, but Luke loved Crater Lake. This was his home. It wasn't her home, even if she wanted it to be. So she'd leave.

Because she loved him so much, she'd leave and let him get on with his life without her. She could find roots in another town, even though she loved Crater Lake.

And she would find another job and of that she had no doubt now.

CHAPTER THIRTEEN

A MONTH AGO you couldn't have paid him enough to be at a gala like this. All the people, the drinking, the noise and decorations were enough to set him on edge. Luke didn't really like being around people who pretended to be nice. Who were putting on a show.

He avoided social situations like this for a reason.

So, no, he wouldn't be at an event like this, not for all the money in the world, but for Sarah he'd walk through fire. For her he'd do anything. She deserved it all and if she let him, if she forgave him, he would spend every waking moment making it up to her.

Since Christine left him he'd always stated his only mistress was the mountain, but the mountain was cold. So cold his heart had been frozen.

Until Sarah came.

Now all he wanted was her and he was going to do everything and anything to get her back.

She was across the room now and he caught glimpses of her through all the people. She was so close, but so far away. To get to her, it would be like walking through fire for him.

He waited until she was alone and not talking with

Silas Draven. He didn't want anyone to interrupt this moment.

Carson and Esme had helped him get ready, since the only suit he owned was from when he was eighteen and married to Christine. So that was unacceptable, coupled with the fact it no longer fit him.

So he wore Carson's suit. It was designer and, even though he felt completely awkward in it, Esme had swooned over him. He knew then it was good. That he would fit in for her. He'd even shaved his beard off.

Now he stood on the other side of the gala, remaining in the shadows at the edge of the dance floor watching her. She took his breath away. She was wearing a bloodred, sparkling evening gown that was a halter, so he got to admire her creamy white shoulders, but the seller for him was her white-blond hair was pulled to one side, but down. So it just brushed the top of her shoulder. Just like in that self-portrait she'd done. The one he loved the most.

Of course, when he was presented with the real thing, the drawing paled in comparison. Sarah was beautiful. She was radiant and he noticed other men admiring her, which ticked him off, but no one else approached her. So he didn't have to inflict any bodily harm on would-be suitors.

She looked unhappy standing off to the side and he knew that was his fault. Something he aimed to fix in a moment, because right now he just enjoyed the sight of her. He enjoyed drinking it in. He didn't want to disrupt the magic she was weaving.

He didn't deserve her, but he would work hard to rectify that for the rest of his life. If she would only let him, and he hoped she would. He pulled at his tie and headed toward her.

Luke had faced many dangerous situations in his life. Things that would scare others, but here, in this moment, crossing a dance floor to beg forgiveness and put his fragile heart on the line for the woman he loved was the scariest thing he'd ever done. But for her, he would do anything.

Sarah didn't want to be at this dance. Mostly because everyone who was at this gala was with someone and she was standing off to the side of the dance floor in her red evening gown, like a wallflower. It was like junior high all over again.

Still, it was a great success. She could see this Valentine's Gala becoming a yearly event for the hotel.

Valentine's never really bothered her, but right now watching all the happy couples dance, kiss and enjoy themselves made her envious.

She should just leave.

Silas Draven had introduced her to all his important guests and then she'd discreetly snuck away, wandering along the edge of the dance floor as the band played endless romantic songs. She was hoping that Esme would be here tonight, so at least maybe she could talk to someone she knew, but Esme hadn't shown up and Sarah hoped that it wasn't because of that goofy chimpanzee card she'd picked out.

The thought of that card made her laugh to herself. A waiter walked by with a tray full of champagne flutes. Sarah took one and as she glanced back across the dance floor her breath caught in her throat at the sight of a man in a well-tailored tuxedo walking across the floor toward her.

And it wasn't just any man. It was Luke and he was clean shaven.

Oh, my God.

Her knees buckled. Those intense blue eyes fixed on her as if he were going to devour her whole and devour her in a good way. A way that made her blood heat with need, with a craving she'd been trying to suppress since he'd walked away from her and broken her heart.

His beard was gone and she could clearly see those delectable lips, which had kissed every inch of her, turning up in a mischievous smile. He stopped in front of her and pulled on the cuff of his jacket, adjusting what looked like cuff links. His brown curls were tamed in a debonair coif, he had a tie on and it didn't look like a clip-on. He rolled his neck and pulled at the tie again. He must be so uncomfortable.

Good.

Even his boots were gone, replaced by dress shoes.

He spun around. "How do I look?"

So good. Only she didn't say that thought out loud. "Fine."

He cocked any eyebrow. "Just fine?"

No, she wasn't going to be drawn in by his cute banter. She wasn't going to let herself be drawn in by him again. She couldn't.

"I… What're you doing here?"

"I've come to the gala. Am I not dressed appropriately?"

"You're dressed fine. I told you that."

It's more than fine.

In fact she was having a hard time controlling herself from throwing the champagne flute aside, hiking up her long skirt and jumping in his arms, but she controlled herself. She was angry at him.

"Can I have this dance?" He held out his hand, his blue eyes twinkling.

Say no. Say no.

"Okay." She took his hand and he led her out on the dance floor, spinning her around gracefully before pulling her back up against him. "I didn't know you could dance."

"I have hidden depths."

"I'm aware of those hidden depths," she said sarcastically. "I don't know why I'm dancing with you."

"Because you're a forgiving sort of person."

"Am I?"

"I think so."

"I hope you're right. I don't feel so forgiving right now."

"I loved my painting. I put it on the wall," he said changing the subject.

Her heart skipped a beat. "You did?"

Don't fall for it.

Only she couldn't help it when it came to Luke Ralston. She was so weak when it came to him.

He nodded. "Thank you for that. It's beautiful, but that wasn't my favorite the night you showed me your drawings."

"It wasn't?"

"No, it was the self-portrait you'd done." Then he reached out and ran his hands gently through her hair and brushed her shoulder. "It was the pencil drawing with your hair down, your shoulders bare. That's the drawing I loved."

Her pulse thundered in her ears. That was a drawing she'd always hated. One she'd never got right. At least she didn't think so. Maybe because she couldn't truly see herself through her own eyes. She was her own worst judge. But looking into Luke's eyes at this moment, in his arms, she could see what he saw, even if only for a brief moment, and it almost made her cry.

"Why didn't you tell me?"

"I didn't want you to know at the time."

She blushed. "I'm surprised you're here. I thought you didn't like Valentine's Day. It's the one thing you and Esme have in common."

"Me, too, to be honest." He chuckled. "Actually, Esme may be warming up to Valentine's Day, or at least Friday the thirteenth."

"Why?"

"Carson proposed last night and Esme accepted."

Sarah smiled. "Oh, how wonderful. I'm happy for her. I'm surprised they're not here celebrating."

"Well, they wanted me to come here."

She blushed again, her heart racing. "So what're you doing here?"

"I've come to beg for forgiveness."

Her heart skipped a beat. "What?"

"I've been an idiot. I thought love was pointless, but only for me."

"Only for you?"

He nodded. "My first wife left me because I was selfish. I was so focused on what I wanted that I didn't let her have a say. I wanted to be in the army and serve my country as a surgeon, I wanted to train at the army hospital in Germany and nothing was going to stop me. Not even the woman I loved, or thought I loved at the time. Actually, I'm surprised she didn't leave me sooner."

"I understand that kind of drive. You loved serving your country, so why did you leave it?"

"Because I left for her, but by then it was too late. I gave up my commission, but it wasn't enough. So I turned to the mountain. Being alone meant I could live my life the way I wanted. I never wanted to feel that pain or be responsible for inflicting that kind of pain on someone. I thought it was easier to shut people out. To be alone, and then you came along."

Tears stung her eyes. "Oh, Luke. Things aren't so black-and-white."

"I know that now. When you walked into that OR last summer, I knew there was something about you. I knew that you would break through, even if I didn't want to admit it. I love you, Sarah. I'll go wherever you need me to go. If you need to be a surgeon in New York again, I'll go there. I just can't lose you. I need you. I'll change my life, give up everything to be with you."

Her knees went weak and she wasn't sure she'd heard him correctly. No one had ever offered to give up everything to make her happy.

Everyone expected pieces of her, for her to conform, but Luke was offering all of himself to her and she was overwhelmed by it.

She knew there were tears running down her face but there was no stopping them.

"For so long I've been fighting to prove to the world I'm not someone they think I am, I didn't know who I really was, but with you I found who I was again. I shut everyone out. Even me. I shut myself out. I was convinced I didn't need love. That I didn't want love…

that I could make it through this life on my own. I was wrong. I love you, Luke. I love you so much it hurts. You see me."

He pulled her tight against him, cupping her face, and then kissed her. His kiss gentle at first, before it deepened. She melted into that kiss, wrapping her arms around his neck, not caring who saw her kissing him. Her whole world had righted itself. She was where she wanted to be. She was who she wanted to be.

She had found out who she was thanks to this man.

When the kiss ended she laid her head against his shoulder, moving with him as they swayed gently on the dance floor. She didn't want to let him go. She'd missed him. She'd missed this Luke Ralston. A man she'd only met in brief glimpses. A man who had been surrounded by high walls.

A man she desperately wanted to love.

"So am I forgiven?" he teased.

"Yes. Though I should've made you work harder."

"Yes. You should've."

"Now you tell me." She glanced up at him and kissed him again. "Thank you for coming here tonight. This is the best apology ever."

"So, where should we move to?" Luke asked. "There's no surgical jobs in Crater Lake sadly."

"There will be next year when my contract is up here at the hotel."

"What?" He was clearly confused. "There's no hospital in Crater Lake. They talked once last year about building one, but nothing ever came of it."

"Not yet. A trauma and surgical center is going up outside of town. A board of directors from a large hospital in Great Falls realized there was a shortfall up in this area for one."

Luke grinned. "You want to stay in Crater Lake?"

"Of course. It's home now. You're my home." And it was true. She'd found a home. She'd found what she was looking for. She'd found herself in him.

Luke kissed her again. "And you're mine. I love you, Sarah."

Sarah kissed him back. "Happy Valentine's Day, Dr. Ralston."

EPILOGUE

Valentine's Day, a year later

SARAH WALKED SWIFTLY through the halls of the new trauma center. Her ER was running smoothly. Her board was in good working order, which made her slightly apprehensive. She'd learned early on as a trauma resident that a smoothly run ER and good board would mean that a huge trauma was due any second to muck it all up.

They'd only been open a month, but already there had been several large traumas, a couple of emergency births and an avalanche. Thankfully no bear mauling.

Sarah shuddered recalling that moment.

The man had pulled through, but required several plastic surgeries.

She'd seen several bears in the summer when Luke was working on building onto his cabin. Their cabin. And a bear had crashed Esme and Carson's wedding that summer, but thankfully none of the encounters had been violent.

Once she'd got the trauma center open, her father had come to tour the facility and he'd donated money to the pro bono fund, which had shocked her, but what was the most shocking moment was when he told her he was proud of her. That she had done well for herself.

And she had.

She was happier than she could ever remember.

Now, if only her boards would stay quiet tonight.

"Dr. Ledet, can you come to OR Four? There's a problem."

Sarah saw a very pregnant Esme running toward her. Esme operated on her cardio patients at the trauma center, but Sarah wondered when she was going to give it up because soon she'd be giving birth.

"You shouldn't be running," Sarah said. "You're due in, like, three weeks. Why are you even working now?"

"It's only an angio," Esme said, as if an angio were nothing. Which was odd for her.

Sarah glanced up at the board and then back to her. "You said there was a problem. If it's only a simple angio, then what's the problem?"

Esme bit her lip. "Oh, I'm not in OR Four. I'm in Three. That board is wrong. I finished my angio, but I was passing OR Four and they were having a problem."

Speak of a quiet board, get swift retribution.

"Okay, let's go." Sarah jogged behind Esme. They put on their surgical caps and then scrubbed. "So what's wrong again?"

"It was a mauling," Esme said. "It's pretty bad."

"Oh, no. Are you serious? Why do tourists insist on disturbing a bear during its hibernation cycle?" She walked into the OR, her hands up and waiting to get gloved when she saw Luke, gowned and standing in the OR alone.

"Bears don't hibernate, Sarah. Have I not taught you anything?"

Sarah glanced back, but Esme had disappeared. "What's going on here? I thought there was a mauling."

"No, no mauling, but I wanted to get you here fast, without arousing your suspicions."

"Well, now I'm suspicious. You're supposed to be in Missoula visiting Nestor. What's going on?"

"Nothing is going on."

"Is Nestor okay?" Sarah asked.

"He's fine. I swear. He hates city living, but you know that."

Sarah sighed in relief. She was glad to hear the older man was okay. She'd grown fond of him and went with Luke to visit him every month.

"So what's going on?" She asked.

"Well, picture this room full of rose petals." Luke grinned. "Only I know it's not."

"Which is good because if it was I would have a panic attack thinking about having to sterilize this OR again top to bottom. Do you know how many patients are allergic to scents?"

Luke crossed his arms. "Really? Don't you have any scope of imagination?"

"No, not on a night when the ER is quiet and my board *was* running smoothly."

Luke moved to stand in front of her. "Well, I was trying to be romantic, but I realize now it's kind of hard to be romantic when we're both wearing surgical masks standing in an OR."

"Yeah, why are we here?"

"Because it was in OR like this that I first met you. You told me to get out of your OR."

"And I'm telling you that now, too." She laughed nervously and then it hit her when she spied Esme in the scrub room, crying. "Oh, my God."

Luke got down on one knee and pulled out a ring. "Don't worry, it's been sterilized. It won't contaminate this surgical field."

"Oh, my God," she said again in disbelief.

"Sarah, I can't live without you. You brought me back from the dead. You taught me to love again, to feel again and I want you to be my wife. Marry me."

She began to cry, soaking the paper surgical mask. "Yes. I'll marry you. Yes!"

Luke slipped the ring on her finger. "Good. Nestor will be thrilled I finally found the nerve to ask you."

Sarah laughed. "Remind me to kiss him next time I see him."

"Kiss him?" Luke asked then ripped off his mask. "Sorry, but you're going to have to sterilize this OR again. I need to kiss my fiancée properly."

Sarah removed her mask and let him kiss her. It wasn't the exact OR where they'd first met, but it was an OR where they worked together constantly, together saving lives, but most of all it was a place where they'd saved each other.

And being in his arms was right where she needed to be.

"There's something else I need to tell you," Sarah said. "It's important."

Luke groaned, but grinned. "You want to move back to New York."

"No. Look, it's…"

A tap on the glass interrupted their conversation and she turned around to see Esme in the scrub room looking quite distressed.

"What's up with her?" Luke asked.

Esme hit the intercom. "Um, I think we need to sterilize that room right now. My water just broke."

Sarah chuckled as Esme was pointing frantically at her belly. "I believe that we're about to be an aunt and uncle. Even though technically I'm not an aunt until we actually get married."

Luke's eyes widened as the reality of what she was telling him sank in. "What?"

"I would go find Carson and bring him here. Esme has gone into labor."

Luke shook his head. "Only her baby would be born on Valentine's Day. I'll get Carson."

"And I'll get Esme comfortable." She kissed him again. "Be careful."

"You, too. I have a feeling she's going to fight back when that pain starts to hit."

Sarah went to Esme and helped her stand, because she was bent over the scrub sink, holding the side as pains rocked through her.

"Sorry, I thought I had more time," Esme panted.

"You can't control it."

Esme cursed under her breath. "It figures, though— my kid had to come on Valentine's Day."

Sarah laughed. "I know, but let's get you to a birthing room and wait for Carson to come."

Sarah walked Esme down the hall and tried not to think about the fact that in nine months she might be walking down this very same hall, with Esme holding her up, and she couldn't help but wonder what Luke was going to think when she told him, because that was something they'd never talked about in their year together.

She'd been going to tell him but then Esme had gone into labor.

Right now their conversation would have to wait, but pretty soon she wouldn't be able to hide it any longer.

"Come on, one more push." Carson was behind Esme, holding her shoulders, and Luke was pacing by the door.

"Stop pacing," Esme shouted over her shoulder. "It's annoying me."

"Sorry," Luke mumbled.

"Come on, Esme. Ignore him and give me one more push."

Esme used some choice curse words that were directed at Carson, but she gave it that one last push and soon Sarah was catching Carson and Esme's baby girl in her hands. The baby didn't even need a back rub; she began to cry lustily.

"It's a girl," Sarah announced. Esme began to cry and Carson kissed her. "Carson, you want to come cut the cord?"

Carson moved toward her and Sarah tied off the cord and handed Carson the sterile scissors. He cut the cord and then took his daughter gently in his arms, bringing her to Esme, who waited for her with open arms.

"If this doesn't change your mind about Valentine's Day, Esme, I don't know what will," Carson teased as he kissed Esme's sweaty brow again.

Sarah's heart swelled with happiness.

She wasn't used to this kind of love, this kind of family, but she had it all here and as she glanced up at Luke she could see the wonder in his eyes as he looked down at his little niece with love.

A nurse that was on duty took the newborn to weigh

her, rub ointment in her eyes and give her a vitamin K shot. Luke did the APGAR on his niece with Carson watching over his daughter and Sarah helped Esme.

Once everything was done, the newest, swaddled, seven-pound-five-ounce member of the Ralston family was handed to Esme again.

"What're you going to name her?" Sarah asked as she gently touched the baby's head.

"Not Valentine," Esme said quickly, glaring at Luke and Carson respectively.

Sarah laughed. "Well, we'll leave you alone for a bit, but really you've come through that beautifully. You can go home in the morning if her vitals remain stable."

Carson nodded. "Thanks, Sarah."

"No problem." She washed her hands and then walked out of one of the two birthing rooms they had in Crater Lake.

"That was amazing," Luke said. "You never cease to amaze me."

"What do you think they'll name her?"

Luke laughed. "My brother's so head over heels for her and the baby, he'll agree to call her anything that Esme wants. And really that's the way it should be."

"Really?" Sarah asked. "So you wouldn't object if I called our baby something like Asterix or Cantaloupe or some other fashionable name when it comes this fall?"

Luke paused. "What?"

"I was trying to tell you, but Esme interrupted us. I'm pregnant." She waited with bated breath for his reaction, but she didn't have to wait long. Before she had a chance to tease him with other names she was in his arms and he was kissing her.

"Truly?"

She nodded. "Truly. Though I'm terrified I don't have the best example in parents. What if I end up like them?"

"Highly doubtful." He wrapped his arms around her. "You'll be a great mother."

"And you'll be a great father."

"I love you, Sarah." He kissed her again and she melted in his arms. "You're my life, I would do anything for you, but I'm not naming our baby Cantaloupe."

Sarah laughed. "I love you, too."

And as she kissed him again she realized that she'd found her place. She'd found herself and she was right where she needed to be, in Luke's arms.

* * * * *

MILLS & BOON®

MEDICAL ROMANCE™

THE ULTIMATE IN ROMANTIC MEDICAL DRAMA

A sneak peek at next month's titles...

In stores from 25th February 2016:

- **The Socialite's Secret** – Carol Marinelli *and*
  London's Most Eligible Doctor – Annie O'Neil

- **Saving Maddie's Baby** – Marion Lennox *and*
  A Sheikh to Capture Her Heart – Meredith Webber

- **Breaking All Their Rules** – Sue MacKay

- **One Life-Changing Night** – Louisa Heaton

0216/03

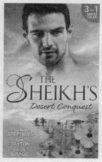

1215_MB16

MILLS & BOON®

Let us take you back in time with our Medieval Brides...

The Novice Bride – Carol Townend

The Dumont Bride – Terri Brisbin

The Lord's Forced Bride – Anne Herries

The Warrior's Princess Bride – Meriel Fuller

The Overlord's Bride – Margaret Moore

Templar Knight, Forbidden Bride – Lynna Banning

Order yours at
www.millsandboon.co.uk/medievalbrides

MILLS & BOON®

Why shop at millsandboon.co.uk?

Each year, thousands of romance readers find their perfect read at millsandboon.co.uk. That's because we're passionate about bringing you the very best romantic fiction. Here are some of the advantages of shopping at www.millsandboon.co.uk:

* **Get new books first**—you'll be able to buy your favourite books one month before they hit the shops

* **Get exclusive discounts**—you'll also be able to buy our specially created monthly collections, with up to 50% off the RRP

* **Find your favourite authors**—latest news, interviews and new releases for all your favourite authors and series on our website, plus ideas for what to try next

* **Join in**—once you've bought your favourite books, don't forget to register with us to rate, review and join in the discussions

Visit **www.millsandboon.co.uk**
for all this and more today!

The way Jack had first seen her—face red with anger, eyes flashing, tight little chignon askew and one sleeve torn at the shoulder seam—had roused his protective instinct to the maximum. She needed him on a level that no woman ever had before.

He knew he would miss the women who welcomed him with open arms and merry laughter. This girl was not of their kind, however. Attaining regard from her would require more than he had offered the others. This time he would need to make irrevocable promises. Vows.

He only hoped he was up to the challenge. Given the fire he had seen in her, he figured she would be anything but boring.

Jack rarely met a woman he didn't like, even the guileful ones with nefarious schemes to trap him. Now the shoe was on the other foot. He meant to marry her even should it require employing a bit of guile himself. She needed charming, and he could do that.

AUTHOR NOTE

Sometimes love takes you by surprise. It might begin with a chance meeting, an unintended altercation or, in the case of Jack and Laurel, a reluctant good deed.

A man of honour does what he should, and Jack is no exception—even when it means abandoning a life of adventure to do the right thing. After all, he benefits too. Laurel provides the greatest adventure he has yet encountered when she grants him her hand in marriage and her trust.

However, trust proves more fragile than love when deception enters the mix. The question becomes whether nobility lies in the heart or in a name. They say no good deed goes unpunished. Come see if that's so!